MEMORIES FOR SALE

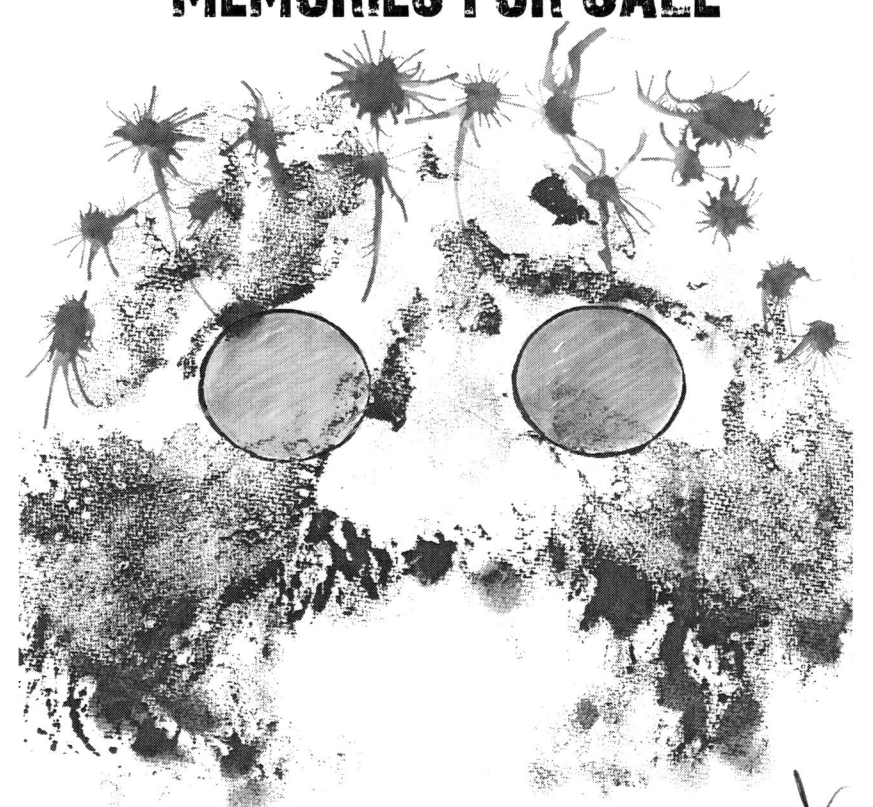

Tales from a Small Town

John F. Gardiner

ARCHWAY PUBLISHING

Copyright © 2017 John F. Gardiner.
Interior art/cover graphics: Rebecca Lee Gardiner

All rights reserved. No part of this book may be used or reproduced by any means, graphic, electronic, or mechanical, including photocopying, recording, taping or by any information storage retrieval system without the written permission of the author except in the case of brief quotations embodied in critical articles and reviews.

This is a work of fiction. All of the characters, names, incidents, organizations, and dialogue in this novel are either the products of the author's imagination or are used fictitiously.

Archway Publishing books may be ordered through booksellers or by contacting:

Archway Publishing
1663 Liberty Drive
Bloomington, IN 47403
www.archwaypublishing.com
1 (888) 242-5904

Because of the dynamic nature of the Internet, any web addresses or links contained in this book may have changed since publication and may no longer be valid. The views expressed in this work are solely those of the author and do not necessarily reflect the views of the publisher, and the publisher hereby disclaims any responsibility for them.

ISBN: 978-1-4808-4479-7 (sc)
ISBN: 978-1-4808-4477-3 (hc)
ISBN: 978-1-4808-4478-0 (e)

Library of Congress Control Number: 2017906348

Print information available on the last page.

Archway Publishing rev. date: 05/16/2017

This glimpse into my soul is lovingly dedicated to:

My mother and father, Chuck and Doreen, as they've been known to their countless friends over all of my life....I can't remember my parents ever even raising their voices, let alone their hands toward us children, when I was a child....they are both gentle souls filled with kindness.

Glen Pupich, Bill Lee and Sam Kinsman, all of who made me a writer. Glen and Sam are dead now and I miss them both every day.... Glen opened my world when I was a kid....he showed me there was more than Hanover and that I should dream big – that I could change the world. Sam told me I was going to be a great writer, and, for some reason, I believed him and I believe him still. Bill Lee was my English teacher in Grade 12 and 13 and he taught me to think big and that great literature could change the world. I believe him still as well.

My children, Jason and Rebecca, who have done so much to fulfill me as I've passed through my life. I didn't want children when I was a young guy because I knew they would cause me much pain and suffering. But I have discovered that it is through your children that you feel true joy and wonderment....thanks to them for standing by an irascible old curmudgeon through their lifetimes.....

Carol...who has sustained me all these years and kept me going through some difficult times....she has saved my life on countless occasions. I could not have made it this far without her. She is the love of my life.

Isaac, April, Tomas and Olive... ...be strong always.

Brenda, Brian and JoAnne, my siblings, who've found it in their hearts to accept me for who I am and love me regardless.

And to my musical friend, Richard Knechtel, who writes wonderful music, and is great to perform with... ....

Rick Flewelling, Mike Schnarr, Stan Kochany, Murray Eydt, Al Lobsinger, Wendy Lantz, Bob Hubbard, Rob Fidler, John Sweeney, Philip Shaw, Ian Mills, Kuntzie (John Kunsenhauser), George Anderson, Bill Evans....and the rest of my friends who have helped me along the way....I love you all....

Best read to Kate Bush.....

Foreword.....

This is a small reflection of my writing life, which began when I was a young guy writing out my thoughts on the sill of my bedroom window. I have poured my heart and soul into my writing for nearly a whole lifetime, but have generally been unsuccessful at getting that work out to a wide audience. I have self published five small books over the last 25 years and I've done readings and radio pieces and pretty well anything I could do to try to push my writing out into the world. All of these things have helped to sustain me as a writer because I've received nothing but positive comment on my work. Indeed, all have been successful in their own way.

I have called my writing "ordinary writing for ordinary people" and that's really the way I feel about it. Over the years, I've had people from all walks of life and all backgrounds read my writing, and it has touched them all. It is a good feeling when Doris, the elderly woman with a Grade 6 education, and Wendy, the university educated career woman, can both read your work and find it comforting and of value.

This book is illustrated by my daughter, Rebecca Gardiner, who has had a really tough go in her brief life. I know that one day she will be a great artist, but I cannot rush her into it. She will find her way as I did mine. It has been hard for me to watch her struggle, but I have known that it will make her tougher so she can survive to make great art. I pray that she has finally found her place in life......

I've been told on many occasions over the years that I should write a murder mystery or a piece of science fiction or something that has some chance of being successful in a commercial market…..that's not the way I work. I write from deep inside my soul….I'm not even sure where the words come from myself. Sam used to think I had a muse that wrote through me. I'm not sure what it is but I've believed for all these years that my writing is worthwhile and should someday find its place in the world….

I hope you will take the time to get involved with the book and to try to see what it is saying about the human condition. My faith in humanity is somewhat shaken as I reach into old age. I'm not as confident as I once was that we are smart enough and innovative enough to solve all of our problems. Indeed, stupidity seems rife…..

Contents

Secret Fears xi

Short Stories

When I Was Crazy..3
Brothers 15
My One Great Love. And How It Ended. 27
Reminders.. 46
The Melancholy Man..55
When I Was a Star 72
Conversation with a Friend...82
Uncertain Waters... 94
Jammin'.. 106
Old Friends 116
Memories for Sale... 130
Waiting for Winter 145

Poetry

The Hippies Knew.. 165
Listening to Janis Laugh 167
The Mystery of Makeup 169
On Watching ER… …..171
Waiting… …...173
Remembering Leo….. 175

On being the one.. 177
Ode to the King of Hearts 179
Wishing for Company 183
Silly People 185
On Mattering.. 186
Soon Tomorrow… 187

The Gawd Book

In the Beginning... 193
A Fresh Start 203
Parties and Prayers.. 219
First Love.. 233
True Love 252
A Wonderful Guy 264
The Temptation... 278
And Gawd Is Cast Out 292
Into the Wilderness 306
Revelations... 328

Secret Fears

I watch old people as they wait to die
And I know that I'll be there soon.
They stare vacantly into nothing and slobber on their shirts
And I am going there to be like them.

I cannot stop getting older, no matter how I try.
It seems to happen to me while I'm asleep.
I go to bed and I am young and I wake as an older man.
I see it in the mirror – I see it in my face.

I put on a brave front and smile at my birthday,
But I am secretly afraid.
Afraid that I will pass from life
And no one will notice that I've been here.

Because it is something we all fear –
Not the inevitable, physical death – but being forgotten.
That no one will remember us or pray for us
And it will be as if we never happened.

Short Stories

When I Was Crazy

The moment you're born, you start to die. I didn't used to like dying slowly. Especially with all the suffering that goes on around here. That's why I slashed my wrists when I was seventeen. That's when they sent me to the Ontario Hospital in Kitchener. That's when I found out how very sane I really was. Man, that place was full of crazies. Like the drug addict who thought they were putting marijuana smoke into his room through the heating vent when he wasn't looking, 'cause he thought he could always smell it. And the lady who'd had six shock treatments, and couldn't remember who her husband was when he came to visit.

My Dad took me to the hospital to meet the doctor, and the way he talked, the doctor I mean, you'd have thought I was in for something really special in the OH, in his new program for troubled teenagers. He talked my Dad into leaving me there, bandages on my wrists, an old beat-up brown suitcase holding my pajamas and such. It was my first time away from home. I was scared.

One of the first things I noticed was that there were other people with bandages on their wrists. I saw them walking the halls, and when you looked at them, they looked back with a kind of hollow stare. They seemed like a nice bunch of zombies -- if you liked zombies.

They took my disposable razor, the one I use for shaving my legs and under my arms, when they rummaged through the old brown suitcase. It was maybe a sensible precaution. But they also took my belt, and that kind of pissed me off, because my jeans were a little big for me, and I didn't want to have to be holding them up all the time. Anyway, they should have known that I'd made my try, and that I wouldn't try again. I'd told the doctor, and he shouldn't have doubted me. That set us off on a bad footing almost right from the start. They have to put a little faith in you, even after you try the suicide thing. It can have a lot to do with why you try in the first place -- because they have no faith in you to begin with.

I met Bill in the lounge after supper; after my first day. I was sitting on the couch, and the only empty seat in the room was beside me, when he came walking in. He came in quietly, and settled in on the couch, seemingly careful not to make any noise, so people's television watching wouldn't be disturbed. It was Jeopardy time and people were pretty caught up in it. So, we just sat on the couch, not being introduced or anything like that. But I could hear him breathing beside me, and I found myself wondering who he might be. I looked over to catch a glimpse one time, but he did the same, so that we ended up sitting face to face really close, just for a second, before I looked away. It was embarrassing.

When the first commercial break came, people's concentration left the television, and there was some talk in the room.

"You're new," I heard him say.

I looked over and regarded him, nodding slightly.

"You crazy?" he asked as straight-faced as you might please.

I said nothing, but the question made me smile slightly. He saw his chance.

"I'm Bill," he said, smiling back and offering his hand. "And I'm definitely crazy -- and proud of it!"

He emphasized the last part of what he said and it made my smile widen.

"Angela," I said, feeling this guy might be okay to know, so that I could let down my guard just a bit. I took his outstretched hand.

"Glad to make your acquaintance, Angela," he answered, and as he took my hand, he held up the bandaged wrist for a closer look. "Nasty bit of business that," he said, looking at me kind of out of the tops of his eyes, as if he was looking over invisible glasses. You know, those half kind that some people wear when they get old.

"You into Jeopardy?" he asked.

"Not particularly," I answered.

"Want to hit the caf for a coffee?" he asked. "I'm not into this mind-numbing TV stuff. It's for cattle."

And we were off to the "caf" for a coffee.

There was quiet for a couple of moments after we'd settled in.

"You in school?" Bill finally asked, interrupting the silence.

"I was," I answered, "but I don't think I'll be going back."

"Why not?" he asked.

"I'm just not into that stuff anymore," I answered, and I used a tone that said I meant it.

"That's too bad," he said, "because school can be cool."

"Is that so," I said.

"It is," Bill answered.

"I suppose you went right through school," I challenged.

"I didn't have to," he answered. "Because I knew what school was really trying to teach me -- that knowledge is power -- so I read.......I learn. I don't need school. But I'm not stupid."

"Maybe I don't need school either," I said, again challenging him.

"Maybe you don't," he answered, but it was in a patronizing sort of way, like he somehow didn't believe there was any truth to the statement. "But," he added, almost in a drawl, "maybe you do."

And we were quiet for a while longer. There was no one else in the caf, so that the whole place was bathed in the quiet. I felt sort of peaceful for the first time since my Dad had dropped me off at this place. It was him. He seemed to exude a strange sort of serenity.

We talked a little more, but it was mainly about nothing, except that I was a die hard Toronto Maple Leaf fan, which he thought was odd for a girl, so I called him a sexist. But it was a pleasant time, and I found myself wishing that it could linger longer and longer.

Finally, though, Bill looked at his watch. "Lock-up at ten," he said. "I've got to get going."

I must have looked puzzled, because he smiled at me. "I'm over in the dangerous offenders ward," he said, suddenly drawing himself up and trying to look particularly menacing. "You know.....the place for the criminally insane." He continued to do a bad Dracula-like impersonation, then abruptly ended the charade. "I'm in the protected custody ward," he explained, now serious. "The doors lock automatically at ten every night, and you've got to be inside. I'll fill you in sometime."

He walked off across the empty room, winding his way through the tables and chairs. I watched him go. I smiled. He made me smile.

The night was okay, although after I got back to my room, I decided I'd like to take a bath, because I was feeling grimy and dirty, and I thought it might help me stay relaxed after the coffee, which I probably shouldn't have drank because sometimes it keeps me up half the night. The bath water was weird. You kind of floated in it, like they must put some chemical in it, or something. And it was hard to relax because your feet kept floating up to the surface of the water and kind of off-balancing you. I guess they must treat the water to keep you from drowning yourself. At least that's all I could think of.

So, the bath idea was sort of a failure. But the coffee didn't keep me awake, and I slept good.

I had my first therapy session after breakfast the next morning. I went into this very tiny office and sat across from the psychiatrist. He asked me a few questions, but I didn't answer. I didn't really trust him. And I really didn't trust myself. Where I grew up, the only people who saw shrinks were crazy people. And maybe that was me. Or maybe he was there to trick me into thinking I was crazy.

I sat through the whole session and didn't say a word. I didn't find his questions too interesting, so I didn't answer them. Mostly, I thought he was a boorish old fart who probably drove a Beemer and had a prissy wife with big tits and a kid with horn-rimmed glasses. He wanted to know about my early life, and I figured he was going to point to something in my upbringing as being the whole key to why I was having trouble. But I liked my upbringing, and I thought I might dirty it by holding it up for scrutiny. So, I was quiet. And, finally, he was quiet. So that we sat across from each other in an office that wasn't all that large, and seemed to try to avoid making any actual contact. It was kind of odd. It was odd then, and it's odd now that I think of it.

So, most of my morning was wasted. I didn't get to see Bill and that was about all I could think of during the whole thing with the shrink. Finally, though, it ended, and I was told I could go to the cafeteria because the rest of my group was involved in some activity which I'd missed most of. I went to the caf and there was Bill, sitting off all by himself, with a coffee sitting in front of him, but not seeming to pay it much attention.

But, as I got closer, I thought something didn't look right with Bill. He was just sitting there, sort of looking out in front of himself, but not like he was seeing anything. Even as I walked closer, there seemed to be no flicker of recognition, so I was quiet, said nothing. He sat as still as could be, back erect, stiff and straight and proper. But to look inside of him, through the eyes, you'd have thought he was empty, filled with nothing, and his face blank, but serene and calm.

Then, as I watched, he cried. Tears came from somewhere deep inside of him, where there seemed to be only a void. His expression blank, betraying no emotion.

I felt sad. I did not understand. But I was quiet. I did not intrude.

After a few moments, I left the caf.

"Too bad about him," the waitress remarked, as I passed. "He had a treatment this morning. They're always like this after one of those. It makes them forget."

I said nothing, just walked hurriedly by. When I got back to my room, I cried. How could they, I thought? That had to be the awfullest thing I ever saw in my life. It was the look on his face......and the eyes.........and the emptiness. And it was like he was fighting to get out. How could they?

That afternoon, we went bowling. It was alright, because I'm a pretty good bowler, because my Dad is a really good bowler. But it was the way they lined us all up and paraded us down the street to the bowling alley, just a little ways from the hospital. Retards on parade. That was about all I could think as we were walking along. I kept to myself. Most of the other people were talking and laughing, probably glad to get out of the confinement of the hospital, but I was thinking about Bill. I was wondering how long he'd be like he was in the morning when I saw him in the caf. I'd never seen anyone like him before.

I saw him sitting in the cafeteria when I went there for supper. He was off by himself again, but he had a tray full of food in front of him, and he seemed to be paying it some attention. I walked over to him, when I finished loading up my own tray.

He looked up and smiled at me as I approached, but there was still something about the look -- the eyes. It made me uneasy.

"Hi," I said, knowing I was nervous saying it.

"How are you?" he asked.

"I'm alright," I answered, and I took up a position across from him.

I said nothing else, but started in on my food, hungry after the bowling, not even minding it being the hospital stuff. Also, I was unsure what to say -- where to start.

I kept my eyes down toward the table, and couldn't help but notice that he was just toying with his food, not really eating, but sort of playing with bits of it, moving them around on his plate, almost deliberately.

He noticed I was watching.

"Not too hungry tonight," he offered. "Kind of lost my appetite."

"I understand," I told him, and I tried to mean it.

"You saw?" he asked.

"I saw you in here this morning," I answered.

"Not a pretty sight, I imagine," he said.

I didn't answer, but felt a lump in my throat at the thought of it.

"I feel a lot better now. Just not too hungry -- especially not for this." He slid the tray of food away from him.

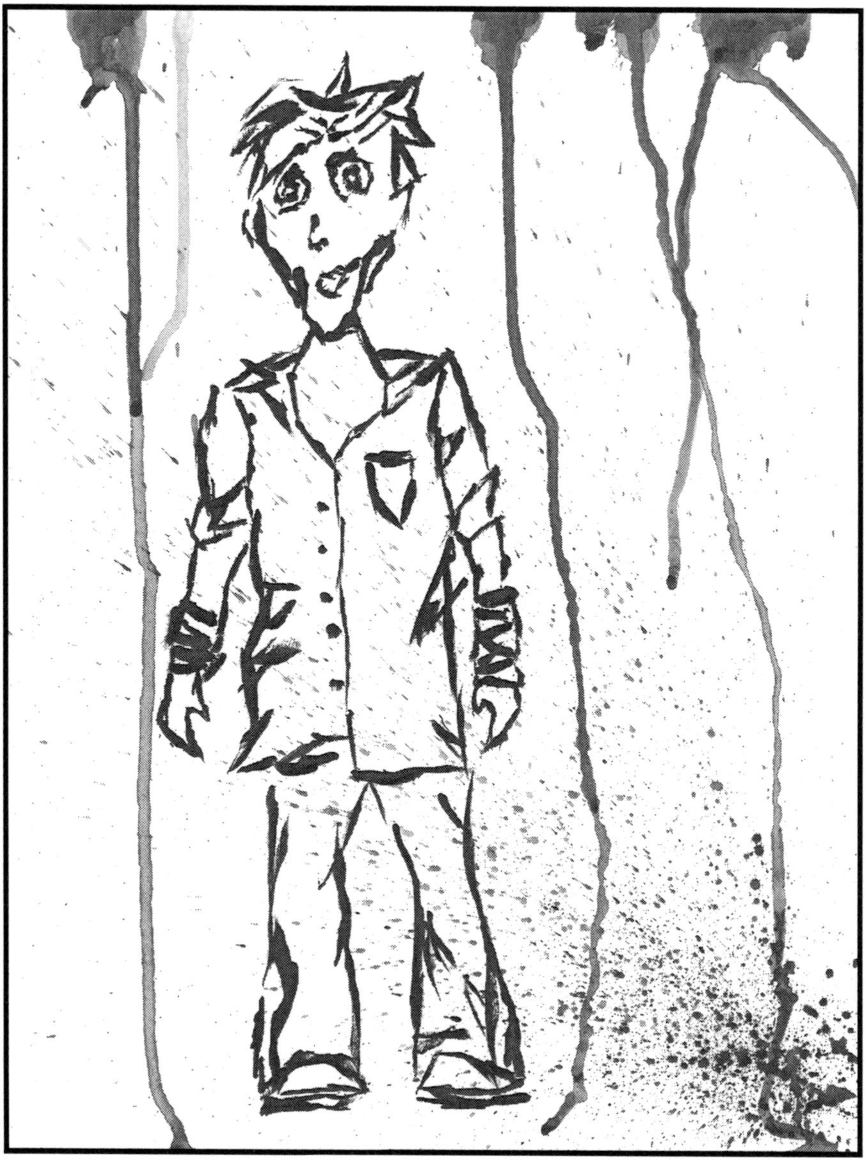

Suddenly, I seemed to remember about the hospital food.

He pulled out a pack of cigarettes, got one out, and lit it.

"I didn't know you smoked," I said.

"It comes and goes," he answered. "I guess I feel a little stressed out. I'm not particularly good with stress." He took a long drag on the cigarette, and exhaled through his nose, flooding the tabletop with smoke.

"Look at it," he said, passing his hand through the smoke. "First, it's there, and then it's not. Kind of like life." He paused. "Did you ever know anybody who died?" he asked.

"No, not really close. There was a kid in my class who drowned when I was ten," I answered.

"You almost knew someone too well," he said, reaching over and touching one of my bandages. "You've got to know how precious life is."

I didn't answer. I was quiet. Embarrassed.

"It seemed like the thing to do," I finally said, putting a defiant edge on my voice.

"I've been there," he said. He pulled back the cuff of his sweatshirt sleeve. I saw the scars. "A long time ago."

"Not any more?" I asked.

"Not for a long time," he said, covering his wrist.

We sat in quiet for a couple of minutes.

"Not for me to lecture you, anyway," Bill finally said. "I guess if I'm in here, I'm not such a great role model, right?"

"I don't care if you're a role model," I answered. "At least you're a bit friendly. That's better than those bitches in my group."

"Yea, but I'm not sure we should be hangin' out together," he said. "Remember, I'm potentially aggressive."

"You don't seem too aggressive to me," I said. "What'd you do to get in here?"

"You're never supposed to ask another patient that," he said. "It's against the unwritten code of the inmates."

"Comeon," I chided. "How am I supposed to know whether it's safe to be with you?" I told him. I was kidding with the tone of my voice.

"Hey, how am I supposed to know if it's safe to be with you? Looks like you're pretty handy with sharp objects," he kidded back.

"Not much of a threat," I answered. "Didn't even do a good job at it......or I wouldn't be sitting here talking to you."

There was another short silence.

"Why'd they shock you this morning?" I asked, probably a little too bluntly.

"I guess it's part of my treatment," he answered.

"It makes you forget?" I asked.

"It's supposed to," he said.

"Does it work?" I asked.

"I remembered you," he answered.

From there, the conversation wandered. I told him a bit about the town I was from. He asked me questions about school, and other dumb junk, like if I had any boyfriends. I told him I didn't -- that no dumbass boy from that hick town was having his way with me. Finally, though, the conversation headed back to where it had started.

"I'm not sure why I tried the suicide thing," I found myself telling him, and him almost a total stranger. But, somehow, he got my guard down. I felt comfortable talking to him. "It's like it all looked so hopeless."

"How do you mean?" he asked.

"Well, just look at most people," I answered. "They aren't happy. They're all caught up in their little lives. But they're not happy. They go along and gather all this useless junk. And that's what you're supposed to do.......I don't know if I can do that. I don't want to do that!" My voice had gotten louder and louder. I looked around. Others were watching.

"Don't get angry," he said, reaching over and putting his hand on mine, trying to calm me. "But I don't think there's anything wrong with how you feel. You've just figured it out and they haven't. That's all."

"What do you mean?" I asked, and there was still a trace of anger in my voice.

"Most of them are happy," he answered. "I think you're wrong when you say that most people are unhappy. They're happy because they're doing what they want to. And that's sort of what it's all about. I agree with you that most of them spend their lives in ways that seem a waste to you right now. But it might not always be like that. You might meet Mr. Right and want some kids some day, and you'll need a house, and that sort of stuff. It just sort of happens to most people without they're even realizing it."

"God, I don't want it to happen to me," I said, and there was more anger in my voice.

"You probably don't have to let it," he answered. "You're in control."

There was quiet.

"Do you have a family?" I asked, breaking the short silence.

"No," he answered. "That's not for me."

"Why not? If it just happens. Why didn't it happen to you?" I asked.

"I don't want all that responsibility," he said. "I'm no good at that sort of stuff."

"Seems to me you'd be pretty good at it," I answered.

He just offered a sort of half smile.

We'd been sitting in the caf for quite a while. Most of the other people had left.

"Just remember, Angie, that you're in control," he said, after some quiet.

I looked over at him. And I smiled.

"I should go," he said. "I'm really whipped. It's been quite a day." He got to his feet.

"I might go and watch some TV," I said, and I kind of hoped he'd change his mind and come along.

"Suit yourself," he answered. "I'm off to lock-up."

We walked to the cafeteria door together. Then, it was time to part.

"Take care," he said, as he turned to go. And he came back to me and hugged me. It only lasted for a couple of seconds, but it was a firm and solid hug and it seemed so sincere the way he did it. Then, he turned and was gone. I went and watched TV. It was one of those cop shows. A lot of people died.

The next morning was my first group session. There were about six of us in the group. We were supposed to take turns talking about stuff that was bothering us, and why we thought we were here -- in the program at the hospital. But I thought it was a pretty dumb thing -- a couple of girls got all upset and cried -- so when my turn came, I was quiet. I said nothing. I watched the others carefully, just to make sure they didn't try to sneak up on me. The doctor was annoyed with me, and pulled me aside after the session to tell me so. I didn't care. I didn't talk to him either.

It was lunchtime. I went to the caf. Hoped I'd see Bill there.

But he wasn't there. I looked around, while I was picking out my sandwich.

"Too bad about your friend," the cashier said, as I approached with my money.

I didn't know what she meant.

"The guy you were in here with last night almost until closing," she said.

"Why?" I asked, now knowing that she meant Bill.

"He offed himself last night. I thought you'd have heard," she said matter of factly. "Hung himself."

I dropped the sandwich and the money. I felt the tears starting to come. I looked at the cashier, and the shock and sadness must have been all over my face.

"I'm sorry, baby," she said softly, suddenly seeming to feel some compassion for me.

But I burst away from her and out of the caf and toward my room. I lay on my bed and cried. I cried for Bill. Why? I asked. Why? I thought of him sitting there telling me so calmly how precious life is. I knew nothing about him. He was dead. Offed himself. That's what the cashier had said.

I checked out of the hospital the next day. Took the bus back to the town where I lived, and kind of surprised my parents when I came walking in. I've never been back to a place like that. I haven't needed it. I just keep telling myself that I'm in control. And I guess I am. Have a husband who works in the foundry and three kids and a house up behind the hospital in a kind of fashionable suburb. And I guess it's alright. Just like Bill said.

I think of him often, as I think of that time in my life often. First I was lost, but now I'm found -- that sort of stuff. And I've decided that I think I'll try to die very slowly, a year at a time. Sometimes, I look down into the eyes of my five-year-old, and she looks back, and the whole world explodes with beautiful colour for me. And I know that life is precious. Just like Bill said. Back when I was crazy.

Brothers

"Comeon, Chuckie, don't be afraid," said the older boy's voice.

"But, Ray, I don't want to. I am afraid," whimpered the younger boy, as he stood trembling on the big, black railway bridge, high above the river below.

"There's nothing to be afraid of," chided the one called Ray. "This is what you've got to do if you want to belong to the club. You're the one that wanted to join."

"I don't know, Ray. It looks so far down," answered the younger boy.

"You don't have to look down. Just jump.....and you'll be in," said Ray. "Anyway, I'll be right behind you. I'll jump as soon as you're clear."

"You're sure it's all right?" Chuck asked in an uncertain voice. "I won't hit bottom."

"Chuck," answered the older boy, impatience starting to sound in his voice, "I've done it a hundred times. It's great." He paused, before using the strongest argument he could. "Anyway, you don't want the other guys to think you're chicken, do you?"

And that seemed to do it. The exchange seemed at an end. Now the younger boy stood on the very edge of the bridge, appearing to make one last attempt to gather his courage. Then, suddenly, he jumped.

He saw nothing, his eyes squeezed tightly shut, his teeth clenched with terror and apprehension, the upward rush of the surrounding air the total of his physical experience. He tried to keep his feet pointed straight down, his arms held stiffly at his sides, because Ray had told him it would hurt if he didn't.

The water caught him by surprise, because it seemed to rush up to meet him so quickly. It seemed like he hardly left the bridge, and he could feel himself slicing into the river's surface. Then, he was through it, and down, down he went. He spread his arms out from his sides, perhaps thinking to try to slow himself, but more likely just as a reflex action caused by the fear that he still felt.

And before his descent had slowed sufficiently, he was into the river's bottom, his feet driven deeply into its mucky substance by the force of his downward motion, first to his ankles, and, finally, almost to his knees. And there he stopped.

At first, he did nothing. Was motionless and still on the bottom of the river, perhaps surprised that he was conscious after the descent from the height of the bridge. Then, he felt the coolness of the river muck around his feet and legs, opened his eyes, but could see nothing but a few feet of dark murkiness. It seemed quiet and calm. He went to pull up out of the muck, toward the faint light he could see coming from above, knowing that he must seek air. But the river bottom held him firm. No matter how he struggled, and soon he did struggle, he could not pull free. At first, he felt fear, a return of what he had felt on the bridge. Then, after more struggling, there was panic. He fought to hold his breath until his chest felt as if it would explode. He reached toward the mud at his feet, to make a last deperate attempt to free himself.

And it was then that the older boy came, also having jumped from the bridge, but having landed some distance away, where the water was deeper. And, of course, he also knew all the tricks of how to slow himself down once he hit the water. He'd quickly surfaced, and seen that the younger boy hadn't come up yet. He'd found him quickly, tracing the air bubbles being released during the struggle on the bottom. He easily pulled him from the river's oozing grasp, and it was only a moment before the two boys had broken the water's surface, the older one holding the younger's head above the river while he gasped for air and choked and sputtered from the water he'd inhaled.

Later, they lay on the river bank in the sun.

Memories for Sale

"Are you sure you're okay, Chuck?" asked the older boy.

"Yea, I'm alright, Ray," answered the younger one.

"You won't tell Mom?" asked Ray.

"No, Ray," answered Chuck.

There was a moment of quiet.

"Can I still be in the club, Ray?" asked the younger boy.

"Sure, Chuck," answered the older one. "You can still be in the club."

"Will I have to jump off the bridge again?" Chuck asked somewhat timidly.

"No, Chuck, you won't," came the answer.

A hand on his arm brought him back from the river bank. "Excuse me, sir, would you like some breakfast?" asked a pleasant female voice.

He looked up to see the smiling face of a flight attendant and he remembered the reality of his situation. Aboard an airliner, passing over the Atlantic Ocean. He glanced to the seat beside him to see his wife of forty years, just waking up from the sleep she had fallen into as they'd travelled through the night.

They listened to the young lady as she recited their choices for the morning meal. He settled on some toast and coffee, while his wife asked for a fruit salad. They watched as she made her way off up the aisle, taking orders as she went. He asked his wife how she'd slept, and they talked for a few moments about being on the flight, this being the first time flying for both of them. Then, they settled back into their seats to await thearrival of breakfast.

He hadn't really slept, but had dozed off and on throughout the night, with the reality of the airplane intruding now and then. It had been a night of dreams, if they can rightly be called such when you aren't really sleeping, but are rather existing in a type of twilight zone between the here and now and another place that stayed all fuzzy and unreal. That was where he had been when he had seen his brother, Ray.

When he had been again on the big, black railway bridge, a place he had not been in over fifty years and which no longer even existed in real life.

Even the thought of Ray caused a wave of emotion to swell in him. His older brother by four years. His protector and guardian. His accomplice and co-conspirator. His roommate and playmate. But most of all, his friend. The two of them had done everything together. His mother, when she'd been alive, had often reminded him of how he'd tagged after Ray even when he'd still been in diapers. Even though there'd been the age difference, the older boy hadn't seemed to mind.

He still thought often of Ray. In the small town where they'd grown up, he'd been sports star and talented musician, easily winning friends and admirers from all parts of the community, everyone agreeing that the boy would go places in life; that he just simply couldn't miss to make it big, whether it was in sports, music, or any of the many things he did so well.

His own growing up years had been a struggle, because while the older brother shone at everything he did, he could do nothing right. He was small and scrawny and was always the last kid chosen in sporting contests, and he was tone deaf. He had difficulty making friends of any type, and his life seemed the proverbial uphill battle. Where Ray was always bringing home all kinds of exciting news of this accomplishment or that one, he became known as the dependable one -- reliable, old Chuck.

But it had been like the older brother had sensed the disappointment of his younger brother at never seeming to do as well, or to be as good, so that he always took an interest in him. Tried to include him in things like sports contests and other activities, so he'd not feel left out.

And, god, how he'd looked up to Ray, who seemed like a great, white, shining knight in an ordinary, dull-gray world. There was no one who was truer, or nobler, or more righteous than Ray.

"Excuse me, sir," said the flight attendant's voice, and again she brought him back to reality. Breakfast had arrived.

"Why, Ray, why?" he asked his older brother, and there was real anguish in his voice.

"I've got to, Chuck," Ray answered emphatically. "It's my duty to go. It's all of our duty."

"Then, why can't I go?" the younger boy implored.

"You're too young," Ray answered.

"But you're only eighteen, and Mom says she needs you at home since Dad died," Chuck answered.

"I've got to go, Chuck," the older boy said. "And you're not making this any easier. You can be the man of the house now, and look after Mom and the girls. You've got to understand, Chuck, I don't want to go, but I have to. There's a war on and I think I can help to win it for us."

"I can't be the man of the house, Ray," Chuck answered. "I'm only fourteen. I'm just a kid."

"I know you better than that, Chuckie," said the older boy, and as he said it he reached forward and toussled the younger boy's hair. "You're Mr. Reliability. You'll be better at looking after Mom and the kids than I would. I know you, little brother."

And despite what he was saying, Chuck couldn't help but think how magnificent and grown-up Ray looked in his air force uniform, and he knew that his brother would probably win the war single-handed, and come marching home a full-blown hero with a chestfull of medals.

That night, the whole family talked of such things over dinner. Ray would be the best pilot in the air force and stop the hated enemy once and for all. It would be a short war once Ray arrived to join the battle. That was the way they all talked.

But Chuck fought back tears the next morning, as Ray kissed their mother and the girls good-bye, and gathered up his duffle bag and climbed aboard the train. He didn't cry, because that wouldn't have been right. Ray had to think he was strong. After all, he was the man of the house now.

But he was afraid. Very afraid. And he felt alone for the first time in his life.

"Chuck, are you alright?" asked his wife's voice, startling him back to the present.

"Yea, just lost in my thoughts, I guess," he answered, smiling at the woman who'd been his sweetheart from the time he'd been a boy.

"Thinking about Ray?" she asked, reading his mind as she usually did.

"Yea, I guess I was," he answered.

"It must be hard not to," she said.

"I guess," he answered.

"I just wish you'd enjoy the trip more," she said. "We're passing through some beautiful countryside. The tulips are all in bloom."

He leaned over to her side of the train compartment and looked out the window at the passing scenery. "It is awful pretty," he agreed. "And I'm sorry if I seem pre-occupied. I am enjoying the trip." Again he smiled at her, and this time he gave her a quick, little kiss.

She blushed, and looked around to see that nobody had seen, even after forty years of marriage.

He settled back into his own seat for the rest of this part of their trip. Before long, they would arrive at their destination.

It was a tiny village in Holland, far away from their small town home in Canada. It was where Ray was.

"Chuck!" called out his supervisor. "There's someone here to see you!"

He wiped his hands on his apron, trying to smear off the grease that came from working around the butter machine in the dairy where he'd laboured for the past two years, since Ray had left.

"Yessir," he said, as he approached the supervisor's office. He could see that another person was standing just back inside the office door, but, because of the shadows, couldn't make out who it was at first, then was surprised to see it was his minister. What was he doing here? he thought. He was young, only seventeen, and nothing more sinister crossed his mind.

"Chuck, Reverend Gillway is here to see you," his supervisor said.

"Yessir," answered Chuck, wringing his hands just a little nervously. "Reverend Gillway?" he asked quietly.

"It's Raymond, Chuck," the man's voice said flatly.

"What about Ray, sir?" he asked.

"Son," said the minister, walking forward and putting his hand on Chuck's shoulder, "your brother's been listed as missing in action. His plane was shot down over Holland last night. I've got a telegram from the War Department."

Chuck stood silent, stonelike, his eyes shifting to and fro anxiously, as if considering his options, and knowing that one was to flee. "Ray?" he sort of asked quietly. The rest of that area of the dairy fell silent, as the news spread, whispered word of mouth through the place.

"I'm sorry, son," the minister said softly, putting his arm around him and sort of embracing him with it.

"Oh, god," Chuck managed. He was numb. He could think of nothing, but Ray filled his mind. He saw his brother as he had last seen him, all decked out in his air force uniform, duffle bag slung over his shoulder, boarding the train. Smiling confidently. Offering a slight wave.

Chuck struggled briefly with himself. He must have composure. "Does mother know?" he asked.

"No, I came here first," Reverend Gillway answered. "After all, you've been the man of the house since your father died and Ray left. I thought you should know first."

"I've got to go to mother," Chuck said firmly.

"You go Chuck," said his supervisor; "and with full pay for the rest of the week."

"I'll come with you," the minister added.

"I'd appreciate that," Chuck answered. "Mom and my sisters will need you there."

And so it went. There was hardly a week had gone by since the war had been begun, and the battle joined, that such sad news had not travelled through the community. But he had not once thought that it would one day be news of Ray. He hardly remembered telling his mother, or his sisters, when they returned from school. And once he had calmed them somewhat, as much as it could be done after such calamitous news has been received, and left them in the care of some neighbours and ladies from the church, he headed out into the falling night. And he walked, and walked, and walked. Down by the big, black railway bridge, and in the ravine near the cemetery, and over to the arena, and by the dance hall -- to all the places where Ray might have been. But he couldn't find his brother in any of those familiar haunts.

He was seemingly dead.

It was the train conductor's voice that finally brought him back this time, for he had, of course, been drifting back and away from this time, and to a remembering of his brother.

"Ter Apel!" called out the man's voice, cutting through the dreamy, dozy mood that had come over him. "Ter Apel!"

He roused himseld back to a full consciousness and looked out the train window to see that the train had come into a smallish-looking village. His wife, who had also fallen into a light sleep but also awoken, looked over at him. "We're here," she said, smiling.

"Yes, we're here," he answered.

"You alright," she asked, taking his hand and giving it a gentle squeeze, knowing that he was filled with emotions about the trip.

"I'm fine," he answered.

And they both started to get to their feet and search about for their carry-on bags, as they felt the train start to slow.

The people of Ter Apel had long honoured the memory of the six fallen fliers who lay buried on the edge of the village cemetery, and often throughout the years, they had sent letters and photographs of the grave to Chuck's mother, and they had thanked her often for sending them her son in their time of need. So that when they received news of the brother's visit, they offered him accommodation with a family from the village. And that couple and their children were on the train platform to greet them, as their long jourrney drew to a close.

The first place they visited was the cemetery. But it had started to rain, so they stayed in the car, but even from there, Chuck could see there were fresh cut flowers on the graves.

"The one on the left is where your brother is buried," their host explained in halting English.

And Chuck thought that even in the gray sombreness of the weather, there was somehow a specialness to the place, and it almost seemed to shine out even in the overcast and rain. He found himself smiling to think that Ray had come to a place such as this.

They sat in quiet for a few moments, even the children who seemed to know the importance of this time. Then, they drove on, until they arrived at the house where the host family lived. Then, it was in to freshen up, and to have supper.

He felt restless during the evening. The two couples exchanged pictures of their families and learned more of each other. But it was a hard time for him. It was like he felt him close by, and wanted nothing more than to go to him. So that the evening passed slowly, and it was like there was to be no end to it.

Finally, he could bear it no longer. He announced he must go for a walk before bed. His wife expressed concern about walking in such a strange environ, but he quickly calmed her, and declined any offer of company, and was off into the night.

And it was the cemetery he sought. The house was close to it, and he had watched closely as they'd made the trip earlier in the day, because he had known that he would want to return by himself. It was why he had come all this way. It was why he had come.

There was still a light drizzle falling as he started the walk. He walked purposefully, in the direction he was sure the place was. It was almost like something drew him to it. That he must at least be by his side.

And so it was that he came directly to the village cemetery, with neither his memory nor his sense failing him. And he walked to its edge -- to the place where six brave fliers were buried so far from home. He walked the length of the six plots, and even in the darkness of the night was able to read the names etched on the six stones. He could see the neatly groomed grass, and the remains of the flowers that must have been placed there earlier in the day. All was as it should have been. He knew the stories of how the enemy had not let the villagers say even so much as a prayer over the bodies, when they had been dumped into mass graves, carried to the place in a horsecart. Nothing placed in memory. No neatly groomed grass. No flowers on that day.

But, finally, he came to Ray's grave, nothing more elaborate than the others, but somehow so noble and so true. He could not fully explain why he had wanted to make this trip to visit the grave of the brother who had been killed all those many years ago, so that had he lived, he would be a nothing more than a withered up old man in this day and age. Ray had stayed eighteen years old for him always. And although he had known his brother was dead and buried in a faraway land, it was like he was also not dead, but had merely gone away, like the son who had quarreled with his father and gone away to the far ends of the earth forever.

He had missed his brother, and had often wondered what life would have held had he come home from the war. For it was true that he had lived a gilded life before he had gone, and Chuck had later learned that he had been a great hero in the war as well, putting himself at great risk to save others, even as they said that he and the others had stayed with the plane on that fateful night so long ago, and not bailed out, so that they could be sure it would not crash on the tiny village below. So that they had given up their lives, so that others could be spared the carnage and death of war.

He took a small pill bottle out of his coat pocket. Stooped and gathered up some of the soil from the grave with the little plastic bottle.

"Don't be afraid, Ray. I'll take you home," he said softly.

Thanks for coming, Chuck.

It's alright, Ray.

And it was alright.

My One Great Love. And How It Ended.

I pretty well lived at the pool hall back in my younger days, much to the grief of my good parents, who thought that such places were dens of iniquity where great and wondrous transformations were carried out on young boys to make them turn from the Lord and smoke cigarettes and curse and swear like old salts from the sea. It was a curious sort of place for certain; and one where the Lord was surely not safe. There was for sure lots of cursing and swearing and smoking of cigarettes and there were occasional bouts of drinking and gambling, but I took the attitude early on that it was all in good fun -- maybe not good, clean fun, but fun all the same. I revelled in it -- much to the grief of my parents, who were probably right in what they thought.

The pool rooms from back in my youth were what I think you'd call bastions of male machismo, where men hid from wives, and boys from their mothers, and every male of the species knew he was safe and secure from all things womanly. The old men contended that no female had ever set foot in the pool room where I got the better part of my learning. I couldn't prove that to be true, but my mother wouldn't even go in the place to get my Dad his smokes when he was in hospital for his ulcer. It was just that kind of place where one step inside could taint your soul for an eternity in the hereafter -- at least that's what I'm sure my mom felt.

But this is the story of a girl I once knew -- and she was a special thing, and I loved her with all my heart back in those other olden days. She came into my life when I was in the twelfth grade, struggling to make sense of logarithms, wrestling with the chemical symbols for all sorts of foul and evil-smelling concoctions and generally having a most difficult time with the whole adolescent thing. And it was true that I had never been on a for-real date in my whole life by the time I was in twelfth grade. And it wasn't like I wasn't interested, because Lord knew that I was more than interested in anything and everything female. But I just couldn't get my nerve up. The other guys called it getting shot down when a girl refused their advances, but I called it being humiliated, and I avoided it at all costs.

Now, I'd known this girl for some considerable length of time, both of us living in the same small town, but I'd not known her well because we ran with different crowds. I'd admired her, too, because she was a looker -- that's what the other guys said. Would have liked to have gotten closer to her, but was forever without the chance. Anyway, after we got older, she was constantly on the arm of a boyfriend, usually a big tough, hunk of a guy with the looks and the money and the inevitable car, and I had none of those. So, I kept my distance -- knew I hadn't a chance.

And so it happened that while I was in twelfth grade, I really did struggle with my maths and sciences, but I was a wizard in English literature. There wasn't a hidden meaning lurking that I couldn't find as we read our way through some of the great literature of modern western civilization. But others were not so fortunate, and could discover nothing hiding among the words and phrases in their English texts -- they saw only the plain language on the surface of the pages and could not mine beneath for the richness of thought contained in their depths.

And it also came to pass that my twelfth grade English teacher pulled me aside after class one day, just before Christmas break.

"That was a great way of expressing that the way you did," she said, alluding to a particularly insightful remark I'd made in a discussion of John Steinbeck's Of Mice and Men, which I have always considered to be a work of true genius, a slim volume compared to Grapes of Wrath, but packing much more emotional punch.

"It's just the way I see it," I answered, appearing quite non chalant about receiving such praise.

"Well, I just wish more of the class had your way of looking at work like this," she said. "It would really make my job easier."

I stood in silence, rocking back and forth on the heels of my cowboy boots, but not exactly sure where this was leading, wondering why she'd called me aside.

She seemed to wait until the rest of the class had left, and only when that had been accomplished, did she continue.

"I wanted to talk to you about something," she started.

I knit my eyebrows and got a serious expression on my face to show her I was paying attention.

"I've got a student who's approached me for extra help -- from my other Grade 12 class," the teacher said. "The problem is that I'm already tutoring six kids this semester and I've gotten myself too busy." She paused.

I regarded her. Said nothing, but waited for her to continue.

"I was wondering if you might consider helping this student understand some of the books on the course?" the teacher asked. "I think it would even be okay if you charged a little something for your time."

I thought for a moment, surprised at what was being asked, caught unawares by her question. "Gee," I started to answer, continuing to rock in my boots........

"You don't have to answer right now," she interrupted. "Think about it and let me know later in the week, but before the holiday if you can, so we can get the two of you started during the break."

With that, I was off, hurrying to my next class, but wondering about the offer to tutor as I hurried. I could surely use a little extra cash -- that was for sure -- but it would mean sacrificing time from the pool room and from hanging out with the guys -- both major intrusions in my social life and so a cause for serious consideration. I could use the extra cash, but I'd mull it over just the same.

As it turned out, I mulled it over until dinner that night when my

Dad announced that he had run into my English teacher uptown, which was not all that strange considering my Dad worked in the post office. That meant he regularly ran into almost every single person in town when they came to pick up their mail, which was what my English teacher was doing when my Dad ran into her.

"Miss Robbins tells me she's offered you a job," my Dad said between mouthfuls of leather soup, an odd mixture of fatty, end-of-the-line roast beef and flat, doughy dumplings that had been invented during the depression when my mother's mother had wanted to fool her family into thinking there was still food to eat.

"Well, it's not exactly a job," I answered, thinking to discourage him from putting pressure on me to accept. After I made the brief answer, I abruptly shoved a spoonful of leather soup into my mouth, hoping he'd get the point and drop the subject.

"Oh, isn't that nice," my Mom said. "If it's not exactly a job, what is it she's offered you, dear?" she asked, maintaining the conversation and almost certainly assuring my position as a tutor.

Likely for some big, hairy, ugly basketball player who had to pass English so he'd be allowed to play for another season, before he dropped out to become human fodder for the furniture factory on the town's main street. Because that's who I'd decided my student was most likely to be. The more I'd thought about this, the more sure I was that this tutoring thing was going to be a big mistake.

"Well, what is it?" my Dad asked impatiently. "If it's not a job."

"She wants me to help somebody with their English," I finally answered. "But I'm not sure it's a good idea," I quickly added. "I mean, it might just slow me down -- I mean, I don't need anybody getting me confused about this stuff. And that might happen."

My Dad was looking at me like I was crazy, and I probably sounded like I was, both of us realizing that I was offering up some pretty lame material.

"It sounds like Miss Robbins must think you could do it, son," Mom said. "You've always gotten really good marks in English."

"I know, Mom," I answered.

"She told me you could make a little money over the holidays," joined in my Dad, adding his usual practical, finance-oriented point to the discussion.

"It likely wouldn't be much," I countered.

"Well, it sounds like a good opportunity," my Dad said. "You should think about it."

"I am thinking about it, Dad," I answered.

"It sounds like a good opportunity. Maybe there'd be something more next year," my Dad said, relentless in his reasoning.

"I know, Dad," I answered. "I've thought about that."

"You two better eat your soup before it gets cold," my mother chimed in, effectively telling us the conversation was at an end. And we both listened to what she said, because there's nothing that can curdle your blood quicker than to be faced with the prospect of eating some of my Mom's leather soup after it's gotten cold and taken on the consistency of wet cement.

But I knew that if I didn't accept the tutoring assignment, each time I approached my Dad for some cash from now until I reached middle age, he'd remind me of how I'd passed up the one great opportunity in my life -- I was trapped in the proverbial no-win situation.

So, I accepted. And the plan was that I would meet my new student on the last day of classes before the Christmas break, right after the Christmas assembly, so that we could set up a schedule of appointments for over the holidays.

So, I dutifully trudged up to the classroom where I studied English immediately following the assembly, painfully aware that my friends were headed for the chinaman's restaurant where they would sip cherry cokes and plan the festivities for the first night of the much anticipated Yuletide vacation.

I entered the room, and it was empty, except for a single person -- the very girl I'd admired from afar for so many years. I stopped short -- said nothing.

"Hi," she said brightly. "You must be the English wiz."

"I...I guess," I managed to stammer, knowing full well that I was turning twenty-seven shades of red, embarrassed to be confronted by her, wanting to scurry from the room and hide from her.

"I've seen you around," she said. "We were in the same Confirmation Class at church."

"I remember," I answered, and the tone of her voice seemed to set me somewhat at ease, so that I could feel myself relax a bit.

"So, do you remember any of that stuff?" she asked.

"What stuff?" I answered her question with one of my own.

"That Bible stuff they taught us," she answered. "You know."

"Oh, yea," I said. "Guess I remember the important stuff. Haven't killed anybody recently."

She laughed at my little joke, and the rest of the tension I was feeling seemed to disappear.

Still, there was a silence and I was a little unsure what to say.

"So," I started......

"You likely want to know what a smart girl like me is doing needing English help," she said, seeming to sense my uncertainty. "Well, I'm a wiz at science and math but I don't seem to be able to get English through my thick head. I just don't seem to understand what the writers are getting at."

"Well, I'm not sure I always know, either," I answered truthfully.

"Miss Robbins says you're really good at this stuff," the girl said.

"I do my best, but I'm not sure there's any trick to it," I said. "I think it's mostly being able to let yourself go and getting inside the author's heads."

"Can you teach me how to do that?" she asked.

"Don't know," I answered, again truthfully. I paused. "Do you like to read?" I asked.

"I don't read much," she admitted. "I used to read Nancy Drew, but not much past that."

"Maybe we can change that," I said.

"When do you want to start?" she asked.

"Is tomorrow too soon?" I asked back, and the pool hall and my friends were both forgotten.

"That would be great," she answered.

"Should I come to your place?" I asked.

"No, you can't come to my place," she answered and I was aware that she said it a little more loudly and deliberately than was perhaps necessary. "I'll come to your place, if it's okay," she added, and her voice was immediately softer and more like it had been earlier.

"Yea," I answered, unsure what nerve I'd struck. "That would be great."

And so we parted, and I walked on air as we left the room. I didn't even bother with my friends or the pool room. I went home. I had work to do.

My mother's jaw must have dropped a foot when I told her my student was coming to our place for tutoring the next day and that the student was, in fact, an attractive member of the opposite sex. I could well imagine her sitting up half the night knitting baby booties for the grandchildren, and knew for sure she'd be up early the next morning to make sure the house was good and clean before my guest arrived.

I was also up early, reading voraciously away, scribbling notes, trying to prepare for the first lesson. After all, I had to make a good first impression, appearing able to make many wise and knowledgeable insights into the work of various great writers -- a tall order, even for one much more learned than I. I didn't have hunk-type looks, or cash, or a car. I would have to dazzle her with my superior brain. I would have to show her that there was more to life than tooling around in a fancy red convertible with the captain of the football team. Everything depended on how we made out at this first session.

She was to come at four and by ten after I was sure she'd changed her mind and not bothered to call.

"Are you sure it was today?" my mother asked.

"Yes, mother," I replied, and just then there was a knock at the kitchen door.

I showed my new student into the living room where we were to work, finally managed to convince my mother that we didn't need anything, and we settled in to study.

The hour passed quickly, too quickly for my liking. I know for certain that I had never spent that much time that close to a girl who was also surely a woman. I could smell her. Her breath touched me. I could feel her without touching her. I was continually aroused during the lesson, constantly afraid it would be revealed to her. But I did my best to conceal it, and it seemed to go unnoticed. Finally, my Dad came home from work, meaning an end to our time together.

We had said nothing to each other, excepting what needed discussing for high school English, but I felt I could feel something between us as I showed her out. And just as she stepped out the door, she looked back and our eyes connected for the first time since we'd come together the day before. I melted into a puddle of soft, warm emotion at that very instant and could tell she felt something too. But she turned and left, not looking back as she walked down the sidewalk and made her way toward her home. I watched her go, until she was no more.

I waited for our next meeting, two days hence, filled with anticipation. She was on my mind constantly and she came to me in my dreams. I'd heard my buddies discussing the concept of getting "hung up" on a girl, and had laughed at them as they went through the various gyrations of puppy love, but now I felt an awful grasp upon my soul. I wanted to be with her. Indeed, I craved to be with her, and had little interest in the rest of my life.

The two days passed slowly, but finally they were at an end, and I was pacing the floor, again awaiting my tardy student. Then, at fifteen minutes past the hour, just after my Mom had again asked me if I had the right day, I peered out through the kitchen window and saw a bright, flashy, red sports car pull into the driveway, and at once my spirit soared and was crushed. I realized my Venus had arrived, but had come with one of the thick dullards she usually hung with.

I watched from the corner of the window as she climbed from the car. Then, just as she was about to close the door, it seemed whoever was in the car spoke to her, because she wheeled around, an angry, hurt look on her face, and said something back into the vehicle. The car door slammed abruptly shut and the car backed quickly out of the driveway.

She stood for a moment in the driveway, a light snow falling about her, seeming to try to compose herself after the brief altercation with the car's driver. She brushed her hand across her face, perhaps clearing away an errant tear. And even as I watched her there, I could see only heavenly beauty both in her and surrounding her. She seemed a vision of soft radiance to my lovestruck eyes.

Finally, she came up the walk to the house. I pulled back and gave her time to knock, not wanting her to suspect that I'd seen the exchange in the driveway. But I didn't wait too long after she knocked and I swept the door open and invited her inside.

Soon, but not until I had fended off the obligatory offer of pop and chips or cookies and milk or whatever from my mother, we were back sitting in our study area in the living room.

"Are you okay?" I found myself asking after we'd gotten settled, not sure I should ask such a question, but unable to prevent myself from doing so.

"Is it that obvious?" she asked, but she offered up a small smile that made me feel better.

"You just look like you've been upset," I answered.

"Oh, I'm all right," she said. "I'm just not a very big fan of Christmas. I find it a hard time of year."

"That's too bad," I said. "Most people really like Christmas."

"Well, most people's fathers don't come home drunk and miserable every night over the holidays," she said.

"Your Dad?" I asked, not sure I wasn't treading where I shouldn't.

"Oh, he drinks all the time," she answered, "but at Christmas, it's always worse. He can't hold a job, and at Christmas, he gets feeling sorry for himself because he's got no money and he really takes it out on my Mom."

"God, that's too bad," I answered. "It must be hell."

"It's not great," she answered. "And Jeff just doesn't understand what I'm going through."

"Jeff your boyfriend?" I asked.

"Yes, and all he cares about is whether I'm going to make the big Christmas party," she answered. "He doesn't understand that I've got other responsibilities. My Mom has to work and I've got to help with my brothers and sisters and get meals ready and stuff like that." She paused. It seemed a cloud had settled over her. Gone was the bright cheery person I'd encountered at our previous meetings. "And I've got to help my Mom deal with Dad. I can't leave her alone with that."

"That's really too bad," I said softly, trying to show her that I could understand. "Well, I'll tell you something," I continued, "if there's ever anything I can do -- anything at all -- you call me. You shouldn't be going through this alone."

"You're sweet," she said, leaning over and giving me a light kiss on the cheek -- a touch that sent a warm, gentle wave of emotion washing over me. I could feel myself blush.

And we waded into that day's English lesson, and no more was mentioned about her difficult circumstance. And it was a pleasant enough hour, just to have her so close, and to see her face as she listened attentively to my every word -- just to have her as mine for even a time so short.

Finally, it was at an end. Jeff's car horn sounded from the driveway.

"I've got to go," she said, gathering up her books.

I escorted her to the door and got her coat for her.

"I've enjoyed this," she said, looking back at me as she prepared to go. And, again, as they had on the previous occasion, our eyes locked together, and I was flooded with feelings for her -- and I knew she could feel them too.

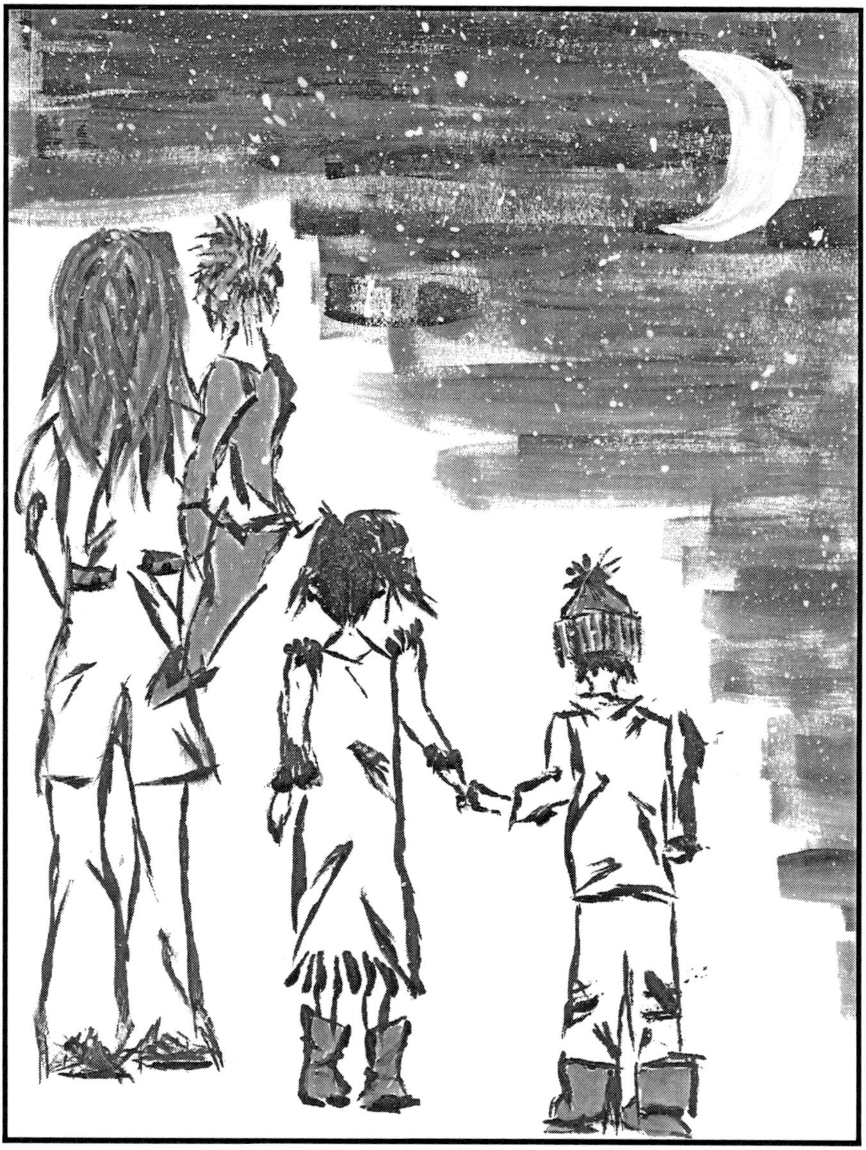

And just as she stepped out the door, I took my best shot. "Don't forget to call if you need to," I said. "I'm always here to listen."

And she left my life and went back into Jeff's, and I could feel jealous anger rise up in me to know that she was with such an uncaring lout, who made no effort to see what she was going through. How could she be with him?

But I went on about my business. We wouldn't be able to meet now until after Christmas had passed. That meant three days before our next session and I couldn't just sit about the house and pine away. So, I pulled on my parka and headed uptown for the pool room. With any luck, I'd be able to get into a good game of card pool. Somebody might even have smuggled in a bottle and there'd be a little drinking to be done -- that appealed to me on this particular day.

And the rest of that day passed and we were into Christmas Eve day. I was generally discontent, but knew the mood was caused by the girl. I shot a little more pool in the early afternoon, until the place closed for the holiday, then a few buddies and I headed for the chinaman's restaurant to sip on cherry cokes until that place closed for the holiday, then we were left in the street, faced with the prospect of going home.

Later that night, after my parents had settled in for a long winter's nap, and the presents were under the tree for another year, I was surprised to hear the phone ring just as I was preparing for bed myself. I hurried and snatched up the receiver on the second ring, not wanting it to disturb any who slept.

"Hello," I said.

"Hi," answered a voice I recognized immediately as belonging to the girl of my dreams.

"How are you?" I asked, realizing it was likely a stupid question.

"I'm not great," she answered. "Sorry to call so late, but I didn't know who else to call." There was distress in her voice -- I could hear it as she spoke.

"What's wrong?" I asked, almost afraid to hear.

"It's my Dad," she answered. "He came home drunk again tonight, and he brought a couple of his drinking buddies after the bar closed for the holiday. They were drinking here all night, and, finally the other guys left, but my Dad got really angry. He started to knock my Mom around. I tried to stop him, but I couldn't. I got my brothers and sisters and ran out." It was desparation I heard from her now. Her words quick and tense.

"Where are you now?" I asked, my heart pounding in my ears.

"I'm at the laundromat," she answered. "It was the only place I could think of that might be open."

"Stay there," I said. "I'll be right over."

"You'll come?" she asked.

"Stay there," I repeated. "I'm on my way."

We said a quick goodbye and I hung up the phone and walked to the bottom of the stairs.

"Dad," I called into the darkened upstairs where my parents were sleeping.

"What, son?" my Dad called back . "Who was that on the phone?"

"It was a friend, Dad," I answered. "I need to borrow the car for a while."

"Is anything wrong?" he called down.

"No, Dad," I lied. "I just need to go out for a while."

"Well, okay, but be careful," he answered. "It's been snowing and it's slippery in spots."

"Okay, Dad," I answered. "Thanks."

And I was out the door, into my Dad's car, and fishtailing off up the street toward the laundromat.

I found them in good order, the girl and her brothers and sisters, but all looking thoroughly miserable and forelorn to be out and in such a condition on Christmas Eve.

"Oh, God, thanks for coming," the girl gushed as I came through the door, rushing up and giving me a huge hug. She had been crying.

"That's what friends are for," I said, and I guided her over to where the younger ones were huddled in a bunch.

"How are you all?" I asked, giving them a great big smile, and trying to make them feel more at ease.

I got a round of return smiles from the bunch, except the youngest girl, who scrunched up her face and let out a loud wail.

"Comeon," I said to them. "I'll take you home."

"We can't go home," piped up one young boy. "Daddy's very mad."

"We've got to go and check on your Mom," I answered. "Now comeon, let's go."

And I followed the lead of the oldest sister, who was my reason for being in this strange circumstance, and we gathered up the brood and were soon all in my Dad's car, the love of my young life just a few scant inches from me. I could hear her breathing beside me.

We pulled up in front of her house, and all was in darkness.

"Let me go in first," I said, knowing that I was now frightened at the prospect of having to enter such a probably hostile environment. "I'll make sure everything is okay."

I left the car running and padded apprehensively up the front walk, and was finally at the door. Then, I wasn't sure what my course of action should be, to knock politely and await the confrontation that might follow, or to barge right in and attempt to surprise whatever might lay in wait for me behind the door. I knocked.

There was no answer, so I knocked again. I also looked back toward my Dad's car and smiled, hoping to re-assure those from the family who waited there.

Finally, I tried the door. It yielded and I pushed it open and stepped gingerly into the near-dark house, looking about in the dim light cast by the Christmas tree.

"Who's there?" called out a woman's voice. "Frank, if that's you come back, you might as well leave right now. There's nothing more for you here."

"It's not Frank, ma'am," I answered. "I've brought the kids back home. Are you all right?"

The woman appeared in a doorway off the room where I was

standing. She looked more than a little the worse for wear, misery etched in a tired-looking face.

"You've got the children?" she asked.

"Yes, ma'am," I answered.

"Keep them out of here for a few minutes, until I get cleaned up," she said. "I can't let the little ones see me like this." She made an attempt to straighten her hair.

"I'll do my best," I said.

And I headed back out to the car, where I explained the situation.

"Your father's gone," I said, "and your mother would like you to wait for a few minutes before you go in."

We settled in, but it was only a couple of minutes and we saw the lights come on in the house, and soon the mother was at the front door waving for us to come.

I walked up to the front door with the wayward children, and watched awkwardly as they embraced and wept with both sadness and joy at being re-united. While they were in the middle of the reunion, I slipped quietly out the door and sat on the step. I wondered at what had happened on this night. It was crisp and clear and cold. I looked up to see a cascade of stars spilled across the sky like rare and wondrous jewels. I breathed in huge mouthfuls of the frigid winter air. It felt good.

Just then the girl came out of the house to where I was sitting. She took a seat beside me.

"How is everybody?" I asked.

"Oh, not too bad," she answered. "The little ones want to hurry to bed so Santa will come."

"Yea, I guess it's Christmas," I said.

There was a long silence. I could see our breath billowing vapourous as it mingled in the night air. The two became one.

"Listen, I really want to thank you for coming and helping," she finally said, interrupting the quiet. "It was awfully nice of you."

"What are friends for," I said. "I'm just glad I was able to come when you called."

"I'm beat," she said. "I'm not sure I've ever felt this tired."

"Should I wait out front for a while in case your Dad comes back?" I asked, looking over at her.

"No," she said. "You go home. Mom's promised that she'll call the police if he tries to come back. That's probably what we should have done earlier."

"All right," I answered. "If you're sure."

"I'm sure," she said, and with that she leaned forward and gave me a kiss full on the lips, so that it took my breath away, and I almost fell off the step. "Thanks. You're sweet," she said.

"Merry Christmas," I said softly, and it seemed a moment of the most special time had arrived.

"Merry Christmas," she answered, and she disappeared in through the door and closed it behind her.

I walked on air back to my father's car, glad to have been kissed, glad to be alive, sure that I had made the most of my chance. There could be no doubt that I had rescued the fair maiden in her time of crisis. What more could I have done to win her heart?

It was a long Christmas day. I wanted to call the girl to make sure everything was okay. As it was, I borrowed Dad's car and drove by her house in mid-afternoon to see if anything was amiss, but all appeared quiet, so I was soon back home, eating turkey with all the trimmings. Finally, the day was at an end, and I slept.

The bowling alley in town was open on Boxing Day, so my buddies and I took advantage of their pool table, playing a few games, whiling away a generally boring day when most things remained closed for the holiday. Finally, that day was also at an end, and I slept.

The next day, there was a lesson and I waited anxiously for four o'clock. It came and went, but I wasn't surprised because she was always late. I kept a look-out at the kitchen window, expecting to see her come walking along.

But the red car came instead. And I watched as she climbed out of it, then leaned back inside to offer the driver, no doubt the dreaded, uncaring Jeff, a kiss. My heart sank as low as it could go. I even felt the beginnings of a tear in the corner of my eye, but I chased it away. How could I have been so stupid? Stupid, stupid, stupid!!!

"How are you?" I said to her as she came into the house, a smile on her face.

"Oh, I'm great," she answered. "Looking forward to discovering Steinbeck."

"Great," I answered, lying, wanting her to leave so I could be alone, the way I belonged.

But I struggled through the lesson. I even managed to smile in the appropriate places, and once let out a laugh. I kept my real emotions hidden. I couldn't let her know how I felt. She'd laugh at me, to think I could have cared for her. I'd be a joke.

Finally, the lesson ended -- even before the horn sounded in the driveway signalling Jeff's arrival. Just as we were gathering up our things, I saw she had a ring on her finger. I'd not noticed it on our previous encounters.

"You've got a new ring," I remarked. "Christmas gift?"

"Sort of," she answered. "Jeff gave it to me. It's an engagement ring. He asked me to marry him when he gave it to me on Christmas day."

"You said yes?" I asked, my voice flat and monotone, the life already beaten out of me, knowing the answer.

"I had to," she answered. "I can't live at home anymore. Jeff can take me away from that."

"What about your Mom?" I asked.

"I can't help her," the girl said. "She took him back again, even after the other night, just like she always does. I've got to get out."

I said nothing. I was destroyed beyond belief. I had no idea what to say. I thought I had done all that I could to win her heart. But I'd failed and lost.

I walked her to the door.

"When should we get together again?" I asked.

"I can't study together anymore," she said. "Jeff doesn't think it's right that I come over here. He's awfully jealous."

I wanted to cry out to her that he was also an insensitive jerk who'd likely start and finish as a frustrated factory worker like her old man and who'd end up beating the daylights out of her and their snotty-nosed brood of kids. But I was quiet for a moment.

"Oh, I'm sorry to hear that," I finally answered. "I thought we were making some progress." But I knew there was no point in continuing the lessons, because she'd be pregnant before the school year ended -- Jeff would have to put his mark on her -- make sure her life was over. That's what happened all too often in this little one-horse town.

Finally, she left and the red car drove out of the driveway. I hurried up to my room so my Mom wouldn't see me cry. More anger, than sadness.

After I was cried out, I went back downstairs and grabbed my parka off the hook behind the door. "I'm going uptown," I announced.

"You're going to miss supper," my Mom said.

"I'll grab a burger," I answered.

"Your Dad will be disappointed," Mom said.

"Tell him I'm sorry," I answered, and I was out into the coming night, knowing that I didn't need supper on this night.

I needed the pool room with all of its courseness and roughness. I wanted to smoke cigarettes and curse like a sailor. And I wanted to engage in a bout of drinking and gambling. I wanted to be somewhere safe from all things womanly.

So, I got drunk and I gambled away my Christmas money and I staggered home in the wee hours of the morning. When I awoke at about noon the next day, I had one hell of a headache, but the heartache seemed gone. I was thankful for that and when it came back, I drank it away again, and I'm afraid to say but this became a regular pattern in my life from that time forth. And some might say I have a drinking problem, but I really do think it's more of a woman problem. And although I never lost my love of reading, and although I can still find those hidden meanings faster than anyone, I am a bit of a bum these days. I just can't take the humiliation that comes from life.

So, I drink. So, sue me. Except I haven't got any money, because I lost it all playing card-pool. And to this day I never have asked a woman out. And that's the story of my one great love and how I came to ruin because of it.

What's that they say?

That's life.

And so it is.

Reminders

I loved my Dad. Even in spite of what went on back then. We were close after my mother left him, but he was a mess and it was hard seeing him like that. He held a job, and he kept some semblance of a household, I think mainly for us kids, but he was just sort of wandering. My Granddad told me years later that my Dad was a man who believed everything in life depended on family, so that he was completely devastated when Mom left and took us with her. We came on weekends, me and my brother, and Dad would always try to do fun things with us, cook us macaroni and hot dogs, take us bowling and ice skating, and do kind of family type stuff with us. But even though I was just a kid, I'd see him sitting there in the arena while I was skating by, and you could see that faraway look in his eyes; the one that said he was just a little this side of empty. It was hard. But he did his best.

I've always accepted that. Even after it happened, and even after all these years, I still love him and think fondly of him. I wish I could have known him better, and I wish I wouldn't have been just a kid back then, because, who knows, I might have been able to help more, and that might have made the difference. I believe he was a good man. That he just lost his way.

I remember one time when I was in about Grade 3. Some years have passed since then, and it's only a child's memory clouded by time, but I think it was the Christmas right after Mom and Dad split up for the final time. I hadn't seen him for a couple of weeks. Mom said he was sick. It was the last couple of weeks before the holidays, and my school

Christmas concert was approaching. I had a big solo part in our class skit, and I was nervous, at least as nervous as you can be in Grade 3 when you're not really aware of what's at stake, and excited at the same time. I wanted him to come. But I hadn't seen him for what seemed a very long time.

"You should come. She really wants you there," I heard my mother saying into the telephone one night when I came in from playing. "It shouldn't matter that Tim will be there. You better get used to it. Tim and I will be together for a very long time." A pause. "Well, she's your daughter and you should forget how you feel for once, and consider how she feels."

It was at that moment that my mother noticed me for the first time since I'd come in. She quickly closed the door to the kitchen, and continued in a hushed voice, so that I couldn't hear any more of the conversation.

I knew that Daddy didn't like Tim, who was always around our house these days, and was really kissy and huggy with mom, which was something I didn't understand back then. She told me she still loved Daddy, but in a different way now, and she also loved Tim. I didn't really understand, but I didn't mind Tim because he took me to the store and bought me candy sometimes. He seemed like a nice guy, I guess, even back then. But Daddy surely didn't like him. It was obvious; even to a kid.

When mother got off the phone, she came to help me out of my winter things, my snowsuit and stuff.

"Was that Daddy?" I asked.

"Yes," she answered, before pausing. "And it doesn't look like he's going to be able to come to your concert. He's still not feeling well."

"Did he go to see Doctor Ralph?" I asked.

"It's not that kind of sick," she answered.

I was disappointed, but I was quiet.

The day of the concert came. It was in the evening, and I was dressed in my Sunday best, standing in line with my classmates, waiting in the hallway outside the gym. We were next. I had butterflies in my stomach. I was repeating my lines, just to make sure I hadn't lost them in the bedlam of the classroom earlier, when we'd been waiting our turn and generally misbehaving, much to the chagrin of our teacher.

Then, as I stood there ready to go on to play my big part, I felt a hand on my shoulder.

"Hi, princess," he said, as I turned to face him. He crouched down so he was more at my level, and we could see eye to eye. "I'm sorry I haven't seen you for a while."

"Daddy!" I exclaimed. But then my excitement subsided. "Do you feel better?" I asked.

"I'm alright," he answered. "But the important thing is how are you feeling?" He brushed my hair back away from my face with the back of his hand in a gentle, sweeping motion.

"I guess I'm alright," I answered.

"Well, listen, it's normal if you're a bit nervous," he said. "It's not easy to get up in front of a lot of people. It takes a special kind of person. I'm very proud of you. You know your lines?"

"I think so. I've been practicing at home," I answered.

"I'm sure you have," he said.

There was a brief pause in the exchange.

"Well, I should get in there," he said. "There are no chairs left, but somebody said I could stand at the back." He leaned forward and kissed me on the forehead. "Remember, I'm proud of you. Just do your best. And......I love you, princess." And when he said the last bit, I remember thinking that his voice sounded different, I thought maybe like he was sad. He stood up quickly, and walked away. He didn't look back.

I didn't really have time to look for him while I was on stage, but I knew he was there, and I was so proud. I always remember being so proud of my Dad. We shared some special time, from when we sat in his big, comfortable maroon easy chair to watch the Leafs on TV (I'm still a Leaf fan today, which is a bit odd for a girl, I guess), to when he sat on the edge of my bed gently stroking my hair and telling me stories, mainly about when he was a kid growing up at Granddad's. I didn't really know back in those days the turmoil he was going through and the pain he was feeling. He hid it well, except for the occasional moment when he got that faraway look in his eyes, or when he got the sadness in his voice. Then, I think I knew there was something wrong, but I was just a kid and I thought a trip to the doctor could make anything better.

He used to take me and my brother bowling quite a bit, even though my brother really couldn't bowl, because he was too small to hold the ball right. That year, for my birthday, he got me to invite a bunch of my friends, and he took us all to the bowling alley for a party. There was Samantha, Anna, Debbie, Alex and a couple of others, and we went for lunch and had pizza, and laughed and giggled until it must have nearly driven him crazy. But he kept quiet, and watched over us, and even laughed at our shenanigans, which was nice because he didn't really laugh, or smile, very often, if I remember right. Even when we'd sit and watch shows like Funniest Videos and Funniest People, he wouldn't laugh. He'd have more of a puzzled look on his face. If I remember right.

Anyway, after we'd had our pizza, and our laughing and giggling, and our bowling, we were getting ready to set off, when Dad excused himself to go to the bathroom.

"I like bowling," Samantha said, as she zipped up her coat. "I'm glad your Dad brought us."

I smiled because I knew I'd scored points with my friends on this afternoon.

"My mom wasn't going to let me come," Debbie said.

"Why not?" I asked.

"She thinks your Dad's a bum," she said straight back, very direct and frank, the way only a kid can.

"He's not!" I said defiantly. "You're just saying that!"

"He's poor, you know," Debbie said in her snottiest tone of voice.

"He's not!" I answered defiantly.

"He drives that old, beat-up car. He lives in a bad part of town. That's what my Dad says," Debbie said, her words attacking me, striking me, ripping into my child's innocence.

But just then, he came back, so the conversation ended. Debbie gave me one of her haughty, I'm-smarter-than-you-are looks, and disappeared out the door of the place. I grabbed him, hugged him tightly.

"I love you, Daddy," I said in my little voice.

"And I love you, princess," he answered, hugging me back, before quickly pulling away with a man's embarrassment at possibly being caught displaying emotion in public.

And I did love him.

I'd never really thought much about where my Dad lived, after he moved out from Mom's, where me and my brother and Tim still lived. I went on weekends and it seemed okay to me. It was up a long flight of stairs, and there didn't seem to be much furniture. I remember he had one plant, because he put a couple of ornaments on it at Christmas and called it his Christmas tree. Me and my brother slept in his room when we were there, and he slept out in the living room on the couch, because he said he liked to watch TV late. The TV was always fuzzy. The picture wasn't too clear.

But to think back on it, he probably was pretty poor. I remember the old car, where everybody had to crawl in through the driver's side door because it was the only one that worked. One time, for a couple of weeks, he didn't even have a car, and he got us to pretend we were pioneers, before there were cars, so we hiked everywhere. It was kind of fun, now that I think back on it. But he was probably pretty poor, despite the fact he worked in the big factory in town.

I was really upset when my Mom and Dad split up. I cried a lot. That's what I remember most about Grade 3. Crying. Usually in bed at the end of the weekend, realizing that I would leave tomorrow and not see him all week. It seemed to bother me more to leave his place, than to leave Mom's. We were close, my Dad and me. That's because he always treated me like his little princess, like I was somehow special. When I'd cry, he'd come to the bedroom, and hold me in his arms and whisper softly that everything would be fine. He'd tell me it would all work out as long as we stuck together and helped each other. It was his

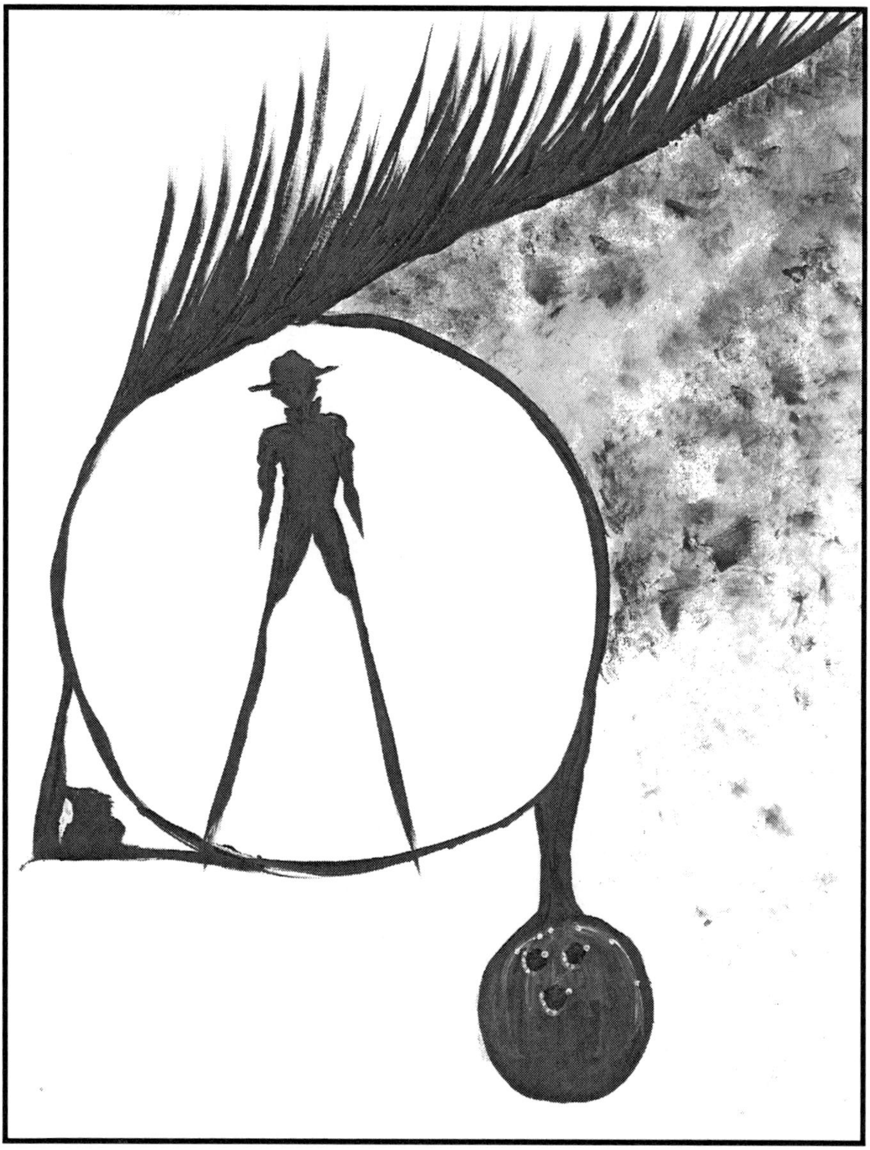

job to help me, and it was my job to help my little brother. But there was one thing that he forgot now that I think back on it. That there was no one to help him.

One night, late, soon after my birthday, when I was supposed to be sleeping but wasn't, I got out of bed and crept out to the living room, perhaps thinking I might catch a glimpse of the TV. But it was black and dark in the living room, except for the flickering of a single candle. I could see him sitting in his big, comfortable maroon easy chair, and even in the near-darkness, I could see that he was crying, with a tear glistening in his eye. I stood quietly. Daddies didn't cry. They were big and strong and never got hurt. He sat still, not moving, but still the tears came.

Finally, I could no longer stand on the edge of the room and watch.

"Daddy," I called out softly, "are you alright?"

He turned and saw me standing there, and you could see him gather himself up in the chair, collecting himself, again becoming the one who was big and strong and never got hurt.

"What are you doing out of bed you little munchkin?" he asked, sitting forward in the chair.

"Daddy, why are you crying? I'm scared," I told him in my tiny, unsteady voice.

"Come here, princess," he said, holding out his hand and gesturing for me to come.

I went to him and fell into his arms and let him hug me close.

"Oh, princess," he whispered as he held me.

"Why were you crying, Daddy?" I asked, repeating my question.

"I guess I've got a broken heart, and sometimes it hurts," he said, and his voice had the sadness in it.

"It's hard being in a split family," I said, remembering something he'd once told me.

"Yes it is," he said.

And we sat quietly for a few moments in the candlelight, and it's one of the most vivid memories I have from when I was a child. I could feel his heart beating against me, and his slow steady breathing beside my ear. I didn't want him to ever let go of me. I wanted to stay his little princess always, and I wanted to sit with him always in the big, comfortable maroon easy chair. Finally, though, I fell asleep. And left him alone.

He took us bowling the next day, and we had fun. What I remember most from that day was the laughter, and most of it was his. I didn't think of it at the time, I guess because I was just a kid, but he was probably trying to show me that he was alright; that what had happened the night before was now in the past.

We watched Funniest Videos and Funniest People that night on his fuzzy TV. We both laughed at the part where the little kid turned a garden hose on his parents, completely soaking them.

Then, it was my bedtime.

He kissed me goodnight and tucked me in. I fell asleep, beside my little brother, in my Dad's big bed. I remember feeling all snug and secure and comfortable.

"You have a good day," he said to me the next morning, as he dropped me off at school.

"I will," I answered.

He leaned over to me, kissed me lightly on the cheek. "Love you, princess," he said softly.

"Love you, Daddy," I answered.

But just as he went to get back in the car, I felt I needed to show him one more time, so I turned back to him. He was in the car, but saw that I wanted to say something to him, so rolled down the window.

"I love you, Daddy," I repeated, and I leaned into the car and gave him a quick, little kiss on the cheek.

"You keep smiling," he said, and he brushed the end of my nose lightly with his finger, and offered me a smile.

I smiled back.

And he was gone.

I never saw my father again. He left. Left his beat-up car, and his run-down apartment in the bad part of town. When he didn't show up at work for a couple of days, and didn't answer the phone or the door, the police forced their way into his apartment. He hadn't even taken his clothes. He just left.

And it was kind of like I understood. I didn't cry as the days passed into weeks, and the weeks passed into months, and still there was no word either from him or about him. Finally, I was all grown up.

I heard it said that he killed himself, but I never believed that stuff. I think he just went off to start a new life for himself, and he didn't want any reminders of his old life, on account of his broken heart and how much it hurt him sometimes.

I love him still.

I miss him.

Sometimes, it's hard being in a split family.

The Melancholy Man

He had travelled through life straight and true, and rarely varied from the main path; the one where all good and decent people tred. And he could never remember having the least bit of doubt as to whether he had made the right choice all those many years ago, when he had forsaken the opportunity to pursue his career in the city, and had decided, instead, to work quietly with his father, in the family business, until one day when it would be his. But now, as he looked out through the holly wreath, and into the winter's scene that unfolded beyond, he felt a type of sadness. And it wasn't just sadness brought on by the fact this was his last Christmas season on Main Street; it was something that ran deeper than that.

He had poured his life into this little business and into life on this street, but now it was gone, and soon he would be gone. And what did it matter? Or what had it mattered? He was one of the last of the family-owned businesses left on the street, and there would be no others. He hadn't even been able to find a buyer for his store, so he was just going to close the doors the day before Christmas, and that would be that. He would sell the inventory to an auction house, and the business his father had started all those years ago would start a rather brief, and abrupt, slide into the oblivion of the past, to be remembered only by old men over games of checkers at the seniors' centre.

He watched the snow wisping, twisting and turning into the alleyway across the street. What did it matter he thought. A way of life, and not just his way of life, was slipping away, and he wondered if people knew, or if people cared, or if maybe he was the only one that even noticed.

He turned away from the window. Two weeks 'til Christmas, he thought. The downtown and my store would have been teeming with shoppers twenty years ago on a Saturday this close to closing.

He walked to the back of the long, narrow, rectangularly-shaped jewellery store, while the faces of a hundred clocks gazed down on him. He was fixing himself a cup of tea, when the little bell over the store's front door sounded the arrival of someone, possibly a customer.

"Daddy, why don't you close up and go home?" It was his daughter. She walked over and gave him a little kiss on the cheek.

"There's not a soul downtown. You should go home and sit by the fire with mother," she continued.

"It's Christmas," he responded. "The stores are supposed to be open late. What if somebody came all the way uptown, in this weather, and found I'd closed early? Why, the word would get around and I'd lose business."

He took a sip of the steaming hot tea.

"Daddy, you're retiring in two weeks. Remember?" She gave his arm a good-natured squeeze. "Now, pour your tea down the sink, and go home and sit by the fire with momma."

"No," he said, "I think I'll stay 'til closing. It's only about another half an hour anyway." He paused to take another sip of his tea. "Somebody might come," he said somewhat more quietly.

"You're just being stubborn," she said, in a way that made her sound a lot like her mother.

He was tempted to tell her so, but instead found himself gazing up the length of the store, and out into the street again.

"Anyway," his daughter said, brushing past him and starting toward the front of the store. "I've got to get going. I just had to come up to the drug store to get some cough medicine for the kids. They've got the worst cough and cold," she chattered in his direction, as she buttoned the top of her coat, and prepared to brave the blustery evening that lay beyond the confines of the snug, old store.

"I only dropped in because I figured you'd be the only one still open on the street on a night like this, and I thought I might be able to get you to go home to your dear wife a few minutes early," she continued.

"I guess I'm just being stubborn," he said, managing to pull his gaze away from the wintery street outside for long enough to say a goodbye.

He walked to where she was standing by the front door, and gave her a polite little peck on the cheek, and her hand a little squeeze.

"If no one comes in the next few minutes, maybe I'll close," he said, knowing it could make her feel she had accomplished her mission, even though they both knew she hadn't.

And, with a blast of cold air from the street beyond, she was gone, and he was left alone with his cooling tea.

But he might as well start to close up, he thought, as he shuffled in a tired kind of way, across the well-worn hardwood floor, toward the back of the store, where business was conducted.

There really wasn't much closing up to do, because it had been a slow day, and there had been few customers, so there were few sales to total. But he gathered up the few papers, and took the float from the till and walked to the huge, old safe, that had stood, cemented firmly into the middle of the office area, for over seventy years, since the day his father had had it installed.

He delicately searched out the combination on the safe, and swung the massive door effortlessly open. He placed the till inside, along with the papers, before starting to gather the valuable pieces of jewellery from their display cases in the store, and place them in the safe, as well. It was a nightly ritual he had gone through for virtually a lifetime, but tonight, unlike other nights, even in the recent past, he was vividly aware of the fact the ritual would soon come to an end. He carried out each of the actions involved in closing up the store with a deliberateness, and a special care; placing each item solemnly in its place within the silence and security of the safe.

Finally, everything was in its proper place, and he stood back and swung the giant door slowly shut. He heard it click closed and spun the combination wheel, sealing the safe for the night, and he felt the sense of satisfaction he always did when the day's business had been concluded.

But, instead of making for the back door of the store, where his coat and boots were located, he headed again for the front of the store. After all, it was still ten minutes until closing. He had only closed the store early once in all these years, and that had been when his daughter had been born, and there was no such occasion on this night.

So, he stood again, just inside the door, watching the swirling snow, and the twinkling of the Christmas lights in the store window across the street. The storefront had been decorated by a local Scout troop, because the store had been empty for the last couple of years, but there had been a feeling among some of the remaining downtown merchants that even the vacant stores must get into the Christmas spirit; that it would somehow help business. So, local Scouts and Guides had decorated the fronts of the emptiness that lay beyond. So, he stared out into the snow and across the street into the festive storefront and the hollow harbinger stared back, and he wondered if the local Scouts would decorate the front of this store, after he had gone, and this business was also just an empty memory.

Finally, there was no avoiding it. The faces of row upon row of jewellery store clocks all told him it was closing time; that it was the end of another business day.

He walked to the rear of the store and fetched his coat and boots, also making sure the back door was secure. Then, he walked again to the front where he got into his winter garb, and made ready to greet the cold, night air.

He took a final look around the store, extinguished the lights, and went through the door and into the street, where he stood on the sidewalk, and let the winter's wind take his breath away and bite at his face. He pulled the collar of his coat higher up around his face, and snuggled down into the parka.

But it felt great, he thought, and he just stood there and let the wind whip around him, and lick at him, trying to find his most vulnerable places, so it could drive him from the outside, and back into the stuffiness and staleness of the inside. But, tonight, it gave a feeling of aliveness, and the cold biting at his lungs seemed to force him to take great gulps of air that seemed to invigorate him.

He stood for a couple of minutes longer, then turned and started out on the four-block walk home, and to the warm fireside. But he had only gone several steps, when he stopped. For some reason, he didn't feel like going home. Even in the frigidness of the outside, he felt a sense of melancholy over what was coming to be, and he felt he wanted to be only with his thoughts for a while longer, so he turned back the other way, and started to walk along the main street where he had passed through life and become who he was. He should have phoned his wife, but she was far from his thoughts on this particular night.

As he walked past the lonely storefronts, and the empty cavities where there had once been storefronts, it seemed as if the past walked with him. He could almost see Mel's Grill, and the old Red and White, and the Capitol Theatre, with its lineup of young lovers waiting to see the new Cary Grant film. And he could surely feel each and every one of the imagined sights as he walked. And even the cold of the winter's night was forgotten, and he found himself alone with his memories, and the warmth of a tear traced its way down his frozen face, and he felt a saltiness on his lips. Old fool, he thought.

He walked the complete length of the street, and started to make his way back up the other side, not feeling the cold until he had reached about the halfway point on his return walk. Then, he paused briefly to try to burrow more deeply into his coat, and he found he was standing outside the Queen's Hotel. Of course, it wasn't called the Queen's anymore, and instead of the Rotary Club meeting here, you were more likely to run into one of those exotic dancers, he thought, as he stood outside the building, suddenly feeling an urge to go in; and the feeling that maybe he needed a beer, a beverage he consumed about once every six months.

He had only seen a stripper once before in his life, he found himself thinking, and he wondered if the stories he had heard about how rough this place was were true.

The interior of the place was dim and hazy, with smoke wisping and swirling around each of the dull orangey lights. He couldn't make out much as his eyes took their first turn around the room, but he managed to locate a seat near the far end of the bar, and to partially unfasten his coat and make himself somewhat comfortable.

When the bartender, a rather muscular tattooed young lady, came, he ordered a draft beer, which she brought, looking at him in a funny kind of way that sort of asked him what he was doing in a place like this. He offered no explanation, and took a sip of the beer. His eyes had kind of adjusted to the poor lighting of the place, so he looked about to see what he had missed on his way in.

There were few people in the place, a few swaggering young cocks gathered around a pool table drinking beer and bragging, and a couple of fat, out-of-shape older guys, with unshaven faces and hopeless expressions, sitting at the bar. And a table full of younger banker-type guys, who were undoubtedly wasting away an evening drinking beer in the local strip club and feeling thoroughly mischievous knowing their wives would never find out, and who looked as completely out of place in here as he did. And there was a stage, where he guessed the young ladies unclothed, but, at the moment, it was empty, and the room lacked any focus it might have had.

So, he sat quietly, taking the occasional sip of his beer, and wondering if this was a typical Saturday night out. He wondered how this place had managed to survive and remain a part of the downtown, even in its present condition, if this was the type of crowd it attracted on a Saturday night.

The jukebox was playing almost inaudibly in the background, but its unrecognizable tune was suddenly and unceremoniously interrupted, and replaced with some rock music, that was extremely loud, and caused him to grimace, which got a reaction of sorts from the young lady with the tattoo behind the bar, in the form of a somewhat gap-toothed smile, which he acknowledged.

But his attention was drawn to the stage, where a young woman had appeared and was beginning to move to the music. He found himself watching her as she went through her routine, removing the few clothes she had worn when she had climbed the stage. It had been many years since he had seen a lithe young body like her's nude, and he found her mildly arousing to watch, but he did so nervously, somehow feeling what he was doing was wrong, and somehow knowing that this young woman was someone's daughter; someone's hopes and aspirations, gone astray, and ended here in this rundown strip club, disrobing in front of old men and swaggering young cocks.

"Not bad, eh?" said a voice, interrupting his thoughts.

He turned toward the direction of the voice, and found that a man he knew from his dealings on the street had slid onto the bar stool beside him and was coddling a beer and looking toward the stage. The man peddled flowers for a living, and they were probably about the same age, he guessed.

"She's pretty nice lookin', eh?" his uninvited guest said, repeating his earlier sentiment.

"She's very attractive," he answered, feeling very embarrassed, both for the girl and himself.

"I know you," the man suddenly said. "You're the jeweller."

"Yes," he answered, "and I've really got to be going."

"Yea, you don't belong in here," the man said, somewhat gruffly.

"No," he found himself agreeing; "I don't think I do belong in here anymore." And he got off the barstool and made his way toward the door, but not before receiving another somewhat gap-toothed smile from the muscular, tattooed bartender, which he acknowledged.

And it was back out into the night, past the lonely storefronts and the empty cavities where there had once been storefronts, while the winter's storm blustered and blew around him and he burrowed deep into his parka. This time, though, his destination was home, where he was sure his wife would have alerted half the town that he was late getting home from the store.

As he came up the front walk, the snow crunched crisply under his feet, and he continued to try to rid himself of the melancholy he had been feeling because his wife would be able to sense it in him quick as a wit. During the walk home, he decided he'd not tell her about his visit to the hotel, and he had chewed a stick of gum to cover the beer smell. What she doesn't know won't hurt her, he thought.

She came scurrying from the kitchen area, the moment he came through the door.

"What happened to you?" she asked, brushing some snow off the shoulder of his coat.

"I got held up at the store," he lied.

"Grace called, and she said you weren't busy at all," his wife said, referring to their daughter's visit to the store. "She said she tried to get you to leave early, but you were being stubborn."

"I had a last minute customer," he said, lying again and removing his coat.

"Well, that's good," his wife answered. "It's a good thing you didn't close then," she added, not questioning his story for a minute; apparently believing there was no need.

He felt a twinge of guilt and wondered why he'd bothered to lie, because he knew that if he'd merely told her where he had been, she would have accepted that without question, as well. It was the type of relationship they had after fifty years of marriage.

But he made no effort to correct himself, instead heading for the couch in the living room.

As usual, on the rare occasions when he was unexpectedly late, she had kept his supper warm; relying on the warmth of an oven and not having made the transition to the new-fangled microwaves which her daughter's generation used for such tasks.

He appreciated the gesture, and thanked her as was his custom with a polite, little kiss, when she bent over the TV table to deliver the meal. But he only toyed with it, not feeling any real inclination to eat.

"Quite a wintery day outside," she commented, as they both sat watching the TV.

"It's going to make for a white Christmas," he answered, as he tried to pretend he was making progress with his dinner.

She tried on a few other occasions to start a conversation, but he was uncommunicative, and felt that he wished only to be left alone with his thoughts, so unsuccessful had been his attempts to shake off the melancholy that had been haunting him since earlier in the store.

"You thinking about retirement?" she finally asked, already knowing the answer.

He paused for a moment before answering, choosing instead to flip through a couple of stations on the TV.

"Yea," he finally said, "I guess maybe I am."

He paused, changing the channel again.

"I went to the hotel for a beer after closing," he said, confessing the earlier lie.

"I smelled it on your breath," she said, also confessing her's.

"I can't fool you, even for a minute," he said softly.

"I just can't figure out why you'd want to," she answered. "I thought we'd learned a long time ago not to keep secrets from each other."

"We did," he said. "I'm sorry."

They sat for a moment in silence, as if reflecting on the brief exchange.

"You didn't have to retire," she finally said. "You're your own boss, and nobody forced you to. We talked about it."

"Hey," he answered. "It's time. I've been at it long enough. I want to spend some time with you and my grandkids." He set the TV convertor on the end table.

"Then, what's bothering you?" she asked, persistently trying to help him with his burden, as she had for so many years, and in so many of his life's crises.

"Oh," he said. "I'm not sure what it is. It's kind of stupid, really. It's kind of like I never thought about what I was doing for all these years, until just the last little while. It's like all of a sudden I woke up and noticed that everything's changed; all the people I knew are gone and everything's different. It's kind of stupid wondering where all the years went."

He looked over at her, and she offered him a soft, vulnerable smile, that somehow gave him a feeling of assurance.

"It's not stupid at all," she said. "This is going to be a big change in your life.....in our lives," she added the last bit, correcting herself. "I've had some of the same thoughts, but it's worse for you. You've spent more hours in that store over your life than you have at home. And that's coming to an end. It's only natural that you're going to have some trouble adjusting to that."

"Anyway," he said, "it's nothing to worry about. I'll be fine."

"Well, I just want you to know that I'm here for you if you need me," she said, reaching across the couch and putting her hand on his arm.

He looked over at her, and felt some of the electricity he had felt between them across the span of years they had spent together.

"I'm a part of your life that won't change," she added softly, as if trying to emphasize the feeling.

"I know," he added, leaning over and kissing her with a passion undiminished by the time and the years it had added to their relationship.

He broke off the contact, and moved back to his own end of the couch, where he retrieved the TV convertor, while she rose to clear away his dinner dishes. And so the conversation ended. But the feeling of closeness endured, as it always did.

Soon, the fire was snapping and crackling in the hearth, and they were sitting in their cozy, little living room watching the Saturday night movie.

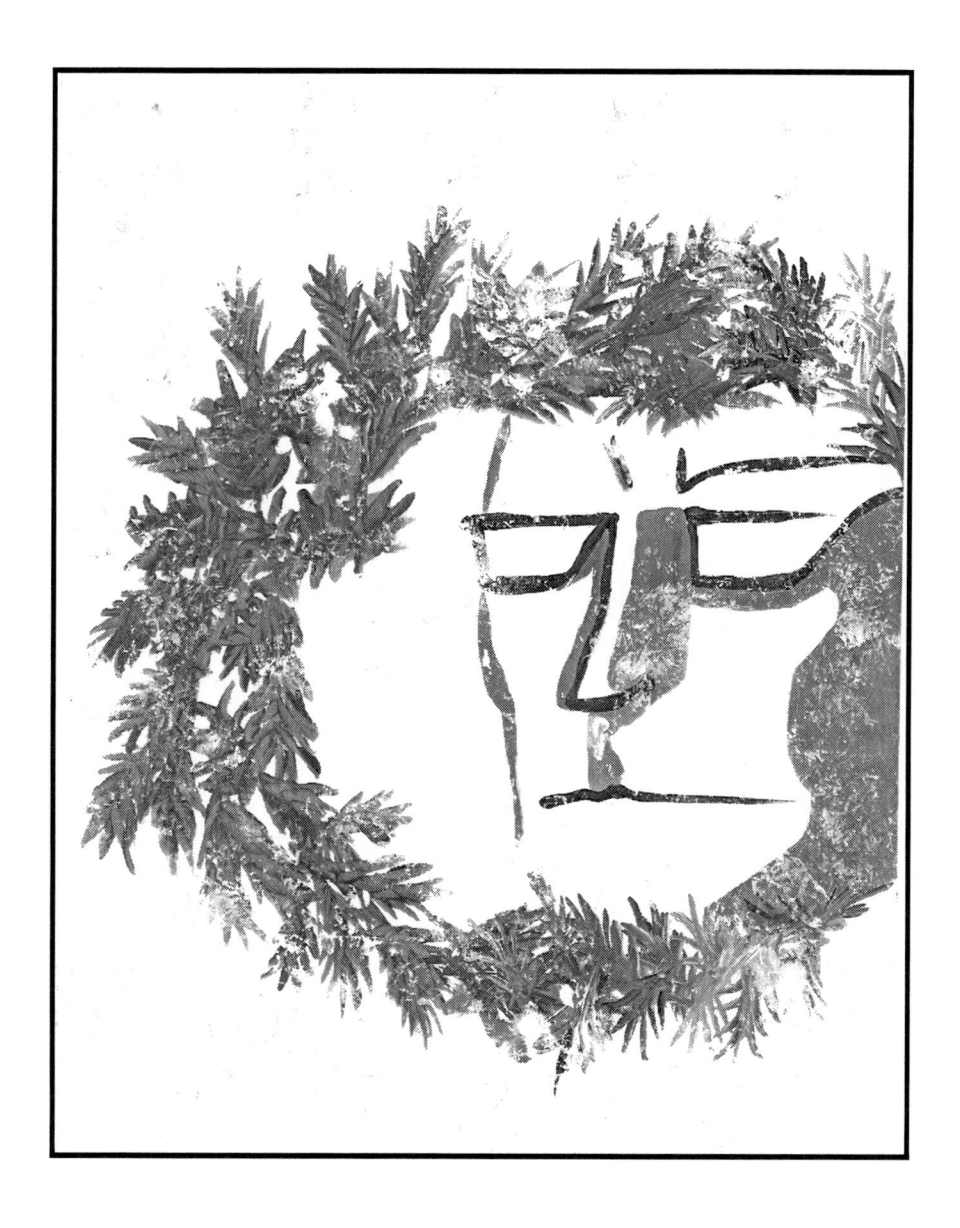

As he sat, he found that he was more aware than usual of his surroundings; of the house the two of them had built when they were first married. When they had built it, it had been in one of the most fashionable areas of town, but, over the years, many of the professional people in town had moved over into the subdivision behind the hospital, so that that area had become the fashionable one, while their little corner of the community had become rather tired looking, with the big, old, brick houses turned to apartments, and most of the little, frame ones badly in need of a coat of paint. Until tonight, he had not really seen it in those exact terms, but now that he thought about it, he supposed that was what had happened. That he had been left behind in that area of his life, as well.

But as he sat, feeling all snug and secure in their comfortable, little abode, where the troubles of the world, such as they were, had never succeeded in reaching him, he was sure this was where he belonged; in the place where he had loved his new bride, where his daughter had been born, and where he and his wife had watched her grow to maturity, while, at the same time, they had reached across time toward their golden years. A point they had now reached; a time they had come to.

But, while she sat, apparently engrossed in the movie, he was again feeling the stirrings of melancholy, like the ones he had felt earlier in the day. Even now, as he sat in the snugness and security, he felt quiet despair at whether his journey through life had been what he had wanted it to be. He found himself remembering again, looking back into his past, thinking mostly of the store and that part of what had been.

And even as he settled in for his night's sleep, knowing that tomorrow was Sunday, and he'd not have to worry about going to work, he found himself thinking that in two short weeks, he would never ever have to worry about going to work again, and he wondered how that would feel.

He felt somewhat better about things in the morning, and during the two weeks that followed, he found he had somewhat mixed feelings about the end of his business dealings. He felt the melancholy from time to time, but he also felt that, somehow, on that night when he had walked in winter's frigid grip, and had come home late from the store because of his stop in the hotel, he had awakened to the reality of the situation, and something had forced him to become aware that the world had changed, and he had become old during that change, and now it was time for the change to be completed, and for him to be swept aside, just like all the others. He could remember thinking so clearly how he had once thought it would never end; that he would somehow remain in his prime, at the centre of the bustling street, for all time; even while those around him grew old and were swept aside. And now it was his turn, and that was what he had come to grips with that night.

It was a death of sorts, he had found himself thinking. And it was at those times, when such thoughts started to intrude into his day, that he found himself flooding his mind with the many things he could look to and hold out as accomplishments during his life. And it was a type of struggle that raged within him; one side of him seeming to ask whether there had been worth to the time spent here in this little, rectangular jewellery store, while the other side told him, yes, it had been worthwhile, there had been a reason for it.

Two days before the final day, the reporter from the local newspaper came looking for a story. He was a sincere young fellow who'd been with the paper for some years, and they conversed easily for nearly two hours about the jewellery store business and the changes in the downtown over the course of the store's history. And there was also the chance for the reporter to ask him how he felt about his retirement and whether he'd enjoyed all those years serving the public and working in the downtown. And while he had known the question was coming from the moment the reporter had called, and while he had rehearsed a long, and rather complex, answer, when the actual questioning took place, he found himself somewhat at a loss for words. He mumbled the usual words about spending more time with his family, and, of course, he had enjoyed his years in the business and serving the public. He realized by the time the young man had left, that his story in the local paper would sound just like all the other "retiring from business" stories he had seen in it over the years. But he guessed that was the way it should be.

On the final day, he got out of bed and washed and dressed and had his breakfast exactly the same way he always had. As a matter of fact, he followed pretty well his same old routine throughout the day, except for at lunch, when a few business people from the chamber of commerce dropped by with a cake, and there were more pictures by the guy from the paper. His wife was there, and his daughter, along with a couple of old friends from the street, and it was nice, and he appreciated it, but he was glad when his wife, the last of the guests, finally left to do a little shopping before coming back to stay with him, whatever that meant.

It was Christmas Eve day, so there were a few last minute shoppers out looking for bargains. He had insisted on keeping the store well-stocked right to the end, and was glad he had, as he was able to satisfy the needs of several customers over the next couple of hours. His wife came back, but he was busy, so she left, telling him she would pick up a few more things and be back. He told her he would close at four, as had always been the custom on Christmas Eve.

A few more customers came and went and a few more sales were made, and he was glad he'd stayed open after the little celebration.

Finally, though, the end of the day had nearly been reached, and even though his wife had not returned, he decided he could not put off the inevitable, and started to carry out the end-of-the-day ritual with the great safe.

He heard the bell over the front door ring as he went about his chores back in the office and assumed his wife had returned. Shortly, though, he heard someone clear their throat out in the front area of the store.

He went out to see who had come and found a young woman had entered and was standing near the till.

"Can I help you?" he asked, as he walked out into the front of the store.

"I don't know," answered the young woman.

"Are you looking for something in particular?" he asked.

"A locket," she answered. "But it has to be a certain type of locket."

She paused and came toward him, offering him something she held.

"My husband got his for me last year," she said. "My little girl fell in love with it and he promised he'd get her one just like it this year."

"And he forgot all about it," he offered, seeming to sense she was having difficulty explaining the situation.

"He died," she said quietly, her eyes shifting nervously away.

"I'm sorry," he managed. "That's tough."

"Anyway, " the woman continued, "I thought my daughter had forgotten all about the locket, until we were at a Christmas party today, and she asked the Santa Claus there not to forget to bring her a locket just like her Mommy's, like her Daddy had promised. If she doesn't get one, she'll be heartbroken, and she's had enough heartbreak for one lifetime already this year."

The woman paused briefly, before continuing. "I've looked in a couple of jewellery stores in the mall, but they didn't have anything even close. They said this was an older design, and I thought of you."

"Here, let me have a look at that," he said, taking the locket from the woman.

He looked at it, and walked over to the display case where his own supply of lockets were kept. He was almost certain he had one similar.

"I guess it pays to be behind in the designer jewellery business," he said, as he held out the two lockets for her to examine.

"You're a miracle worker," the woman said. "They're almost identical. She won't even notice the difference."

He took the locket back from the woman and searched out its box, before walking back to the till to ring in another sale, and the thought suddenly came to mind that it was probably his last.

"Would you like it gift wrapped?" he asked, as was his usual habit at this time of year.

"No, that'll be fine. Just like it is," the woman said. "I'm just so grateful to get it. I just can't tell you how happy that little girl's going to be tomorrow morning," she beamed.

Just as he was about to ring in the sale, the bell over the door rang, and his wife came in. He looked up into the face of the young woman who had come in search of the locket, and she smiled a wide smile back at him.

"Ma'am," he said, putting the locket into a bag with the name of the store on the side. "I want you to take this as my Christmas present to you and your daughter. No charge."

The woman looked up from her purse with surprise.

"You can't mean that," she said.

"Just being able to satisfy you and to see how happy I've made you is payment enough for this locket," he said. "I'm honoured to have been able to help you."

She took the locket from him, and thanked him several times more, before turning to leave the store. Just before she left, she turned back toward him.

"You know, I thought people who worked in stores these days were all the same," she said. "They're always trying to get you to buy something you don't really want or need. Or they treat you like you're some kind of inconvenience. You're different. And that's nice. Thank-you again."

And she was gone into the night.

His wife was looking at him and smiling.

"What's wrong?" he asked.

"Nothing," she answered. "Are you almost ready?"

"Yea, I guess. I just had one more sale to make," he said. "But I guess I'm ready to go now."

He went to the rear of the store to collect his coat and boots. He took one more look around the office area, before turning out the light. Then, he walked to the front of the store, where his wife was waiting. He opened the front door for her, then followed her out onto the sidewalk.

He took one more look around the store, before turning out the light, closing and locking the door, and putting his keys in his pocket.

His wife was still looking at him with a warm, little smile, that spoke of an affection for someone special.

"That's what it was all about," he said, as he took her arm, "wasn't it?"

"You're what it was all about," she answered.

And this time, it was he who smiled.

That night, as he sat on his end of the couch in his cozy, little living room, in his cozy, little house, in a slightly run-down, but once fashionable, area of town, with his wife, who was seemingly engrossed in the movie of the week, he couldn't help but think that he felt a lot better. Somehow, that brief exchange with a young woman trying to do something very special for her daughter had made it clearer to him who he was and why he had bothered. And it had convinced him that maybe it did matter, after all.

His wife slid down the couch to be closer to him and put her arm through his. It all felt so very comfortable.

"I love you," he said to his wife.

"Nice to have you home," she whispered quietly into his ear.

"It's nice to be home," he answered.

And it was.

When I Was a Star

I've got particularly fond memories of this one period in my life back when I was a kid. That was when I played organized hockey for this one year. It was a fun time and something I'll always remember. Now, I was a good skater and a fair hockey player even before that one year, because we lived by a lake until I was nine. My Dad taught me to skate on the lake and he and I used to chase a puck once in a while, so I could handle a stick. But I never played any organized hockey in my life until we finally moved into town.

But after we made the big move, I bugged my Dad day and night to let me play hockey. I mean, I was all caught up in the hockey thing when I was a kid. I collected all sorts of hockey stuff and Dad and I were always in front of the TV on Saturday nights for the Leafs. I lived hockey back in those days -- I wished with all my might that I could play hockey like my idols on the Leafs. And the first step toward that was to get into the house league at the arena in town.

So, Dad took me up there about a week after we got settled in our new house, and signed me up. Then, he took me to Canadian Tire and bought me the few pieces of equipment that were necessary in those days. I already had a Maple Leaf sweater, a pair of skates and an old pair of hockey gloves passed down to me by an older cousin. When I got home, I suited up in the living room, and Mom and Dad and my brother and sisters were duly impressed with my new hockey stuff. I was proud as proverbial punch as I stood tall in my skates and shoulder pads.

Dad came over to me after I'd changed back into my ordinary

clothes and was sitting having a hot chocolate. "I hope you have a real good time playing hockey," he said. "I never really had a chance to play in a real league when I was a boy. There were seven of us at home and Grandpa just couldn't have managed it."

And I knew he was telling the truth. I'd heard lots of stories about growing up in the Depression, when they played hockey on frozen ponds and rivers and used Eaton's catalogues for shin pads, because there was just no money to do it right. And I knew my Dad had dreamed of playing for the Leafs when he was a boy, just like I did. He was a huge hockey fan.

It was about this time that calamity struck our little family, and my Dad was laid off from his job in the factory. This was back in the days before stuff like unemployment insurance and that, and we'd never had much money, so it was a real disaster of epic proportions to be caught without a job. But my Dad was a scrapper, and he hit the road in search of employment right from the start, and he didn't quit until he'd landed himself something else. The only problem was that it was fifty miles away, and we had no car at that point, so it meant he had to board up there most of the time and only get home when he was lucky enough to hitch a ride with somebody. We didn't get to see him much in those days, but Mom told us he was doing it for us and we should be thankful.

Now, this was okay for me. Dad was able to arrange for a ride almost every weekend that winter, so he was there for us most of the time and that included for my hockey on Saturday mornings. He and I would get up early, and eat our breakfast together at the kitchen table, talking hockey all the time. Then, I'd climb into my hockey stuff, and Dad would help me lace and tighten my skates. After that, it was out into the cold winter's air and off up the street to the arena, me skating on the frozen, packed snow on the street and Dad walking along beside me, giving me little tips that might be helpful in my game.

And that was a good year for me. There were four teams in our division and mine was called the Shamrocks. And our coach was a real enthusiastic young guy, and he came across a scheme where by collecting Jello boxtops you could get a whole set of matching sweaters for your minor hockey team. I was a little disappointed to have to give up my Maple Leaf sweater, but the prospect of looking like I was part of a real team more than made up for it. After we got those sweaters, we were the only team in the whole house league that had matching jerseys. The other kids watched in awe the first time we hit the ice in our green get-up. And, man, were we pleased when they started calling us the Green Machine and forgot about the Shamrocks.

It turned out that there were two good teams and two not-so-good teams in our division, and our Green Machine was one of the better ones. Our main rivals were the Flyers, and they had a great team, as well. Each time we met, it was fierce battle with no quarter given -- there were none of those namby-pamby rules about hitting back in those days -- hockey was a rough and tough game and most guys would take your head off as quick as look at you, because that's the way it was in hockey. And us and the Flyers knew how to play hockey.

I was on defence from the beginning, because I was one of the few guys on the team who could skate backwards fairly well even at that tender, young age. And I enjoyed it back behind the play, where I could see the whole game unfold in front of me, and I was able to man my position pretty good for a guy in his first year of hockey.

Now, the Flyers key to success was mainly this one guy. He could skate like the wind and stickhandle like crazy and his moves were like greased lightening. And, after our first game with the Flyers, where he walked through our team three times to score, each time with apparent ease, our coach called me aside, and gave me the single-handed job of trying to stop him. "You're our best backwards skater," he said. "I know it's a big job, but I'm sure you can handle it."

I didn't even know what to say, but I vowed to do the best job I could. Dad beamed with pride when I told him about the assignment I'd been given. "Just remember one thing," he said solemnly, imparting some of his limited knowledge of the game; "always keep your eye on the puck. That's the way to beat him."

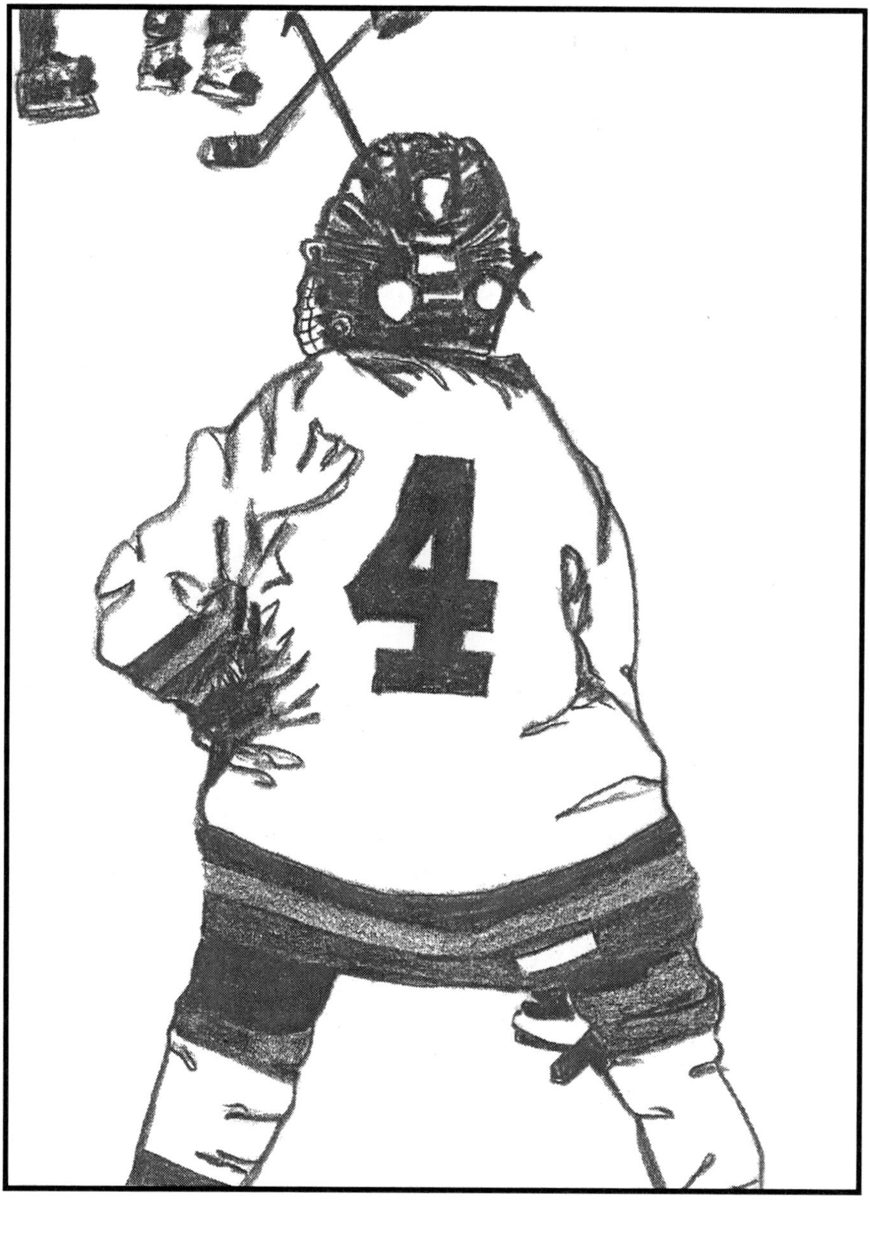

We played the Flyers five times during the season that year, and we each won two games, and we tied the other, so it was dead even between us. I did a fair job of stopping their star kid -- he got through sometimes, and I stopped him sometimes. Sometimes the goalie bailed me out and stopped him after he got through. And sometimes he scored. I did the best I could. I played my heart out with my Dad in the stands cheering me on.

After one game, with about two weeks left in the season, I saw a crowd of other kids standing in front of the bulletin board in the lobby of the arena, and there was an excited buzz about them. I walked to the rear of the group and craned my neck to try to see what the commotion was about.

"What's up?" I asked the kid beside me, unable to get a glimpse of what might be on the bulletin board.

"Oh, they've just announced that the finals are going to be held on a week night, instead of on Saturday morning when we usually play -- so more people can come," he answered, chewing on a big wad of bubble gum.

"Wow, the arena'll be full," I heard one kid say.

"It'll be just like when the Hurricanes play," his friend answered back.

But while it was obvious there was jubilation among the rest of the hockey crowd, I staggered back and sat in a dejected heap on a bench. A week night! That might be great for everyone else -- that might just be the cat's meow for everybody else. But what about my Dad? He worked out of town and he'd never be able to get home to see the game. He was going to miss the finals.

Dad knew there was something wrong the minute I met him outside for the walk home.

"What's wrong?" he asked. "You look like you just lost your best friend. Remember, you won your game this morning."

"They're going to hold the finals on a week night," I said, extreme exasperation in my voice. I'd have cried if it was proper.

Dad didn't answer right away. We went a ways down the snow-covered street, Dad's boots crunching and squeaking along on its frosty surface, while I skated along beside.

"Well, that's a big disappointment," he finally said. "I can't deny it. I'd like to be there."

"Can't you stay home that week?" I asked with a tone of pleading.

"It's not that simple," he answered. "We can't do without a week's pay. You have to understand that."

I didn't answer. I didn't understand. This was an important thing -- way more important than work. He should be there.

"I'm sorry, son," he said. "But you're starting to get older and you've got to understand these things. Some things are more important than hockey. I'd give almost anything to be there, but I can't give miss work. Your mother will come."

I maintained my silence. I wanted to cry. All year toward that one game, and now Dad would miss it because of stupid work. Later that day, when I was alone in my room, I did cry.

And the time leading up to the day of the finals was a miserable time for me. There seemed to be little joy left in the game. The following Saturday, even though Dad was there, I had a hard time concentrating on the game. We were playing one of the not-so-good teams, and I got beat on some very ordinary plays, and we were lucky to win. The coach pulled me aside and said to me didn't I know the finals were coming up and everybody had to be sharp if we were going to beat the Flyers. Everybody was counting on me.

The next Saturday was the last one of the season -- the semi-finals. We were playing one of the not-so-good teams and the Flyers were playing the other, and both games were expected to be nothing more than formalities on the way to the finals, where we would meet our arch rivals.

It didn't quite turn out to be smooth sailing. I got beat right off the opening face-off and we were in a hole before you could count to three.

I just couldn't seem to keep my head in the game. Between periods, Dad came to the dressing room, and called me out into the hallway.

"You've got to try to get it together," he said. "I know you're upset because I'm not coming to the finals, but there are a lot of guys on your team that are counting on you to help them get there, so their parents can come and watch."

"I'm trying my best, Dad," I answered.

"Well, see if you can dig deep and try a little harder," he said softly, reaching out and putting his hand on my shoulder.

So, I went back out and played a whale of a period and we made it to the finals. The coach slapped me on the back and said it was great to see the old me back.

The week started and Dad left early Monday morning for his job. He wished me luck in the big game, just as he was going out the door. I smiled and promised to do my best. He smiled back and gave me a wave as he went off to meet his ride.

I went to the arena on the night of the finals with a heavy heart. Mom helped me lace my skates on, and I skated off up the road myself. She'd follow after she got the rest of the family ready. It should have been the biggest night of my young life, but I didn't even want it to happen. I was angry at the way things went.

The arena was packed to the rafters, just as had been predicted, and that got my spirits up somewhat. So, at least I managed to convince my teammates that I was in the mood for such a big game, as we talked and waited in our dressing room for our turn on the ice.

Finally, the big moment arrived. Huge cheers erupted from the stands as both the Flyers and the Green Machine took their turns hitting the ice and skating around at full speed, whipping the crowd into an even greater frenzy. The cheering seemed to go on forever and I'd never heard such a din in the arena in all of my life. For a moment, I even forgot that my Dad wasn't there.

But, gradually, it quieted in the building and the starting line-ups took to the ice for the opening face-off. The puck was dropped and the game was on.

It started at a furious pace, but our guys carried the play in the opening minutes, so there was no pressure on me. I spotted my Mom and the rest of the family, as I sat on the bench between shifts. I worked hard out there, trying not to let the rest of the guys down. I covered my share of the ice, and then some, racing across to try to help my defence partner when he seemed in difficulty.

But the inevitable was bound to happen. Finally, just as the second scoreless period was winding down, I saw their star player gathering momentum in their end of the ice. He circled around behind the net and I knew he was getting ready to make a rush. I stayed in motion, as I watched, knowing it was my job to stop him when he made one of these rushes, and knowing I had to be ready to move in any direction.

I watched as he came up the boards out of their end and their defencman feathered a pass out to him just as he hit full flight and broke across centre ice. He easily outmanouvered two of our forwards, slipping through between them with ease. I'd been skating forwards toward my end, getting my speed up, so I could turn and stay in front of him when he crossed our line.

I executed my pivot just as he twisted around my defence partner and sent him sprawling awkwardly to the ice. I glided over in front of the star kid, my stick outstretched to run as much interference as possible. He came at me just flying. The crowd was gone and the game was gone and only he was there. Then, in a split second, he made his move, and I made mine, and before I knew what was happening, he'd turned back the other way. I realized he was going to sweep around me, so I tried to switch directions while going backward at full speed. It was a disaster. I lost my footing and fell in a heap, sliding backwards into the end boards. I had a perfect view of the goal that put them ahead 1-0.

There was total quiet in our dressing room after the period ended. We were down by a goal. It would be a tough goal to get back. I'd been the cause. I couldn't even bring myself to look at the other guys.

Suddenly, there was a knock on the dressing room door. The coach answered it. "There's somebody here to see you," he said, directly to me.

I got up and walked to the door. I opened it and stepped out into the hallway and looked about. There was my Dad. Somehow, he'd made it. I was overjoyed and broke into an ear-to-ear grin.

"You took your eye off the puck," he said.

"He's just too quick for me," I answered. "I tried to stay with him."

"You've got to keep your eye on the puck, son," he said. "If you know where the puck is, it doesn't matter where he is. You've got twenty minutes of hockey left. Just bear down and do your job and the other guys will take care of the rest."

"I'll try, Dad," I answered.

"Get back with the guys," he said. "I'm going to sit with your mother." And he turned and walked away.

I went back into the dressing room and I felt like I was walking on air. My Dad was here. I couldn't believe how happy I felt.

Just as the third period was starting, the Flyers got a penalty. We pressed and got the equalizer on the power play. I got an assist. That made me feel better. I looked up toward my family after the goal and Dad gave me the V for victory sign. I felt myself gain confidence.

And the period wore on with no change in the score. Our forwards were checking well, breaking up their plays at centre ice, constantly getting in the road of their players and not letting them get going. The clock wound down, until there were only two minutes left in the game. Overtime was looming. This was a championship.

Then, it happened. A couple of our guys got caught deep in their end, just as their star player started to wind up for a rush. I could hear our coach yelling wildly, telling the forwards to get back in the play. But it was already too late.

The star kid broke out of his own zone with no obstruction, so that by the time he hit centre ice, he was in full flight. He easily crossed our blue line and dipsy-doodled past my partner, who made a desparate lunge, missing completely and taking himself out of the play. It was up to me.

I backpeddled across ice, until I was directly between the attacker and the net. Watch the puck, I told myself and I glued my eyes to it. He came straight at me, just like he had in the previous period. He went this way, then that, twisting and turning. But this time, I stood tall. I didn't make my move until I was as sure I could be that he was committed, that he couldn't turn back. I stared resolutely at the puck, forgetting about everything else. Then, I went for him.

It was over in a split second. I took him cleanly out of the play and gobbled up the puck, quickly turning the play in the opposite direction. I took about three quick steps and spotted one of our forwards up just about centre ice. I knifed a pass to him and caught the whole Flyer team going the wrong way. He gathered in the pass and headed toward the net in a clear breakaway. I stood and watched as he beat the enemy goalie to the glove side with a nice, crisp wrist shot. The place went wild and the cheering continued while we ran out the clock to win the game. We were the champions.

That was a fine time in my life that season of organized hockey. But I never played again. I continued to chase pucks and play shinny on the frozen ponds and rivers, but I never played another organized hockey game in my life. I'm not really sure why. Dad was so proud of me after we won the championship that he took the whole family for shakes and fries at Norm's Restaurant. But I just couldn't go back to it. It was like that was my whole hockey career in that one season, and I won the championship, so there was nothing more to do.

Dad was surprised when I didn't want to play the following year, but he didn't press me on it -- he seemed to know I had my reasons. I'm still not sure what they were, but they made sense at the time. I just knew the sports thing wasn't for me -- not the playing part. But we went right on watching the Leafs on TV and talking hockey all the time and really enjoying it. It's just the way it was away back then.

Conversation with a Friend

I was sleeping. It was the middle of the night. Well, maybe not the middle of the night -- I'm older now and I keep more sensible hours -- but it was late. I remember it well. The phone ringing, waking my wife and I from a dead sleep. Her answering it, because the phone's on her side the way it's always been since we moved here after we got married.

"It's for you," she said sleepily, looking at me with the squinty eyes of an extremely tired and annoyed person.

"Hello," I said into the phone with uncertainty, wondering who could be calling at this hour, sensing that it might be bad news.

"Hey, Shark," said the voice on the other end. It was a low and quiet voice. I was surprised by the use of the name Shark, but knew it wasn't a wrong number.

"Shark," said the voice, "that your wife that answered?"

"Yea," I answered, and I knew the voice. "That you Sid?" I asked, knowing the answer. I fought the tiredness that threatened to overwhelm me. I hadn't heard from Sid for probably more than twenty years -- since back in the old days -- in one of my other lives.

"Hey, buddy, what are you doing keeping regular digs with a lady?" Sid asked, his voice continuing to be low and quiet, so it was sometimes hard to hear.

"Hey, I'm a respectable guy these days," I answered, glancing over at my wife, to whom I had always been a respectable guy.

"That's hard to believe," the old friend answered. "I just can't quite picture that. The guy who could drink a bottle of Jack Daniels straight up and still gamble his grandmother out of her underwear turning respectable. The next thing you know you'll be tellin' me you're working for a living too."

"That would be a safe assumption," I answered.

"Christ, Shark, I've searched the world over for a better friend than you," he said, "and I can't find one. I remember back to those old days, and there was none better than you and I when we set out to get crazy-headed drunk and pull off another of our adventures."

"Those were good, old days," I agreed, also remembering what had been done back in that other time -- smiling. But I was sort of glad my wife wouldn't know what I was talking about if she happened to still be awake.

"Where are you, Sid?" I asked, now more awake and taking more of an interest in hearing from an old friend, even if it was the middle of the night.

"About as far north as you can get before you run out of trees," he answered. "It's a god-awful, hole-in-the-wall sort of place, where there's nothing to do but drink yourself silly and watch re-runs of Happy Days on the tube. But that suits me just fine because I'm one sick son-of-a-bitch."

"You always were one sick bastard," I said back, knowing the answer would please him; show him I was getting more into the mood of the conversation. Now I was definitely hoping my wife was sleeping.

"You goddamned right," Sid answered.

There was a pause in the conversation.

"Sid, can you afford this call?" I asked, remembering that Sid was usually down on his luck, no matter where he happened to be. "I can call you back," I suggested.

"Naw," he answered. "I'm calling from the bar, and I sort of work here off and on, and the guy that runs the place said I could make a call every once in a while and he'd just take it out of what I make."

"Still, I'm doing alright these days, and I'm glad to hear from you, so I don't mind picking up the call," I said.

"Nah, it's alright," Sid replied. "I can pick up this one." He paused. "But I'm glad to hear you're doing alright. That's good." Another pause. "It's good to know one of the old gang made out alright."

"I sort of sold out," I said. "I got a haircut and a job, and a wife and kids......and a house."

"You went where your heart led you," my old friend answered. "I never got it straight. It sucked me in, chewed me up and spit me back out again. Man, I never did get it straight." Another pause. "Can you hold on for a minute while I grab a cigarette?" he asked.

"Sure," I answered, "but I'm going to switch phones, so give me a minute too."

"Alright. Go," he said, and the phone went dead.

I climbed quickly and quietly out of bed and made for the spare bedroom, where I had an office. I'd use the phone in there. I sat in the antique oaken office chair my wife and I'd bought on our trip to the southern States. Reached for the phone. Picked up the receiver.

"Sid, you there?" I inquired.

"Yea, Shark, I'm here," replied the low, quiet voice. "Puffin' away. I always feel better with a smoke in my hand."

"You should give those things up," I said. "They're no good for you."

"Somebody' shoulda told me that thirty years ago," Sid answered. "It's too late now. I'm beyond redemption."

"It's never too late," I told him. "You're never beyond redemption."

"That's where you're wrong, Shark," he said. "I'm dying, boy. It's all over but the screamin'."

"We're all dying, Sid," I answered.

"But some quicker than others and I'm one of those," he answered. "This doc I know up here says I got maybe a year or so -- maybe a little more if I give up the drinking and tow the line -- but I don't see no point in that at this stage of the game."

I hesitated, not sure what to say, knowing he was telling it like it was. He'd maybe been the closest friend I'd ever known. Even though I hadn't seen him in such a long, long time, I'd always known he was

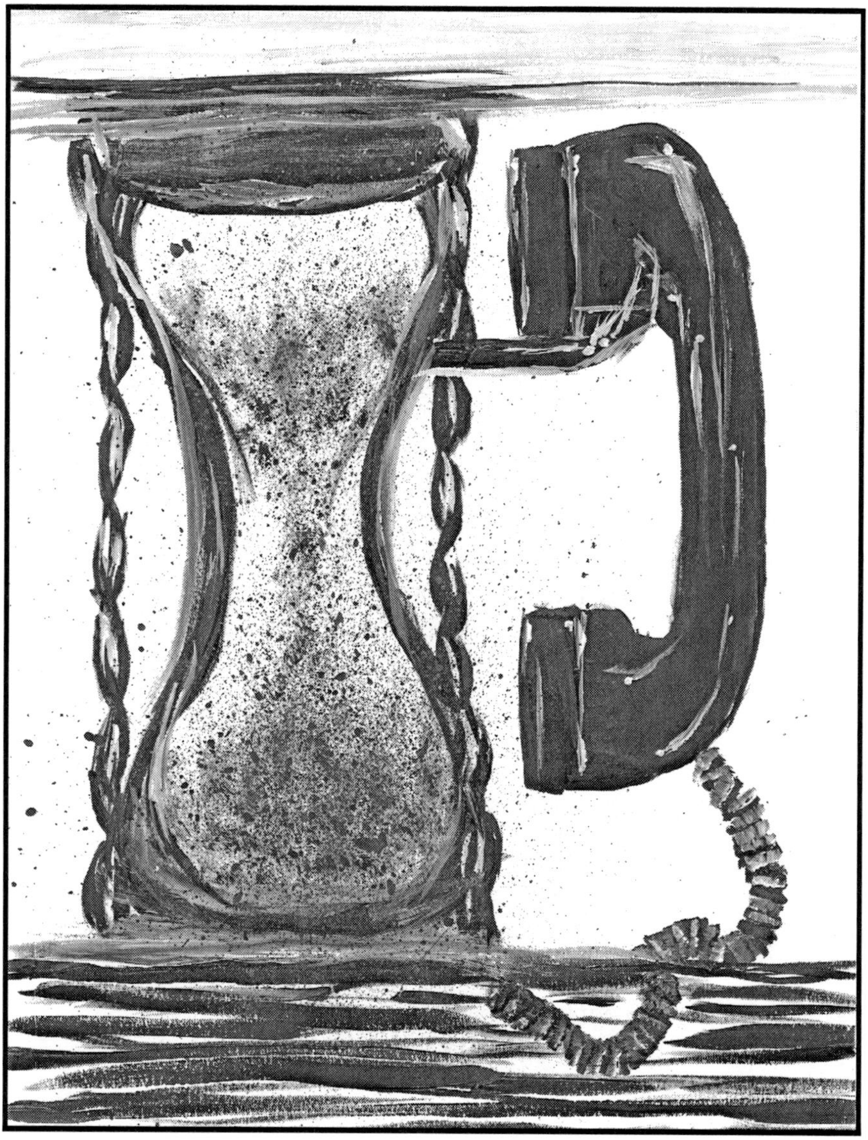

out there somewhere.......partying off into the sunset, like he always did -- like we both used to do together. Every once in a while, as I went about my job as a teacher of higher learning, professor of philosophy, I'd be reading this or researching that, perhaps dealing with Rousseau's concept of the noble savage, or examining Thoreau's anarchical tendencies, and I'd think of Sid. And the very thought would make me smile and feel kind of warm just at the memory.

"Hey, Sharkie, you still there?" the voice asked. "Don't go gettin' all sentimental on me now."

"What's wrong with you?" I finally asked, uncertainty in my voice.

"Mainly abuse," Sid answered. "That's what this doc guy said. Too much whiskey. Too much dope. Too much hard livin'." His voice was matter of fact. "But Shark, don't you go gettin' sentimental on me. We all got to meet the reaper sooner or later and I'm not havin' a real good time anymore, anyway. There's no true partiers left, Shark. You and I were the last. Everything that's come after's been a waste of time."

"What's actually wrong with you?" I asked.

"I can't eat much. I puke up all this green shit and my guts hurt. It's my liver -- that's what the doc thinks. Other than that, it's not so bad," he said.

"You said you went to see the doctor," I said. "Surely there's something they can do."

"Nah, Shark, the games up," he answered. "The doctor I been to see's one of my cronies from the bar up here. Lost his licence for operating on some poor fool when he was drunk. Came up here to drown the sorrow he felt at having such a miserable, disgraced life, much like the rest of us, who aren't really good at nothing but drinkin' and partyin' and hurtin' other people we try to care about."

"Christ, Sid, go see a real doctor," I implored. "Maybe they can still do something for you. Maybe it's not as bad as your friend thinks. You've got to try something."

"Why?" my old friend asked.

"You're going to die," I said, concern in my voice.

"That's life," he answered.

There was a pause. I was at a loss for words. I thought maybe he was just drunk, and exaggerating the situation, the way drunks often do. But he didn't sound drunk. He sounded deathly sober and deathly serious.

"You shootin' any pool these days?" Sid asked at the conclusion of the pause, changing the subject, and reminding me where I'd gotten my long-ago nickname.

"No, not much," I said.

"Miss it?" he asked.

"I don't know," I answered. "I don't really give it much thought." And it was true that the game of pool seldom entered into my world of today.

"I think that's a shame," Sid said earnestly. "Remember how important that game used to be to you. Gawd, Shark, we lived and breathed that game. You should get doing it again."

"Those were good times, Sid," I said, agreeing with him. "I used to like a good game of pool. Maybe you're right, and I should play a little one of these days."

"Get into it," Sid said. "Remember how we read that book about Zen back in the old days. Get into the Zen of pool. Feel it. Experience it. It'll make life worthwhile." He paused for a couple of seconds before continuing. "I still shoot," he said. "It's where I get my peace of mind."

The last remark caused me to smile, as I thought of my alcoholic friend, perhaps about to die by the bottle, yet convinced he had found peace of mind among the multi-coloured balls on a pool table.

"How'd you know where to get in touch with me?" I asked.

"I called your parents," he answered. "I think it's so cool that your parents still have the same telephone number they did when we were kids. Man, that's stability. You just don't see that anymore in this screwed up old world."

"No, that's for sure," I agreed.

There was another pause in the conversation.

"You know, Shark, sometimes in a weaker moment, when I let

myself sober up too much, I get to thinkin' that it's too bad we can't all still be together," Sid said, somewhat reflectively.

"I've had those thoughts, too, Sid," I answered, and it was true that sometimes when I saw my son and his friends clowning around, getting ready to go out on a Saturday night, I yearned for those old days when the gang would meet at my parents' place to plan for our own night out on the town.

"So, what do you do, Josh?" he asked, using my real name for the first time, telling me there was a seriousness to the question.

"I don't know," I answered. "You can't stop time. It just keeps on going no matter what you do."

"I guess you and I are proof of that," Sid said. "You took the respectable road, and I didn't take no road at all, and we're both a couple of old men." I could hear emotion creeping into his voice.

"Sid, is there anything I can do?" I asked quietly.

"I think it's pretty well all played out," he answered. "I'm not quite sure how I got where I am, but I'm here and there ain't no turnin' back. It's the end of the road." His voice was heavy, the words cumbersome as he spoke them.

"Go see a doctor. Quit drinking. Settle down," I sermonized.

"I tried all that shit," he answered gruffly. "I been a family man and I been a regular workin' man, and I just ain't got the stuff for that life."

I was quiet -- not sure what to say. What could I say?

"Anyway," he continued, "I can't see much point. With all these great thinkers and political types trying to straighten out the world, and they can't do nothin' but make even more of a mess of things, I can't imagine where they'll miss one old party animal too much. You know, Shark......I hope that when I finally do go, that I do it with a bottle in my hand and a curse on my lips. That's the way I lived, and that's the way I want to die."

I remained silent. There were no words I could think of.

"The only thing I wish," he said, "is that we could all be together again. I'm kind of worried about dyin' alone away up here in the middle of goddamned nowhere with nobody I know. I mean I been thinking about laying up here dead, and nobody'll really give a shit, so I'll be dead and there'll be nobody to care. And that's kind of a scary thing -- to die alone -- to be dead alone."

"People will care," I said quietly. "I'll care."

"Well, you'll be the only one," Sid answered. "My wife won't care, wherever she is, and my kids won't care -- you probably didn't even know I had kids -- because the old lady'll have filled their minds with all kinds of scum and puss about me. Most everybody I've ever been close to in my life would be just as glad that I'll be dead."

"What about your parents?" I asked, realizing that I was caught in a macabre game with him, trying to guess someone who would mourn his passing.

"I ain't been in touch with them for over ten years, since I broke up with my wife," he said. "We exchanged some words, mainly about my drinking and not being able to hold a job."

"That's too bad," I answered.

"My life's been a mess, bud," my old friend said, and there was no denying that he believed it, and it might have been the truth.

There was an extended period of silence between us. It was a tense, awkward silence. I searched my mind for something to say, but could find nothing.

"So, what are you doing with your life these days, Shark?" asked Sid, seeming to know that he would have to be the one to speak, if the conversation were to continue. "I knew you went off to university after we moved out of that last house we rented with the guys. How did you make out there?"

"I'm still there, Sid," I answered. "I guess you'd call me a professor -- I teach at the university."

"No shit. That's really something," he said, sounding sincerely impressed. "I actually know an honest-to-goodness smart person. That's really something."

"Well, it's not really that much," I answered. "You don't have to be all that smart to be a professor; it just means you're persistent, and probably not much good at anything where you can make a real living."

"Oh, don't give me that crap," Sid responded. "You always were a smart guy -- good marks in school -- when you went." He laughed lightly into the phone. "So, what is it that you fill all these young impressionable minds with, if you don't mind me asking? And don't tell me its business and how to screw your neighbour out of his rightful inheritance."

"I'm a philosophy professor," I answered.

"No shit," Sid responded for the second time. "You're big into looking for some great and wondrous reason for this messed up world. I spent lots of time piss-headed drunk over the years wondering about the big why. Always thought of myself as a bit of a philosopher, you know."

"Yea, I remember," I answered, thinking of the poetry he used to write, and how the rest of us used to think of him as being somehow deep. "You still writing poetry?" I asked, the thought arousing my interest.

"No," he answered flatly. "I wrote quite a bit of it over the years, real tear-jerker stuff, but I got drunk one night and burned most of it."

"God, Sid, why would you do that?" I asked.

"Christ, Shark, it wasn't any good," he answered. "I never did a good thing in my life. That poetry was nothing."

"You used to write some good things," I said. "I remember some of it being in the school paper."

"That's when I thought I had the answers," he said. "I thought all you had to do was be a nice guy, and give people a fair shake, and everything'd be fine. But it's all bullshit, Shark. There ain't no God, and there ain't no heaven. What you see is what you get. This is it -- and it's a sorry enough excuse for reality."

I was quiet again.

"You got the answer, Shark?" he asked.

"I don't think so, Sid," I answered. "I don't think anybody's got the one answer. I think everybody has to find their own answer."

"That's pretty profound," he said. "Me, I couldn't find one."

"Some people don't," I answered.

"Why is there so much bullshit, Shark?" he asked. "Why so much killing, and starving, and fighting, and all the other stuff that makes it so miserable?"

"I don't know, Sid. I don't have an answer for you," I replied.

"And how can most of the rest of us just sit by and watch it happen, happy that it isn't happenin' to us?" he asked.

"It's hard to figure, Sid," I said.

"I remember when we were young," he said. "Sure, there was partying and doing dope, but at the beginning, we thought things were going to be different by the time we took over from our parents. Christ, Josh, things are different alright -- they're worse now than they were thirty years ago.

"Most of those great causes we were so involved in have gotten so big and ugly that they're threatenin' to eat us up," he continued, anger rising in his voice. "People are still fightin' with one another. The environment's a worse mess than ever. What about this political correctness, where everybody's got rights except ordinary people?"

"I don't know, Sid," I answered. "I guess we just all do what we can -- make your own little corner of the world as tolerable as you can."

"That's bullshit," my old friend snarled through the phone. "Remember how we used to rail on about the goddamned Establishment -- the big corporations and how they were so evil and corrupt? Take a look at who's runnin' this old world today -- it's those same goddamned corporations, only they're bigger and more evil and more corrupt than ever. Only now nobody's railin' on against them, whether they pour poison into the earth, or whether they pour poison into people. Nobody gives a shit! They won! We all work for them. We're all their slaves. Just like our parents, only worse, because we knew what they stood for."

"We were pretty idealistic back in the old days," I answered. "We didn't have any idea how things worked."

"Christ, we knew that there were problems," Sid responded. "We were going to make it better. What happened?"

"We grew up," I answered.

"We turned to shit," he said. "We sold out."

There was a pause.

"I guess maybe we did," I finally said.

"Why bother?" he asked.

"Why bother with what?" I asked back.

"To even exist," he answered.

There was another pause, only this time it seemed large and ugly. I felt tired. I wanted my bed.....my wife...my kids....my own little corner of the world. I didn't want Sid reminding me. What could I possibly do?

"But don't fret it, Bud," Sid finally said, after an apparent eternity. "I'm sorry," he said. "I didn't mean to bum you out. I just wanted to say hello. I wanted to remember."

"It's alright, Sid," I said. "It's just late. I'm tired."

"Yea, I guess I probably woke you," he said, his voice sounding calm and placid. "Leave it to me to be stirring up shit right to the end."

"It's nothing, Sid," I replied. "I'd probably just be dreaming about some gorgeous babe if I wasn't up here talking to you." I tried to lighten things up.

"I should get goin'," he said, his voice flat and even, apparently not seeing the humour in what I'd said.

I said nothing. I wanted to ask him something -- I wanted him to tell me something -- I didn't want the conversation to end. He would die. He would be dead to me. Still, I said nothing.

"I love you, Sharkie," he said quietly.

"I love you too, Sid," I answered, knowing I meant it, wishing I could reach out and touch him, that we might again be young and planning to meet at my parents' place for a night out on the town.

"Remember me sometimes," he said. "Tell your kids you knew this guy one time who could drink a bottle of Jack Daniels straight up and still gamble the underwear off his grandmother."

"You're alright, Sid," I said.

"Good-bye, Sharkie," he said.

The line clicked dead before I could answer.

It was the last I heard from Sid. He died about a year later. My Dad phoned me early one morning to tell me he'd gotten the news from Sid's father. I hung up the phone. I felt numb.

"Who was it?" my wife asked.

"My Dad," I answered woodenly.

"Is everything alright?" she asked.

"Fine," I answered. She wouldn't understand. She didn't know.

When I was back upstairs getting dressed, preparing to meet the day, I wept. I cried for him. I cared.

But I also cried for those of us who remained. Because Sid was the product of our hopes and dreams. And as surely as he has died, so have we.

Uncertain Waters

He had invited his father to come on this fishing trip, to this faraway northern place, after his mother had died. He had made plans to offer an invitation one day when he'd looked over and seen his dad as an old man. It had caused him to start -- to be taken aback -- and he'd studied the old man meticulously for the rest of the weekend stay with him. And now that he looked again into his own reflection in the window of the fishing lodge, he knew that he was now the father. His father -- the old man.

The mother had died of a stroke a short year ago. He'd been reminded of mortality, and that even his own parents had not escaped this condition of life. And he felt a need to be with his father. To somehow let him know that he was not alone. So that he could better deal with the heartache he must be feeling since his wife had died. Hence the trip. Just the two of them for a week in the north. In the fishing lodge.

He knew little about fishing, but had told himself he wouldn't complain. His father had taken to the sport in his retirement years, and he knew the old man enjoyed it. That was why he had chosen fishing -- something he had little regard or inclination for -- even though it had been his choice. He wanted it to be a special week for his father. He wanted the old man to do something he liked doing, feeling it would help him to relax so he might lower his guard toward life. Because the father had always had a quiet way about him, even-tempered in all things, revealing little about himself to those who surrounded him in life.

The father slept, tired out from the long drive. They'd talked as they'd driven up in the car. It had been nothing but pleasant small talk. About hockey. And politics. The unusually cold spring. He hoped they could eventually break through the skin of their relationship and reach somehow deeper into the guts of what should be between them as father and son. So that he could, for the first time, know what his father was thinking. He wanted to know the old man. Wanted to offer him solace from life's vicissitudes.

With that thought, though, he stirred from his place by the window, turned out the light, and made his way to bed. It had been a long drive.

"Comeon, Jackie boy! The fish won't wait all day for you!" his father's voice seemed to shout into the veil of dreamless sleep that had shrouded him throughout what had seemed an all too brief night.

"Dad," he mumbled, clawing toward the surface of consciousness, forcing his eyes open, turning his head in the direction of the night table and clock. "It's four-thirty," he said with disbelief.

"Should be out by five, Jack," his father replied. "That's the best time to catch them."

"I thought it was in the evening," Jack answered, making a futile attempt to escape the early rising.

But there was no escaping it. And he knew it. So he swung himself out over the side of the bed, and sat on the edge. It was nearly dark in the room, the old man having left, and the door being just slightly ajar so that little light penetrated. He had promised himself that he would make the best of the excursion. And he would.

It was still the gray, half-light of dawn as the two of them sat, poles cradled in the crooks of arms, boat moving slowly through the water. It was early spring here in the north, and it was cool and damp in the early morning. Such was the weather that they wore winter jackets as they sat and awaited the fish.

Jack sat and watched the old man, who was sitting with his back to him. He had always thought of his father as a strong man, both physically and emotionally, but now some of that strength seemed to be gone. He seemed somehow fragile and vulnerable and alone now that the mother had died.

His parents had been married for fifty-two years. But the husband had not shed a visible tear when his wife had been laid to rest. He had been his stoic self, apparently unmoved, at the funeral. And even in the intervening year, when the son had been around, the father had said nothing to even hint that he had been touched by the death. Jack and his brother and sisters had shed the tears for their mother. It had angered Jack, who had felt such real grief over his mother's death. And he had resolved to make the old man feel -- to know what he felt. Because surely there must be something.

He remembered back to his own difficulties with life, when he and his wife of nearly twenty years had separated and divorced some years back. He had mourned her loss for a considerable length of time. Had even wondered whether it was worth it. That had been eight years ago and he had pulled his life back together. The old man should grieve and suffer, instead of continuing to live with this apparent stone-faced attitude toward what should be a crisis in his life, obviously hiding from his true feelings.

"Boy, they're not biting this morning, eh?" Jack more remarked than asked, as they trolled slowly along.

"We haven't paid our dues yet," answered the father, turning back to face his son. "Fish know. They don't let themselves get caught by just anybody."

The brief exchange ended. They returned to their solitary thoughts. But the son was resolved to talk. He would not let the opportunity pass.

"Do you ever think about mom?" he asked, cutting straight to the heart of the matter, seeming not to care for the old man's feelings.

"All the time, Jack," the old man answered flatly, this time not turning to face the boy. "It would be hard to be married to somebody for as long as I was your mother, and not think about them when they're gone."

"You're awfully quiet about it," the son said.

"Not much need for concern," the father answered. "I had over fifty years with the woman. I was glad for it. But your mother and I agreed long ago to try not to mourn each other no matter who went first. It's something you've got to think about as you get older. We talked about it." Now he turned to face the boy. "I'm just trying to abide by her wishes," and he caught his son's eyes; looked directly into them. "I do what I can."

"It must be hard, though," the son answered, thinking that he might be reaching his father for the first time in a lifetime.

At that moment, the old man had a strike, so the conversation ended, and the father battled for the first catch of the trip. Jack couldn't help but smile as he watched.

He found himself watching with interest as his father filleted the fish later, back at the lodge. He recoiled with an instinctive disgust as the guts poured out onto the kitchen counter.

"We'll feast tonight, Jackie," the father said, as he enthusiastically ripped out the fish's entrails.

"Great," Jack answered, but he knew his level of enthusiasm did not nearly match that of his father.

"I miss her," the son finally said, following a brief silence, "and I'm not even near. It must be hard for you in that house."

"It's alright," answered the father, not looking up from his work on the fish, his voice again flat and even, betraying no emotion.

Jack turned, angered by the reaction. He left the kitchen. Said nothing more. Left the old man alone to his grisly task.

Later that night, as they sat and ate the trout -- and it was a feast -- it was the old man who initiated the conversation.

"How's the fish?" he asked, a certain gruffness to his voice.

"It's great, Dad," Jack answered between mouthfuls.

"Where'd you go this afternoon?" the father asked.

"I hiked up one of the nature trails," Jack answered. "I knew the fish wouldn't be biting. Morning or evening for that, isn't it?"

"Oh well, it gave me a chance to do a little reading," the old man said, and he returned to his dinner.

"What are we doing up here, Jack?" the father asked a couple of minutes later.

"What do you mean?" Jack countered, not looking up from his plate.

"You don't even like fishing," the old man said. "Never did."

"I thought this would be a good chance for us to get away together," Jack answered, now looking up. "You like fishing. And I don't really mind it -- it's not like I hate it. I just thought we should spend some time together."

"Any particular reason?" the old man asked.

"Sure," said the son. "I was worried about you since mom's been gone. I thought you might want to talk about it."

"Nothing much to talk about," the father said, "but I appreciate the offer.......and I'm glad you decided on fishing."

"I hope you catch every big one in the lake," Jack answered, smiling.

The next morning, it had turned sharply colder, and Jack felt tired and miserable as he wrestled with the boat's motor at first light. A light rain was falling.

"Try the choke, Jack," the father instructed, after watching the son nearly pull his arm out of the socket trying to get the engine to catch.

"I think it's flooded," Jack said, gasping for breath after the exertion of trying to pull the motor to life. "I should just wait a minute."

"Give her one more pull," the old man advised.

Jack knew by his tone that the father expected the son to give it one more try -- nothing else would do. So, he grabbed the cord and pulled with all his might. And just as he had known it had to, the motor coughed and sputtered to life. The old man was always right, always had been, always would be.

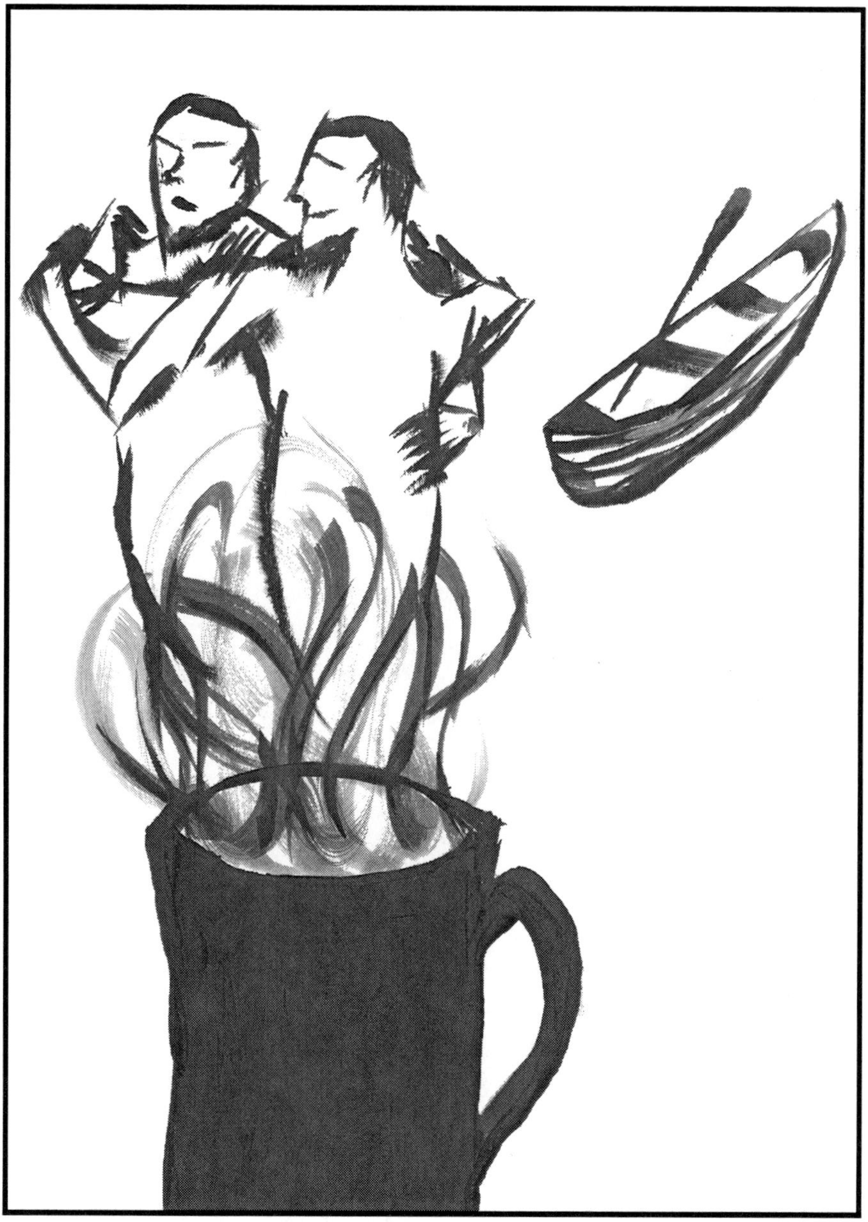

"I'm not even sure we should be going out this morning," Jack said, as he reached up out of the boat, extending a hand to help his father down from the dock. "The weather's not the greatest."

"This is the best weather to be out in," answered the father. "We've got to get you a fish. Can't have you skunked two days in a row."

Jack smiled at the old man as he helped him get situated, but he was really thinking that he didn't mind getting skunked, because catching his own fish would probably mean having to clean it, and that was something he was not sure he could do.

And so they headed out onto the lake, in fact they headed far up the lake, weaving in and out of the many islands that dotted its surface, fishing here and there, but having no luck, so deciding to keep trying further afield.

The rain kept up, so they were glad for the slickers they'd worn, and said so. It was mid-morning, but still gray and cold, as they unwrapped their bologna sandwiches and poured a fresh cup of coffee from the thermos they'd brought. Still no luck. Catching nothing but an aching in the joints.

Jack started to feel the rain pelt into him as he maneuvered the boat back out into the main channel of the lake; out of the tiny inlet where they'd just tried their luck.

"The wind's picking up," he said to his father. "I think we should start back. Remember that guy at the general store in town said to watch for sudden winds because they can really whip the lake up."

"I think you're right," the old man said, already nearly having to shout, his hand shielding his face from the rain that was coming at them harder all the time.

And there was no escaping it. They had to travel straight into the wind to reach the lodge. The old man turned so his back was to it, and he was facing the boy. He looked miserable. Jack smiled, trying to offer some encouragement, even though he also felt the cold and wet. Even the slicker seemed to offer scant protection. The father sat hunched over, pulled together in an effort to stay as warm and dry as possible.

The boat crashed through waters that grew choppier by the moment, until the lake was threatening to invade it. Jack found it more and more difficult to handle the small craft, and he found it more and more difficult to see as the rain sliced through his field of vision.

"Sure came up quick!" shouted the father.

"Yea!" shouted Jack, and he worked to keep the boat moving straight down the lake toward the lodge, although now he worried that perhaps he might have difficulty navigating through the islands, so hard had the rain become that his visibility was greatly reduced.

"Maybe we should turn into one of the bays!" Jack shouted above the storm. "I'm having trouble! We could wait it out!"

"Yea!" shouted the father. "Before we drown!" He pointed to his feet. The waves had been crashing up over the front of the boat, and water was already ankle deep in its bottom.

With that, Jack tried to turn the boat toward the nearest inlet on the mainland, where they might be able to seek refuge. But as he turned the craft, the waves smashed into its side, nearly swamping them. "Christ!" Jack cried, as water poured over the gunnel. The old man found the bailing can in the bottom of the boat, and started waging a futile war with the lake. Jack straightened the boat back directly into the wind, then turned more gradually toward shore. This time, he was more successful, and they started to make some headway.

But the wind whipped and whirled around them, so that it was slow going, and there was no certainty that they would reach their goal.

Finally, Jack thought he was in danger of overshooting the bay he was steering for, so he made a last desperate gamble and turned the boat almost directly into its mouth. Again, the wind and water caught the boat's side, and both men were forced to lean to that side to keep from being cast over and into the lake. For an instant, Jack let go of the motor's throttle, reaching for the old man, trying to steady him, to keep him from falling back into the boat.

Then, they had cleared the mouth of the bay and were into it, and it offered some shelter from the storm's fury, so there was somewhat of a respite. Jack returned to his seat by the motor. The old man also returned to his seat in the middle of the boat.

"That was close," the father said, no longer having to shout, such was the shelter offered by the inlet. "Good work, Jack," he added, with a small smile to show he meant it.

Jack returned the smile, but he was trembling and trying not to show the father how frightened he had been.

"Man, was that close," the old man repeated.

"We're alright now," Jack said.

"You did good, Jackie," the father said.

So, they sat and waited out the storm, and it wasn't the greatest way to spend a couple of hours, but they were in no danger, and there was some coffee left in the thermos, so they were able to warm themselves somewhat, and get relatively comfortable, despite the constant downpour.

Later that night, as they sat savouring the steak dinner they'd just eaten, that battle on the lake seemed a long way away. But Jack returned them to it.

"That was quite a blow this morning" he said, as they cleared the table, and made ready to do the dishes. "That guy at the store was right. It really came up quick."

"You saw it coming," his father answered. "You said maybe we shouldn't go out this morning........but I was the stubborn, old cuss." He rolled up his sleeves and turned on the tap to run the dishwater.

"I had no idea it was going to get like that," Jack answered, scraping the plates into the garbage. "I was the one who wanted to keep going up the lake. I didn't see it coming at all."

There was a pause, as Jack slid the dirty dishes into the bubbling water in the sink, and reached for a dish towel.

"You know something, Jack?" the father asked.

"What's that, Dad?" the son responded.

"I was thinking about your mother today out on the lake," the father said, pausing in his dish washing for a moment.

"Really," Jack answered. "In what way, Dad?" He slowly polished the plate he held.

"I was thinking that maybe I was close to her," the father answered, returning to the dishes.

"You thought you might die?" Jack asked.

"I don't know," the father answered. "It wasn't like my life was flashing in front of me, or anything like that. I just got to thinking about your mother."

"What did you think about her?" Jack asked, starting to stack the dishes in the cupboard.

"It was funny," the old man said, washing up the last of the silverware, "here we were, almost in the drink, maybe not knowing whether we were going to live or die, and I was remembering our honeymoon."

"Why then?" Jack asked, and for perhaps the first time in his adult life, he was listening intently to what his father said, and the old man was more than just an old man.

"We went to stay with your Uncle George and Aunt Marg for the last couple of days of our trip -- there was no money for hotels in those days," the father started, draining the sink and putting down the dish cloth. "They had a river in back of their house, and there was an old rowboat. I took your mother out in it one night after supper, just about dark. We talked and laughed and it was a wonderful time."

The old man paused. Jack could feel the emotion in his voice. He felt his throat tighten and his eyes grew moist, just to know what his father was feeling.

"Finally, it was dark," he continued, "and I stopped rowing. We drifted down under a huge, old willow tree, and you could look out through the branches and see the silvery moon." The old man's voice faltered. "And we embraced and kissed under that old willow........and I guess we got intimate too." Tears traced their way down his face, and he moved a hand to brush them away.

Jack stepped across the small kitchen, where a few moments before dishes had been done. He put his arms around the old man, and held him close. And he also cried, feeling for the old man. And the two men stood in the kitchen of the fishing lodge in a faraway northern place, and for the first time in their lives, knew each other.

Finally, the father pulled away. "How stupid, eh," he said, brushing away the last of the tears.

"No," answered the son, "not stupid at all." He had also regained his composure.

Now there was the embarrassment that men sometimes feel, after having been caught in such a situation.

The rest of the evening was spent in quiet reflection. They played a few games of checkers. Both were subdued, but especially the father. He seemed pensive, more stoic than usual.

So that the next morning, Jack was sure something was wrong when he awoke and it was quarter after six. Why not the wake up call at the usual early hour?

He came out of the bedroom, still tucking in his shirt. It was fine and sunny out, the previous day's stormy weather now just a memory. Jack walked to the front door of the place and could see that his father was sitting down at the dock. He felt relief at seeing the old man, and went back into the kitchen, where he poured a cup of the freshly-brewed coffee that was waiting for him just as it had been both other mornings. Then, he walked out toward the dock.

"Morning," he said to his father as he approached.

His father looked around and acknowledged him.

"No wake-up call this morning?" Jack asked.

"Thought I'd let you sleep in after yesterday," the old man answered, with a smile.

"Hey, no special treatment," Jack answered, returning the smile. "Remember, I've been skunked two days in a row."

The father smiled again, this time more broadly.

Jack sat beside him, but said nothing more for a moment, so the two sat in silence.

"How are you feeling?" Jack finally asked.

"I'm alright," answered the old man, "but I've been up for most of the night."

"Couldn't sleep?" Jack asked.

"Thinking about your mother, I guess," answered the father. "Haven't been able to shake it."

"I think that's alright," Jack said softly.

There was another moment of silence, and feeling hung in the air between them, as it had on the previous night.

"I'm glad I had her in my life," the father finally said. "I'm glad I had those times with her. I think I was sort of mad at her until yesterday. That time out on the lake in the storm made me remember."

"That's great," Jack said. "You deserve that."

More silence.

"Up to doing a little fishin'?" Jack asked, breaking the silence. "I sure would like to get even."

"It's a good day for it," said the father.

And it was.

Jammin'

I first started playing the guitar as a peer thing. Some friends and I decided to start a rock 'n' roll band. Like it was the way to win girls and influence people back when I was growing up. At one time in the small town where I grew up, in my neighbourhood alone, there were three garage bands practicing, all with dreams of making it big -- of hitting the big time.

I got my start on an old Sears' Silvertone six string guitar with only three strings on. Bob had actually taken guitar lessons, so he was the lead guitar player. Mike had money, so he was the drummer, and Brian had none, so he was the singer. I had no money either, but Mike was my best buddy, and he had an old Silvertone guitar with only three strings on, so I was the bass player. We added Delbert on rhythm guitar because his Dad had a station wagon to transport our limited musical equipment around in, but he never really fit into the group.

Our first song was a Stones' thing, Get Off My Cloud, and from there on in, we could handle just about anything with only three chords. We'd listen to a potential new song on Mike's monaural record player, and if Bob could pick out the key and even some of the chords, we were away. I'm sure, looking back on it, that we were completely awful back in those old days, but our friends would let us set up at their parties and then sort of ignore us as we mercilessly butchered song after song. Then, they'd tell us how great we sounded.

But the best part were the jams. And that's how we got better, to the point where we probably actually weren't too bad to listen to. We'd spend whole weekends holed up somewhere jamming the blues. I'm not sure to this day who started us doing it, and maybe it just sort of evolved because most of the old rock songs are basically just the blues, but we jammed the blues for hours and even days at a time. And it was a heck of a good time. Not much structure, but a lot of substance. Freedom to do almost what you liked, as long as you stayed within the pattern, and even then nobody really much cared if you went for a wander. It's the way life should be. But it ain't.

I often think back to when I was in the bands, and to when we used to jam like that. It's not the same today. It's like there's all these expectations that you can't possibly meet up to. That's what happened to Mike. He seemed to realize away back in those other days just what there was to life. So that he sort of opted out, even back then. And through his life, he was a fringe player, not taking things real serious, not caring whether he worked or not -- although he tried to play that game -- just sort of always on the edge. He knew what the expectations were, but he shucked them. He was a jammin' sort of guy. Not much structure, but a lot of substance.

I was a sheltered kid, went to church on Sunday, never late for school, that sort of stuff. My family was kind of Waltonesque. No raised hands, or even voices. Ritual discussion around the supper table, Hockey Night in Canada on Saturday, and Ed Sullivan and Bonanza on Sunday -- when we finally got a TV when I was nine. So that when I met Mike, there was no way I couldn't be impressed. His parents owned the local Queen's Hotel, and he had his own hotel room to live in, his own TV and mono record player. They'd moved from Toronto, so he had that connection, and he wore the clothes and had the look of a city kid. Yea, I was pretty impressed when old Mike showed up beside me at the beginning of Grade 7.

He wasn't too pleased to have moved to our little backwater, but his parents, who were immigrant hotel owners in Toronto, somewhere around Allen Gardens I think, rushed out of the city after Mike's Dad got shot in a hold-up at his hotel. So Mike was stuck with us, so I guess he decided to make the best of it. And he decided that in order to make the best of it, he'd lead us through our adolescence. And, early on, I decided to be a disciple. I liked him. He was cool. And I think he liked me. But it was hard to tell.

Anyway, we grew up together. Went through the puberty thing together. Chased girls. Skinny dipped in the river -- always without the girls. Drank beer and threw up on his Mom's flowers. Did the band thing. Did the drug thing. Did all sorts of things. And they were special times. That much I know. I treasure those growing up times like no other period in my life.

But there is one time that stands out as most special. It was about death. It taught us about life at so young an age.

Donna was a special girl. A poet. She and Mike met through the school paper, he the poetry editor, she the poet. They were soon filling the pages of the paper with passionate verse, extolling their great love for one another. They became an ideal in pure platonic partnership, and spent countless hours discussing the deep and dark mysteries of the world......and of life.......and of death. For she was like an angel, even in life, or so Mike would tell me after he'd had another session with her.

"She is the angel, and I am the unholy sinner," he said to me once. "She shines out to me, yet I cannot be more than bathed in her glow. She is bottomless in her vision of this life. I am only the surface."

That was high praise indeed, back in those other times, when we were into the deep and the meaningful, and could not buy into the silly shallow lives of our parents. And Mike gave sparse praise. He grew into a serious and intense kid, highly critical of what surrounded him in life, hard on himself and on others. That was why he quit playing the drums in the band. He couldn't be as good as the guys on the records, and we couldn't be as good as the guys on the records, so he quit. He still hung out with us, and for a while he was our light man, but we just weren't good enough for him.

But Donna was. She was pure and untouched by the bad and the ugly in life. That was what Mike saw in her. Purity. Virginity. But such was the respect he had for her that he made no move to touch her, so that the relationship also seemed pure and virgin. But it must have been hard for him, because she had a soft, earthy beauty that enraptured many a young man during those first few years of high school. With a sincere shyness that became her, she spurned them all. Except Mike.

And it was hard for me to figure out exactly how Donna and Mike ever became an item. Mike surely wasn't shy around the girls, and his usual attitude by Grade 12 was put out or get out. But with her, he was different. More reserved. More thoughtful. More considerate. She seemed to bring a part of him out that few others ever saw, excepting maybe me, and I can't really think of anyone else. He hid from most of the world, but sometimes when he and I were alone, I'd get to see inside, into the parts of him that were most vulnerable, to see the soft underside of his soul. And he must have exposed it to her as well. It was like there can be love between seventeen year olds, despite what older folks say.

And so this idyllic, platonic relationship reached through the school year, starting soon after school started in the fall, and continuing through the dead of winter, and into the promise of spring. And there was this school dance planned as a kind of spring break-out and we were playing and it was going to be a big deal by all accounts. Everybody was going and by everybody I mean Mike and the rest of our crowd. Even Donna, much to my surprise, because she rarely ventured into town outside of school, and never for social outings. Apparently, her parents were very strict about it. But she had somehow gotten permission to attend this particular dance, and Mike seemed really head up about it, even more than usual, and I guessed it was because she was coming. Mike also said he couldn't work the lights for the band, which I found a little unusual, but again chalked it up to the girl's attendance.

So, the night of the big dance came. We got set up, tuned up and the thing started. I watched for Mike at the breaks, because even though he wasn't really in the band anymore, he was still a big supporter, and I thought he'd be coming up to kibitz between sets -- to tell us what we were doing right and wrong. But he didn't show. Not until later. I spotted him when we were about halfway through our last set. He was standing off by himself in the side entrance to the gym.

But I didn't see him after the dance. He was seemingly gone when it ended, because I searched him out, but couldn't find him.

Likewise the next day, Saturday. No sign of him. I called. I went by.

Sunday I heard. The girl was dead. Suicide. Saturday afternoon, while her parents were in town doing the shopping.

I went right away to search him out. I was his friend.

He wasn't in any of the usual places -- his room, the pool hall, the bowling alley -- but I knew where to find him. We had a place out in the woods, just outside of town, by the river, by the railway bridge, where we'd used to go to just be by ourselves, when the parents and the other friends got to be too much. We'd called it our thinkin' spot even back when we'd been kids. That's where he'd be. I was sure.

And he was there, sitting down underneath the bridge, by himself, just sort of sitting there looking all thoughtful. He watched me stumble down the steep slope that led from the bridge to where he was located. Finally, I arrived.

Nothing was said. I sat beside him.

"Smoke some hash?" he finally asked.

"Sure," I answered.

He produced a pipe and the hash, and we smoked. In silence.

"Odd, eh?" he asked.

"Yea, it is," I answered.

"It's for keeps," he said.

"Yea, it is," I answered.

"There's no where to hide -- no way to get away," he said.

"I know," I answered, unsure what else I should say.

"No, you don't," he replied matter-of-factly.

I didn't argue.

"You can't know," he said. "And neither, really, can I. But she did."

"How could she know?" I asked.

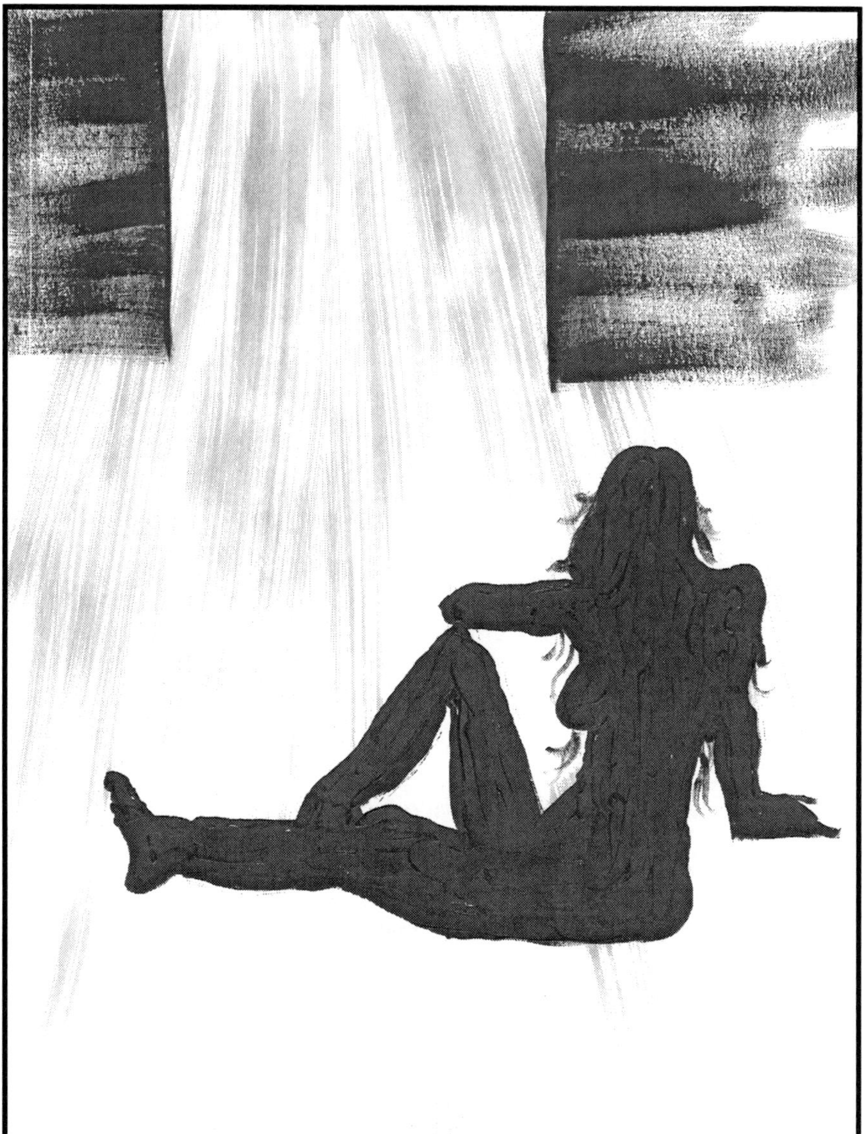

"She was wise," he answered, and he looked at me earnestly that I should believe. There were tears in his eyes as he said it. "She was the only one who knew. She was so pure and innocent. I loved her." He reached out and clenched the grass tightly in his one hand, the other turned to a fist.

"I think I know," I answered, again unsure of what to say, not knowing what he knew, not having known her so well.

He recovered himself somewhat. "Smoke some hash with me and we'll remember," he said.

And we smoked, but mostly in quiet, and there were no more outbursts like the one there had been. We talked about the band, and the latest Jimi Hendrix album, and other stuff that really didn't matter. But there was no mention of her. And when we parted company at the end of the day, I wished him well, and passed on my sympathies. And he embraced me, and held me tightly, and when he pulled away there were again tears in his eyes. "Friend," he said to me, just as he released me.

"Friend," I answered.

But it was at that parting that some portion of our friendship was lost. He was never the same. He seemed to lose his sense of direction -- the structure to his life -- and from then on, he sort of wandered through life. We were never as close a friends again. But there always seemed to be a connection between us, so that we never really lost touch with each other. I always knew where he was, and life was not kind to him, that much I knew from the reports I got of him. He married and worked for a short while, and I thought perhaps the worst was over. But he could not seem to see the value in that stable responsibility, so that he crashed to earth, drinking heavily, and he landed on the bottom -- and there he stayed. He married again, and although I had rare occasion to meet her, that wife seemed an angel to him, and perhaps must have seen him for what he really was, not the way most others saw him, the broken down husk of his former self.

Finally, he died. Relatively young. Far away.

I sent his wife a letter of condolence. I remembered him, although most other people didn't. He was my friend. I mourned him. But I was glad, because he had never fit into things, never quite got the hang of it, not since the girl had died. I could almost believe that true love comes only once each lifetime, and that he believed it too, but that he had lost his chance, and so had lost his life.

I got a letter about two weeks after he died. It was in his hand. I didn't open it right away, even though I recognized the handwriting. I was going up to my parents' place that weekend, and I thought I'd save it until I was back where I'd known him so well.

So that when I arrived at my parents' place, I said my hellos and I was soon saying my goodbyes, so I could head out to where I knew I should read the letter. The thinkin' spot was my destination, and I found myself there soon enough. And once there, I settled in on the old bridge abutment, and I fished for something in my pocket, something that had not been there recently, but only in a past life -- an old, well-worn hash pipe I'd kept for some strange sentimental reason. I found the hash wrapped in tin foil in my inside jacket pocket. It had been tough getting it, because I was out of the scene, and it's always hard getting it when you're out of the scene. I prepared the pipe, then set it beside me on the abutment.

Only then did I open the letter.

'Dear Commie', it started. Commie was my nick name from back in that other time. No one had used it to refer to me in twenty-five years. I read on.

'I haven't had much luck in this life, but I'm a firm believer that you make your own luck in this life, so I guess I got what I deserved,' the letter continued. 'I sort of just never got with it, I guess. Never really saw the point. Thought most of it was a load of shit that buries most people so deep they don't even get to come up for air. It's too bad. It's the people who make it that way themselves.

'It's a hopeless situation with so many morons in the world. Most people don't seem to realize that you only get one chance, and that we're all in this together. I do think that I figured that out quite early on. Back when I was hanging out with Donna -- remember her? Man, Commie, how I loved that girl. She was about all I wanted out of life, but she decided it was a no go. She couldn't handle it, you know. She was so pure and so innocent that life beat her up pretty bad. Her dad was an abusive creature, who hit on her mom, and made her and her sister wash him when he was in the bathtub, even when they were in their teens. Sick, eh? She had a pretty tough go of it. Life was hard on her. She had no peace -- nowhere to hide. Anyway, I tried to tell her that she could get away from him and that part of her life, but she just couldn't pull away. The only outlet she had was her poetry, and nobody ever paid much attention to it until I came along. I think that's why she sort of fell for me.

'I knew it was wrong, Commie -- that I was all wrong for her. I've always been such a slob, with no real manners and graces. But I couldn't stay away from her. I've dreamed about her my whole life, even in recent years, even when she died so many years ago.

'Anyway, remember back to the dance when you guys were playing at the school and Donna and me were supposed to be going. Well, we were never planning on going. It was all pretend, so she could get away with me for a few hours, because she'd decided she wanted me to be the first one to be with her. She thought we had a true love for each other -- I only know now that there is no such thing. So, she planned to sneak down to the hotel and to my room after her dad dropped her off for the dance.

'I'll never forget her coming to me, Commie. She was like my Venus. There was moonlight coming in through the window to my room, and I remember standing back to look at her after we'd taken off our clothes. God, she was beautiful. And when I touched her, she was the softest, smoothest thing I could ever have imagined existed. I couldn't even go to her at first, because I was like intimidated by her -- like she was too perfect for a mere mortal like me. So, she came to me, and, god Commie, I loved her. It was the only three hours of my life that I really lived. After we'd finished, we lay in each other's arms for a while, and it was then that I achieved my nirvana and knew true peace. It was the only time in my life. Nothing afterward ever seemed to make much sense. I should have died then, Commie. After that perfection, there could be no more. She must have realized that also, so she died. I was the coward, choosing instead to drink myself away to nothing. I should have died with her, but she caught me by surprise. I doubted her courage.

I loved her, Commie. And I loved you and the time we spent together, too. It was a hoot back in the old days. Don't mourn too much for me. I had my three hours of perfection, and most people wish for a lifetime for even one minute of the same. Maybe now I'll be seeing her again, although I really doubt all that religious stuff. It's more like now I'll be part of the eternal one, just like her, and maybe our two energies will arc through each other, and just for one split second, I will again know her, and I can be at peace -- and her too.

Anyway, Farewell Friend.

I set aside the letter. I regarded the period after the word Friend, feeling its finality. There were tears. I could taste the salt.

I lifted the hash pipe. I held it aloft, out into the eternal energy that fills life's void. Then, I put it in my mouth and lit it. It made me cough. But I held enough of the smoke inside, until finally I started to feel the effects of it come over me. You can always feel it first in your teeth. It felt good as the first waves of the stone crashed over me. I held the pipe aloft again. Here's to you, friend. Hope you have again found perfection and peace. It's something that all of us search for, but few find. Look for the substance. Not necessarily the structure. Just like a blues jam. Just like Donna and Mike.

Old Friends

Lloyd Nolan hated going to the nursing home. It was a place of death, filled with those waiting to die, and you could feel the life draining away all around you. But he faced the reality of death every day, faithfully at suppertime, as he came to the place to be with his Mary -- or at least what remained of his Mary, the shell of her, all that existed after the stroke. He came each evening to spoon her full of pablum, so that she might draw breath for another day, so he might come again to fulfill the ritual -- or so it had become as the weeks had turned to months, and the months to years.

When Mary had collapsed among her begonias on that fine summer day, the doctor had said she would probably slip away in short order, so severe had been the damage. But she had not slipped away, not her vital signs. Most of the time, she sat staring out blankly, looking so very empty inside, so he imagined that her soul had gone to some other place, and the shattered body lived on without it. But other times, as he sat with her after dinner, and he'd take to talking about their grandchildren, he thought he could see her looking out from inside, straining to give him some sign, like her soul was trapped deep within her, and could not get to the surface, try as it might.

Each night, he went back to their house, which had once been a home, but could no longer be called such, so lacking was it in all the things that make one into the other. His son had told him he should sell the place and get an apartment, because it would be easier to look after, and wouldn't be so hard on him. But who would look after Mary's flowers, that had been her pride and joy for all those years, if not for him? And it was true that he had done his best for these last few years, since her incapacitation, to keep them weeded and watered, as if she might one day come back from the near-dead to reclaim them. His son thought it was morbid, and told him so.

He seldom went out. Watched TV, and had taken to building model boats to fill the time when he wasn't in the garden or at the home. Had built twelve of the damned things over the past couple of years. He'd never have had the patience for it when he'd been younger, but time had slowed almost to a stop since the stroke. He was no longer in a hurry to do anything. Could spend hours fiddling with the rigging of a miniature sailing ship -- something he would have thought was a waste of time back in that other time.

One night, after giving Mary a tiny kiss on the cheek and telling her he loved her, as he did each and every night, he was leaving the home, feeling the usual depression that came with the visits, when someone called his name. It was a woman's voice, but one he didn't recognize, and he turned to see who it might be.

"Hello," said the fine looking older woman who had called after him. He studied her, and there was a faint familiarity about her, so he thought he should know her, but he couldn't come up with a name.

"You don't recognize me, Lloyd," the woman said. "That doesn't surprise me. It's probably been fifty years."

"No," Lloyd answered, "I'm sorry, but my memory's not so good any more."

"We were in high school together. Not that we were real close friends, but we knew each other," the woman said.

"I'm sorry, but I can't come up with your name," he admitted.

"Shirley Dodd -- I mean, Field, Shirley Field -- that was my maiden name," she answered. "I'm here with my husband, Jack Dodd -- you might not remember Jack -- he only moved here for Grade 13. His dad was with the Hydro." She paused. "He's had a series of strokes, and I can't tend to him properly any more. I brought him back here, so I could be near my sister -- you know, Gertie Allen." The words seemed to rattle out of her machine-gun style. Almost as if she might be nervous.

"That's too bad about Jack," Lloyd said, and he remembered her; or at least he thought he did.

"What are you doing here?" she asked. "You must have someone in here. How's Mary? That's who you married? Mary Dean? The grocer's daughter?" The questions ran together, and the expression on her face became grave as she realized the possible answer to the first one asked.

"It's Mary," he answered soberly, and he explained about the stroke.

"Oh, god," she said, "I'm really sorry. I remember her as being such a live wire back in high school."

"We don't seem to have much control over it," he answered. "It gets the good and the bad -- there doesn't seem to be any reason for it."

"No, I felt the same way when it happened to Jack," she said. "He always tried to do the right thing and to be a good person, but, somehow, it just didn't seem to matter." She paused. "You look well," she commented.

"Oh, I'm all right," he answered. "I've got the usual aches and pains that come with getting older, but really I can't complain."

"No, me either," she said.

They stood for a moment in silence.

"I should go," he said, although he had nowhere to go but back to an empty house.

"Yes," she answered. "I should probably get going too. My sister will wonder what's happened to me. Since I moved back, it's been just like we were kids again, with her mothering over me."

They walked together out into the parking lot.

"I'll see you again, Lloyd," she said.

"Yea, sure," he answered, and he turned toward his car.

That night, as he sat alone in his big easy chair and sipped a cup of tea, he couldn't help but think of her. He thought he remembered her from back in the old days, when they'd been young. She and Jack and he and Mary. They might even have shared a cherry coke back in Paul's

Grill and Tea Room. But he thought he remembered Shirley and Jack moving to the coast after getting married. Jack took a job with a bank, he thought. He'd seen them around town a couple of times since, but not too often, and as is often the case, even that contact had ended many years ago.

His sleep was restless that night. In his dreams, he was again back in his high school days, and the four of them were sitting together in Paul's, sipping on cherry cokes and laughing gaily. He could see her clearly, sitting beside Jack, vibrant and fresh and young, as was his Mary.

And the image of Shirley was with him during much of the next day, as he went about his business, tending to the garden and working on the latest model boat. He thought of how fine she had looked on the previous night when he'd seen her at the nursing home. He wanted to see her again -- he knew that. But he was embarrassed that he should have such a desire. There was only Mary. That's what he told himself. But he couldn't shake his thoughts of the other.

He didn't see her again for some time -- a couple of weeks. He thought she must come to see Jack often, but perhaps not as often as he visited his Mary, and perhaps not at the same time he visited, and he guessed their paths just hadn't crossed again. But even after those two weeks, she came often to his thoughts, as he puttered in the garden, or fiddled with his boats, or watched TV.

One night, after returning home from the nursing home, where he had again been disappointed by the lack of a chance encounter, he even found himself looking in the phone book for her sister's name. He found it, and sat for a few minutes reading the number over and over, drumming his fingers on a table like he always did when he couldn't make up his mind about something. But he didn't call. Somehow, he didn't think it would be right.

It was only a couple of days after that incident, and he was again leaving the nursing home for the night, when he saw her standing at the nurse's station, speaking to the on-duty nurse. He had waited all this time to see her, and now wasn't sure what to do. Should he approach? Should he leave and wait for her outside? If he did approach, what should he say? The questions raced through his mind.

Suddenly, she wheeled away from the nurse, and walked a short distance away, covering her face with her hands. She was upset. Something was wrong. The questions vanished and he started to walk toward her. As he got closer, he could see that she was crying.

"Shirley," he said, as he approached, and put what he hoped would be a re-assuring hand on her shoulder.

She looked up with red-rimmed, tear-filled eyes. "Oh, Lloyd," she sobbed, and she collapsed into his arms. He embraced her, held her in his comforting arms. "Why did it have to come to this?" she wept. "Why didn't he just die?" There was anger in her voice.

"I don't know," he said softly, continuing to hold her close. "Who knows why anything happens the way it does? I've asked myself the same thing about Mary. Mary'd say it was God's way -- that he had a reason -- but she believed in that sort of stuff more than me. I just don't know."

Gradually, after a couple of minutes, her sobbing subsided, and he released his hold on her. She stood dabbing her eyes with a Kleenex; trying to regain her composure.

"I'm sorry about that," she said. "I just can't believe that they can't keep him cleaned up better. I'm afraid he sits here all day in his own mess. And he was such a proud man." Her bottom lip trembled. It appeared she might break down again.

Lloyd reached out and gently squeezed her arm. "I think they do the best they can," he said quietly. "It's just that there's so many people here, and they nearly all need almost constant attention. I felt the same way you do when Mary first had to come here, but I've gotten to know most of the staff, and they really do care -- they'd have to, to work here at all."

"How long's Mary been here?" she asked, also speaking in a quiet, subdued voice, almost whispering the question as if she was afraid to hear the answer.

"Almost three years," Lloyd answered. "It'll be three years next month."

"God," she sighed, shutting her eyes tightly, "I hope Jack doesn't.......I mean......oh, God." It was obvious she hadn't considered a virtual eternity in this place. The thought of it distressed her. He could see tears welling up in the corners of her eyes.

"Come for a coffee," he said quickly. "Let's get out of here. You don't need to be in this place any more today."

"I'd like that," she said, and a small smile slipped across her face.

They each had their own car, so he explained the location of the coffee shop to her while they stood in the parking lot of the home. He felt excitement as he drove. He felt the giddy excitement of a teenager going out on his first date. And he thought he was a silly old fool for having such feelings. He thought of his Mary, and how he loved her. And he thought of Jack, and how much Shirley must surely love him. But he wanted to be with her, to share her company, even though he couldn't make it feel right in his mind.

She arrived at the coffee shop right behind him, so they went into the place together. Even though he'd asked her for a coffee, he didn't drink coffee, didn't like the stuff, so he ordered a tea, and was pleased when she did the same. They went to a secluded corner booth, and settled in opposite one another. She smiled broadly, and he couldn't help but give her one in return, so absolutely joyful did he feel.

"So, what have you been doing all these years, Lloyd Nolan?" she asked.

"Nothing very exciting, I'm afraid," he answered. "I've just been here all my life -- working for the factory." He paused, feeling suddenly disappointed that he didn't have a better answer.

"Oh, I think you're not telling me the whole story," she said. "I've been asking my sister about you and Mary. You raised a fine family. Your son's a teacher, Gertie was telling me. You've got grandchildren. It must be great for you."

"Oh, yea, that's okay," he answered, "but I never did much travelling, and we didn't live too fancy. I guess Mary and I were kind of simple folks -- at least you might think so."

"I think no such thing," she answered. "It's true that I've travelled, and maybe we did live a little what you might call fancy, but a lot of times I've wished I never left this town -- that I'd had that kind of stability in my life."

"You don't have a family?" he asked.

"We couldn't have children -- I had a blockage, and they couldn't fix that kind of thing back when I could have children." She paused. He thought maybe it bothered her to talk about this part of her life. "So Jack concentrated on a career in banking. We travelled everywhere, lived in the finest houses, and had everything you could want." Another pause. She took a sip of her tea. The smile gone.

"But I used to think of the gang at Paul's Grill, and wonder what I missed by not staying closer to home," she said. "Gertie would write me and tell me what was going on in the old, home town. We came back to visit when Mom and Dad were alive, but not too often, it usually wasn't very practical, and after they died, we came less often -- it's probably been eight or nine years since the last time. I never had a lot of close friends, and Jack wasn't here long enough, and his parents moved away right after we did."

"I heard a little about you over the years," he said. "Mary and Gertie were involved in a couple of things together some years ago -- I never got too involved in much, except when the boy was younger and into scouts and such -- and I heard a few things. It sounded pretty exciting. Jack did well in the bank."

"Yes, he did do well. He worked hard," she answered, and she looked wistfully out the window of the coffee shop into the street where it was a windswept and rainy night in early fall, dark and forelorn. "God, Lloyd, I don't know what I'm going to do," she sighed, suddenly serious. "I can't go into that place. I can't see him like that. I can't see all that death." She paused, touched her hand to her eye, fought back the tears.

He sat quietly, knowing what she felt, having felt it himself in the not too distant past. "It's hard," he said softly.

"It is," she said, as a tear trickled slowly down her cheek.

He thought he could taste its salt.

They fell silent. Quiet. Thoughtful.

Eventually, the conversation resumed, and it ranged far and wide, concerning old friends, and what had become of them, and grandchildren, and the obligatory photographs were produced and exhibited. It was pleasant, and more tea was ordered and drank, and they smiled and laughed, and forgotten for the moment were the others, the two who lay silent forevermore.

Finally, though, too much time had passed, and enough tea had been drank, and it was time for a finish.

"We could go together," he said suddenly, as they were getting up, putting on their coats.

"What do you mean?" she asked.

"We could go to the home together," he said. "I'll go and visit Jack with you."

"You'd do that?" she asked, seeming suprised.

"Sure," he said. "I've got to go anyway. I go every day."

She looked at him thoughtfully for a moment.

"You wouldn't mind?" she asked. "Gertie said she'd come when she could."

"I go every day," he repeated. "In fact, your sister's house is on the way from my place. I could pick you up. I don't mind."

Her expression softened. "You're a nice man," she said, leaning over and kissing him lightly on the cheek. He felt himself go flush.

"It's a deal?" he asked.

"On one condition," she answered.

He furrowed his brow. "And what's that?"

"If you come with me to see Jack, I'll come with you to see Mary -- if you like," she answered. "I won't mind."

"That would be very nice of you," he answered. "Only if it won't bother you," he added.

She smiled, and they walked to the door of the place.

"I'll pick you up tomorrow about five," he said.

"All right," she answered. "We'll try it."

And they parted company for the night.

And the experiment worked well, and the shared visits to the nursing home became a regular habit, and it was a comfort to them both to have the other as companion on those trips to that awful place. In fact, he found himself looking forward to the time when he'd get cleaned up and get the car out of the garage, and drive over to Gertie Allen's. Shirley'd always be waiting out on the porch, except in bad weather, then a honk of the horn brought her hurrying to the car. He enjoyed the time spent together immensely.

One night, as he was driving her home after the required visit, and after some weeks had passed, she surprised him with a question. "Would you like to come over for dinner tomorrow night?" she asked.

"Dinner?" he asked back.

"Yes," she answered. "You must get tired of eating your own cooking night after night. I thought I'd make you a good, home-cooked meal."

"What about the home?" he asked, his thoughts of Mary.

"We can either eat late -- about this time, if you can wait....or....... we can miss a day at the home." She made the statement with a tone of voice that made the last part sound a little mischievous -- like they'd be doing something they could get in trouble for.

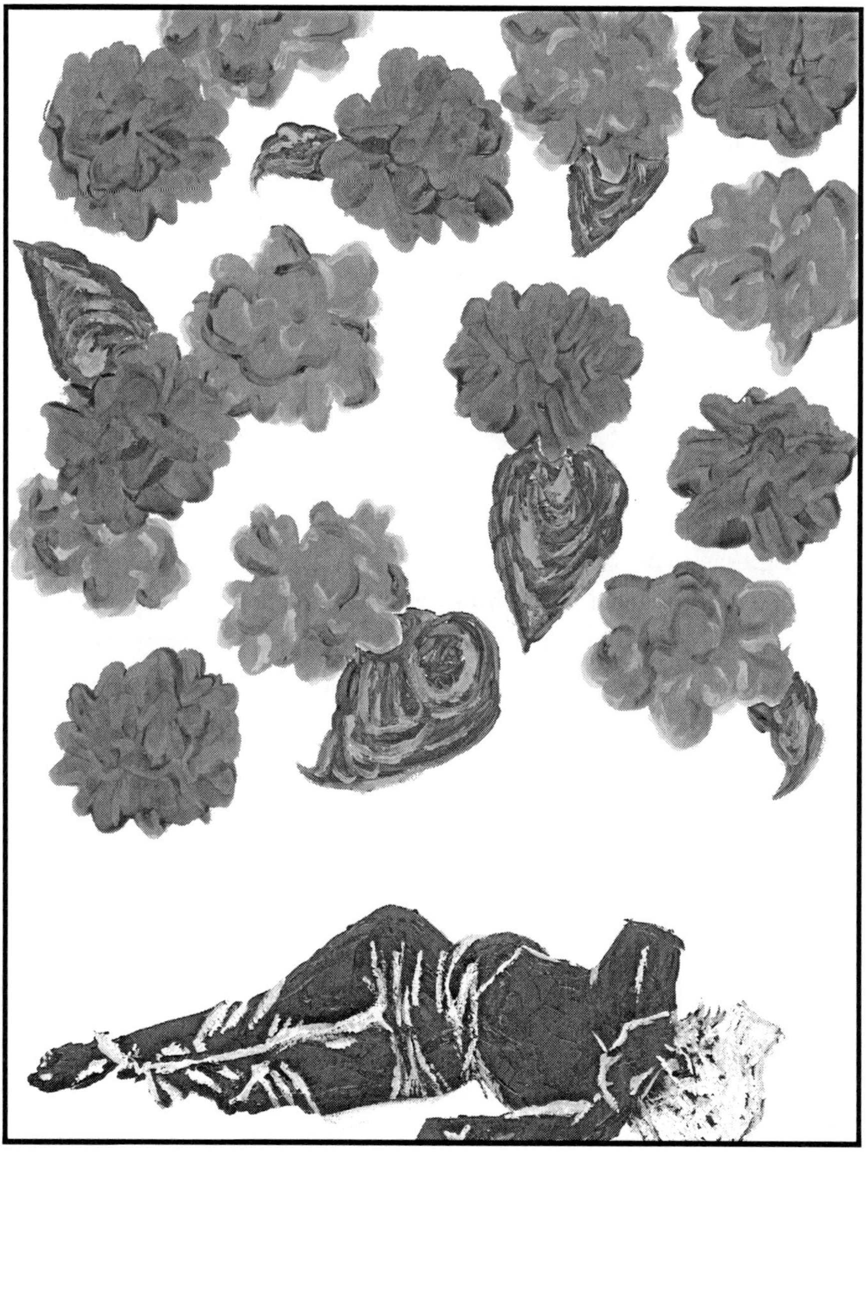

"I don't know," he said. "I've only missed a few times when I've been sick, or something like that."

"Well, I don't think there'd be anything wrong with it," she said. "But if it'd make you feel any better, I'll take my own car tomorrow and come back to Gertie's a little early. I'll have everything ready, so I can just heat it up. We can eat late."

"I'd feel better," he said.

"Then, it's settled," she replied. And it was.

He looked forward to the next day with some anticipation. He was again having feelings that he was somehow doing something wrong, but he kept telling himself that Mary would understand. If there was a way to reach inside the empty shell, all that remained of her, to ask if she minded, he was sure the answer would be no. That was what he kept telling himself as he got ready to go to the nursing home. And he got a little more cleaned up than usual, even getting out the bottle of ice blue shaving lotion he used for special occasions, but hadn't used at all since the stroke.

Usually, as he sat with Shirley and Jack, he and Shirley would sit solemnly, but there would be some exchange of conversation, perhaps concerning some television program that had been on the night before, or some other such thing. But there was even less said on this particular night, and Lloyd thought he felt some awkward tension between them; something he had not sensed at any other time since he had become re-acquainted with her those few weeks ago. But nothing was said about the mood, and she left early as promised, and he went on to visit with Mary.

And as he sat with Mary on that evening, and as he spooned her dinner into her, he seemed to look harder than usual for some sign that she even knew who he was. He wanted so badly to see even a flicker of recognition. He talked quietly to her during the feeding, telling her how their grandson had a birthday coming up, and how he'd almost finished getting the garden ready for winter. And he tried to look into her, inside of what remained, and he wanted a sign from her, to somehow acknowledge that he was a good and faithful husband who had proven his eternal love for her. But the sign did not come. And, finally, it was time to leave.

He drove to Gertie's, mounted the steps, and rang the doorbell.

Shirley answered. She looked great. She'd changed since he'd seen her at the home. And she smelled good. He could smell her as he came into the house, and took off his coat.

"Where's Gertie?" he asked, as she showed him into the living room.

"She's away at an IODE conference," Shirley answered.

He felt himself flush at the news. The sister's presence had been expected. He was alone with her. He swallowed. He was nervous. Anxious.

The meal was fabulous, and she'd obviously done her share of cooking. He wasn't exactly sure what they were eating, it had some kind of French name, but it tasted all right, so he was a good boy and cleaned off his plate. There was some conversation over dinner, but it seemed some of the earlier awkward feeling had returned and the talk was somewhat stilted.

Finally, the meal was at an end. He went to get up to help clear the table, but she stopped him, guiding him instead into the living room, where he was instructed to wait while she got the tea. He found himself sitting on the edge of the couch, leaning forward, unable to sit back and relax.

"Well, here we go," she said, as she entered the room carrying a tray. "We'll fix a nice cup of tea. Just the right thing after a dinner like that.. Most people prefer coffee, but I've always enjoyed a good cup of tea."

"Yea, me too," he answered.

She poured his tea, and passed it to him, and he was soon cradling a cup of the hot liquid on his lap.

"That was a fine dinner," he remarked.

"Thank-you." she said. "I enjoy cooking. It relaxes me."

"I find it to be a bit of a bother," he answered.

"You just don't look at it the right way," she said. "It's all in the way you approach it."

He didn't answer, and they sat for a moment in silence, and he continued to feel awkward and cardboard stiff, still sitting on the very edge of the couch, as if poised to depart at any moment.

"You look tense," she said, seeing it in him. "Are you all right?"

"Yes," he answered.

There was a pause.

"Something's wrong," Shirley said. She reached over and put her hand gently on his. "What is it, Lloyd?"

He hesitated before answering. "I'm not sure I should be here," he finally said.

"Why not?" she asked, pulling her hand back.

"It might be false pretences," he answered, not looking at her, his eyes looking into the cup of tea he was holding.

"Why's that, Lloyd?" she asked.

"I'm growing rather fond of you, Shirley," he answered. "I greatly enjoy your company."

"And I enjoy yours," she said.

"Well, I've got Mary to look after," he said. "I shouldn't oughta be here. I'm getting feelings for you -- strong feelings." He continued to look away, embarrassment overwhelming him.

"I have feelings too," she answered. "I'm very fond of you as well. I've got Jack, but I can't die because of what's happened to him. I feel bad, but I've got to have a life."

"I want us to just be friends, Shirley," he said, and finally he looked up at her.

"That's what I want too, Lloyd," she said, and she again reached over and placed her hand on his. "And I'm sorry if I made you feel uncomfortable." She smiled.

He returned the smile. "I really enjoyed the dinner," he said.

"I'm glad you did," she answered.

And he settled back in on the couch, and they spent the rest of the evening in quiet conversation about this and that and some other things as well. He found it pleasant. But as he left later that night, and she said good-bye to him at the door, he knew it would never be quite the same. And part of him regretted that. But it was best. That's what he told himself.

She called the next day to say that she was going away for a few days and he didn't have to pick her up to go to the nursing home. She never called to resume the ritual. After that, he again went to the nursing home alone. It should be a private time. It's best. That's what he told himself.

He only saw her a few times at the home, and they would stop and exchange a few words. How was Jack? How was Mary? That sort of stuff. Jack died that winter -- slipped quietly away one night. He tried calling to offer his condolences, but couldn't catch anyone in. Then, he heard that Shirley and Gertie had left on a trip. Then, there was a "For Sale" sign on the lawn of Gertie's house. He felt a touch of sadness at that. But it was best. That was what he told himself.

Memories for Sale

As his eyes slowly opened to meet another day, his attention became focused on the slender crack that was delicately etched in the ceiling over his bed. And had been ever since sometime around the time of the birth of his second child, about the time they had sent the oldest off to school. Or so he thought. He had been meanin' to fix that crack, and re-paint the room, but had never been able to quite find the time.

And now there was no time. Time had run out. All his life he had assumed it was others who got old and faded off into the mists of life, and, finally, into the oblivion of death. And even if he was not quite ready for oblivion, he could no longer deny that there was a certain translucent covering on his consciousness; something that clouded his perception with feelings of nostalgia, making him feel like an old fool who was quickly losing his way in the mist. After he had made that stark realization that he was mere mortal and that he had nearly crossed the entire span that had been his life, he had known he could no longer manage in the house, that had, for so long, been his home.

But it was too big, and there were too many corners to it, and he couldn't begin to keep it clean, and it was unfair to expect the children to be forever looking after him, now that he had reached old age, and now that their mother had died, and left him alone to rattle about in the big, old house. He knew that. No matter that he and their mother had struggled through years of adversity raising them, always seeing to it they were clothed and fed and supplied with all the necessities of life, while the parents often did without. But it wasn't fair to ask for anything in return, she would have said. Raising them had been a labour of love, she would have reminded him.

As the thought of his wife crossed his mind, he found himself reminded of her quiet strength, and he felt his eyes grow moist, and he felt an empty ache inside him, in places where there were only feelings for her, and where no one else could intrude. It had been two years since she had died, but each time he thought of her, it was as if he had been with her only yesterday, and she had gone away, probably to her sister's for coffee. But, then, he would remember, and his eyes would grow moist, and he would feel the empty ache deep inside in that hidden place, and he knew that whether it was two years, or whether it was twenty years, he would feel it all the same, such had been the depth of affection he had felt for the woman, who had been his high school sweetheart, and with whom he had shared a virtual lifetime.

A noise in another part of the house brought him back to reality, and caused him to look away from the crack in the ceiling, and to forget the memory of his wife, and to remember that this would be the final time he would be visited by such a memory, while he lay in this bed, his attention focused on the delicately-etched crack.

For today was the auction. And after a gaggle of strangers had searched for bargains, and exchanged bids on a lifetime of his possessions, returning cold, hard cash for memories, he was to go dutifully with his son, to the stark sterility of the extended-care facility; to the place where his children had decided he would spend the autumn of his years.

The door to the room opened, and his son's head appeared through the doorway.

"Mornin' Dad," came his son's cheerful voice.

He didn't answer, thinking that perhaps he could somehow hold back the start of the day if he simply refused to acknowledge that it was beginning.

"You awake, Dad?" his son asked, starting to walk toward the bed.

"Yea, I'm up," he finally answered, breaking the momentary silence.

"Good," his son answered. "I know it's early, but the guys from the auction service will be here soon, to get things ready, and you've got to be up and ready."

He swung his legs over the side of the bed and prepared to stand. Each morning, even this simple task seemed harder and harder and requiring of more effort. His son seemed to sense that this was a difficult day for him to begin.

"Dad," he said, "are you sure you're alright?" He placed his hand on his father's shoulder. "You know, you don't have to stay here for the auction. I know it's hard for you, seeing all the things you and Mom worked so hard for getting sold." He paused for a moment as if to emphasize the sincerity he was trying to project. "But we talked about it." Another pause. "And you know this is best." He said the last line more softly and gently squeezed the old man's shoulder. "It's not too late to go over to Margie's," he added.

"I'll be alright, Jack," he said, looking up and offering his son a slight smile. "I'm just feeling sorry for myself and your mother would have given me the dickens for it."

"What do you think? Want to go to Margie's?" his son asked, repeating his earlier question.

"No," the old man answered. "I want to stay. I can still take care of my own business affairs at least, and this is my auction; they're my things that are being sold."

"Alright," Jack answered, "but you'd better get dressed because it's almost six and that's what time the auction guys are coming. Remember, the sale starts at nine."

Jack turned to leave, but stopped short of the door. "Remember, if you change your mind and want to leave, I'll find somebody to drive you over to Margie's."

"Okay," he answered. "Now get out of here so I can get dressed."

He got up from the bed and walked over to the room's closet to search out some clothes.

He found he went through each morning ritual, from filling the basin and washing, to pulling on his pants, with a certain exaggerated deliberateness, as if he was trying to etch them in his mind, so he would not forget the last time he had carried them out in this place.

Perhaps he should have gone over to his daughter's. She would have fussed over him and made sure he didn't have a lot of time to think about the sale, and she would have said all the right things to make him feel better. That was the way it was with Margie. Just like her mother. He knew she would have loved to have been at the sale, herself, but had said she wasn't all that interested, just to offer him a refuge from the events of the day, if he chose to take it. He also knew that she would appear to hover over him as soon as she realized he was going to make good on his promise to attend the sale and to stay for its duration.

Jack already had the coffee on, so he helped himself to a cup, and found one of yesterday's bran muffins, before making his way out onto the large, old front veranda, where he had gotten into the habit of drinking that first coffee of the day on fine summer mornings. And this could have been described as one of those fine summer mornings, when everything is fresh and crisp, and still resplendent in its spring newness, had it not been for the impending sale, and the thoughts of foreboding it had cast upon him.

The guys from the auction service arrived on the front steps to the house, about five minutes after he'd settled into a corner of the porch swing and was just beginning to slurp the scalding, hot coffee, and munch on the hard-around-the-edges, day-old muffin. He directed them inside to see his son, having no urge to deal with these apparent harbingers of doom. Or so he had found himself regarding them, as he had watched their tiny caravan edge down the street and pull up in front of the house. He knew it was foolish to think so, that they were only carrying out a job which he had agreed upon, but as soon as he had caught sight of them coming up the street, he had felt a knot form in the pit of his stomach, and had felt a certain anxiousness about what was soon to transpire.

He finished the muffin and was sitting cradling his cooling coffee, when the door to the house swung open, and two men appeared, struggling to move a large cabinet through it. It was the china cabinet from the dining room. He and his wife had gotten it as a wedding gift from her parents, as part of a set, the remainder of which would likely soon appear.

The two men wrestled the cabinet out onto the front lawn, and returned to the house. He sat watching the sun reflect off the finely polished sheen of the dining room piece, as it sat alone and forlorn on the lawn, and he found himself wondering how often it had been lovingly rubbed, to make it shine so. Again, or perhaps still, he felt himself retreating to the private places that lay within. He remembered. He felt her with him. And he wished that she were with him, so she could make it better, just as she always had. His eyes grew moist. Old fool, he thought.

The door re-opened, and another piece of the dining room set appeared through it; this time, the buffet; emptied now of the sterling silver tea service, that had, for so long, occupied a cherished place within it.

He watched the two men manhandle it down beside the china cabinet. By the time the chairs were brought out, he had recovered himself somewhat, so that even when one of the men carried out his chair, the one with the arms, that had always sat at the head of the table, he found that he was able to watch, and at the same time maintain an emotional distance from the scene.

Still, he grew tired of sitting and watching the artifacts from his past parade by, each taking up a place on the front lawn, on display for those who searched out bargains among the memories of others. So, he got up from the swing, left the porch, and walked around to the back of the house. It would have been quicker to have gone through. He knew that. But the interior of the house no longer beckoned to him as the safe haven he had known. There were strangers there. And they were tearing out the insides of his life.

Already, the stove and fridge and a few other items from the house had appeared on the back lawn. He walked over to them, and walked around them, seeming to inspect them.

"Dad," he heard a voice call from the direction of the house.

He looked over and saw Jack, standing by the kitchen door.

"Dad," his son repeated. "Margie's on the phone. She's coming over and wants to know if you want anything."

"Can't think of anything," he answered. "Just tell her I don't want her fussing over me." He knew his last comment meant nothing, but felt an obligation to add it just the same.

"Okay," his son said. "Your paper's here," he added.

After his son had disappeared back inside the house, he walked back around to the front of the house to retrieve the day's news. Almost from the day his wife had died, he had developed a habit of reading the newspaper, nearly from cover to cover, when it arrived each morning.

When he arrived at the front of the house, he noted that the dining room set had been joined by many other items that were about to make their way out of his life.

He found the paper on the porch swing, and gathered it up, before taking his customary spot on the end of the swing, to begin the morning reading of the day's events; to find out what life was like.

He read for a while, until the sun had crept a little higher into the sky, to the point where it had just cleared the roof of the house next door, and so he knew it was about eight-thirty. He had become relatively oblivious to the constant passage of the men from the auction service, as they went in and out, in and out, carrying a well-worn footstool, that brought instant recognition the moment he glanced up and caught sight of it, or, perhaps, a child's two-runner sled, which, when it finally did spawn a flicker of recognition, he thought he remembered stuffing into the basement rafters, probably thirty years ago.

When he finally did raise his head from the paper, to take in a full view of the lawn, being distracted from his reading just when the sun glinted over the neighbour's eave, he was surprised to see the wide array of artifacts which had come to rest there; each of them representing something or sometime in his past.

He also saw a car drive up and come to a stop across the street, and a woman and two children got out and he saw that they were coming toward the house. Almost immediately, the woman, presumably the mother, he thought, headed off in the direction of the dining room suite. The children, on the other hand, wasted little time discovering anything that might have any faint association with being a plaything, and the boy had soon found that among all this mostly uninteresting stuff on the lawn of this house, there was at least one thing that had been made just for him.

It was a hockey game; one of those miniature hockey games, where players spun on stationary posts, embedded in plywood ice, and the Montreal Canadiens and Toronto Maple Leafs battled for eternity for a four-inch high replica of the Stanley Cup, using a marble, or a checker, or anything else that would serve as a puck.

The old man sat on the porch and watched as the youngster seemed to try to touch and work every part of the game.

It had been a Christmas gift to his son from Santa Claus. He remembered Jack had been about seven that Christmas, and one day shortly before the big day, they were in the hardware store to buy something, and Jack, as could be expected this close to Santa's visit, coaxed him to allow one final look at the toy department, just in case anything might have been missed and not seen the required number of times. And there was one toy the boy could not keep his eyes off, nor his hands. And it had been the hockey game. The shiney, new hockey game where all the Toronto Maple Leafs wore Tim Horton's look of determination, while the Canadiens looked like the fiery Rocket Richard.

The boy had breathed a profound sigh of relief to discover the game was still there, and rushed to it the second they walked under the arched "Toys" sign at the entranceway to the rear part of the store. He had walked around it studying it carefully, tempted to reach for one of the player controls, just to give it one little spin, but resisted, sure such an action would only bring rebuke from his father.

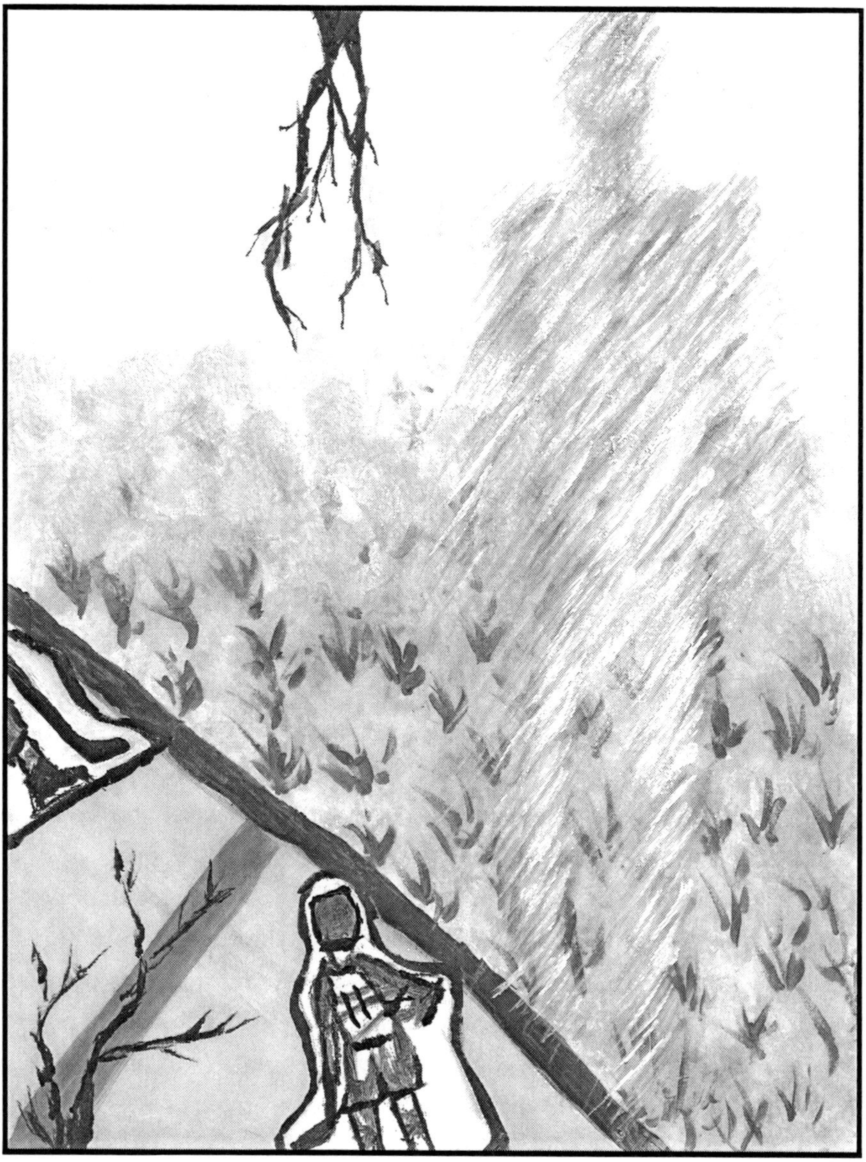

His attention stayed on the game just long enough to make sure it hadn't changed, and was still safe and secure for Santa to pick up and bring him on Christmas Eve, then moved on to some other favourite toys, but it was obvious where the boy's heart lay, especially when the father told him it was time to go, and he had to give the game one more look over before leaving.

The old man remembered the excitement he had felt on Christmas Eve, as he had wrapped the shiney, new hockey game, so he could put it under the tree for his son. He remembered imagining the joy his son would feel, content with the knowledge that he had gotten his hockey game, there was a Santa Claus, and that dreams did come true.

They had played the game often; he and his son. He had had to keep his goalie off to make the games fairer, until Jack got a bit older. He remembered his son's glee the first time he beat his father. It was the first time the Leafs had won a Cup for quite some time. And it didn't even matter that the Canadiens played the entire match without their goalie.

The old man realized he had drifted off, and he returned to the present reality just in time to see the mother scolding the boy and pulling him by the sleeve away from the area of the hockey game.

"I thought I told you not to touch things unless you're going to buy them," he thought he heard the obviously irate woman saying, as she continued to hustle her apparently delinquent offspring away.

He watched until the lady and boy had disappeared around the corner of the house, then got up to go and see what had happened. He had been sitting in one position on the swing for too long, and he felt stiff and sore as he got to his feet. It seemed to take considerable effort to force himself toward the porch steps. Another reminder of age, he thought. As if I need any more reminders.

He made his way slowly to the hockey game, which was perched on a card table. He looked at the game and saw the damage.

"My brother broke it," he heard a tiny voice say.

He turned and saw the little girl, the boy's sister, who had been left at the front of the house when the mother and boy had made their hurried exit to the rear.

"My brother leaned on it and broke it," she said, repeating her earlier confession.

He looked at the crack in the plywood playing surface.

"It's too bad," the old man said to the little girl, his voice relatively emotionless.

"I don't think it matters," the little girl said. "My brother said it's old and people don't even play with that sort of junk anymore," she added, no doubt using the exact words her older sibling had used to defend his action.

"I suppose you're right," the old man answered. "But I think it's a shame," he added.

There was a pause.

And during that pause, he was suddenly overcome by a wave of unexpected, unwanted emotion, and, as he again regarded the crack in the plywood ice, he felt profoundly sad; sad that it had come to this; to be regarded only as a piece of junk, that little boys didn't care about any longer. He felt a tear slowly trickle down his well-worn face, and a taste of salt touched his lips.

"Why are you sad?" the little girl asked, reminding him of her presence, alongside the broken hockey game.

He looked down at her, and saw her face, covered with childhood's innocence, looking up at him, waiting expectantly for an answer.

"This used to be my son's hockey game when he was about as old as your brother," the old man finally answered, smiling softly down at her.

She didn't reply right away, but instead seemed to have to consider this latest bit of information, and consider how it was possible that this man, who must have seemed older than time to her, could have a son the age of her brother.

"That must have been a long time ago," she finally said in a somewhat thoughtful tone.

"It was," he answered, and his thoughts returned briefly to a Christmas that was lost somewhere in his past.

There was another brief pause.

"Have you seen my Mommy?" the little girl asked, returning him from the vision of the past.

"Yes," he answered. "She went around to the back of the house," he explained, gesturing toward the corner of the house where he had last seen the angry mother chastising the boy.

"Thanks, mister," she said, turning to start in the direction he had indicated.

But, before she left the old man alone, she looked back toward him a final time.

"I'm sorry my brother broke the game," she said, with a type of sincerity only a child has access to. "Maybe you can get your son another one," she added. And she turned about and was gone.

Other people were starting to filter onto the yard, and he suddenly felt an urge to be alone. He found himself drifting off the yard and onto the sidewalk, and then he started to walk, in the kind of shuffling step that had become his walk in recent times. And he walked. And he didn't really care where, only it had to be away from the house. He wanted to leave the area of the house.

He walked away from what had become of his past. And before he had gone too very far, he came upon a small park that was only a short distance from the house, and although he had not intentionally set off in its direction, when he came upon it, he was glad he had happened to walk this way.

It was only a tiny park, a kind of oasis in suburbia, and he remembered he had often wondered why the city fathers had situated it here. It had only a single tree and a small flower bed and a park bench within its triangular boundary.

He walked to the park bench and sat. He felt extremely tired, and extremely old, and although it was now a bright, sunny day, it was like the world had gone grey, that the colour had faded from it, and that he had faded with it, and become only a one-dimensional, monotone reflection of what had been.

"Mind if I join you?" asked a voice from outside his reality.

He looked up, surprised because he had not sensed that anyone had approached, and saw his daughter, Margie, standing over him.

"Hello, Margaret," he said, moving slightly toward an end of the bench so she could sit.

"Hello, father," she answered, as she sat.

"How did you know I was here?" he asked.

"Jack saw you start in this direction," she answered.

There was a momentary pause in the exchange.

"Penny for your thoughts," she said, reaching over and taking his wrinkled hand in her's.

"I guess I should have gone to your place," he admitted.

"It would have been easier, I think," she answered.

"I just thought I should be there," he said. "It's my stuff.....it's my life."

"I know, Dad," Margie said softly, squeezing his hand ever so gently.

"I feel like my life is over. I think I feel worse than when your mother died," he said.

"Your life's not over yet, Dad," she answered. "I have a feeling there's quite a bit of life left in that old body. You'll adjust, Dad. Just like you did when Momma died. Me and Jack were worried about you then, but you pulled through and you adjusted."

"This doesn't feel the same," he said. "Then, I could just come home and there was so much of her around. It was like I could pretend she was out doing the shopping, or playing bridge. I had time to adjust, as you call it. This time, I woke up in my own bed this morning, and by the time I go to sleep, it'll all be gone.....my life."

"You can't think that way, Dad," his daughter responded. "You've got to think of this as just another phase in your life. One more challenge to face, just like you've faced all the others in your life."

"But this is the last one," he said, and he felt his eyes brim with tears.

"I wish I could have gone with your mother. I don't understand why I had to stay for this."

"Remember what you and mom always used to tell us, Dad?" she asked. "You used to tell us everything in life had a purpose; even the bad things. Remember?"

"Yea," he said. "I guess I do. Dumb advice, wasn't it?"

"Smarten up," she said, half-scolding him. "You're just being silly. I can't remember you or mom ever giving us bad advice. Most of the time, we just weren't smart enough to listen to you."

He looked over at her and saw the image of her mother, sitting there beside him on the park bench, looking ever so stern and serious and sincere, as if to try to convince him she was not taking his current dilemma lightly.

"You're a wonderful girl, Margie," he said, meeting her eyes. "A man couldn't have asked for a better daughter, or one who was more caring."

She reached over and they embraced, pulling each other closer, each with the hint of a tear in their eyes.

"You're a pretty wonderful dad, too," she said, as they ended the moment.

There was a tiny, little silence, caused by the awkwardness adults feel when they bare their emotions and become vulnerable to one another.

It was the daughter who finally broke it.

"Why don't I get the car, and the kids, meet you here and we'll go to McDonalds for lunch?" she said in a light, lively tone that indicated it was time to change the mood.

"Yea, maybe that would be a good idea," he replied, deciding to comply and follow the indicator.

He felt somewhat better as he sat on the park bench in the tiny triangular park, waiting for her to return with the car and two of his grandchildren, or at least that's who he thought she had gone to pick up.

When she returned, he was surprised that his other three

grandchildren, Jack's two girls and a boy, were also in the car. Obviously, Margie had drawn babysitting duty, while the others helped at the sale.

He continued to feel better, as he drove along in the stationwagon-load of children, each of whom had dutifully given their grandfather a kiss when they had picked him up. There was considerable noise and commotion in the car, as might be expected when five small children are close-quartered for any length of time, but on this particular day, instead of perhaps telling the children to settle down a little, he relished their exuberance and energy, and, in fact, felt he was somehow luxuriating in life.

He found himself smiling.

He had put his memories away.

The lunch at McDonalds was confusing and somewhat frenzied, with the five youngsters jostling with each other, and generally carrying on at a high level of excitement, obviously delighted to be at ""Big M's", as he had heard them referring to it on the way over.

Then, they went to Margie's for the afternoon.

And it was a pleasant enough afternoon, considering that unwanted thoughts were continually trying to intrude and return him to his earlier forlorn disposition. But, usually, just when he was about to be plunged into despair, one of the children would appear, or Margie, and he would be able to recover himself, and at least not show that he continued to be troubled by the events of the day.

But, finally, he knew he wanted to go back. It was late afternoon and the auctioneer had thought they would be finished just before supper. That was how long he had thought it would take.

Margie tried to resist, tried to divert his attention and get him interested in something else, but knew almost immediately there was no chance of that, so agreed to drive him back to the house.

When they pulled up in front, it looked rather normal, the front lawn now being empty, and the people gone, no doubt carrying off their bargain-priced booty with them. There was the house, looking like it always had.

He walked up the front walk even more slowly than his halting, shuffling way of walking necessitated.

He climbed the steps to the porch, and crossed to the front door, before reaching to open it.

He had expected the house to be empty and peculiar, but was still taken aback by the starkness of it, as he walked across the barren dining room, his every move echoing back out of the emptiness. Hollow. It sounds hollow, he thought. It sounds like there's nothing left of it but a hollow shell, that its insides have been torn out, and, along with them, its feelings, so that its walls and its ceilings and its floors are devoid of the emotion that had once made this more than a house, but a home instead.

It's gone, he thought, as he stopped just outside the kitchen door, and waited, because he had just heard one of the kitchen floorboards creak and knew someone was about to walk through and into the dining room.

It was Jack, and he was carrying a pile of papers.

"Dad, you're back," he said, smiling broadly. "The sale went really well. We got good prices for most of the stuff."

"Great," the old man responded, but there was a numbness to the way he said it.

That night, as he lay on Margie's fold-out couch, she having insisted that he sleep at her place this night and go to the new place tomorrow, he found his thoughts returning to another place and another time; to a place where there was a delicate crack etched in the ceiling over the bed, and to a time when they had all been together, and he had lain in bed and felt snug and secure and content, and the house had been a home.

But that time was past.

And all that remained was the memory.

That I will keep, he thought.

And his eyes slowly closed, and he slept.

Waiting for Winter

This is damned embarrassing, the old man thought, as a nurse helped position him on the toilet. Can't even do this anymore. He felt himself going to the washroom and could faintly hear the sound of water meeting water. The act finished, the nurse helped him up and pulled his trousers up. She helped him back into his wheelchair and moved him back out of the bathroom and across the ward, over near the window.

There he sat. Each day the same. He sat and watched the stubble-filled field and waited. He waited to be fed. He waited to be taken to the washroom. He waited to be put to bed. Always, he waited. And always the scene was the same. Or so it appeared in his mind. Always, it was fall outside his window, and the leaves were off the trees and stubble filled the field, just waiting to be ploughed under.

And always he was alone. Living in a solitary world where no others could intrude. It seemed long ago that strokes had ripped the powers of communication and movement from him. Except to crawl with a humbling feebleness from the chair that imprisoned him to the toilet or the bed. He lived contained in this broken shell that had once been his pride and joy. And others could no longer be a part of his world. He was forced to look inward, in the direction of his soul, to find the peace that came from companionship. It had been a difficult adjustment, because he had always been a social creature who had enjoyed the company of others, but his inward reflectiveness was now all-absorbing. He was alone.

He had been frustrated by this aloneness in the beginning. When he had awoken after the last stroke, to discover he had become a society of one, he had been frightened, and the fear had turned to bitter frustration. Frustration at not being able to be a part of life; at being forced to become a passive observer and not an active participant in the game of life. But, eventually, he had accepted the finality of the situation. There was no point in being frustrated. Indeed, there was little point in feeling any emotion, because it was impossible to express that emotion to any other member of humankind. And he had grown the stubble-filled fall scene in his mind, and he watched and waited for the coming of winter. He waited for the falling of the first few flakes of snow.

One day, as he sat watching and waiting, the scene changed. It wasn't the arrival of winter that caused it to change. A figure entered it, standing on the other side of the field, near the apple tree, along the fence row. He strained with inward-looking consciousness to make out the figure, to bring it more clearly into focus, so he could ascertain who this figure was and why it had arrived so unceremoniously in the middle of the image; this image that had been his alone for so long.

Then, as the time passed, he noticed that the figure seemed to be moving closer; drifting across the stubble-filled field and drawing nearer each time he imagined the scene in his struggle to escape the humility of reality.

Finally, he was able to make out the figure and he discovered that it was him standing there watching him watch the imagined scene. He was standing there in the prime of life, with an expression of concern on his face, watching the frail, old shell sit numbly by.

As the time continued to pass, and he continued to grow closer to his self, he found himself wondering if he would be able to communicate with it.

Then, as he found himself focussing on the figure again, his question was answered, when a thought broke across his consciousness.

"How are you, old friend?" the thought asked, as it slipped smoothly across his mind, seeming not to cause a single ripple on his inner self.

As he shifted his focus from the entry of the thought into his consciousness, to the scene, he noticed that the image of his self now stood on this side of the field and was gazing reflectively in his direction. He admired the strong, young man who stood before him; his self on the other side of life, before what had come after.

"You look tired," came another thought. "How have they treated you?"

"I feel tired," he thought. "That's really the way I feel. I'm not sad. I'm not happy. I'm not angry or upset. I'm just tired. Very tired." He paused, interrupting his train of thought briefly. "Can I come home?" he thought ever so quietly. "Have you come to take me home?" the thought repeated.

"Yes," returned a reassuring thought. "I have come for you. I will take you home. But, first, remember," a thought invited him. "Remember," it said softly.

The scene came back into focus and he found he was directly meeting the gaze of his younger self. As they continued to stare into each other, he felt the rest of the field start to revolve around the figure; slowly at first, but, gradually, faster and faster, until it was a mind-disorienting blur.

Then, it froze, and the scene had changed. Instead of the stubble-filled field, he was gazing down the street where he had grown up. Although he doubted how it could happen, he felt he was a boy again, out playing some boyish game in the old neighbourhood.

"Frank," a voice broke into his thoughts. "Frank!" it repeated. "It's your turn. Will you hurry up and shoot, before Mom calls us for supper?"

He looked and saw his brother, Robert, standing beside him. They were playing marbles.

He looked and saw he was holding a marble in his hand.

"Take your turn, Frank," Robert implored. "What's the matter with you?"

"Frank! Robert!" a woman's voice called from down the street. "Come on, boys, it's suppertime!"

"There, I told you," said Robert. "If you'd only have hurried," he said, before turning and running toward the sound of the woman's voice.

He found that he followed his brother. He could feel himself running, drawing ever closer to home. He ran faster. And faster. Until he felt his feet would surely fail him.

Then, he saw her. His mother. Standing on the front step in her apron, calling her flock for the evening meal. His mind was crowded with images of this kind, gentle woman, as she tended his wounds, both physical and emotional, and quietly prepared him for the rigours of life.

He ran even faster. He strained to reach her. He wanted to smother himself in her apron and again hear her soothing voice, calming him, telling him everything was alright.

"I'm coming, mother!" he cried. "I'm coming! I'm coming!"

He felt himself drawing closer and closer. He could see her more clearly. He stretched out his arms and reached for the warm, secure strength she offered.

Then, just when he could feel her presence, and he could smell the comfortableness of her, the vision vanished, and he was again sitting, staring into the autumn scene. And his other self stared back. A tear trickled gently down his cheek.

"Why do you cry?" a thought asked.

"I love her," he thought in return. "I thought I was going to be with her again. I thought she could hold me and make me well again."

"Like she did when you fell off your bicycle and skinned your knee?"

"Yes. And like she did when I had the measles and had to stay home from school," he thought.

"She was a kind and good lady, wasn't she?" came a thought.

"Yes. And I loved her."

He sat the rest of the day alone, continuing to watch the fall scene, and his other self, but he felt strangely at peace. His mind feeling blissfully calm, without even a ripple. She stayed with him, and he even felt her presence after the nurse rolled him into bed for the night and he had all but forgotten the image of the fall scene.

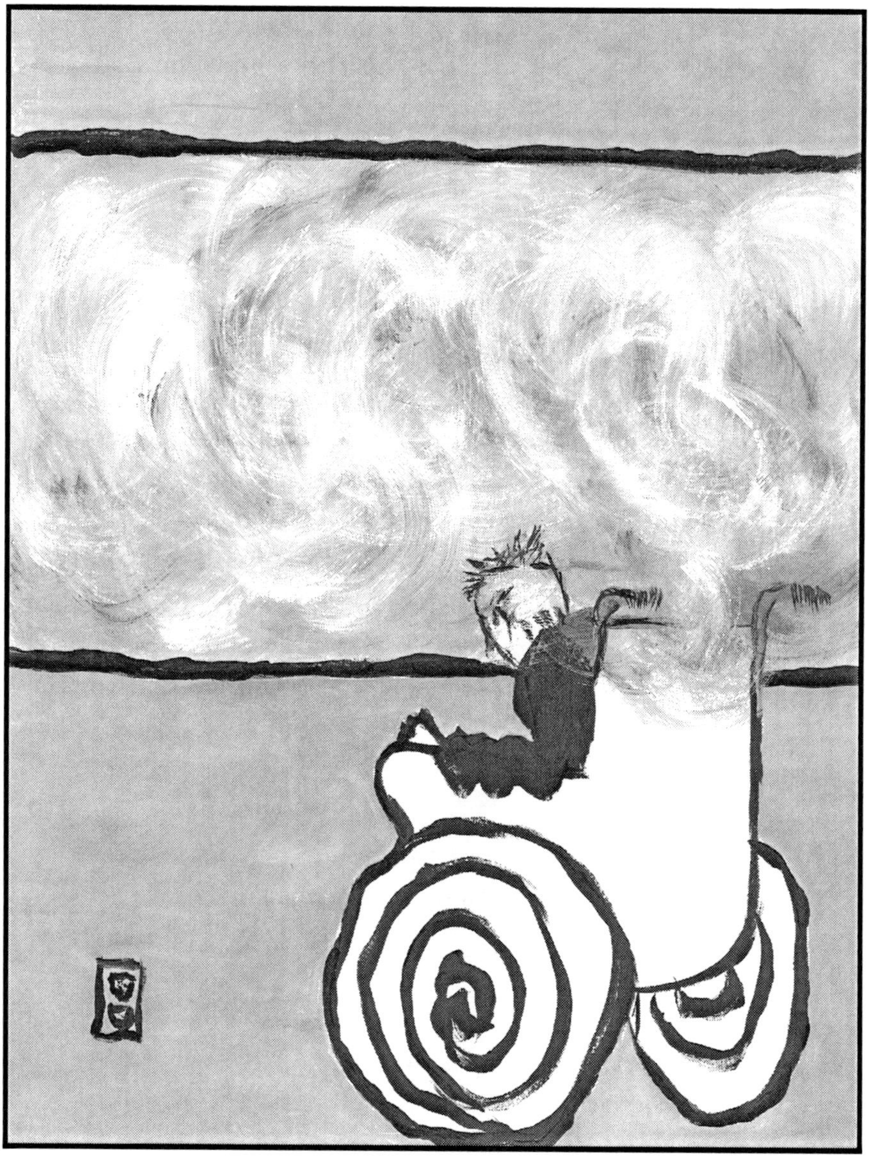

Morning came, and soon he found himself sitting and watching and waiting. Again, the younger version of himself watched back, from the edge of the stubble-filled field.

They watched each other quietly for the longest time. Frank felt a kind of fear of thinking, after the experience of the previous day. Although the vision that had occupied his mind had left him with a feeling of warmth and peacefulness, the realness of it had forced a type of anxiety to invade his mind, and cause him some uneasiness.

After a while, the other sensed the apprehension in him.

"You are afraid?" asked a thought.

"Yes."

"There is no reason. We will only go where you have already been. What can be so frightening about that?" The thoughts gently cascaded over his mind, as if trying to calm him, to restore the feeling of peace.

"I am afraid because of the emotion they cause in me," he thought in return. "I am afraid that once they come, they will be ripped from me, like the one yesterday, and I cannot bear that." The thoughts flowed from him, seeming to ease the uneasiness that had intruded, as if it had been bottled in his mind.

"You need not fear," his self thought. "What you have had, you will always have; and where you have been, you will continue to be," came a thought that felt soothingly warm, and caressed at the corners of his mind.

"But how do I know where we will go?" he asked in silence.

"You will go where you want to go," a thought replied.

"And where will that be?"

"Is it important?"

Pause.

"I'm ready," he finally thought.

He settled in and looked upon the fall scene and the figure who stood within. It gazed back at him reflectively, but he could not see into in it; and he knew that it could see into him; and he could feel it probing and examining him, but he did not know what for.

Then, after a time, the scene again started to revolve, slowly at first, like it had before. He braced his mind, as the revolutions quickened and he started to feel the disorienting, disquieting sensation of dizziness taking hold of him.

Suddenly, his mind cleared, and he found himself standing in the waiting room of a hospital; the hospital where his daughter had been born.

"Mr. Claxton," someone said, causing him to start, and the scene to snap into focus.

He looked and found himself confronted by a nurse.

"Yes," he mumbled.

"Mr. Claxton," the nurse repeated. "Your wife has had a baby girl. Both she and the baby are doing fine. Come this way, and you can see your wife."

He followed the nurse, as she padded her way down the corridor in those foam-bottomed uniform shoes nurses wear. Then, she arrived at the door to a room, where she stopped.

"Your wife's in here," she said, opening the door for him.

He walked into the room and looked to where she lay in the bed, and he thought how radiant she looked in the afterglow of childbirth; but, oh, so very tired, as well.

He walked across the room to the bed, and bent over and kissed her. She smiled up at him, but, strangely, neither of them spoke. Instead, he stood beside the bed, holding her hand with one hand and caressing it with the other. He glanced down at her, and caught her eye, and in that brief moment, as they stood in that grey monotone hospital room, with the smell of antiseptic heavy in the air, they caught sight of each other's souls. This must be love, he thought. Today, I am truly in love.

At that moment, a nurse broke through the door and shattered the mystical connection that had grown between them. His wife looked away, with what seemed a touch of embarrassment, he thought, and he turned toward the nurse, for a first glimpse of the creation of their love.

Then, it was over. He was back and again a tear trickled down a well-worn face.

She came to visit him that afternoon; his daughter, that is. She hadn't been to see him for some time, but, for some reason, she appeared that afternoon. He appreciated the gesture whenever she came, but it was all rather meaningless, since he had lost the power of communication. They sat silently, as if trying to read each other's thoughts, but on this day, like all the others, it was to no avail.

They had been close once. But that had been when it had been possible to be close; and to love, and to hate and to suffer all the other emotions of humanity. But he no longer felt capable of life, and had been convinced that he was in some type of state of living death, until the experiences of the last couple of days. Now, as he sat staring with an apparent emotional blankness, he thought he felt. He thought he felt something stirring in him. And even though she could never know, he thought he might again feel close to her.

She bent over and kissed him gently on the cheek as she rose to go.

"I love you, Daddy," she said softly in his ear, even though there was no way she could be sure he could hear, or even understand.

There were times when she had spoken those words over the last while, when he had not been sure he had understood. But, this time, he did. After she had passed out of his line of vision, he felt a sadness, a feeling he thought had been lost forever.

That night, as he slept, he dreamed. He dreamed he was sitting alone in a park. He was crying. Tears rolled down his cheeks. Even though it was a dream, he felt its realness. He felt a great sadness swell over him, even as he slept.

In the morning, as he waited for the nurse to come and get him ready for another day, he seemed to feel a sense of urgency. He anxiously waited for her to take him to the washroom, and feed him, and wash and dress him. Then, wheel him in front of the window, where the fall scene awaited.

It was as he had known it would be. His self gazed back. They watched one another but respected the privacy of each other's thoughts. He wondered what awaited him today. What would it be? Where would he go? Or what would he be forced to seek out in the distant recesses of his mind, where he had seldom gone recently?

This time, however, as he watched and waited, he was not fearful. He felt a calmness in his mind, and the sadness of the previous night had evaporated with the morning dew, although he could recall the realness of it even now.

"You slept well?" a thought finally asked.

"I had a dream," he thought in return.

"Was it a pleasant dream?" asked a second thought.

"Yes," he answered. "I found it so."

"What did you dream about?" asked a thought.

"I dreamed I was crying," he answered.

"And that pleased you?" came a thought.

"Yes," he thought in return.

"Why?"

"Because it made me feel alive again," he answered. "Even to dream of crying makes me feel alive after this."

"You do not seem to be afraid to see me today," came a thought.

"No," he answered. "I'm prepared for whatever may come. I'm ready."

He sat and watched the figure in the field. And the figure watched back. And that was all that seemed to happen for some time, and their thoughts stayed silent.

Considering that he had been impatient to revisit the scene, he felt no anxiousness as he waited.

Then, as he had known it would, the scene started to move in his consciousness and to revolve on an imaginary axis. Gradually, it moved faster and faster until it started to again cause a dizziness of his mind.

Just when he thought it would cause him to break the contact and return to his wheelchair beside the window, it started to slow, and another scene started to come into focus; to make itself felt on his consciousness. It wasn't like the two previous experiences, because it didn't snap sharply into focus, but rather appeared slightly fuzzy around the edges, and difficult to become involved in.

Gradually, though, he realized that he was standing beside a young woman; his daughter, and she was attired in her wedding dress. She was reaching over and trying to adjust his cummerbund. He felt her delicate hands fussing with it, trying to fasten it behind.

"Really, Daddy, you're such a bother," she said. Then, she looked up and into his eyes. "But I love you all the same," were the words that came from her lips, and at the same time, her eyes came alight the way they always did when she was overflowing with happiness and joy. He found himself thinking back to her visit and how he had almost forgotten the special bond that had existed between them.

A door opened somewhere out of his range of vision, and a voice intruded into the scene.

"It's time you two," said the voice.

"Come on, Daddy," she said, smiling warmly at him and taking him by the hand.

He found it beyond his capacity to speak to her. He silently followed after her, feeling as if he was drifting dreamily along, without his feet making contact with the floor. As a matter of fact, he was suddenly aware that the scene had remained unclear in his consciousness, as though he were encased in a translucent bubble that was drifting in a fog.

Still, he felt his daughter take his arm, and he took her hand. He felt emotion well up in him, as he walked with her to her wedding. He felt a profound sense of loss within him, as he now fought to continue moving forward. Whereas before, he had drifted effortlessly forward, something now seemed to be holding him back, not letting him move forward with her. He felt her starting to move away from him. He felt he was starting to fall backward, and away from her. He felt her hand slide through his; felt her fingertips lose contact with his. Just as she was about to disappear into the fog, and out of his view, she looked back.

"I love you, Daddy," she said, smiling and waving gently back.

He felt as if he was lying prone on the ground, and tried to reach out for her. But it made no difference, the harder he tried to reach out to her, and the more he struggled to move after her, the more securely he seemed to be held.

"Goodbye, my little princess," he thought, as he watched her outline disappear from view.

Then, it was over and he was back. And, again, he felt the tears on his cheek.

He sat in the chair and watched the stubble-filled field, as a few weather-dried leaves blew across, and the solitary figure within stood quietly, and watched back.

As he sat, he reflected inwardly on the scene that had just filled his mind. He saw the image of his daughter in her wedding dress, and remembered the special look of happiness and joy she had given him as they had waited alone for the beginning of the ceremony.

And again he thought back to her recent visit and he mourned what had been, and that it could be no more. That they could no longer share those special times, like they once had. They had been close once, he thought.

That night, as he slept, he found himself dreaming again. This time, he was sitting in his office at work, but it was curiously quiet. The office was empty. He was alone. There was silence.

In the dream, he sat at his desk. He felt the silence overwhelming him. He found it stifling. He found himself straining to see if he could hear anything, but there was nothing, except complete and thorough silence for as far as he could hear.

Then, he felt the sadness starting to come over him. He felt it first in the pit of his stomach and it gradually started to make its way up to his mind. Again, he cried. And, again, there was a realness to the dream.

When he awoke, he again felt anxious to be placed in front of the window, where he could imagine the fall scene. He felt impatience during the morning ritual, which seemed to proceed even slower than usual. He regarded the nurse with a feeling of disdain as she spooned the textureless mush into him during breakfast. I haven't time for this, he thought. I must find out what awaits.

Finally, he found himself back in front of the window. He found the calmness coming again to take his mind, and he felt his consciousness wander to where it was always fall, where the crops had been harvested, and to where a solitary figure stood in a stubble-filled field and waited for him.

"Welcome," a thought said. "Have you slept well?"

"Yes, but I've dreamed again," he thought.

"Does that bother you?" came a thought.

"I'm not sure it bothers me, but I find it strange because I've not dreamed in such a long time; not since the last stroke," he answered.

There was a brief pause.

"Actually, I find it nice to be able to dream again," he finally thought. "I just wish I wouldn't be so alone, even in my dreams. That's what I think bothers me."

"You feel alone?" a thought asked.

"Yes," he answered. "I feel very alone, and I think that's what bothers me. Until you came, I thought I was completely alone, and I could not bear it. I had stopped being and only was. Now, I feel like I'm starting to be again, even if it is only in my mind," he thought.

There was another pause.

"Good," came a thought. "Good."

They sat and watched one another, but were quiet for a while.

Then, a thought again intruded into his mind.

"Are you ready?" it asked.

"Yes," he answered. "I would like to go."

And he waited. And, gradually, the scene started to make those slow, circular motions he had come to expect. It turned, always gaining speed, and again starting to make him feel the slightest bit of dizziness. Then, as his mind again started to feel an uncomfortableness caused by the spinning motion, it started to slow, and he found himself starting to adjust to a new mental picture, as he arrived where he was going.

He found himself in his bed, in his bedroom, in the house where he had raised his family. He was lying beside his wife, and he could feel her breathing gently as she had as she slept beside him through nearly fifty years of marriage. He could not see her clearly as he looked over, but he reached out and took her hand and held it firmly in his.

He felt a type of inner strength and serenity to his mind as he held her hand; almost as if he could feel her strength flowing into him, and somehow adding to the wholeness of his person. But hadn't that really been how it had been, anyway, he thought? She had always been there; always by his side, and always encouraging, and always urging him to strive to do his best. And she had made him become what he had been. And he had been a good person and an upstanding member of his community.

Then, as he lay, holding her hand, he sensed a difference. He listened for her breathing, but it had stopped. He found his hand suddenly holding the nothingness of the vision, and when he reached for her, he found there was nothing to take hold of. She was gone. And he was alone. And there was nothing but the sadness for him to be with.

The scene returned, and with it, the figure. He sat, and it stood, and they regarded one another, but were quiet. He felt extremely at ease, and he wandered through the thoughtscapes of his mind, recalling this, and remembering that. While he had been remorseful at the conclusion of the last thought trip, he now felt a certain peacefulness and pleasure as his mind crowded with images from throughout his life, overflowing into one another and spilling over into his reality, and the vision of the field.

"You are back," a thought commented.

"Yes," he thought, as he sent the thoughts and images of his past scurrying hither and yon into the corners of his mind, from whence they'd come.

"You seem changed," came another thought. "You seem different."

"Yes," he answered. "I am alive," he added matter of factly.

"How do you know?" came a question.

"I feel again. I know what it is to feel again," he thought.

"And you didn't always?" came another question, passing through his mind.

"No, I thought I had lost the ability to feel anything forever," he answered.

"Your spirit lives," another thought commented. "Your spirit lives," it repeated.

"Yes," he found himself thinking. "I guess you could say that my spirit is alive again. It has been dead, but now it is alive again."

"Good," came a thought. "Good."

There was a pause. They continued to regard each other, and the figure seemed to be smiling, he thought. If I could force the muscles of my face, I'd be smiling too, he thought. I feel as if I've learned to walk again, or just received the ability to see, after having been blind since birth. He felt exhilarated. His mind reached toward the sky and he rejoiced in the ability to feel again, even if it remained beyond his capacity to communicate that feeling.

Gradually, he returned to earth, and saw his self was now crouching on one knee beside the field. In the scene, the wind seemed to have picked up and the weather-dried leaves were swirling here and there.

"Winter's in the air," a thought came.

"Yes, I can feel it as well," he thought in return.

"Come with me," the figure beckoned.

"Where shall we go?" he thought back.

"To a place where it's always spring, and where you can be whenever you want to be," the figure answered.

"I'd like that," he found himself thinking. "Yes," he reflected, "I think I'd like that."

"Come, then," the figure said, holding out a hand toward him.

"How? he asked. "I cannot leave this chair. Surely, you know."

"But you can leave the body," the figure said.

"The body?" he asked.

"Yes," his self said. "Leave the body. Come with me."

And he felt the scene again starting to revolve, as his mind started to turn on its axis.

"You have done it before, my friend," came a thought. "This time, just let go. Just let go," the words repeated in his mind.

The scene was starting to spin faster and faster in his mind. Again, he felt the dizziness starting to overtake him and he wondered if he would be able to continue, or if he might have to return to his limited reality.

"Let go," a thought came. "Let go," it repeated. "Let go."

He felt his consciousness spinning faster and faster, and faster and faster, and he thought he could no longer stand it, but he let it continue, and, finally, he felt a sensation of rising; he felt like his mind was still spinning, but that it was now spiralling upward.

"Good," came a now familiar thought. "Good. Let go."

Suddenly, he found himself standing in the fall scene. He looked for the other, but he was not there. He looked back toward the home and saw his body, sitting and staring emptily out into the field.

A few flakes of snow were starting to fall. There was winter in the air.

Poetry

Memories for Sale

Some poetry and other thoughts on life...

The Hippies Knew

I can't help it if we were morons and didn't listen to the hippies –
The hippies knew all the bad stuff was coming.
Pollution – over population – war – pestilence – carnage….
The hippies knew all about that stuff.
They tried to get the rest of us to listen….
Then they went about their lives
Because that was all there was to do
Back in that other time
When I was young
And the world seemed somehow fresher and more alive
They were times of hope
When we thought we were gods
And nothing could defeat us…..

Life is a hard place for old hippies….
There's not much peace and love in this age.
The Age of Aquarius has come and gone….
And we are the poorer for it
I sometimes watch the evening news,
Or the one before bed that unsettles me
And I watch people get killed and I hear about others still….
And I wonder what it's like to get snuffed out on the evening news
When nobody really cares….
Because that's the world we live in

Where no one is safe
And there is no way to really save anyone
Even yourself….

I'm going to tell you something that's far out….
We are slaves to the Establishment.
We do its bidding.
We oppress others.
We murder and kill.
We rape and steal.
We brutalize our brothers and our sisters – and even our children.
Who all started out together those many years ago
In a rift valley in Africa….
Where we somehow became separate from the rest of the beasts….
And walked out into the world
As the greatest known miracle in all of time…
But we are fucking it up –
Really good…..

When we were young and thought we were hippies, we knew the truth…
We knew the Establishment was coming for us
But not that it would take our children –
And our children's children – and into the forevermore….
Because that is what has happened while we were being morons….
Back in that other time
Of peace and love and harmony and real passion.
These days, the times are dangerous
The world is a different place –
It isn't really safe for any of us…..
Things might have been different if we'd listened to the hippies
And somehow kept our souls…..

Listening to Janis Laugh

I'm watching the American Music Awards on TV
And thinking about Don McLean.
I'm wondering about the day the music died…
And realizing that it's been a long last gasp.

I can almost hear Janis laugh
And wonder what Sid Vicious would have thought
To know that it really is all about the glitz
And the music is sort of an afterthought.

The more I watch, the clearer it becomes
That art does imitate life.…
Because life is mostly about the glitz these days,
And there is precious little substance to any of it.

It's gotten to the point where the surreal is the real
And the real can't be trusted
And nothing is at it seems
There is nothing but untruth.

I hear that when a musician does a live album these days
They go back over the recording and fix the mistakes
And that some of the greatest singers in the world
Are prone to use pitch correction machines.…

Sayin' bye bye, Miss American Pie
Drove my chevy to the levee but the levee was dry.
And I am love with the ghost of Janis Joplin
And worship at the tomb of Sid Vicious
They were the ones who tried to save us
But we didn't listen to what they were saying
And we have paid the price
And seen the end of greatness…

The Mystery of Makeup

I don't understand why modern women wear make-up –
And I don't get the jewellery thing either.
I don't understand why any modern woman
Would want to sexualize herself
Unless it is to celebrate
The sheer beauty of the human form.

Back in the mythical Sixties –
That decade of peace, harmony and violence
The hippie chicks cast off the trappings of sexuality.
They burned their bras and braided the hair in their underarms
And said, "Take me as I am,
And not who you would like me to be!"

But, today, the modern woman craves adornment
As once did the Egyptian slave girl.
She washes herself in scented bath oils
She wears a pushup bra and edible panties
Joni Mitchell says that sex sells everything…
And I'm sure she's right.

It is a primitive way of doing business,
But perhaps all we're capable of.
We think we are enormously smart
Because we have huge brains

And the ability to use KY jelly.
But all is not as it seems.

In fact, almost nothing is as it seems.
Most of the world is one big pornographic illusion.
It's all done with smoke and mirrors.
Isn't that what they say?
And I believe them.
Whoever they are.

No, I thought by now we'd be a little more civilized
Than we seem to have become.
My friend Sam would have called it the devolution of the species.
I prefer the age of great superficiality
And meaningless fluff.
But what do I know?

I don't know nothin' 'bout nothin' –
That's what I think.
Because if I knew anything at all
It would be that there's a way to make this work;
That everything could be okay
And we could live happily ever after.

That's what used to happen in Disney movies.
But now they're full of sex too.
And that's a strange reality going forward;
And the fact we are where we are
Makes me wonder if there's any hope at all
Or if I'm just wasting my time.

On Watching ER......

I'm watching an episode of ER on the TV –
One of the doctors is volunteering in the Congo.
Incredibly bad things are happening all around him….
Things so incredibly evil that I can't even speak of them..
Even to utter them causes me hurt and pain –
I switch off the TV – I cannot watch.

How can the world be this evil?
I do not want to even know that this much evil exists;
Because I cannot do anything about it….
No matter how hard I wish it, it will not go away.
We are the most savage creature on the planet….
No other species could even carry our shame.

I take a lot of heat for my perspective on life…
Because I see incredible bleakness…
I see the children living in fear…
I see the hungry; and the sick; and the dying –
And I don't have much fun
Because I don't think that would be fair.

Only the poor and downtrodden struggle for justice;
The rich and privileged already have it.
This is their world – it's their party.
We're just here to hold them up – to keep them in their place…
It's the way it's always been – it's the so-called way of the world.
But we could change it – that's what we've gotta hope for.

Waiting........

I'm waiting for the second coming....
I'm hoping it will happen soon.
I want to see Jesus in action;
I want to see him kick some serious ass.

There seems to be little hope we'll sort this mess out ourselves.
But perhaps that's not our fault....
We're a little slow as a species;
Not really all that bright.

No, it's going to take an all-out apocalypse to set us straight;
Some real fire and brimstone, thunderbolts and lightening.
And even that might not get some people's attention,
Because they're so caught up in the useless crap.

I'd like to have a chat with Jesus before he casts me into the pit.
"How could you let this happen?" I'd ask him.
And I'd tell him he's one mean son-of-a-bitch –
But I'd mean it as a compliment.

Because he probably thought we'd figure it out on our own.
Use some of the wisdom that he left us when he was here before.
Little did he know the true nature of our character....
And how we would twist and pervert his word.

So if the Presbyterians and the Catholics are right
And he is going to come again,
I'd like to be here to see it;
I'd like to see some major-league, serious, holy ass-kickin'.
When death goes unnoticed... ....

Remembering Leo.....

A good friend of mine died recently
And I didn't find out about it until yesterday.
I don't know when and I don't know how he died –
And that bothers me.

He was a gentle giant of a guy....
Kind of like a big teddy bear.
But a few years back
He went crazy and sort of lost touch with reality.

He seemed okay most of the time –
But sometimes when you were talking to him
He'd laugh this strange little laugh
And you could just tell that the elevator didn't go all the way to the top anymore.

He had no real friends and no family.
People felt uncomfortable around him.
Which was probably okay
Because he felt the same way around them.

So I think he might have died alone
And that makes me sad
That no one was there to cry for him –
No one to hold his hand as his soul departed.

I wish I could have been there
To say good-bye
To hold him close
To show him that someone cared.

He went by the name of Leo Isobel...
A man gone mad in a world already crazy.
And I will remember him always
As someone who mattered

On being the one.....

I got the right answer on Final Jeopardy tonight.
I think it impressed my wife.
They were looking for the name of a work of political philosophy
And that's something I know a little about.

The answer on Jeopardy was the Social Contract
Which was a book written by Jean Jaques Rousseau
Who was an 18th Century liberal philosopher
Who believed we have a type of deal with society.

According to the deal,
If society carries out our wishes, we agree to support it
If it doesn't do what we want, we don't support it.
In fact, we have an obligation and responsibility to withdraw our support.

Most ordinary people seem to know that our economic system is unsustainable.
It's a no brainer.
The economy can't grow into infinity…
Its edges are already in sight.

But our world leaders relentlessly ignore this simple truth
They quibble over oil and gold
When all of life is at stake
And time is running out.

Surely, the social contract has been broken.
The governments of the world have not protected either us or the planet
When that was their only job.
They've caused all life to be violated.

But we do nothing
We watch our celebrities
Ever mindful that we may yet get our esteemed fifteen minutes of fame
If only the world can hang together a little longer.

And you could be the biggest loser;
Or the american idol;
Or the bachelorette;
Or the world's top model.

Because that's sort of what keeps the whole thing going –
Some faint hope of success.
A chance to be the one
That everyone else worships.

Ode to the King of Hearts

Back in Grade 9 when I was a pup
I was shy and nervous and always threw up
Girls were something I tried to ignore
I'd not go on dates – that's what I swore

It wasn't that I didn't want to see
Why guys my age went out of their tree
Just to get close to someone named Teri
Or to sit on the bus by another named Mary.

Then along came Valentine's and there was this dance
At first I didn't give it a glance
But it turned out all my friends wanted to go
I'd have been happier seeing a show.

But they bugged me and bugged me to finally relent
My mother my suit to the dry cleaners sent
Her and Dad seemed as pleased as punch
I was sure I'd lose my lunch.

And as the big day began to draw near
My knees felt weak – I was filled with fear
And one of my friends pulled me aside
He'd teach me to dance – it was time I tried.

So there we were – two pimply young teens
Learning to twist with girls in our dreams
But I knew in the very depth of my soul
That survival that night was my only goal.

The day of the dance finally arrived
No decent excuse could be contrived
So I headed off up the street
Afraid to see what I would meet.

During the evening, I tried to hide
I kept 'round to the back and off to the side
I thought it was safe; I thought things were fine.
Then over to me comes a friend of mine.

He wanted to dance with this certain girl
He was bound and determined to give it a whirl
The problem was she'd come with a friend
It was about this time I sensed my end

You just might like it – that's what he said
I wished at that moment that I was dead
I wished there was some way I could say
"Beam me up, Scotty, help make my day."

But I followed him over – one final walk
Not even knowing if I could talk
He asked his true love – he seemed so darned bold
When she accepted you'd think he'd struck gold.

I blurted out something and the next thing I knew
I was out on the dance floor with nary a clue
I stumbled and fumbled my way around
Trying not to look too much the clown

Finally 'twas over and we made our way back
We said our thank-yous; very matter of fact
I headed back into a shadowy place
I'd danced with a girl – what a disgrace!

And at that exact moment up by the band
The dance's convenor was up on a stand
Announcing for one and all to hear
The King and Queen of Hearts were near.

Seems at this party there was a chance
For the girls to be crowned queen of the dance
All of their names were put in a hat
And that's the way they decided that.

And when I heard them call the name
I knew that she was not to blame
Soon she was up getting her crown
And I felt my heart sink down, down, down

And soon there I was – I was the guy
The King of Hearts – don't ask me why
Roses are red and violets are blue
I had my crown and my sceptre too

So there is my story of sorrow and woe
'Bout the time to the Valentine's Dance I did go
I guess I survived and came through the night
But at the time it gave me a terrible fright

I thought I'd be scarred and damaged for life
But now I'm grown up and I've got a wife
I've learned there are few things better than love
At making you soar through the clouds and above

There is no real moral to this tragic tale
Just a story 'bout me travelling life's trail
But strange things happen by luck or by chance
Like being KIng of Hearts at the Valentine's Dance

Wishing for Company

I saw a UFO the other day
And I'm glad my wife saw it too.
Otherwise, I'd be pretty skeptical…
And afraid to admit it.
But I know what I saw
And it's sort of changed my life.

After my wife and I witnessed the unusual vision
She didn't want to talk about it….
But I couldn't stop smiling.
It made me really happy….
To think there's even a remote possibility
That we might not be alone.

I don't want us to be alone;
Because we're so terribly bad at this life stuff.
We're really messing it up quite badly…
And if we're it….
The whole future of intelligent life is at risk….
And that's a sobering thought.

Because that would mean there would be no one to remember us…
When the finish does come…
And we find ourselves at the end of time.
Wouldn't you somehow feel better,
If you knew there were others watching down on us
To at least chronicle our failed attempt.

And if my vision was indeed otherworldy….
Then it would mean that others had reached the stars.
And although we may have failed at life…
Some others may have succeeded.
And perhaps they will remember there was some good to us…
Along with the bad.

I only wish I could have called out to them –
To tell them to take me with them –
To carry me far from this veil or tears…
Where there is so much suffering and pain.
Indeed, I feel like one of them….
An alien among the humans

Silly People

Silly people scurry here; live their lives in utter fear
They play the lotto, drink some beer – for most of them the end is near
How do you tell them to cut and run
When all of them think they'll be the one.

There ain't no easy way out of here – that's what the Joker said.
But there was no way for him to know that the King was already dead.
The good ones die after they try – they ask the questions, they wonder why.
But through it all – oh my, oh my – no one hears the people cry.

Help me find a place to go – a place where I can learn and grow;
A place where there is utter peace; a place where I will know
That there is love and caring and never compromise
And most of us folks have all we need – and rich folks don't tell lies.

Come what might, come what may – what do you say at the end of the day
You work so hard, you toil and sweat, struggle for all the life you get.
Must be some reason we live life like we do
Find meaning to life and make it come true.

On Mattering

So much suffering – So much pain –
I know it's a tired and worn-out refrain.
But what do you do when you're scared to death….
Afraid even to take one more breath.
When you think that no matter which way you turn
There's a very good chance that you're gonna burn.

Trying to wade through a pile of shit…
Trying not to be squeezed like a king-sized zit.
There don't seem no way to make life fair
Seems more like a case of buyer beware
There don't seem no way to get yourself out
I've killed myself already without any doubt.

But it don't much matter – not in the least.
None of us nothing – no more than the beast.
We think we're so special; so very smart
That we've been blessed among creatures right from the start.
Seems more like illusion; not really real.
It's funny how we value the gold that we steal.

All that we take and all that we hold
The stuff that we buy and the stuff that is sold
None of it matters – not one small bit
None of it matters – not even a wit.

Soon Tomorrow...

I watch another show about the environment on the TV –
It kinda seems like we're screwed.
But it's sort of hard to tell….
Because we're a slippery bunch.

"You gotta watch those damed humans –
They're a slippery bunch."
That's what they're sayin' about us….
Whoever "they" are.

Since slithering from the primordial ooze
We have survived many tight spots….
But there are more of us all the time….
And things are starting to get serious.

At some point in all this environmental crap
We're going to walk right off the edge;
And we'll fall forever
Into the abyss of tomorrow.

I was telling people this back in the Sixties,
And I'm still telling them today…
But the edge is much closer…..
And tomorrow is almost here….

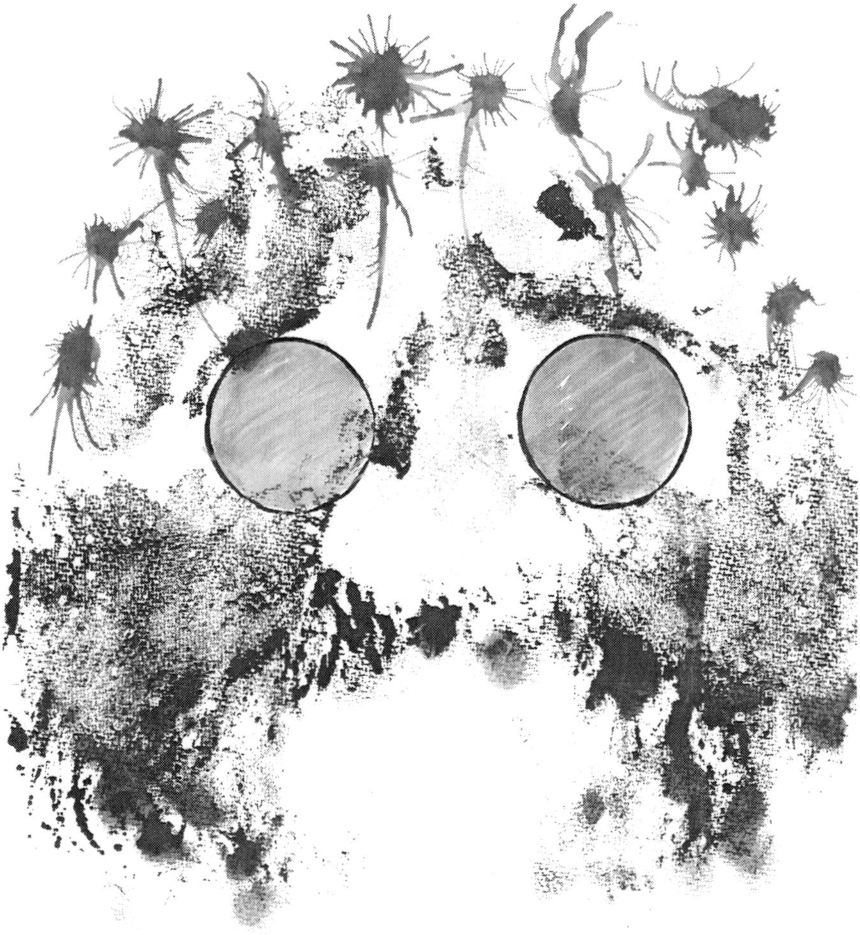

The Gawd Book

In the Beginning

His name was Gawd, the name given to him by a drunken, miserable, abusive man who claimed to be the father of the unwanted child. But he thrived despite his wretched birth, and watched as a succession of fathers came to bed with his mother, who had once been young and beautiful, but was now old and hard and who fell into tearful depression whenever she had a couple of drinks -- and that was often.

She was a weak woman, and Gawd watched as she bowed low to each of her lovers. But she truly loved only the boy, even though he was nothing more than a pill missed through drunken unconsciousness, and tried to nurture him as best she could, and to protect him from the beatings that seemed to come his way regardless who might be the father. And he loved her for it, and tried to help her in her difficulties, so that the mother and son grew close together.

And Gawd wanted nothing more than to take her out of her life of misery and into something better, perhaps like in the books he read whenever time permitted. Because that was where he found his escape -- at the town library, among the book stacks. He read about anything and everything, and found interest in all manner of things. But his favourites were the stories about the people who made good for themselves in life and who had good families, even after they'd had a rough start, like the one he was part of. Because he wasn't too awfully old before he realized where he stood in life. Kids taunted him about the starkness of his home life and by the time he was ten he'd heard the word "whore" more than once in reference to his mother.

But he loved her still and sometimes, between men and bouts of drunkeness, they shared some time together. His favourite time was when they sat together on the corner of the couch, under the big blanket, huddsying they called it, even having invented a word to describe the closeness of the experience. After he got old enough, he'd read to her about the people who had conquered evil circumstances and risen above intolerable surroundings and who had good families.

"I shouldn't oughta brought you into the world, Gawd," she would tell him. "'Cause I have trouble enough lookin' out for myself. But you gotta do good at school, and work hard, and you'll do better than me. You won't hafta live this way. I wish I could get you out of here. But I do the best I can. I hope you understand that, Gawd." And she'd brush his usually too-long hair back out of his eyes and give him a big, warm hug.

It wasn't the usual mother-son sort of stuff, but he liked it just the same. It was all he had so he clung to it tenaciously, and he pleaded with her in his boyish, childish sort of way to foresake her drinking and to throw out the latest bum, at least giving them a chance to find their way in life.

"It's too late for me, Gawd," she'd say. "I got my place in life."

And so he went about his life, and it wasn't long before another low life came to occupy his mother's bed. But then came Tom. When he was about thirteen, just getting ready to set out for high school and that big slice of life. Tom came in the night like most of the other ones, but he didn't come swaggering out of the bedroom in his underwear scratching himself where it wasn't polite in the morning. Instead, Gawd awoke to the fine waking-up aroma of bacon sizzling on a grill. He came out of his bedroom wide-eyed to the sight of the man in the cook's apron and oven mitts loading another batch of pancakes into the oven.

"Mornin' sport," the man said cheerfully.

"Mornin'," Gawd answered, taking up a seat at one end of the kitchen table.

"I'm Tom," the man said, "and I thought I'd fix us some breakfast. Are you hungry?"

"Sure," Gawd answered.

"I'll keep your mother's warm in the oven," Tom said. "I don't expect she'll be up for a while. She had kind of a rough night."

Gawd's guard went up at these last words.

"I'm here, Tom," came a woman's voice from the bedroom. They could hear her getting out of bed. She came to the doorway of the kitchen. Her face was bruised, an ugly gash over her one eye.

Gawd hurried to his mother's side when he saw her, and he turned and shot an angry look at the man in the apron. "Bastard," he hissed.

"No, Gawd," the mother said. "It was Tom that brought me home after another guy beat me up and left me laying in the gutter bleedin'. It was late. I offered him to sleep on the couch."

Gawd continued to watch the man suspiciously, but some of the anger left his look.

"You should sleep," Tom said to the woman.

"I'm hungry," she said.

"Then, let's eat," he said, with a big, wide grin.

And they did.

It turned out that Tom became a sort of a regular guest at their place. He told them he wanted to be honest with them. He'd been a drinker. Lost his family. Lost his life. Lost his way. But that he'd been sober six months and had just started a re-training program over at the high school -- something that could maybe lead to a job. It had been a long time since he'd had a job.

And he was like a gentleman toward Gawd's Mom, he never stayed over but always went back to his own place for the night, unless he slept on the couch, and he treated the boy well, played some catch with him and took him fishing a couple of times.

One time, as they were sitting on the bank of the river just outside of town, and it was very early in the morning, Gawd looked over and saw Tom regarding him. Gawd thought he saw a tear in the man's eye; something he'd not seen before, from this man or any other.

"You alright?" the boy asked.

The man didn't answer right away. Instead, he gazed somewhat wistfully out over the river's post dawn mist. Gawd stayed quiet.

"You know, Gawd," he finally said, "I got a boy about your age. At least I think he is. I sorta lost track of him over the last few years. He might be a year or two older than you."

Gawd stayed quiet.

"I last saw him when he was about four," Tom continued. "I know it's best that I don't see him. I heard my ex, his mother, is remarried to a real successful guy, assistant manager at a Crappy Tire -- and that's a good job." He paused. "I never amounted to much," he said, and he seemed quite thoughtful about it.

"You couldda though, Tom," the boy offered.

"Na," Tom said. "I can't take the responsibility. The drinking takes over. I'm best on my own." He paused again, and again seemed thoughtful. "But I still think about my boy sometimes, and I hope he's doing okay."

"You should see him sometime," Gawd said.

"Na," Tom answered. "It's best this way. I'm a loser."

Gawd said nothing, but he felt compelled to go to Tom and wrap his arm around him, and it was the first time he could ever remember holding a man so close.

"Aw, Gawd," Tom said softly. "You're a good kid." And he returned the embrace and the two sat for a silent moment on the riverbank within the dissipating mist.

It was the first real family time of Gawd's young life, and he cheerfully absorbed it. He and his Mom and Tom went places together, like a for-real family. One time, they even went on a picnic to a park with strange and rare animals in it, like the kind that Gawd had only seen in books before. And Tom bought one of those instant cameras and took pictures of Gawd and his mother with the strange and rare animals. It was a very special time.

And what made it even more special was that Gawd's mother went on the wagon with Tom, and it was the first time the youngster had seen her stay sober for so long. She even talked of getting into some sort of re-training course herself, and getting a job. It was a very special time.

And Tom joined them when Gawd read his books, and the boy took delight in the fact that his family, of which Tom must now surely be a part, seemed to be just like the ones in the books that Gawd liked so much. It seemed there was a chance that they would rise above what they had become in life, and Gawd revelled in it. He felt he was living a dream.

But he still saw a sadness in Tom from time to time, and he imagined that he had again reminded the man of his own son, as he had on that earlier occasion on the riverbank. He usually said nothing, but sat quietly and regarded his friend, wondering if there was anything he could do or say. Until one day, when they were again out fishing, and Gawd was again busy living his dream.

As Gawd applied a worm to his hook, he glanced up and caught sight of Tom sitting watching him and there seemed to be that sense of melancholy about him. And it seemed that the boy felt compelled to say something at last; that he could no longer watch the suffering and not react.

"You should go and see him," Gawd said.

Tom seemed startled. "What's that?" he asked.

"You should go and see your son," Gawd said.

"We shouldn't talk about it," Tom answered, looking away and fiddling with his fishing line.

There was a moment of silence over the river.

"Sorry," Gawd said.

"It's alright," Tom said.

"You're like my dad," Gawd said quietly.

The man looked over and smiled, but he looked quickly away, perhaps embarrassed. "That's good of you to say," he said, looking back after brushing his sleeve across his eyes.

Then, Gawd had a bite and that ended the exchange, but the boy thought he perceived a change in the man after that excursion to the riverbank. The two seemed even closer after that day, and it was like they truly were father and son, and Gawd's mother was the wife as well as the mother.

But the man continued to journey off to his own humble abode each night, or he slept on the couch, and Gawd wondered about that. At first, when Tom had started coming over, he had been glad about it, feeling his mother should share her bed with no man. But now that some months had passed, Gawd thought it strange that the man and woman still slept apart, because he well knew, even at his tender age, what it was that brought men and women together.

There came a day when Gawd's mother had to go to her sister's for overnight in the middle of the week, and Gawd couldn't go because he had school, so his mother asked Tom to stay over. Gawd was thrilled, because he always liked it when the man stayed over.

They went to McDonald's after seeing the mother off at the bus station. They ate like pigs over the sports pages, spilling stuff all over them and the table -- and made a mess of things the way only men can make a mess of things.

That night, they started to watch the mid-week hockey telecast on the tube and they ate some popcorn that Tom made on the top of the stove. It was again, as had become the custom lately, a family scene, with the man and boy sitting side by side on the couch, sharing a bowl of popcorn and a big bottle of root beer the way a father and son might do in a similar circumstance, with the mother gone away.

"You know, Gawd, my life has been pretty crazy over the last ten years or so," Tom said, after the second period had ended, giving way to intermission, "but this is really the best time I've had. I've really enjoyed this time I've spent with you and your mom."

"Yea, it's been pretty great," Gawd answered.

"And I can't believe I've done it without the booze. It's almost made me believe I might be able to put things back together," he said, before pausing. During that pause, he reached over and put his hand gently on Gawd's shoulder. "I'd like to try to put things back together," he said, and Gawd thought he could hear sincerity in the man's voice. "Would you like it if I tried to get together with your mom?" he asked.

"I sort of thought you already had," Gawd said.

"Not really," Tom said. "I know we've done lots of things together, and I seem to be over here all the time, but I've been careful with your mom. I was sort of back on my feet when I met her that night. But I thought she needed time to try to get herself back together a bit -- sort of on her own. I wanted to be around, because I like both of you, but I didn't want to push myself into your family, but I wanted her to be sure of herself -- and I wanted to make sure I could trust myself. Your mother's been through a lot, and so have you, and I didn't want to put you through anything more."

There was a pause. Gawd was unsure what to say. Surprised the man was confiding in him.

"Another thing. I've been thinking about what you were saying," Tom continued; "about seeing my boy. I'm thinking that maybe that wouldn't be a bad idea. Maybe I could do it. I didn't think I could a couple of months ago, but now I think I might be able to."

"Then you should," Gawd encouraged. "I bet he'd be glad to see you."

"My wife told me never to try to see him. She said she'd make my life miserable if I ever tried. She's probably poisoned the boy toward me, anyway." Tom looked dejected, depressed, tired.

"I'd like to see my dad," Gawd offered. "Mom says he's dead, but he's probably not. But if my dad turned out like you, even if he used to have troubles, I'd be really glad if he came to see me. It would make me know he cared about me. And that would mean something."

"Maybe it would," Tom answered somewhat thoughtfully. "Anyway, what would you think of me hooking up with your mom -- if she'd have me?"

"I think it'd be great," Gawd said, and Tom gave his shoulder an affectionate squeeze. There was closeness.

But at that moment, the third period resumed with a great scoring chance, and the conversation ended.

And that topic didn't come up again in the weeks that followed, but Tom started to proceed with his plan of hooking up with Gawd's mother. He didn't share her bed. Instead, he sort of asked her out on dates, for dinner or a movie. Gawd's mother was in her own form of heaven at having a man treat her with some apparent dignity and respect. And Gawd was pleased. He wondered about Tom and his son, but felt that was the man's concern to deal with and that he would speak first about it if there was anything to be said.

One night, though, Gawd's mom got all dressed up to go out with Tom, who was supposed to pick her up at eight. He was never late and prided himself on his punctuality, so by nine both the mother and Gawd were worried. By ten, there was concern. And by the time they went to bed about midnight, and he had still not appeared, both were extremely anxious and fearful.

Two days passed and there was no sign of him. The mother and son didn't speak of him, both perhaps fearing the worst, but afraid to talk of it.

Then, on the third day, he came. He was drunk. Bad drunk. Sad drunk. Mad drunk.

Even as Gawd stood outside the door to the house after school, he knew there was trouble.

"You should leave, Tom," he could hear his mother say. "The boy'll be home any minute. You don't want him to see you like this. Go home and get yourself straightened out. Sleep it off."

The man sat, slouched on the end of the couch, when Gawd came through the door. He'd not shaved or cleaned himself for some time. He looked a hell of a mess, the boy thought.

"I came to see him," Tom said drunkenly to the mother. Then, he pointed and leered in Gawd's direction. "I came to see you," he growled. "You, boy, the one with all the answers. The smart one."

"Leave him alone, Tom," the mother said defensively, walking over and putting herself between the boy and the man, who was now halfway up off the couch. "Go home and sleep it off."

Tom had now managed to pull himself into an upright position. "I saw my boy," he said, moving toward the mother and son. "Just like you told me," he said too loudly over the mother's shoulder to the boy who stood frightened behind. "You know what?" he asked, and there was anger in his voice.

The man had been standing, leaning forward, gesturing with his arms, almost menacingly, but now he shrank back and looked small and broken. "I found out where he went to school and went to see him play in a basketball game. I wasn't going to go near him, but after the game -- I just had to say something." The man stood, tears had started to trace their way down through the misery that was etched in his face. "I didn't even tell him I was his father -- just said I'd like to talk to him for a couple of minutes. He laughed at me. He told his friends I was bothering him and they all laughed at me. They made fun of me. Called me a bum, and told me to clear out of their neighbourhood or they'd rough me up. The boy's a loud-mouthed smart-ass."

As the man said the last line, anger returned to his voice, and he seemed to gather himself up. "Why'd I listen to you?" he asked loudly, almost as if the mother did not stand between the man and the boy. Again, he seemed menacing.

"Tom, it's not Gawd's fault," the mother said. "He didn't know what your son would be like. You probably just surprised the boy. He didn't know who you were."

"I want to talk to your son," the man said, this time directly to the mother, finger pointed threateningly. "And you'd better get the hell out of the way," he said, and there was deliberateness to his voice, even though his words were badly slurred from the drink.

"Get out of here, Mom," Gawd said, knowing there was to be trouble.

Then, the man lunged toward the boy. "No, Tom!" cried the mother, recoiling and wrapping her arms around the boy.

But it was no use. It was an awful and bloody scene before a neighbour tired of the noise and called the police.

When the two officers came through the door, there was only Gawd. The mother lay dead, her skull crushed in by a brass table lamp. The man lay dead, a butcher knife protruding from his throat. Gawd sat at the kitchen table -- reading. It was a very special time. Very special indeed.

And Gawd created the earth..........

A Fresh Start

It was spring when Gawd got out of the Spring Valley Youth Centre, and that was kind of fitting because it seemed like the whole world was starting fresh, and that was what Gawd needed -- to start fresh. Even though everyone had agreed that his heinous act had been justified and that he was young and had acted in the heat of passion, they had still decreed that he was a troubled youth, and he had spent the last two years at Spring Valley. It had been a most unpleasant time, filled with bullies and adolescent tyrants who had made him pay again and again for his crime. So that by the time he was finally released on that fine spring day, he knew he needed to start fresh.

His mother dead, no father, his grandfather came to claim him -- his grandfather, his mother's father, who he'd seen only once before in his life, and that had been at his mother's funeral two years ago, and they had exchanged no words.

The old man was waiting for him in the superintendent's office. There were some papers to sign, and as the old man signed, Gawd thought of it as sort of like being sold into slavery and he listened patiently as the superintendent explained that his grandfather now had custody of him and that he should listen to the old man and pay him heed -- or risk coming back here. It was only out of the goodness of his heart that the grandfather had agreed to take the boy -- that's what the superintendent said -- and he'd better show some appreciation. He was lucky to be getting another chance -- most boys who'd been in trouble weren't so lucky.

They got in the old man's shiny, new car and drove away from Spring Valley. It was fresh start time.

They drove in silence for a while.

"Your name's Gawd?" the old man finally asked, breaking the silence.

"Yes, sir," Gawd answered.

"Well, that'll never do," his grandfather said. "I respect the name of the Lord in my house. We'll have to find something else to call you."

"Yes, sir," Gawd answered quietly.

"Have you got a middle name?" the old man asked.

"No, sir," Gawd answered, his voice remaining subdued during the line of questioning.

The old man sort of grunted and returned his attention to the road, seeming to lose interest in the boy.

They drove again in silence. But only for a short while before the old man pulled the car off into a roadside eatery.

"You hungry?" he asked the boy, after bringing the car to a stop beside the place.

"Yes, sir," Gawd answered, nodding in the affirmative.

"Well, let's get something to eat," the grandfather said. "We've got quite a drive ahead of us." And they climbed out of the car and went inside the restaurant.

They ordered, the old man a bowl of soup and a sandwich, the boy a cheeseburger with fries and gravy, the meal he'd been craving for some time.

"You know, I'm not sure why I'm doing this," the old man said, as they waited for their food to come.

Gawd said nothing, but watched the old man and waited for him to continue.

"But your grandmother wanted us to take you in," he said. "She said that maybe we didn't give your mom a fair upbringing and that maybe we could make it up somehow. Your mom never wanted any part of us back when she left. I guess we were too stuffy for her. She wanted to have her head, and I guess we wouldn't give it to her. She just up and left."

Their food came, so the old man's monologue was momentarily interrupted.

But it wasn't long before he continued.

"Your grandmother really took it hard. She was never the same," he said. "She always hoped we'd be able to patch things up, but we never saw her again. It's a good thing she never lived to see what became of her daughter. Murdered by a drunk."

They ate for a moment in silence. Gawd was unsure of what to say. His mother had never said much about her parents, just to say that they lived in a small town a long way from the city, and that she hadn't seen them for quite a while. He didn't know what to say to the old man -- he'd read about grandparents, but never had any of his own -- never had any family except his mom.

"I never been too good at raising kids," the old man said. "We had your mom when we were older, and we had a hard time with her. I don't know how we're going to make out, or what you'll think of me, but I know this is what your grandmother would have wanted." He paused and returned to his meal.

"So, I've come for you," he said. "But how it turns out is all up to you. I'm kind of set in my ways, especially since your grandmother died, and it'll be up to you to fit into my way of living. "There'll just be the two of us, and hopefully we can get along. I'll try to give you a good home, but it'll be mostly up to you."

Gawd regarded the old man. He remained quiet.

"You're quiet boy," the grandfather said. "What have you got to say for yourself?"

Gawd thought for a moment. "I'll do my best, sir," he said solemnly.

"I can't have you calling me sir, either," the grandfather said. "How about Bert?" he said.

Gawd didn't answer, but he couldn't help but offer a small smile.

"And we've got to have a name for you," the old man said. "We can't go around calling you Gawd. That's not proper at all. It'll never do." He seemed to plunge himself deep into thought for a moment. "What say? Are there any other names you like?" he asked.

The boy thought. He had taken many a taunt and blow over his name, but now that he had a chance to perhaps part with it, he could think of no better alternative, his mind a blank.

"How about Adam?" the old man asked. "It's a good Christian name, and one that you can get used to." He paused and regarded the boy. "Got any objections to Adam?" he asked.

"No, sir," Gawd answered.

"Bert," the old man corrected.

"No, Bert," he answered.

The grandfather smiled warmly for the first time since the two had come together. Gawd couldn't help but smile as well.

Soon, they had finished the repast, and were back in the shiny, new car, driving toward Gawd's fresh start.

And, finally, after much of the day had passed, they came to the small town where the old man lived. The small town made Gawd think of places where real families might live, on tree-lined streets, in white frame houses with white picket fences. It had been some time since he'd had such thoughts and he found it difficult to think them. He thought of his mother who had grown up on these very tree-lined streets back in another time and he found himself imagining her as a young girl, filled with innocence and awe at life, not with the grief and misery that had become her lot.

The old man guided the car into the driveway of one of the white frame houses, complete with white picket fence, and soon Gawd was following him into the house, carrying all his worldly possessions in an old worn-out duffle bag. He followed his grandfather up the stairs to the second storey, where they soon stood in one of the bedrooms.

It was a girl's room, frilly and sweet in every regard. Gawd stood quietly by the old man, who said nothing at first, but stood in silence, almost as if he might be remembering. "This was your mother's room," he finally said. "It'll be yours now. I'll expect you to keep your things picked up and keep it neat and tidy. Understand?" He turned and looked at the boy.

"Yes, sir," Gawd answered, forgetting to use the old man's name, as he'd been instructed, causing the old man to look toward him and offer a slight frown.

"Don't worry," the grandfather continued, "we'll make a few changes in here. We can't have you living in here with all this girl's stuff." He paused. "Now you get cleaned up, and come to the family room." And he turned and left the room.

Gawd stood in the middle of the room, giving it a lookover. It was hard to imagine his mother had ever lived in a place like this -- that she'd once been a real little girl, with real parents. He regarded the big doll house in one corner of the room, saw the teddy bear in the tiny rocking chair. Oh that she had come to her end so far away and in such dire straights, when this had been here, seeming to wait for her.

He walked over and put his duffle bag in the closet. Then he sought out the bathroom, before descending the stairs in search of the family room.

His grandfather was there, sitting in a comfortable-looking recliner chair, his feet up.

"You settled in?" the old man asked when he saw the boy enter.

"Yes, sir," Gawd answered.

"Bert," the old man insisted.

"Sorry," the boy answered.

"I know, it'll take some getting used to, eh?" the grandfather more said than asked. "For me too." A pause. "But I've been getting used to a lot of things lately."

There was a silence in the room -- a solid silence that surrounded both of them with their own thoughts.

"Thanks," Gawd finally said, pushing the small word out of him and into the quiet of the room.

"What's that?" the old man asked.

"Thanks for getting me out of Spring Valley," Gawd answered.

"It had to be done," the old man said. "Your grandmother would have wanted it. She wouldn't have wanted you with strangers. I never let her down in life, and I wouldn't in death either."

"What happened to her?" Gawd asked.

"She died. She had cancer. It wasn't too good," the old man answered, shooting the sentences out in staccato.

"I'm sorry," Gawd said.

"We live to die," the old man said bluntly. "It was her time."

But Gawd could tell the old man was only putting on a front. "You must miss her," he said.

"We were married for forty-six years," the old man said. "I guess I sort of got used to having the old girl around."

Now there was a matter-of-factness to the old man's voice, but there was also emotion, like it was creeping in and he couldn't stop it.

Gawd thought for a moment. "I'll try to do good," he said softly.

"I know you will, boy," the old man answered, and his voice was also quiet, and there was an unsteadiness to it.

Then there was silence in the room and Gawd could hear only the old man's breathing, and it was shallow and uneven. The boy got up quietly and crept back upstairs to the room where he'd put his things, leaving the grandfather alone to his thoughts. And Gawd was reminded of the sorrow and unhappiness in the world. And he was reminded that this was nearly all he had seen of life.

Gawd had an uneasy night's sleep in his mother's old room. It was like he was haunted by her image throughout the night, and every time he closed his eyes, all he could see was her and he wanted her to be with him again, so they could again share the quiet times they once had. Try as he might, Gawd could see her only as the unhappy wretch she had become. There was no more little girl who played with doll houses and teddy bears. And it was sad. And Gawd almost wept at such a memory.

The next morning, the old man fixed Gawd what might have been the best breakfast he'd ever had, and he ate and ate and ate. He chased the food down with a great, steaming mug of coffee, even though he was told that coffee was for adults, and that it would stunt his growth.

Then, it was off uptown to the post office to get the morning mail. They walked because most things are close in a small town, and as they went, they passed this person and that person, and the grandfather introduced the boy as they went. "Like you to meet Adam, my grandson," he'd say, and Gawd thought he could almost hear pride in the old man's voice.

Then, it was back home, where the old man sat on the porch swing and read the morning paper and Gawd was expected to find his own amusements for a while. The boy disappeared into what could now be called "his" room, and had soon discovered a shelf full of books in the closet where they must have been placed some long years ago when another had no longer been there to read them. They were books like "Black Beauty" and "The Sword in the Stone", and there was a battered copy of "Mother Goose Nursery Rhymes", and Gawd thought of his mother reading and re-reading them, alone in the confines of this room. He'd never known his mother to read anything more than the tabloids, but here was something more -- another side that spoke of contentment and bliss on a rainy summer's day.

They ate lunch out on the back deck in the warm sunshine.

"I suppose we'll have to get you into school in the fall," the old man said, between bites of his sandwich. "But we'll have to keep ourselves occupied for the summer. Are you a fisherman?" he asked.

"Not much," Gawd answered.

"Are you interested in fishing?" the grandfather asked.

"I've liked it when I've tried it," he answered, and it was true that he had warm memories of fishing with another.

"Well, how say we head out this afternoon," the old man said. "We won't catch much in the heat of the day, but I'll at least have the chance to show you around to a couple of the spots.........Would you like that?"

"Sure," the boy answered, and he was sure he would.

So that by mid-afternoon, the two were sitting statuesque on a riverbank, idling away what remained of the day and hoping for a bite. Gawd had wondered what he would fish with, but the old man was prepared with two sets of tackle and he explained that one had belonged to his wife, who hadn't used it much, but on occasion had joined him on his fishing expeditions, if the weather was just right, and there was a good chance she wouldn't catch anything.

"I've never been a real serious fisherman," the old man said, as they patiently waited, "but like your grandmother used to say, it gives me something to do in my retirement. And I really don't mind it. It's sort of relaxing. I came fishing the day she died. Just to get away from everyone -- to be by myself."

"What did you do when you worked?" Gawd asked, finally working up enough courage to initiate a piece of the conversation.

"I ran a hardware store," the old man answered. "Spent over forty Christmases on the Main Street of this little town. I know it's not much of an accomplishment the way people think of things these days, but I was able to put food on the table and a roof over our heads for all those years -- and there was a time when that sort of thing counted for something."

Gawd found himself reminded of something he'd read about small-town hardware stores. "Did you have a toyland in your store?" he asked.

"Every Christmas," the grandfather answered. "The biggest one in the county."

"Wow," said Gawd, "that must have been cool."

The old man smiled. "I suppose it was," he said.

They sat for a while in quiet.

"Your mother wasn't very happy, was she?" the grandfather suddenly asked.

"No, sir," Gawd answered.

"I suppose I was to blame for that," the old man said. "Did she tell you that?"

"No, she never talked about you," Gawd answered.

"I'm not surprised," the old man said. More quiet. "I was over forty when she was born. Her mother and I thought we couldn't have kids, the doctor told your grandmother she couldn't get in the family way because of some medical problem she'd had. But she got pregnant anyway, right out of the blue, and we had your mother. I tried to bring her up right, you know, but, as she got older, we argued about everything -- it was the times as much as anything, now that I look back on it."

He paused for a moment, flicking his fishing pole, as if he might have had a bite. Then, he continued his tale.

"Kids were rebellin' against their parents everywhere. We couldn't understand what she wanted out of life, and she couldn't understand what we wanted out of her. Finally, it all just blew up over one thing or another -- I found drugs in her room and she was hanging out with all the wrong kids -- she didn't want to go back to school -- she wanted to go hitch-hiking in Europe. I hit her -- I shouldn't have, I know that now. It was the only time I ever did anything like that, but she made me so mad -- I never remember being that mad either before or since. She just wouldn't listen."

He hesitated again in the telling, looking as if he might be remembering what had happened all those years ago. "She was a strong-willed girl, like her mother, and she packed her things and left with a guy in an old van all painted over with flowers. We never saw her again. She never let us know where she was. She was seventeen. Didn't even know about you until her funeral." The words poured from him.

"It's sad," Gawd said.

"Yea, it is," the old man agreed. "I know that now." And he looked to be honestly remorseful.

They sat again in quiet.

"Your grandmother took it hard," the old man continued. "Wanted me to hire a private investigator to try to find her. I wouldn't. I figured she'd come back." He paused again, seeming to be reflecting on a time long past. "But I reckon judging by your age that she had you shortly after."

"Yes, sir," Gawd said.

"Was she a good mother to you?" the grandfather asked.

"Yes, sir," Gawd answered.

"I'll bet you miss her," the old man said affectionately, a warm, generous smile spreading over his face.

"Yes, sir," Gawd answered.

"I do too," answered the old man, and he said it evenly and solemnly.

And that was the first time Gawd felt like a family with his grandfather. That time when they were fishing. And that was the beginning of the most wonderful summer of Gawd's life. It was like his grandfather couldn't get enough of him. They fished and hiked and built model cars, and went to the fair and the science centre in the city. It was beginning to seem like the fresh start was going to work. Gawd sensed a comfortableness coming over him. He smiled often, even to himself. And he started to call the old man grandpa.

But there were times as well, as the boy learned, when the old man would suddenly grow quiet and sombre, and he'd go into the family room and sit quietly in his recliner chair, seeming to be of heavy heart, and it was like a sense of melancholy came over the whole house when such was the case. And Gawd crept around the place, careful not to disrupt the old man, feeling respect for him and what he might be feeling.

One night, they sat watching a baseball game on TV, something they'd done often since they'd been together. Summer was almost over and Gawd was reflecting on the fact that school would soon begin, and he assumed he'd have to go, so was feeling his own sense of melancholy. And he could tell the old man was the same. He was sitting silently in the recliner, hands folded on his chest, not waving excitedly in the air, while he coached and instucted the players on the TV. It was dark in the room, the only light the flickering of the television. As Gawd watched the game, one of the players smacked a long home run over the centre field wall, and the boy looked toward his grandfather for a reaction. The old man sat quietly -- no reaction -- and Gawd could see a tear glistening its way down his well-worn face.

"Are you alright, Grampa?" the boy asked, over the noise of the cheering fans.

The old man stirred, turned in the chair, and looked over.

"Yes," he answered.

"You're awful quiet," the boy said.

"I guess I was just thinking about your grandma," the grandfather answered, and he clicked off the sound on the TV.

"You miss her," Gawd said.

"It just wasn't fair that it was her," the old man said. "She was the good one, the long suffering one. When we found out she was sick, and things didn't look so good -- she was the one who took it the best. I was crushed. I felt like my life was over, instead of hers."

There was silence in the room -- the boy unsure what to say -- the old man seeming reflective.

"She's been gone a year," he said, interrupting the quiet. "And it's been a long year. You know, I never knew what people meant when they said somebody had a broken heart, until your grandmother died. Now, I get this aching right in here -- right around where my heart is." He paused and pointed to his chest. "It's the emptiest feeling, so empty it hurts."

Gawd thought of his mother, and knew the feeling, but said nothing.

"You've made me think about your mother, too," the grandfather said, seeming to read the boy's thoughts. "I was so angry at her for so many years -- and where did it get me?" There was no answer. "Maybe if I hadn't been so stubborn, and your mother hadn't been so stubborn, your grandmother wouldn't have gotten sick. She just wasn't the same after your mom left. She didn't say anything, stood by my side the way a good wife should -- tried to talk some sense to me when she thought the time was right. But I wouldn't listen -- and I knew how it was eating away at her."

"I wish my mom would have called you," Gawd said, innocence in his voice.

"It probably wouldn't have done any good," the old man answered.

"I was too thick. I really thought I wanted her out of my life." He put his hand across his brow. "How could I have done such a thing?" He sounded angry with himself.

There was more quiet in the room, the old man withdrawing into himself, the boy not feeling he could offer anything that might help.

"But I shouldn't be talking like this to you," the old man finally said, after a few moments of the quiet. "You're a boy, and boys aren't supposed to have to worry about this type of thing. You've had your own share of sadness and heartache. It almost seems like that's what life is all about."

There was another brief moment of quiet before the old man turned his attention back toward the TV. "What the heck's going on with this ballgame?" he asked, a little more loudly than was necessary, turning the sound from the television back on.

"Maybe we could go fishin' tomorrow," Gawd said over the sound of the cheering crowd.

"What's that?" the old man asked.

Gawd repeated the suggestion, more loudly than before.

"Sure," answered the old man. "That'd be great."

And so they went fishing the next day. And they watched a ballgame that night. And, as the weeks passed, they grew closer and closer, the two who had each experienced his own share of grief in a lifetime, whether long or short. Gawd wondered that it would never end, and even went to school equipped with his new name, and found some peace in that, although he kept mainly to himself as he always had in the past. In fact, that was what made it almost perfect, that there were only the two of them nearly always, so that the man and boy could share in each other. Gawd even resented the cleaning lady and the occasional relatives who lived in town and came to the house, and was glad that the old man didn't seem to see a great need for socializing, with family or not.

Gawd had a for real life then. And he revelled in it, and thought less about his mother and that beginning part of his life, when everything had seemed so tragic. He thought that perhaps even the old man found some solace for his own grief in the relationship the two had developed. It was not uncommon to see the two just walking in the park on a sunny fall afternoon, the leaves rustling under the shuffle of their feet. And they would talk about all manner of things, how their favourite team would do in the coming hockey season, whether Gawd should take up something like Scouts, which model boat they should build next. It was an idyllic time for the boy.......and it seemed also for the man.

Finally, though, the snowy winter came. The two comrades had stacked a cord and a half of wood along the side of the garage in the fall, so they were prepared to weather any storm. The fishing season was over and they were immersed in the hockey season. There was the first talk of Christmas -- a season the boy had never liked. Gawd had even dared to think that this year might be different so hopeful had he become. Perhaps there was more to life than he had thought.

One morning, as they sat eating breakfast at the kitchen table, watching the birds twitter around the backyard feeder, fresh white snow all about, the boy was feeling particularly buoyant. It was Saturday and there was a road hockey game in Pinewood Park, and even though he continued to keep to himself on most occasions, he was so keen on road hockey that it was worth enduring others to be able to play. Sometimes, the old man came to watch.

"Want to come to Pinewood to watch the game?" the boy asked, between mouthfuls of cereal.

"There's a game today?" the old man asked back.

"Every Saturday," Gawd answered.

"You mind doing the walk before you go?" the grandfather asked.

"Do I have to do it this morning?" Gawd asked, with a pained sound to his voice. "I don't like to be late, or I'll have to play with whoever's short."

"Your Aunt Rose is coming over later this morning. We don't want her to slip and fall," the old man said. "She's a big woman, and it might mean the end of our sidewalk," he joked.

And it was true that Aunt Rose was a big woman. She was really his great aunt, because she was one of his grandmother's sisters, a spinster who lived all by herself in an oversized house across town. Gawd steered clear of her, and she seemed to have taken an instant dislike to him, he thought just because he was a boy and would one day turn into a man, and she didn't seem to have much use for that sex. She was always complaining about how old and decrepit she was. Gawd knew the walk would have to be shovelled. There was no use arguing. The old man and he had agreed at the first snowfall that it was the boy's job to do the walk -- a man came and ploughed the driveway because it was too big and long even for the two of them.

"Okay," the boy answered, but it was clear from his tone of voice that he was not pleased with what had transpired.

"It'll just take you a few minutes," the grandfather said.

"I know," Gawd said dejectedly, and he got up from the kitchen table to go to his task, a once buoyant mood deflated.

It had snowed quite a bit in the night, so he knew it would take longer than a few minutes. He went grimly about his work, and had made it only a short distance toward the street, when he heard someone call.

"Adam," he heard the voice call.

He looked up and saw three of his school friends, three of his fellow road hockey buddies, standing at the other end of the snowed-in sidewalk, hockey sticks in hand.

"Hi," Gawd called out to them.

"Hey, man, you comin' to play hockey?" one of the boys hollered back.

"I hafta shovel the walk," Gawd answered glumly.

"Comeon'," one of the boys urged. "It'll wait. That snow's not going anywhere. Anyway, if somebody comes, they can use the driveway -- it's ploughed."

"Yea, we need you to help stomp down the road," another boy said. "That's why we're going early. There'll be a ton of snow and the grader won't be around 'til later."

"I promised my grandpa," Gawd answered, but he was looking toward the freshly-scraped driveway.

"Hey, my old man wanted me to shovel," said the third boy. "I told him I would, and I will, but just not right now. You can do it later. You want to be on our team, don't you?"

And it was true that Gawd did want to be on their team, and that was why he'd wanted to go early in the first place. These boys had treated him as a friend since he'd started school in the fall -- and these were the boys who had first invited him to play road hockey. Perhaps he'd be letting them down if he didn't go. There was the driveway -- it was clean -- he could cut a path to it in short order.

"I have to do this," he hollered, indicating the short distance between where he stood and the driveway.

"Hurry up! We'll meet you there. We're going to try to get a couple of more guys, so we have our whole team together," answered one of the boys.

"Alright," Gawd answered, and he went fervently about his task, all the time re-assuring himself that grandfather would understand when he saw what had been done.

He finished quickly, leaned the shovel by the garage door, and got his hockey stick from inside the garage. And he left.....with no word to the old man......no chance to be dissuaded. Aunt Rose could walk up the driveway. The old man would understand.

The boys had finished stomping down the snow in the street, and the game had been underway for some time, when a police car drove into the Park. The boys stopped their game, as the car stopped in the middle of their makeshift rink. An officer got out. He asked for Gawd.

The boy was hesitant before stepping forward. He distrusted police from his younger years. Finally, though, after the officer had asked for him a second time, he identified himself, and stepped forward.

He got into the car with the policeman, as he was told to do, his hockey stick put into the trunk. The officer gave no indication why he'd come. He asked if it was a good game of road hockey, and Gawd grunted that it was okay. They rode most of the way in silence and were soon pulling into the driveway of the old man's house.

"What's the matter?" Gawd finally asked, knowing that something was almost always the matter when the police came.

The officer looked over at him -- there was a look of evenness to him.

"What's the matter?" Gawd repeated.

"It's your grandfather," the officer said.

"What?" Gawd asked suspiciously.

"He's had a heart attack," the officer answered.

"Is he alright?" Gawd asked quietly.

"He's dead," the officer said. "Died on the way to the hospital. They couldn't save him. We didn't know where you were at first."

"Dead," Gawd said quietly.

"He was shovelling the walk," the officer said.

And Gawd wept.

Parties and Prayers.....

And so it was that Gawd came to live with Aunt Rose, who made it abundantly clear that she was his last chance, and that he was going through next of kin at a rather alarming rate.

"Just remember, young fellow, that it's only on account of my sister's dying wish that I'm taking you in," she said. "I think there's something awful peculiar about you that first your mother dies in a way that was never properly explained to me, and then your grandfather up and suffers a heart attack when there's no history of it in the family. Awful peculiar, if you ask me." She stood for a moment, hands on hips, a stern expression on her face. "Well.......have you anything to say for yourself."

Gawd stood on the step of her house, his duffle bag slung over his shoulder, fishing pole in hand. "No, ma'am," he answered as politely as he could.

"Are you a Christian?" she asked bluntly. "Ever been to church?"

"Not much ma'am," he answered somewhat sheepishly.

"We'll change that," she said stiffly.

"Yes, ma'am," he answered dutifully.

And so he was welcomed into her house, a big overgrown, two-storey Victorian structure located in the old part of town, down by the Big Shop, the furniture factory that had once been the biggest structure in the British Empire. Even now, it was an immense building that he had to pass each day on the way to school, and he was able to look down into its bowels through its basement windows to where he saw old men who seemed dirty and dusty in their work, and who never looked happy, and who seemed to look toward him longingly as he walked by.

And it was school where he focussed his attention after his grandfather's death. It wasn't that he disliked Aunt Rose – he was sort of neutral about her at first and even grew fond of her eventually, but they had nothing in common. There was no fishing and hockey and building model boats, although he maintained an interest in all the things he'd done with the old man. But at school, he found friendship with another who had come from outside this small community, and who felt awkward at being suddenly thrust into a new environment. It was Sid.

Sid moved from the city in the New Year after the old man died. His mother and father had divorced, and his mother had moved to this particular small town because she'd wanted to get as far away from Sid's father as she could after they split, and the bank where she worked as a teller had an opening at the branch here. Sid made no secret of the fact that he was aghast at having to live in such a rural backwater when he'd just been in the city, where there was considerable action for pubescent boys.

"Hey, asshole, you're blocking the view," were the first words Gawd heard Sid speak, and they were spoken in his direction.

He looked back at the new kid and scowled, but kept quiet, and actually shifted slightly to the side, so the speaker could possibly see better -- two kids from their class were duking it out over a girl – it wasn't much action, but it was about the best you could hope for in these parts.

"Not much of a fight," Sid commented after the dust, or in this case, snow, had settled, and the combatants had been dragged off to the office for punishment.

"It wasn't bad," Gawd returned.

"Girls are better," Sid answered. "They really get involved in what they're doing. They're more emotional. They lose their cool better."

"I see your point," Gawd answered. "Cat fight."

"Yea," answered Sid. "And I'll tell you something else -- they're not worth fighting over. My mom's a bitch, and my dad says that all women get to be bitches as soon as they get married. What about your mom?"

"She's dead," Gawd answered.

"Ooo, that's too bad," Sid said. "Because, even though they're a pain in the ass, they're kind of useful to have around. You live with your dad?"

"I live with my great aunt -- don't have a dad," Gawd answered.

"Tough luck story, eh," Sid said.

Just at that moment, the bell sounded, calling them back to their studies.

"Meet me after school," Sid hissed under his breath as they filed back into the school.

Gawd wasn't sure why, but he nodded in the affirmative, but kept his mouth shut, knowing the teachers would be testy after the fisticuffs in the schoolyard at recess. And so, Gawd met Sid.

And he did meet Sid after school, and they walked home together, after finding out that they lived in the same direction from the school. Sid invited Gawd in when they got to his place.

"Comeon in and check out the digs," he said. "It's Thursday -- busy day at the bank -- mom won't be home 'til about seven. Why don't you call your great aunt, or whatever she is, and tell her you're stayin' over for supper -- tell her we've got some homework to do together."

Gawd thought there was little harm in agreeing to stay over for supper, but when he phoned Aunt Rose, he left out the part about the homework, because it would have been a lie, and he tried to save those for really important occasions. He figured the old girl probably wouldn't really care whether he was there or not anyway.

Sid's room was out of this world to Gawd. The walls were painted flat black and the ceiling was done in tin foil -- and there were mirrors everywhere.

"Wow," Gawd said, as they entered; "this is quite a place."

"It's comfy," Sid said.

"You've got your own record player," Gawd said, incredulous at his friend's good fortune.

"I pick up all the latest records when I'm in the city visiting my dad," Sid replied matter-of-factly. "My dad bought the record player for me. He's always doing stuff like that 'cause he feels guilty for having an affair and leaving mom and me. I got to say, though, that his new chick is a real looker. I wouldn't mind getting into her pants myself."

Gawd was surprised that Sid would talk so -- surprised that he'd talk about a woman like that, because Gawd hadn't heard much discussion about the opposite sex from the guys he played road hockey with, or others of his age. Girls remained objects of scorn in his circle. "You wouldn't know what to do," he challenged.

"I guess I wouldn't," Sid answered sarcastically. "I had my way with Sally Reynolds in Grade 6 -- she was a grade eighter and she taught me the ropes, and I've been trying to pass on what I learned ever since."

Gawd said nothing. Sid rummaged through a pile of records, appearing to search for one particular disc.

"You must be able to get a boner," Sid said, looking up from his search.

Gawd must have looked puzzled.

"A hard on......an erection," he elaborated.

"Yea, I guess," Gawd answered, but embarrassment showed.

"Well, what do you think it's for?" Sid asked, as he pulled a record from the pile, and looked pleased with himself.

"I know what it's for," Gawd answered, a trace of anger in his voice.

"Hey, I know the girls in public school aren't much," Sid said, as he put the album on the record player, and turned the machine on. It was something Gawd didn't recognize. "But next year we'll be in high school, and there are some great chicks there. You got to be ready."

"What do you mean by that?" Gawd asked innocently.

"We've got to get you laid," Sid said. "You can't go to high school a virgin. You'll get laughed out of the place."

And that was Gawd's introduction to Sid -- old Sid who was more worldly than anyone Gawd had ever met in his short life -- even when he'd lived in the city with his mom. And for as long as Gawd knew Sid, his friend was always just a little bit ahead of the crowd in everything he did. That was sort of Sid's distinguishing feature.

And it sort of became Sid's mission in life, over the rest of that winter and the spring and summer that followed, to try to get Gawd laid before high school. The two boys became almost inseparable over that time, and except for the girl stuff, Gawd was happy to have Sid for a friend, because they were always doing different and kind of neat things. Sid didn't care much for sports, but he was heavily into fishing and hunting, which was good, because it was something they had in common right from the start -- not the hunting so much, but the fishing for sure. They spent a lot of time listening to the latest music, and doing things like horsing around with Sid's older brother's movie and recording junk that he stored with his mother when he was out of the country, which he apparently often was. So, while the others kids were doing kid stuff, Sid and Gawd were making movies and recording rude sounds, and doing all manner of other neat stuff. That was another thing about Sid -- he had the neatest junk.

Gawd went to just about the first party he'd ever been to on Valentine's Day in Grade 8. He suffered considerable trepidation as the event loomed, knowing that he was ill-prepared for it, not being much of a social animal and not really possessing the so-called graces such a function might require. But Sid was adamant that they attend, even though Gawd did his best to dissuade him. "I've got a little surprise," was all Sid would say. "Make sure to ask your aunt if you can sleep over," he'd added. It was all very mysterious, but Gawd let himself be talked into attending the party. That was a condition of finding out about the surprise -- he had to agree to go to the party.

So he asked his aunt if he could sleep over at Sid's, and she consented, thinking Sid was an unusually polite kid because that was the way he always acted when he came to her house to visit Gawd. She didn't quite approve of the fact that Sid's parents were divorced, or that Sid's mom lived on her own and "needed a man", but she kept quiet about it when Sid was around, and even seemed to feel sorry for him because of his parental situation, so she was always offering him cupcakes or butter tarts or oatmeal cookies -- which he always accepted with a polite thank-you.

Gawd arrived at Sid's early in the evening, about an hour before the eight o'clock start for the party. He had his pajamas and toothbrush in a paper bag that hung from the handlebar of his bike as he rode into Sid's driveway. He also had a change of clothes, because he was dressed in his Sunday best, because that's the way you dressed for parties in those days. There was no car in the driveway. Sid's mom must be out, Gawd thought.

"Yea, she's gone out of town to some meeting the bank's putting on," Sid said, as Gawd followed him to his basement room. "She said she probably wouldn't be back until about midnight. Time for us to have some fun."

"You better get ready for the party," Gawd said.

"Lots of time," Sid answered, as he disappeared through the doorway to his room, with Gawd following after him.

"So, what's the surprise?" Gawd asked, while Sid searched the records.

"Oh yea," Sid said, "I suppose you're interested to know."

He abandoned the records and walked over to the closet. Gawd followed. His friend turned on the light and went into the back part of the large space. Gawd watched as he moved a couple of boxes, revealing a small, hinged door in the wall. "My mom doesn't even know this place is here," Sid said, as he crouched to open the tiny door. "Isn't it a great stash place?" He reached into the miniature doorway, and produced..............a bottle..........filled with reddish liquid.

"What is it?" Gawd asked, a puzzled look on his face.

"It's some of my old man's wine," Sid answered with a wide grin, obviously feeling very pleased with himself. "I scooped it the last time

I was at his place -- probably when he was doing it with his girlfriend for all I know. I've been saving it for a special occasion."

"Wine," was all Gawd could say.

"We'll have a few drinks and go to the party," Sid said, as he followed Gawd out of the closet, bottle in hand. In short order he had produced a couple of glasses and even a corkscrew, and was wrestling the cork out of the bottle. Then, he poured them each a good-sized tumbler full of the stuff. "Cheers," he said brightly, and they clinked glasses and drank.

Gawd felt the stuff burn all the way down into him. It was awful; nothing like pop. His first urge was to spit it back out, but he knew that wouldn't be the manly thing to do, so he swallowed it down and felt heartburn for the first time in his young life.

"Man, that's strong stuff," Sid said, as he finished about half the glass.

"You've drank before?" Gawd asked, sucking in the fresh air after the hotness of the wine.

"Oh, sure," Sid said. "My old man makes wine. I was raised on the stuff." He raised his glass for another drink.

Gawd didn't know whether to believe him or not, but he dutifully returned to his glass, not looking forward to consuming more of the vile liquid.

By the middle of the second glass, Gawd was feeling a warmth spread through him, and the stuff seemed to be tasting better -- he found himself grinning ear to ear, as he regarded Sid who was holding a newly-emptied tumbler.

"What's so funny?" Sid asked, a silly grin on his face as well.

"You are," Gawd answered, puncuating his answer with what might rightly be called a chortle.

"You're getting drunk," Sid said, who was talking extremely loudly, and who seemed to be leering toward him so his features got all distorted and comic-bookish.

Gawd recoiled, or at least tried to, but he nearly fell backward off the corner of the bed he was been sitting on.

Sid reached out for him and caught him by the arm. "Easy does it," he said, but it was clear that he was more than a little off balance himself, so that they both almost tumbled to the floor. And their near fall prompted a bout of spontaneous and uncontrollable laughter so Gawd did fall off the bed and onto the floor, where he lay in a mirthful fetal position.

Finally, the laughter died down. They both sat quietly as if reflecting on their drunkenness.

"What about the party?" Gawd said, but he struggled with his mouth, seeming unable to make it do just what he wanted.

"Christ, yea," Sid said. "I should get dressed." He looked to the half empty bottle of wine. "I better put this thing back in my secret stash spot." He went to get up, but teetered on the edge of the bed, and fell back twice, spilling a good portion of his booty onto his bedsheets, before finally making it to a standing position on the floor.

With what seemed like great difficulty, he put the bottle back into the compartment at the rear of the closet, and started digging around for his clothes. "I hate getting dressed up," he said. He looked out of the closet in Gawd's direction. "You alright?" he asked, as he regarded his friend, who was by this time in a sitting position, but was very quiet.

And Gawd had been overtaken by a feeling of melancholy, as he remembered his mother, and the difficulty she had faced with the bottle. He thought again of the quiet times he'd shared with her, as they'd sat on the couch in their little apartment, and he'd imagined that they were a real family.

"You alright?" Sid repeated.

"Yea," Gawd answered, but it was like he sobered up at that moment. And even though he walked a little unsteadily to the Valentine's party, and even though both boys smelled of the mints they'd eaten to hide the smell of the alcohol, he never took another drink -- not on that night, or on any other night.

And Gawd got religion during that last year of public school. Aunt Rose was good to her word, and he was soon a regular feature at the United Church. In fact, he was baptized in short order, and in the spring was enrolled in confirmation class where he was expected to join the church as an adult. It was a bit of a crash course, because he'd not had much of a religious upbringing. His mother hadn't seemed to bother with it, except for a few kid's stories when he'd been younger, and although he'd been required to attend chapel at Spring Valley, it'd been a bit of a joke with all the young lawbreakers and juvenile criminals. The only reason he went along with Aunt Rose and got involved was because he knew it had been in the old man's plans as well, and that somehow made it alright.

The other thing that made it alright was that Sid's mother had decided to get religion after splitting up with Sid's father, and in a happy coincidence Sid ended up in Gawd's confirmation class. Sid was also not very expert on biblical issues, so the two of them struggled together to gain some understanding of them. Gawd found the god stuff interesting, albeit somewhat mysterious and mystical, while Sid absolutely abhorred it and complained constantly about not being able to understand how anybody could believe such bilk.

One day, they were sitting in the Quiet Room at the church, the whole confirmation class, with Reverend Cowan making pronouncements on how all good Christians were born into sin, but that they could redeem themselves and get their reward in Heaven. It was all pretty usual stuff for this couple of hours of time. For some reason, though, Sid was more restless than usual, and, finally, he did the unthinkable -- he raised his hand to make a comment or ask a question.

"Yes, Sidney," said Reverend Cowan, using Sid's full name, something the boy disliked.

"Well, Reverend sir, I was just wondering if there was any proof that Jesus was God's son?" Sid asked, and you could see he'd put considerable thought into it.

"Well, Sidney, that's a very good question," the minister answered.

"Jesus, himself, tells us on many occasions that he is the son of God, and anyone who believes in the miracle of divine birth should acknowledge that."

"Well, sir, I've been reading a lot of this bible stuff since we started this class," Sid answered, as Gawd watched, surprised his friend would get involved in such a discussion, "and it seems to me that there's just as good a chance that Jesus was just a regular guy."

"What do you mean exactly, Sidney?" the minister asked, his eyebrows arched.

"Well, I'm not sure I can buy into all this God stuff -- it's all pretty shakey -- but I like a lot of what this Jesus guy had to say," Sid answered, and by now the whole class was fidgeting nervously in their seats. "I think there's a pretty good chance that he was just an ordinary guy, only a little smarter than most, and he had a whole lot of common sense, and he said some pretty good things -- like if you love your neighbour, and do unto others like you want them to do to you -- but I can't imagine that he was God's son. I'm not even sure there is a God -- that's a pretty tall order."

Gawd was watching the minister's face while Sid was expounding on the theory that there was no God, and that Jesus was just a brighter-than-average guy. It turned several shades of red, and Gawd could tell there was going to be a problem. But the good reverend showed great restraint, letting Sid finish his postulating before responding.

"In this class, young man," the reverend started, his voice stern and awful, "we do not even entertain the possibility that Jesus wasn't God's son. We believe. I believe. You believe. That's what we're here for -- to affirm our faith in God the Father, the Holy Trinity, and Jesus the son." The minister paused, and things were awfully quiet in the Quiet Room. It was a tense quiet.

"You, and all of us, were born into sin, and it is only through acceptance of the Father through the Son that we can be absolved of that sin and find our reward in Heaven," he continued. "We will not entertain such questions in this class over the final weeks. I can only ask Sidney, that you make some effort to find God over that time, so you can find your way to eternal life." He paused again. It remained so quiet you could have heard the proverbial pin drop. It was another moment of tense quiet.

"We should take a break," the minister said. "Be back in ten minutes." He closed the book that was on the desk in front of him, got up and strode out of the room.

Still there was quiet -- perhaps a shocked quiet -- everyone in wonderment that one of their number had so obviously challenged the good reverend and his teaching, perhaps saying what many of them had been thinking.

Then, they started to talk in hushed whispers, casting sideways glances at the perpetrator, but he quickly left the quiet room.

Gawd watched him go, but was quickly after him. Not quickly enough, though, because by the time Gawd reached the hallway outside the Quiet Room, Sid had vanished. Gawd looked for him for a couple of minutes, but could find no sign of him, so assumed he must have decided to lay low during the break, and gave up the search. Instead, he went to the washroom.

As he was just finishing washing his hands, he heard a voice cry out from outside in the hallway. "He's on the roof! He's on the roof!" Gawd came out of the washroom and almost collided with Bill, one of his classmates, who seemed in an unusual hurry.

"What's the rush?" he asked.

"It's your buddy, Sid," Bill answered excitedly. "He's up on the roof. He looks like he's going to jump. He's kneeling right on the edge, looking down."

Christ, thought Gawd. And he went out to see what truth there was to what he'd been told.

And once he was outside the church, and he looked up toward the sky, he could indeed see Sid on his knees on the edge of the church roof -- the one with the steeple -- the really high one. He looked like he was praying.

By this time, Reverend Cowan was on the lawn with the rest of the confirmation class. "You up there," the good reverend called out. "You're not supposed to be up there. You're going to get into serious trouble."

There was no reaction from Sid, but Gawd had stopped watching and was hurrying through the church on his way toward his friend. He needed a better vantage point -- he felt he needed to try to talk to Sid, and he didn't feel he could do it from the ground -- he had to get closer.

Finally, on the upper floor of the church, he found an open window that led out onto the ledge that led to the roof; the window he knew Sid had used to get to his high-up perch. He stuck his head out, and realized he'd not even be able to see Sid unless he went along the ledge to the corner of the building. He wasn't overly keen on heights, but he could hear the minister imploring Sid to get down from the roof, and he felt that was going to do little good in this situation. He crawled out onto the narrowness of the ledge, and looked straight ahead. In the movies, whenever anyone had to do any serious climbing in a high place, the advice was to not look down -- and he was completely willing to follow that advice now that he found himself climbing in a high place.

He moved slowly on the precipice, inching along, kind of shuffling on his hands and knees, eyes straight ahead, hoping the ledge was solid and that no piece would break away in his hand as would surely happen if this was the movies. Finally, though, his hand felt the end of the ledge, where it turned the corner of the building, and he peeked his head out and around the corner, and there he saw Sid, kneeling just up above him, on the edge of the steeple roof.

"Look, there's two of them up there!" Gawd heard a voice cry out from the ground below, and it took him a moment to realize that he was the second presence on the roof.

The voice from below caused Sid to break from his statuesque pose on the edge of the roof, as he seemed to want to know who had joined him.

"What are you doing up here?" he asked, when he saw Gawd peering nervously around the corner of the building.

"I could ask you the same thing," Gawd answered, craning his neck to see his friend, but also trying to remain as still as he possibly could.

"I'm getting closer to God," Sid answered.

"I can see that," Gawd answered.

"I'm trying to find Him," Sid said. "I thought the higher I could be the better. This seemed like a good place."

"It's kinda dangerous," Gawd commented. "Aren't you scared?"

"It's funny," Sid answered, "but I'm not. I feel calm."

"Is it working?" Gawd asked.

"What?" Sid asked back.

"Do you feel closer to God?" Gawd asked, thinking it was a sensible question under the circumstances.

"I don't feel anything, except sort of calm, like I told you before," Sid answered. "I don't hear anything. I don't see anything. I don't feel anything. Where is He do you think?"

"I'm not sure," Gawd answered.

"Do you believe in him?" his friend asked.

"I'm not sure," Gawd repeated. "I haven't really thought about it much."

"Well, I'm not sure there can be a God," Sid said, "because of all the rotten junk that goes on in the world -- like all the wars and people starving and nobody getting along -- and my mom and dad splitting up -- and me having to move to this nothing town. If there was a God, everything'd be perfect."

There was a pause in the exchange. Gawd regarded his friend. So serious.....so very serious. Sid looked down at the confirmation class, standing there on the lawn, and Gawd chanced a look as well. Their classmates looked tiny and small as they stared skyward.

"I think the minister thinks you're gonna jump," Gawd said. "He'll probably call the cops if you don't come down."

"He's a horse's ass," Sid answered.

"He can't help it," Gawd said.

"I know," Sid answered.

"You're not gonna jump, are you?" Gawd asked.

"I don't think so," Sid answered, "but it might be the best way to find out if all this God stuff is true."

"What if it's not?" Gawd asked.

"Then, I guess there'd be no Heaven," Sid answered. "And I guess it would be the end of me. None of that eternal life stuff. This would be it."

"That would be a bit of a shame," Gawd said.

"Why?" Sid asked.

"I might never get laid," Gawd answered.

Sid looked thoughtful, as he knelt on the edge of the roof. "I think Beth Thomas is your best bet. She's after your body," he said.

"I seriously doubt that," Gawd answered.

"Well, I'm telling you, I wouldn't kick her out of bed for fartin'," Sid remarked.

"Me neither," Gawd agreed.

And the situation seemed to be diffused. And even though it took the town fire truck to get the boys off the church roof, everyone seemed to agree that it was nothing more than a boyish prank, so there were no serious ramifications for the pranksters. Sid and Gawd were confirmed about a month later, and it was a joyous occasion for at least some of those involved. Sid may not have found God that day on the roof, but, in a manner of speaking, Gawd found Sid. He found more than the wise-cracking, smart-mouthed, puberty-ridden juvenile he'd accepted as his friend. He saw a troubled edge to his friend, and wondered where that would lead.

But it was almost the summer before high school. And there was that thing about Gawd's virginity...........

First Love

Gawd was not overly anxious to lose his virginity. He found girls to be a mysterious unknown quantity, and even though he was constantly in their company in school, church and most other places, he felt strangely uneasy in certain circumstances. Sid pushed and pushed the issue as the summer wore on, so that Gawd found himself dreading being in his company when an available female came in range. It wasn't that there wasn't interest, because Gawd's hormones were at work, and he was exhibiting the usual signs of pubescence, even soiling Aunt Rose's sheets on occasion, much to his eternal embarrassment. But the awkwardness he felt when he came in close proximity to most young women of his age prevented him from making even a first move. And Sid chided him for his apparent shyness.

Sid never settled into a continuous relationship himself, but was occasionally in the company of various members of the opposite sex, although he never really talked about it much, and Gawd didn't push it, because that would bring up his own very obvious chastity. But Gawd guessed that Sid was dashing well past first base on most occasions -- it was his smug smile in rare moments when the topic was broached.

Finally, it was back to school time, and the boys entered into the annals of higher learning -- high school -- where they soon discovered that they existed on the bottom rung of the academic ladder. Much to Gawd's consternation, entrance into high school was accompanied by an Initiation Day, where the lowly Grade Niners, like he and Sid, were required to dress in silly costumes and be humiliated by the senior students regularly for a complete day. Gawd was not a centre-of-attention person at the best of times, and the prospect of dressing in a diaper and baby bonnet, even if it was all in good fun, did not impress him in the least. Sid was already dreaming up acts of revenge he'd carry out against any senior who dared inflict even the slightest humiliation on him, but Gawd was terrified.

Gawd wore shorts and his coat over his silly baby costume, as he made his way over to Sid's on the morning of the incredibly embarrassing day. This was not going to be great. The boys looked as if they'd been sentenced to eternal damnation as they trudged, heads hung low, toward the school, where they knew the seniors would block every conceivable entrance to the place, thus necessitating the first humility.

It had soon ended -- the dead horse routine with about five others who shared their fate, and they dodged and deked their way toward their lockers, trying to avoid any contact with their tormentors. It was a scarey and frightening trip through the halls of the building, one time managing to elude capture, but the next, caught, and reduced to ridicule.

It was one of the few times Gawd was glad for the beginning of math class, and even though he felt ridiculous sitting there doing problems in a diaper, he hoped the class would somehow last for the rest of the day. It ended, and he headed for wood shop -- another fine pursuit for someone dressed as he was, but you couldn't argue with your timetable -- which was also not among his favourite classes, except that it too had risen in favour on this day.

Finally, though, it was lunch -- open season. It had rained during the morning. This was a potentially bad combination of events, as Gawd soon found out. He had almost made it off the school property unscathed, having discovered an emergency exit out through the janitor's room, but was caught by one of the dreaded seniors out for a noonhour walk with his girl, just as he was about to bolt to freedom.

"You there," the senior called toward him.

He was tempted to make a break for it -- he was that close to safety -- but the thought of an appearance at the school's Kangeroo Court and that ultimate humiliation forced him back. "Yes, sir," he answered, coming stiffly to a type of attention.

"Thought you could sneak out, eh?" the senior accused.

"No, sir," Gawd answered.

"Where do you think you're going, then?" the senior asked.

"Home for lunch," Gawd answered.

"We'll see about that," the senior said. He turned to the girl by his side. "And what price should he pay to go for lunch?" he asked her. "You decide."

Gawd was petrified by the situation, but his attention followed the senior's and he soon found himself looking at the girl. In fact, he found himself staring at the girl, but only for a moment before she caught him, and he looked quickly away and felt himself flush. She was fresh and wholesome and beautiful looking. He couldn't resist trying for another glimpse, but she was watching him, so their eyes met, and he felt his heart jump with a rush of excitement. God, why am I dressed like this? he thought.

"Let him go for lunch, Gerald," the girl said, returning her attention to her apparent boyfriend.

"Why should I?" Gerald asked smugly and self-importantly. "I think we should have some fun with him."

Gawd stood quietly, mired in embarrassment and feeling vulnerable and stupid and pitiful.

"Let him go, Gerald," the girl said, and there was pleading in her voice.

"Oh, alright," the senior said, with a tone of resignation. "If it'll make you happy."

Gawd needed no second chance, and was on his way down the street toward home, but not before chancing another look at his saviour, who again caught him, and offered him a soft, warm smile for the thanks in his eyes.

The afternoon went better. It seemed most of the seniors had tired of humiliating the Grade Nines, and even though there was a parade downtown that proved a dangerous endeavour, Gawd felt more relaxed -- despite the fact his diaper had by this time drooped so he was in constant peril of losing it. And, finally, he and Sid were sitting at the assembly where the Kangeroo Court was being held, and Sid said he was laying low, sure he'd be taken to task for some disrespect he'd shown a couple of upper classmen earlier in the day. But such was not the case, and Gawd suspected that Sid may have exaggerated his indiscretion. Soon, it was over. And they were off home. To change.

And get ready for the dance. Because there was a "Welcome To School" dance that night, where the junior students were supposed to be treated exceedingly well, as if to somehow make amends for the day's humiliation. And Gawd and Sid were surely looking forward to their first high school dance.

It was a strange experience at the dance. Gawd supposed that when you were at a dance, you were supposed to dance -- but he had no intention of dancing, yet hadn't considered what he could do if he didn't dance. He ended up sitting on the end of the bleachers, watching the other people dance, including Sid who had quickly ended up sitting at a tableful of girls, and was working his way through them on the dance floor. He'd sat with Sid and the girls when he'd first arrived, but knew he didn't want to dance, and felt all kinds of pressure to do so with all the available females at the table, so after he excused himself, ostensibly to relieve himself, he didn't return to the table, choosing instead to sit alone on the end of the bleachers, and watch the dancers. He'd been sitting in solitude for some time.

"All by yourself," a girl's voice said from behind him.

He turned, and saw the girl from earlier in the day -- the one who'd saved him from at least one humiliation in a day filled with humiliations. He felt himself tense up at the sight of her.

"Seems a shame," she said, "at your first high school dance."

"I don't know too many people yet," Gawd said, surprising himself by even talking to her.

"That'll probably change," she said.

Gawd said nothing, but smiled awkwardly.

"I should go," the girl said. "Gerald will miss me." She started away, then turned back. "Nice to see you without your diaper," she said, smiling warmly at him for the second time that day.

Gawd melted when she smiled. He couldn't explain the way he felt when he was near her. Excitement. Nervousness. Anticipation. Deep inside him he felt the stirrings of a young heart, and he could not stop it from awakening within him. He felt warm and glowy that she had even noticed him. He guessed she was a senior, because of her association with Gerald, who was obviously a senior. Why she would even notice he was alive was something he could not fathom, as he sat on the end of the bleachers. He was a nothing in life.

He watched for her over the rest of the night, and occasionally saw her dancing with Gerald, and he found himself wishing that he could be Gerald, even just for a couple of minutes, so he'd no longer be a junior, and she could see him as her equal -- just so she could get to know him. He could almost see himself dancing with her, holding her close, feeling her against him. He found the thought of it troubling, knowing that it could never be, but he could not help but think it, try as he might. She was his goddess -- his Venus -- and he felt an attraction to her that he had not felt for any other. Even when he saw her on the dance floor, it was like she danced alone, and he saw no other, excepting himself, perhaps as Apollo.

He drifted back to the table where Sid's harem was down to two; the good looking one he was hoping to make out with, and her not-entirely-unattractive, but plain, best friend, who had become Gawd's date for the night sort of by default. Gawd sat beside the girl for the rest of the night, feeling awkward and uncomfortable at not asking her to dance, until he finally did for the last couple of slow songs of the night, mainly because he felt it was kind of his duty. She felt stiff and wooden against him, and it was obvious the girl felt as awkward and uncomfortable as he had earlier, and he guessed he should have left well enough alone, and they should have sat it out.

Just as they were leaving the "Welcome to High School" dance, as a foursome, there was a bit of a ruckus outside the door to the school. Gawd heard some scuffling, and craned his neck to get a better look.

He saw two older guys pushing and shoving each other, and didn't realize at first that one of them was Gerald. Then, he could see her standing just to the side of the altercation, looking distressed.

"Gerald, it was nothing," he could hear the girl say.

"Nobody messes with my girl," Gerald was saying angrily, and he was punctuating his words by shoving at the other guy.

"It was nothing, Gerald," the girl implored. "Let's go," she said.

Gerald hesitated in his advance on the other guy, turning toward the girl. "Keep out of it," he said, his voice mean and low. Then, he turned back to his apparent foe.

"I didn't mean anything," the other guy said loudly, as if to show he wasn't afraid.

"Apologize to my girl," Gerald commanded.

"I'm sorry," the other guy barked. "I didn't mean nothing."

The two antagonists stood facing each other, and Gawd thought of National Geographic shows he'd seen on TV where big mountain goats stood just like this, then charged toward each other and crashed their heads together in one almighty blow.

"What started it?" Gawd heard Sid whisper to another kid who was closer to the action.

"The one guy's been drinkin', and he thought the other guy was trying to pick up his girl," the other kid whispered back. "It really wasn't much that I could see."

"Gerald, please," Gawd could hear the girl imploring her brutish boyfriend.

The whole crowd leaving the dance stood stalk still and in total silence -- just for a moment.

"Get lost asshole," Gerald suddenly roared. "Don't pull that shit again or I'll cream ya," he bellowed.

Gawd could see the other guy relax his at-the-ready stance just a bit. Gerald looked a little unsteady on his feet, sort of weaving back and forth on the spot he occupied. People in the crowd started to move about and talk, albeit in hushed tones, apparently sensing that the worst was over. Gawd searched the crowd for the girl, and found her, standing off by herself, looking more than miserable. He wanted to rush to her, just to tell her that it was alright, and that he would keep her from harm. But that would be stupid. Gerald would crush him like a small insignificant bug.

And it was over, and they were walking the girls home, through the darkened backstreets where Sid was hoping to cop a feel, and Gawd was afraid he might. Finally, they reached the one girl's house, and Sid and his companion nearly inhaled one other for a couple of minutes, while Gawd and his companion stood awkwardly by, trying not to look at either their friends or each other.

Later that night, as Gawd lay alone in his bed, his thoughts were of her, the woman who had captured his heart -- and she surely must be a woman, and not one of the girls he was accustomed to. Every time he closed his eyes, he saw her there, and he felt a closeness to her. When he slept, he dreamed of her, but not as he had with other girls he found attractive, because she came as an arc of light into the black world of his night, and he felt he could not dare to touch her, or even look upon her for fear of being blinded, so brilliant did she seem.

He awoke early, and felt unrested. He climbed into his jeans, pulled on his jacket, and departed, while Aunt Rose, and most of the rest of the town, still slept. He walked straight out of town, along the County Line, until he hit the Cemetery Road, then he veered off in that direction. He found the railway tracks, just past the river, at the bottom of the cemetery hill. It was an early autumn morning, despite the fact the calendar said it was still summer. Once you got past Labour Day, it was fall -- no matter what the calendar said. Mist was rising off the river, as the first rays of early morning sun collided with the coolness of the water's surface. It was still........peaceful........idyllic.

He walked to a place he'd discovered with the old man, when he'd been alive. Sometimes when he and the old man had had enough of Aunt Rose and everybody else trying to fuss over them, they'd come here. They'd bring their fishing poles, but rarely cast a line, and would usually end up esconced in a conversation that was deep and varied and dealt with life and other such worrisome things. He sat on the riverbank, in the company of the trees and ferns and perhaps the odd fish.

And he sat in this fashion for some time. He thought about his dead mother. He thought of the old man. But mostly he thought about the girl. Knowing he could not have her -- that she was beyond his reach -- despite what he felt. He pondered his dilemma deep into the day, until he was finally concerned that Aunt Rose might wonder about him, and so headed back in the direction of town.

And that day passed, as did the next and the next, and soon the school year was in full motion. He saw her about the school, her name was Julia, usually with Gerald, and she would smile warmly at him, and he would smile shyly back, hoping Gerald didn't notice. But there was nothing he could do, even though he felt excitement just to be near her.

One Friday, Gawd let Sid talk him into coming uptown to the after-school hangout for a cherry coke and a bag of chips. Gawd usually didn't frequent such spots, choosing to keep more to himself than his gregarious friend, but Sid was on the trail of a new babe, and he needed an accomplice to occupy her friend, so he could make his move. Gawd, as usual, made the perfect accomplice, choosing to take part in the crime, but to not take any part of the rewards.

On this day, both Sid and Gawd were lucky, because Sid's prey turned up by herself, so he whisked her away to be alone with, and Gawd was off the hook. He was sitting in the booth, resolved to finish his cherry coke and bag of chips even if he was all by himself. And he nearly was all by himself. There was a football game up at the fairgrounds, and nearly the whole school was there. The crowd would be along after the game. With any luck, he'd be on his way home by then.

He was bored. He took to reading his geography notes, while he munched the chips and sipped the coke.

Then, she was there. He looked up.......and she was there. He quickly looked down at the tabletop.

"Hi," she said. "Mind if I sit down?" She was already sitting.

He shook his head slowly from side to side, indicating it was alright, but could say nothing.

"Not interested in football?" she asked.

He looked cautiously up, and found he felt comfortable with her, that she didn't seem to overwhelm his emotions as he'd been afraid she might. "No," he answered. "It's a little rough. I can't understand doing it or watching it." He surprised himself by answering so forthrightly.

She laughed lightly. "I guess I asked," she said.

"Sorry," he apologized, and he could feel himself flush.

"I'm just kidding," she said, reaching forward and giving his hand a tiny squeeze. "Are you always this serious?" she asked.

He felt embarrassment, and could only shrug his shoulders.

They sat for a moment in silence. He closed up his geography notes.

"Do you like high school?" she asked.

"Yea," he answered, "it's alright. It's 'way better than public school."

"That's what I thought when I first got here too," the girl said. "I hated public school."

"Yea, me too," Gawd said. "They treat you like such a child."

She smiled. "Yea, I know what you mean."

They talked for a while about where they lived in town, and she told him that she'd been a lifeguard at the beach over the summer, and he believed her because she looked like a lifeguard from the beach, even though he thought it might be wrong to think of her in nothing but a bathing suit. And he continued to feel comfortable with her, and to wonder that he would engage her in a conversation filled with the ordinary, when she was so obviously extraordinary.

He wanted to ask her why she bothered with him, when he was so obviously ordinary -- and especially when he didn't like football -- and he knew that Gerald was one of the dread footballers. "You're not at the football game," he remarked.

"No," she answered, and it was a short, abrupt no, and she made no effort to follow it up with an explanation, so he dropped it.

It was then that the first of those who had been to the game began coming through the door. A couple of early arrivals indicated that the home team had won, and there'd be joy in Mudville on this night.

"Want to go for a walk?" the girl asked, as she looked with apparent disapproval at the revellers. "Let's get out of here."

He went. He wanted to ask why, but said nothing, gathered up his school books, and followed her out the door, pushing past some high school seniors coming from the game. "Hey, Jules," one of them called out to her, "you missed a great game!"

But she pushed past, seeming to pay them no attention, and he followed in her wake, aware that all were watching, and seeing the two of them leaving, apparently together. "What's with her?" Gawd heard someone ask.

They had soon cleared the main street, and were on one of the town's maple-arched backstreets. "Would you mind if we went to the park," she asked, as they walked along, side by side.

"No," he answered, knowing he would have followed her to the ends of the earth and back if she'd have asked.

But they set out for the park.

It was a warm fall night, and the leaves were falling from the trees, and rustling underfoot as they walked. Gawd's heart was beating frantically in his chest, that he should find himself walking in this place with this girl, who might even be called a woman. He thought he could feel energy reaching between them, surrounding them like an envelope of warm, soft gas that intermingled about them, swirling and touching over them. He could almost see its bluish-white glow as he walked.

"It's a beautiful night," she said. "Don't you love this time of year?"

He didn't answer, but was awash in the moment.

"You're quiet," she remarked. "You like to watch things."

He smiled at her, but remained silent.

They walked in quiet, but for the leaves. They reached the park. It was suppertime. Aunt Rose would wonder what'd happened to him. But he couldn't have excused himself to go call -- it would have seemed childish, and that was not how he wanted to seem.

As they walked through the entrance to the park, she quickened her pace and made for the swings and slides. She sat on the middle swing, and started to move slowly back and forth, her arms wrapped around the chains that held the swing in place, looking so fresh and alive, her cheeks with a touch of blush from the walk, the sun's final rays pouring over the treetops and glistening off her hair, capturing her vivacity. A picture, he thought, as he found himself a seat on the end of one of the teeter totters.

"Man, I can't wait for this year to end," she said. "I'll be finished with this town. I'll be getting out. Going to school in the city."

"That's what you want?" he asked, breaking his silence.

"More than anything," she answered. "I find this town so predicatable. Everybody does exactly what's expected of them. I can't stand that. You've got to take chances and get out there and do something with yourself." She paused. "Don't you find it awfully boring around here?"

"I guess," he answered.

"Well, I do," she said. "And I want to see things, and do things when this year is over. I might even go overseas."

"Really," he said.

They sat for a moment in quiet, she swinging silently back and forth, while he watched her.

Then, she suddenly stopped, digging her feet into the sand under the swing. He could see a dark cloud come over her, smothering her once luminous spirit with blackness -- covering what had once been such bright light. He could see a tear come to her eye -- her hand reaching up to brush it away.

"What's wrong?" he asked, getting up from his seat and walking to her. He crouched in front of her, looking up into the sadness of her face.

"I'm pregnant," she sobbed.

His heart sank. Such was the news that he could think of nothing to say. He put his hand on her shoulder in an effort to comfort her.

"I don't know what to do," she said, misery in her voice.

"Can't you get married?" he asked innocently.

"I don't know if I can -- or even if I want to," she said. "I haven't told anybody else. You're the first person I've told."

"Gerald?" Gawd asked.

She nodded.

"He'll marry you," Gawd said. "You can get married."

"Oh, yea, he'll marry me," she answered. "After school, he's going to be assistant produce manager at Bolander's Grocery. That sounds like a pretty exciting life, eh."

"It could be worse," he answered, and he knew it could be. "He seems like a pretty good guy," Gawd lied.

"He's a neanderthal," she said. "I was just having some fun with him. All the other girls, all those cheerleader types, wanted him so bad, that I thought I'd cheat them all out of marrying the captain of the football team. I guess the last laugh's on me. It was just supposed to be a diversion -- now it looks like my life."

"What about your parents? Maybe they'll help, and you won't have to get married," he suggested.

"My parents are going to flip when they get this news," she said. "They'll have me to the alter faster than you can say bastard."

He was again at a loss for words, so remained quiet. He could see the tragedy in her life. He thought of her with Gerald, and was disgusted by it. He wanted to gather her up in his arms, and take her away from her life -- give her a new one where it was like a faerie tale with white knights and happy endings. But he was only a Grade Niner, who lived with his Aunt Rose. He could offer her nothing. He had nothing. He was nothing.

"Look," she said, "I'm sorry to pull you into this." She got up from the swing, and took a step back, wiping her face with her hand, trying to compose herself. "I don't know what got into me. I couldn't go to any of my friends. I feel so humiliated........dirty," she said. "My girlfriends and I have names for girls who end up pregnant in high school. Now I'm one."

"Don't be so hard on yourself," he said. "It was a mistake."

"A pretty big one," she answered.

There was a pause. They stood silently, awkward tension between them for the first time. Night was coming, the light fading, shadows lengthening toward forever

"Anyway, it was wrong for me to involve you," she said, looking over at him.

"I'm honoured," he answered, "I wish there was something more I could do. You need somebody to help, and I can't really do much -- other than listen and I don't mind doing that, if you need somebody to talk to. I can listen, and I'm sort of a loner, so you don't have to worry about me talking to anybody."

"I know you're sort of a loner," she said, smiling again, looking more relaxed. "That's why I picked you. That and you look wise beyond your years," she joked.

He smiled. "I'll help you if there's anything I can do," he said. "Just let me know."

It was nearly dark.

"I should go," she said. "My mom and dad will wonder what's become of me."

"Me too," Gawd said.

"Which way you going?" she asked.

He pointed in the direction of Aunt Rose's.

"We can walk together," she said, and they set out for the park entrance.

Nothing happened over the weekend or during the first few days of school the following week. When they passed in the hallway, they exchanged polite hellos, but nothing more -- except perhaps knowing looks. He continued to feel strongly for her, so that when they did pass in a school hallway, he still felt his heart race and a warm flush came over him. He wanted to be with her always, and he found it difficult not to rush up to her, to know how she was feeling and how things were going.

Finally, it was a week later, Friday night. He was home reading. Sid had a date. He heard the phone ring. Aunt Rose was out playing bingo, so he put down his book and went to answer it.

"Hello," he said, as he put the receiver to his mouth.

"Hi," he heard her voice.

There was pause.

"How are you?" he asked.

"I'm fine," she answered.

Another pause.

"Can you meet me?" she asked.

"Sure," he answered. "Where?"

"At the swings in the park in about twenty minutes?" she asked.

"Alright," he answered.

"See you then," she said, and there was a click to indicate she'd hung up.

He returned the receiver to its cradle. He wondered what was up. The conversation had seemed somehow clipped and urgent, although nothing had been said to suggest emergency. But he went to grab his jacket to head to the park. It wouldn't do to be late.

She was already there when he arrived at the swings.

"Hi," she said, as he approached.

He returned the greeting. "What's up?" he asked.

"I'm getting rid of the baby," she said matter-of-factly.

"What do you mean?" he asked.

"I'm having an abortion," she replied, without looking at him.

"An abortion?" he asked.

"Yea, somehow they take the baby out of you and you're not pregnant anymore," she said. "I'm going to the city to have it done," she said.

"Where? In the hospital?" he asked.

"No," she answered. "In a private clinic. Gerald knew about it. He arranged it. He's paying for it."

"He's taking you?" Gawd asked.

"No," she answered. "He thinks it wouldn't look good if we were both away from school at the same time. I've got to go by myself. On the bus."

"It's a long way to the city to go by yourself," he said.

"I can't ask anybody," she said. "Nobody knows, except you and I and Gerald. I don't want anybody else to know, or it'll be all over the school."

There was a pause.

"I could go with you," he offered. "Nobody'd suspect if you and I were away at the same time."

"I couldn't ask you to do that," she said. "How would you explain it to your Aunt?"

"Leave that to me," he said. "It's settled. When do we go?"

"Tuesday, on the eight o'clock morning bus," she answered. "I was hoping you'd go," she said, reaching over and taking his hand, holding it tightly for a moment.

He smiled.

They talked for a few moments longer, but there seemed little to say now that plans had been laid. They parted, and Gawd went to lay his own plans for the trip. He would get Sid to help him out with an excuse for Aunt Rose. There was no need to tell him why his help was needed, but Gawd was sure he'd help cook up something.

So, on Tuesday morning, about a quarter to eight, he met her at the bus station. It was gray and rainy and Gawd thought she looked small and afraid standing under the overhang, trying to keep dry.

"You alright?" he asked, as he joined her in seeking shelter from the rain.

"Good morning to you too," she said.

"Morning," he returned.

"I'm fine," she said. "In fact, I'm great, and I'll be glad when this is over. I almost called you last night to tell you not to bother coming this morning." She talked the talk, but he wondered just the same.

They stood for a moment in quiet. It was a damp, cold morning -- the kind that comes often between summer and winter -- the kind that washes life from the world in the fall of the year and leaves it a sodden, dead morasse to be covered with winter's refreshing apparel, to be born again anew in the spring. It was somehow fitting to do this thing surrounded by that death on this morning. We wouldn't be making this trip in spring, Gawd thought.

"My appointment's not 'til three" she said, after they had taken up their positions on the bus. "We have a couple of hours after we get there to get something to eat, and find the place. We should be able to catch the seven o'clock bus and be home by midnight."

"Is it a serious operation?" he asked.

"Gerald's friend, the one who knew about the clinic, said it's a pretty quick thing," she answered. "His girlfriend had to have one, and he said they went dancing the same night, so it can't be too serious."

"I guess not," Gawd agreed. "Still......"

But they rode most of the long bus trip in silence. It was an awkward, tense type of silence. He could feel her anxiety, the tension in her, coming from the seat beside him. He took her hand, holding it tightly, he looked over toward her, and she returned the look, so their eyes met, and Gawd knew her in that moment. He tried to pour himself into her, to let her know how he felt about her, and he thought that maybe she did know.

"Thanks for coming. It means a lot to me," she said at one point.

He smiled over at her.

At lunch, she talked animatedly about her plans for the future, once the baby problem was solved, and he did what he'd said he'd do -- he listened to her hopes and dreams, even though he could have no part in them. He cursed himself. Such a fool, he thought. For today, I have a place in her life, but tomorrow I may be just a memory.

After lunch, they started to search out the clinic. She told him they weren't supposed to tell anyone they were going to a clinic -- they were supposed to say they were going to visit her cousin on the Southside for the afternoon, and possibly for dinner. Gawd knew they weren't going to a clinic.

He remembered some of the city. He'd lived here with his mother. That seemed like a lifetime ago, and he'd been just a kid. But he knew the Southside. It was where the down-and-outs like he and his mother had lived. What would a clinic be doing there? he wondered. But he said nothing.

But when the cab pulled up in front of a rundown tenement, his fears were confirmed.

"You can't do this," he said. "This is no clinic."

"It's the only way," she answered. She was stone-faced, ashen.

"Why?" he asked, desparation in his voice.

"They wouldn't let me have this done in a hospital," she said.

"This is dangerous," he said. "You should have told me. You knew."

"I needed you to come -- you wouldn't have," she said.

"You can't go through with this," he pleaded.

"I have to," she said. "It'll be all right. He's a medical student. That's what Gerald's friend said. We can go dancing tonight. You'll see." She reached over and took his hand, holding it firmly. She looked into him. "Help me," she said softly.

They paid the cabbie, and were left standing outside the dirty, frame building. They approached the front door, and knocked.

"You're here to see your cousin. You're early," said the shaggy, little Englishman who answered the door. "You can come in," he said to Julia. "You," he said, pointing to Gawd, "can wait at the restaurant on the corner, until the visit is over. It'll be about an hour. Come back, then. Your lady friend will be waiting for you fresh as a daisy."

He paused, and gave Gawd another lookover. "My, but you do look young to be involved in this sort of thing. Kids these days," he said with a sigh.

"I'm her brother, pervert," Gawd said, with a trace of anger in his voice.

"Sure you are," the Englishman said.

Gawd turned to Julia. "You're sure you want to do this?" he asked.

"Effective birth control at an affordable price," the Englishman chortled.

Gawd shot him an angry glance.

"It'll be fine," Julia said, starting into the house with the man. Then, she turned back to Gawd, leaned over and kissed him. "Thanks," she said.

And she disappeared into the house, and the door slammed shut, leaving him standing on the step alone.

He walked to the restaurant. Ordered a cherry coke, and settled in to wait the hour.

It passed slowly. He wondered at one point if the clock over the restaurant's cash register was working at all, but knew it was.

Finally, though, he had waited the hour, and he paid his bill, left the place, and walked the short distance back to the tenement. He approached the door and knocked.

"Well, well," said the Englishman, as he opened the door. "My young friend."

"Where's my sister?" Gawd asked, continuing the ruse he had begun earlier.

"She's just straightening her things. Making herself presentable for you, I should think," answered the Englishman.

Just at that moment, Julia came out one of the doors leading to the hallway where Gawd was standing.

"Hi," she said, when she saw him.

"You okay?" he asked, looking closely at her for some sign that she was not. She seemed pale, but she smiled at him.

"Ready to go dancing," she answered brightly.

But she had some difficulty walking to the restaurant to call a cab. They had to stop, and when he took her hand to steady her, it was ice cold.

In the restaurant, he guided her to a table where she ordered an orange juice, while he phoned for the cab.

"You sure you're alright?" he asked when he got back from making the call.

"Yea, I'm fine," she said. "I feel a little queasy, but the doctor said I could expect that. He told me to drink orange juice, because I've lost some blood. I'm sure I'll be fine." But she sounded tired. Not very convincing.

"I think we should go see a real doctor," he said.

"I'll be fine," she said.

"I hope so," he said.

She died later that night on the bus, in his arms. She just kept getting colder and colder, and he could do nothing to warm her. "I love you," he finally said to her. But she had already gone. And he was alone. He wept.

True Love

Gawd mourned the loss of Julia for some time, and indeed always carried a memory of her with him, remembering her goodness and kindness and wholesome beauty, and he regretted that he hadn't had the chance to know her better. There were some legal ramifications for him to face as a result of the girl's death, and the fact he had accompanied her to the site of an illegal abortion. He pointed police to the "clinic" but the "doctor" had long since cleared out, knowing the law would be coming. There was some talk of charging Gawd with one thing or another, but Aunt Rose surprised him and came to his rescue, explaining that he'd had a rather rough start in life and just kept getting into difficult situations through no honest-to-goodness fault of his own. She promised to keep the boy in church and on the straight and narrow if they just gave him another chance. It was the first time Gawd realized that Aunt Rose might not be the old battleaxe everyone in town, including him, thought her to be.

It was also about this time that Sid, who thought the whole affair with Julia was just about the neatest, keenest thing in the world, moved away. Even though people'll tell you there's a slim chance of reconciliation after a divorce is final, that's what happened with Sid's parents. Sid's mom kept the light aburning, always sure that her wayward husband would tire of the great sex and again want something more substantial, at least that's the way Sid put it -- and she was right. Sid said she really made him crawl. He had to sleep on the couch and live like a monk for the longest time. No sex for him. That's what Sid said.

But no matter what the circumstances of Sid's father's sex life, Sid and his mom moved back to the city, leaving Gawd behind. It was sort of anti-climactic when he moved, because Sid had really taken to the girls when they'd come into high school, and was constantly manouvering for position on a new conquest, so he hadn't been around much anyway. Gawd continued to feel awkward around girls, and hadn't had strong feelings like he'd had for Julia before or since that experience, so that he went through the next couple of years of high school pretty much on his own. He played a bit of basketball one year, and joined the chess club the year after, and it wasn't exactly that he purposefully avoided people, and he associated with people who might possibly be called friends, but he was close to no one. He read a lot. Just about anything he could get his hands on. He had a part time job at a food market. He played gin rummy with Aunt Rose. And he watched a bit of hockey and baseball on TV.

One day, though, early in Grade 12, his life changed. He'd decided to get involved with the school newspaper, having an interest in writing, and was attending the first meeting of the paper's staff at the beginning of the new school year. He was sitting in one of the desks in Room 115, when someone asked if they could sit beside him. It was a girl's voice. And when he looked to see who the speaker was, his life changed forever.

"Hi, mind if I sit here?" she said brightly, as she sat down in the desk next to him.

"No," he answered, wondering if she would have left if he'd said he did, but also being struck by the girl's appearance, thinking how good she looked, and wondering why he hadn't seen her around the school before.

"I'm Janet," she said, extending her hand.

He introduced himself. "Just move to town?" he tried to ask, but the meeting was getting started, and all he got for an answer was a headshake that answered no.

He found the meeting interesting. The editor explained to them that this was a big year for the paper, there were some big issues facing the school population, and it would be up to them to see that the student body was kept well informed about those issues. He would be counting on them to search out the truth -- to look in every locker -- to leave no question unasked in that search.

After the fervent speech, there were story assignments handed out. Gawd got the librarian, who was celebrating his twenty-fifth anniversary in that esteemed position. He shrugged his shoulders. He'd not been into the library since the start of school, and that was unusual. You usually got sent there for one school assignment or another. This would give him a good excuse to drop by the place just to make sure he could still find out everything he ever wanted to know about the Magna Carta, or some other boring piece of stuff. He usually didn't find very interesting stuff in the school library, and had wondered why they didn't carry any of the popular new books. Maybe he'd have a chance to find out.

"Did you get a good story?" the girl beside him asked after the formal part of the meeting had ended.

"Yea, it's okay, I guess," he answered, turning to face his questioner. He was again struck by her, having feelings that had not stirred for some time just to be so close to her. He felt himself flush. Felt embarrassed, but didn't know why.

"I got the new director of education," she said.

"Really," he answered. "That sounds like a good story."

"I don't even know what he does," she said. "All I want to do is get some poetry published in the paper -- that's why I joined the staff."

"You write poetry?" he asked.

"I try," she replied.

"Me too," he replied. And it was true, because he had written a few pieces of poetry over the past couple of years.

"Really," she said. "I'd like to read some sometime."

"I'm not sure it's very good," he answered, and was sure he spoke the truth. "But maybe if you let me read some of yours, I'll let you have a look at mine."

"Sounds good," she said.

While they'd been talking, most of the rest of the room had cleared out, but Gawd was glad they'd lingered because he was enjoying being in her company and was pleased they had discovered common ground so soon after meeting.

The girl looked around, expressed surprise. "I guess we should go," she said.

"Yea, I guess," Gawd said with a bit of a sigh.

"So, you're new here?" he asked, as they walked toward the door.

"Not really," she answered. "I wasn't here last year because I was an exchange student in Germany."

"I've heard of you," he said. "They used to read parts of your letters over the P.A. last year. It sounded like you had a pretty good time."

"It was a good time," she said. "It was a strange time, because I made such close friendships over there that I didn't want to leave, but I couldn't wait to get back here to see my family either."

"You got a German boyfriend I suppose," Gawd said, with a trace of sarcasm in his voice. They were standing in the nearly-deserted hallway outside the room.

"I think not," she answered, with a trace of indignation in her voice.

There was a pause in the exchange, but neither moved, as if both wanted to remain together, and were trying to think of a new piece of conversation that might accomplish that purpose.

Then, they both started at once, interrupting each other, and sputtering into silence and another pause. Then, they both laughed.

"How about a cherry coke?" he asked, smiling.

"Sure," she said. "Down at Paul's?"

"Yea," he answered.

And he went to the after-school hangout; something he didn't usually do. And he went with a girl; something else he usually didn't do. And it was funny. He felt comfortable with this girl -- as he had with his

Julia -- and it was as if she was pure and noble as that other had been, so that he found himself in a constant state of excited anticipation while he was in her company, but it felt so good, he wanted it always.

And as soon as they had parted for that day, she to her home, he to his, he almost immediately wanted to be with her again, to have her close to him so he would feel that excitement.

"How could I have missed you in the earlier grades?" he asked her at one point.

"I've changed a bit," she answered.

And he searched out her picture in the year book, and imagined that she had changed, and in two short years had gone from being girl to woman. And how could that be? He asked other acquaintances if they'd known her and all said they remembered her from those earlier days, although she'd gone to the separate school, so they hadn't known her at that level. Had he been blind not to have seen her?

He went to see the librarian in the morning, before school started -- despite the fact he had wanted to search out Janet. He thought he should get the interview over with, write the story and get it handed in to the editor, so that maybe he'd get another story and it might be more interesting than the stuffy old librarian. They could meet after school, said the librarian. Great, thought Gawd, another missed opportunity. So, he likely wouldn't see her on this day.

He didn't see her in the halls over the course of the day, and he reported to the library right after school, so supposed he had lost his chance. Still, he tried to get enthusiastic about the interview. After all, this guy, Mr. Smedges, was about to get his moment in the spotlight after toiling among stacks of dusty, mostly uninteresting books for what seemed an eternity.

He asked the usual questions -- Did he remember his first day on the job? What did he like about being a librarian? What was his favourite book? -- those kinds of things. And he got the usual answers.

"What about some of the more modern books, Mr. Smedges?" he asked rather innocently.

"We think most of the modern books are unsuitable for young minds," Mr. Smedges answered, a formal tone to his voice.

"Really," Gawd commented, as he scribbled down the reply. "And how are books selected for the library?" he asked.

"Most books are requested by the teachers for courses," Mr. Smedges answered.

"So, if they're requested by a teacher you order them?" Gawd asked.

"No, they have to go to the selection committee of the board," Mr. Smedges answered. "If they're cleared at that level, and we have the money in the budget.......and I approve of the book's content......then we order it."

Gawd thought for a moment.

"Do the students have any input into getting books?" he asked.

"No, not really," Mr. Smedges answered. "I'm not sure most young people would know what they should be reading."

"Really," Gawd commented, finding this an interesting bit of information.

There was a pause in the exchange, as Gawd seemed unsure what to ask, and the librarian sat stiffly erect in his oaken office chair.

"Well," Gawd said, breaking into the silence in the office cautiously, "I guess I should be going. I've got to help my aunt fix supper." He got up from his chair, and gathered up his notes, backing toward the door. "Thanks," he said, as he turned, opened the door, and exited into the main part of the library.

He hadn't walked far when he saw Janet, sitting at one of the study tables, a pile of books to one side of her. He veered straight toward her, with never a second thought.

"Hi," he whispered, sitting heavily in the chair beside her.

She looked up, somewhat startled. "Oh, hi," she whispered back, smiling. "I thought I was pretty well the last person left in the school."

"Naw, I was here interviewing Smedges," he answered.

"How did it go?" she asked.

"I never realized what a horse's ass that man is," Gawd answered. "You wouldn't believe some of the stuff he told me."

"Really," she said, her eyebrows arched.

"Quiet," intoned a harsh, loud whisper from across the room.

They sat quietly for a moment -- until the heat was off.

"I shouldn't bother you," Gawd said.

"I was just quitting," she answered. "I can't hack this stuff today. How about a cherry coke?"

He knew he went flush when she asked -- it was the first time in his life he'd been asked such a question by such a person. "Sure," he blurted almost immediately.

"Quiet, please," repeated the voice, more loudly than before.

"Meet you outside," Gawd said under his breath, and he headed for the door.

"Helping your aunt fix supper?" asked Mr. Smedges, just before he cleared the place.

"Just on my way," he lied, as he whisked out of the library.

And soon they were sitting in Paul's, sipping on cherry cokes, and munching a bag of chips.

"He actually said that students shouldn't be able to choose their own books?" she was asking, incredulous.

"Yes," Gawd answered. "He thinks most modern books are trash, and he holds the ultimate power over what's in the library."

"God, that's scary," she said. "I'm not sure how I thought the books in the library were getting there -- I guess I never really thought about it much."

"Haven't you ever noticed what boring junk they have in there?" he asked.

"I guess," she answered. "But what other books are there?"

"That's just the point," he answered, perhaps more vehemently than was necessary. "Most of us will never know." He paused. "I've got to talk to Mr. Love."

"Why?" she asked.

"Because he's head of the English Department," he answered. "I want to see if he ever gets any of the books he wants.........and you've got to do me a favour," he added, a sense of urgency in his voice.

"What?" she asked, with a puzzled look on her face.

"You haven't interviewed the director of education yet, have you?" he asked.

"No," she answered.

"You can ask him a couple of book questions for me," Gawd said. "Get his opinion."

She smiled slyly. "What have you got in mind?" she asked.

"We could have quite a story on our hands," Gawd said.

And they did have quite a story on their hands -- it ended up sparking a student walk-out and creating all sorts of uproar, with students and parents jamming the monthly, usually-deserted board meeting, and hollering obscenities at the new director of education. Life was never the same for Gawd after that. But it wasn't just the story -- it was the girl.

After the experience with the school library story, the two of them spent considerable time together. They shared their poetry and their thoughts with one another, and it was a time of peaceful bliss for Gawd, and one of those special times that had come so rarely to his life. Even Aunt Rose noticed a difference in him, as he was perhaps overly helpful and considerate around the house.

But perhaps not all was perfection. Gawd wondered that there was nothing physical between them, and although he certainly felt desire for her, she had given him no proof that she felt that same desire for him. So while they were always together, they were also always apart, and he wondered that this should be so between a man and woman.

"There is nothing finer than a purely platonic relationship," she said to him one day over cherry cokes. And she wrote about it in her poetry. He wasn't sure he agreed, but he wanted their relationship to be absolutely pure, so hid his wants and desires.

Still, he wanted to reach out to her, to put his arms around her and have her with him, but he would make no move to do so, not knowing for sure what the reaction would be, and fearing it might mean an end to that which they already had. He worried, though, that she might at some point have a change of heart and a need for the physical, but might think he wanted nothing to do with it, that he also felt there was nothing finer than a purely platonic relationship, and so would leave him for the arms of another.

But he resisted until the relationship was several months old. He was sure that was what she wanted. Then, there was a ski trip planned from the school during the winter break. She'd done quite a bit of skiing during her year in Germany and thought the trip might be fun. He had no urge to travel to a ski lodge for a week of drinking and unfettered merriment. It just wasn't his style. It was the first time there was a real crisis in their relationship.

"Why don't you come?" she asked, as they sat in a booth at Paul's.

"I'm just not interested," he answered. "You tell me how going on a ski trip is an educational experience, and what I'd get out of it." He was being sarcastic, but really didn't want to go.

"You might learn not to be so anti social," she answered, and he could tell by her tone of voice that she was partly kidding, but partly serious as well.

"I just don't like that stuff," he said.

"You're too serious all the time," she said. "You need to get away and have some fun."

"And exactly what is the point of fun?" he asked.

She looked angrily away. "You're impossible," she said, without looking at him.

"Look, you go and have a good time," he said. "I'll stock up on some books for the break and I'll be fine." But he didn't feel fine, and wished she was staying here for the break. It would be the first time since they'd sort of become an item that he'd have to go so long without seeing her. He hated the thought of it.

And to make matters worse, a couple of weeks later, he agreed to accompany her to an after-school meeting to discuss the details of the trip. Gawd saw all the other guys who were going on the trip, and thought every one of them looked like a large, erect penis sitting in a desk. He knew it was a stupid thought, but it was a thought nevertheless.

As the trip drew closer, he thought she was avoiding him. She wanted to go to a school dance, even though they'd discussed dances shortly after they'd met, and she'd agreed they were far overblown in their level of importance. He reluctantly agreed to go to the dance with her, but refused to dance once they got there, as was his usual custom when he was forced to attend these affairs. She stayed with him for most of the night, but accepted a couple of invitations to dance, and while she danced, Gawd hung back sullenly in the darkness under the end of the bleachers. When they parted for the evening, after he'd walked her to her door, she seemed angry with him. He wasn't sure why. He didn't see her at all for the rest of that weekend.

He went to see her off at five in the morning when she was leaving on the ski trip. He thought it was the least he could do to try to show her that he'd accepted her decision to go on the trip. They stood so formally, as they said their farewells -- or that was what he thought. He wanted to embrace her, and say a fond farewell to a lover, not a mere friend. But he could not tell her for fear that he might lose her -- or that was what he thought.

But he felt a shaft of pain pierce his heart, as he watched her take up her seat next to one of the guys he knew from school -- only he didn't see much of the guy sitting beside her, only that part of him that was possible cause for worry.

He tried to rationalize as he walked toward home, the sun just a glimmer on the early-morning horizon. There was nothing between them -- they were only good friends -- bosom buddies in a purely platonic relationship. That was what he told himself as he walked toward home. There was no reason to be jealous, because that was obviously the emotion he was feeling. He didn't know what she felt for him, and why should he be jealous when there could probably never be anything between them anyway? That was what he told himself. But it did no good. He felt miserable.

And so the first couple of days of the break passed, and he tried to read, as had been his plan. But he found it difficult and was easily distracted, so that he made little headway, and thought he heard nothing but ski reports on the radio. He thought of her often -- was perhaps obsessed with her, more than he had been when he had been constantly in her company and she had not been on any dumb, old ski trip.

Late in the evening of her third day away, the phone rang. Aunt Rose was out at the bingo, so Gawd hurried to the kitchen to answer it.

"Hello," he said.

"Hi," her voice said.

There was a pause. He felt his heart race. "What's wrong?" he asked, not knowing why he asked that particular question.

"I called to see how you were doing -- how your reading was coming along," she said.

"Oh, I'm doing fine" he said, knowing there must be something else on her mind. "I've read eight books so far. I've put a hold on the R's at the library for the last three days of the week."

She didn't laugh at his joke. There was silence.

"How's it going?" he asked, still wondering why she'd called.

"I'm not sure," she answered. "Who are you talking to?" a man's voice said in the background on her end of the phone. "I've got to go," she said.

"Yea, it sounds like it," he replied, and he had already hit bottom.

"Sorry to bother you," she said.

"Hope you're having a good time," he said, but he surely didn't mean it.

That night was perhaps the longest night of his life, or so it felt as it passed, slowly, agonizingly. He lay in his bed fully awake for much of the night. Why had she called? She'd been with someone else. Why had she called? To see how his reading was going. What should he have said?

What could he have said? And the thought of her with another tore at him throughout the night. How could he be so senseless?

By dawn, he was standing on the edge of the highway that led from the town to some faraway ski hills. It was cold and snowy even here, but he was bundled warm against the winter. It was an eight-hour trip by bus to the ski lodge. He had no idea how long it would take him to hitch-hike there, or even if he could, but he would try because he had to be with her. He could no longer deny his feelings for her. If all she wanted with him was a purely platonic relationship, he could perhaps not be with her, but he must tell her all -- that he loved her and wanted to be with her, and only her, for a lifetime.

And he made it to the ski lodge, and she cried when she saw that he had come for her, and she told him that after the phone call of the night before, she'd sent the other away because she couldn't bear to be with any other but her true love -- and she'd only realized who that was and how she felt after she'd tried to be with someone else. They fell into one another's arms. It was love. And life would never be the same. And Gawd wanted a long and prosperous life for perhaps the first time in his own existence. And he knew happiness.

A Wonderful Guy

And Gawd's life was good. He rose to be editor of the school newspaper, which, for some unascertained reason, was called "Thistlebush". He had Janet. Even Aunt Rose was more than tolerable -- had perhaps grown almost fond of him. And it happened that good fortune continued to smile on him and he landed a job at Bolander's Groceteria on Saturdays as a box boy, so he even had some cash. This was good because he was planning to go to university, and even though Aunt Rose agreed with his plan, he didn't think it was fair for her to have to foot too much of the bill -- something she told him she'd be more than happy to do, if he got good grades and was serious about it . So he'd been squirreling money away almost since the beginning of high school, hoping to pay for as much of it as possible.

Even though they were only in Grade 12, he and Janet had already visited the university campus in the city where they both hoped to go right after they graduated the following year. Gawd had been in awe at the university campus. He had stood in the gigantic library, surrounded by much of society's knowledge, overwhelmed by the simple hugeness of it -- the sheer magnificent sum of it all. And he watched the grey-bearded philosophers -- for that was what they must have been -- as they walked to and fro through the book stacks, pausing every so often to look sage and thoughtful, as philosophers must surely do.

And he and Janet had stopped for lunch in the campus coffee shop, Brewster Hall, and it was the most gloriously, deliciously intellectual sort of place on the planet. It just had an atmosphere about it; that you had to be a smart person just to be part of it. Gawd couldn't help but feel that they were surrounded on all sides by extremely smart people, possibly involved in anti-government plotting as most university students invariably are. He found himself wondering if he could ever hope to achieve so much in his life.

"Isn't this great?" he whispered over to Janet, not wanting anyone else in the place to overhear, lest they be exposed as mere high school students, and embarrassed beyond belief.

But Janet didn't answer. She looked less sure, an uncertain expression on her face.

He didn't say anything else right away, but returned to his lunch, a piping hot danish, dripping with cheap margarine, leaving a trail of grease down the cleft in his chin.

"It sure is big," Janet finally remarked a couple of minutes later.

"Of course it's big," Gawd answered. "It has to be big just to hold this much knowledge."

"I mean I just feel so small," she said, a pained look on her face. "Like I don't really matter."

"At first, you wouldn't matter," he answered. "That's because right now we' don't really know anything. We don't know the answers to the deep questions. We can't really see the big picture the way we should."

"I don't know," she replied. "I'm not really sure you have to go to university to experience life. I think you can do that in a lot of ways -- like reading -- and travelling." She paused. "And it costs so much money." Another pause. "And it's so far away from my parents."

He felt for a moment that she had finally let the truth slip......but he didn't say so, not wanting to get into an argument on this so perfect of days, when he had finally gotten his chance to see this esteemed institution. She had surprised him. They'd talked about university, and she'd seemed just as enthusiastic as he was about the prospect of escaping the old home town for a taste of the real life in the big, wide world.

"What's the matter?" he said quietly, reaching over across the table and taking her hand.

"I don't know," she answered, pulling away from him, looking away.

"Jan," he said, concern in his voice.

"I really don't know," she said, looking back toward him, a trace of a tear in her eye. "It's weird. I've always wanted to get away from small towns and small minds -- you know that -- but it's like I'm here facing it, and I'm feeling like a part of my life is coming to an end. It's kind of scary in a way."

"Sure it is," he said sympathetically, reaching again for her hand, this time securing it, holding it gently but firmly. "But we've got to get out of that time capsule we're trapped in. Just look around. This place will give us a chance to grow -- to be anything we want to be. Sure, it's a little scary, but we've got to give it a go." There was almost a pleading to his voice.

"I know," she said, smiling. "I'm just having a case of nerves. I want this thing too."

He smiled back at her. He loved her.

Gawd worked hard at the school newspaper, always trying to come up with new ideas for stories, always looking for causes -- because that's what his idea of a journalist was -- looking for wrongs to right, seeking out injustices, making sure the little guy had a chance. In fact, Gawd thought he'd found his calling in life. He was constantly calling editorial meetings to discuss issues the paper could delve into -- like why there wasn't a late bus so kids from the country could more easily take part in after school activities. But the really big issue that came along was the one about attending the big football game over at the fairgrounds.

It so happened that the Halybury High football team was a winner. With all those chunky farm boys for a line, the tiny rural high school had built a virtual dynasty even though it competed against far larger schools. And because everybody likes a winner, every student in the school was a football fan. And every year, there was the big game against arch rival Walkerville, and every year it was preceded by a giant pep rally held the night before, where it was the job of the entire student body to whip the team into such a frenzied state of aggression, that they would go out the next day and kill the Walkerville team.

Only the year Gawd was in Grade 12, busily editing Thistlebush, with an issue almost ready to go to press, just waiting for a story on the pep rally and the big game, there was a calamity. A couple of members of the student body decided there was a need for some alcohol-induced enthusiasm at the pep rally, so smuggled in several bottles of vodka, the stuff with no smell, and set up a bar in the boys' changeroom. Of course, it didn't take long for people to start throwing up all over the place, and the cat was out of the bag, so to speak. The authorities closed down the bar, and incarcerated the bartenders, Gawd was there to get the story, which he did, and he thought that was the end of that.

But neither Gawd nor his schoolmates had counted on what happened the next day. The principal came on the PA after the regular morning announcements.

"If I could have your attention please," he said in his deep monotone voice. "The incident which occurred at the pep rally last night was a very serious one. The perpetrators have been apprehended and will be dealt with appropriately, but there is deep concern that other students were also involved. I have decided that you all need to learn something about getting involved in a situation like last night." He paused dramatically. The school was completely quiet. You could have heard the proverbial pin drop. "It has therefore been decided that you will not be permitted to attend this afternoon's football game. All students, except those directly associated with the team, will remain in class until the normal dismissal time. The next time something like this happens, maybe you'll think about what you're doing and what the consequences might be. That is all."

The PA clicked off, but the silence remained. Stunned silence. Gawd could feel a kind of tension in his classmates. Normally, everyone would have burst out into conversation and motion at the end of the announcements. On this morning, after the decree that had been issued, nobody moved. It was strange. Really strange.

Then, it started. "He can't do that," said the angry voice of one student.

"How could he do something like that?" asked another. "The old bastard," muttered a third.

"Are you people going to be getting to your first class at some point?" home room teachers throughout the school inquired. It was a rhetorical question. But everyone answered.

There was motion as the student body got to its collective feet to start the day, but as Gawd got to his feet, he heard the grumbling and cursing, all focussed on the principal's decision not to let the school out for the big game that afternoon. Just as he passed through the doorway out of home room, one of the school toughs charged across the hall and grabbed him roughly by the shoulder.

"Hey, man," he snarled. "You're always lookin' to stir up shit with that rag of yours, think you're a for real newspaper guy or something. Well, here's a real chance for you. This is bullshit that we can't go to the game. I mean, what is this goddamned place? A prison camp?"

"Don't start any trouble," said Gawd's home room teacher, who was following Gawd out of the room.

The tough pulled away, shot a menacing glare in Gawd's direction, and disappeared into the crowds of disgruntled adolescents.

"You better get to class," Gawd's teacher said, but Gawd was already underway.

And as it turned out, his first class was library, which was not his favourite, because Mr. Smedges still hadn't forgiven him for the uproar he'd caused over the book selection process, but off he went.

It also turned out that Janet had a spare first period, and they had agreed to meet at the back corner cubicles in the library, where they could sort of work together, but actually just be together.

And that was exactly what they did.

But they hadn't counted on Glenn. He was involved in the newspaper with them, and it so happened that he was in Gawd's library class. He chanced by the back corner cubicles on his way out for a smoke.

"Doesn't that just suck about the football game," he said, when he came upon Gawd and Janet.

"Yea, it's really too bad," Janet said.

"What did we do to deserve this?" he asked, shrugging his shoulders. "Christ, I brought my own booze to the rally. I wasn't even patronizing the bar that got busted. And I can't get out because of that."

"It sure doesn't seem right," Gawd answered.

"Yea, it surely doesn't," answered Glenn.

"It's really too bad there's not something we could do about it," Janet said. "I mean, it's going to be a big story for the next issue of the paper, right?"

"Yea, I guess," Gawd answered thoughtfully, furrowing his brow, obviously reflecting on the situation.

"It's too bad there's not something we could do now," Glenn mused.

"Yea," agreed Janet.

There was a pause, a pensive pause, as the three young people seemed to consider their options.

"What about a special edition?" Gawd suggested

There was no immediate answer.

"How?" asked Glenn.

"Just one page, one side -- an editorial -- telling the school that this ban on the game is unjust and we shouldn't stand for it," Gawd answered.

"Well, that'd be great," said Glenn, but his voice was flat and even and there was a trace of sarcasm in it. "And so what?" he asked. "What will it accomplish? Except to piss off the principal."

"We'll call for a strike," Gawd said.

"A strike?" Janet asked.

"Yea, a strike?" Glenn echoed with a certain enthusiasm replacing the earlier sarcasm.

"It's a matter of principle," Gawd said. "This is unfair. You said so yourself, Glenn."

"Yea, it is unfair," Glenn answered. "Oh, this could be great," he said, grinning broadly.

"So, you'll support me on this?" Gawd asked, looking first to Glenn, who nodded vigorously in the affirmative, then to Janet.

"Gee, I don't know," she said quietly, glancing furtively about, as if someone might discover them while they plotted and conspired.

"Comeon," Glenn urged. "It's a matter of principle. We've got to take a stand. We've got to stand up the dictators of the world. It's up to our generation."

"What if we get into trouble?" she asked nervously. "My parents'd kill me."

"Look, Janet, this is not about parents," Glenn said. "The world's in such a mess right now because our parents, and their parents before them, just sat back and let people tell them what to do. But we're a new generation. We're going to set the record straight. It's our responsibility to our children and the generations after them." He sounded quite fervent.

"It's only a football game," she said.

"You have to start somewhere," Glenn answered.

Janet looked to Gawd, knitting her eyebrows, looking uncertain.

"Glenn's sort of right," Gawd said.

"You think we should call for a strike?" she asked

Gawd shrugged his shoulders. "Yea," he answered.

And so they set about rounding up a typewriter, and a place to copy the one-page, one-side editorial that got the whole thing rolling. Or, actually, the one that was supposed to get the whole thing rolling. Because it didn't quite work out the way it was planned.

They hit the hallways with the special edition of the newspaper just after noon, completely bypassing their staff advisor, calling for a full scale, immediate walk-out, all students to assemble at the football field at the fairgrounds, and to stand firm no matter what the administration did to dissuade them from their purpose, which was to represent a bastion of democracy in a troubled world, by watching a football game.

The problem was that although over half of the student body did in fact walk out of school, only about thirty showed up at the football field. Gawd, Janet and about twenty-eight other lonely souls. The rest dispersed for parts unknown, except for Glenn, who was last seen heading out of town with a few buddies and a case of beer, apparently ready to hoist a few in the name of democracy.

Gawd took the fall for the whole sorry incident, getting a three-day suspension, and almost losing the editorship of the paper in the bargain. Janet only got four detentions, and her parents didn't kill her. Glenn woke up the next morning with a terrific hangover, and got a few laughs out of it, but he marched right down to the principal's office and offered himself up as a co-conspirator in the plot, being rewarded with a suspension similar to Gawd's, for which he was eternally grateful.

Gawd went fishing for the three day suspension. He camped out at the bottom of the cemetery hill, where he and his grandfather had fished before the old man had died and left him with Aunt Rose.

Janet came down and visited him one night, and was so proud of him for his part in the strike, and how he had stood by his principles, that she got extremely affectionate, and he made love to her for the first time. Because although they had become close, even in a physical way since the ski trip, they had not consumated their relationship. She had resisted, but it had taken only a mild resistance, because he was too shy to force the issue, and respected her every wish.

Even on this night, he had not pressed her, seemingly content to neck and pet, as they did almost constantly when they were in private and together. He loved the feel of her, and had often fondled her breasts, and had once even touched her private area, but he had felt her pull away ever so slightly, so had withdrawn the advance, and never chanced in that direction again.

But on this night, she was different. She forced the issue, reaching into his pants, taking him in her hands. Standing by the campfire, undressing, showing herself to him, so that he felt embarrassed and wanted to look away. But she came to him, stood over him, and he couldn't help but reach out and touch her, and feel her, and hold her, and reach deep within her. He was clumsy -- it was his first time. It was her first as well, but they managed through it, until they lay together at the end, exhausted.

"I love you," she said softly.

"I love you," he replied, and he knew he felt something for her, and he knew he felt better with her than without her. Still, he had to hide uncertainty. He leaned over and kissed her lightly on the breast. Her hand moved between his legs.

"I love you," she said.

"And I you," he answered.

When he came back to school after the unsuccessful strike and the suspension, he found he was somewhat of a hero. Kids he didn't even know came up to him and congratulated him for his part in the failed revolution. He had never before been in the position of being exalted on any level, and he found his newfound star status quite awkward and uncomfortable, and was happy after some time had passed and the fuss seemed over.

He and Glenn had to report to the principal's office on their return to school, sort of be officially re-instated, and they were lectured sternly and warned to be on their best behaviour for the remainder of their days at Halybury High. The principal said they were all in the same boat and should pull together in the same direction -- whatever that had to do with the circumstances at hand.

Soon, however, it was back to normal. Back to the books and the pursuit of higher learning. Gawd paid considerable attention to the books. He continued to work toward his goal of attending university, wanting so badly to escape the confines of this small world for a much larger one. It wasn't that he minded Halybury, and it had been a great place to get his head back together after the tumult of his earlier years. And he had actually grown as fond of Aunt Rose as she had of him. But it was like he felt a need to go beyond Halybury, to seek out something that lay beyond, even though he couldn't exactly explain what that something was. He just knew there had to be more to life than all that existed in Halybury.

But Janet troubled him. She seemed to neglect her books, which was not in her character; she had always been an A student. When she got a D on an English -- her best subject -- paper, he finally said something.

"You must have been having a bad day when you wrote that," he commented, after coming upon her in the cafeteria, where she was sitting, drinking a chocolate milk, the English paper in question on the table in front of her.

"I guess you could say that," she answered flatly.

He sat across from her, looked at her, searched for her eyes as he always did, but she avoided him.

"What's up, Jan?" he finally asked.

"What do you mean?" she asked back.

"You seem kind of bummed out," he answered. "You just don't seem like yourself."

"I'm alright," she said, but she still didn't look at him, her eyes casting about.

"Then, what's with the D?" he asked sharply. "You're blowing your average."

"I'm doing alright," she answered. "I just had a bad day when I wrote this," she said, gesturing to the offending paper.

"I just hope you are," he said. "We've got to have good grades. What if we applied to university and one of us didn't get accepted?" Once, he wouldn't have considered such a question.

For the first time since he'd sat opposite her, she looked back at him, right into him, and he could see into her, and there was hurt in her -- he could see it clearly, but didn't understand it.

"Is that all you think about? The university?" The words shot out of her -- angry, hostile words.

He recoiled, taken aback, not sure how to respond.

"Maybe there's more to life than university," she said, again with anger. "Maybe you should think about that."

"I don't understand," he stammered uncertainly. "I thought you wanted to go."

"You don't know me at all," she said, and he could see her eyes go watery. She got to her feet. "You don't listen to me." She turned to go.

"Janet," he said after her. "Don't go." But she had gone.

And it was like she dropped out of his life. She didn't come to school the next day, or the day after that, or the day after that. And she wouldn't come to the phone -- her mother said she wasn't feeling well and was sleeping. Gawd tried to go about his normal affairs, but he was rattled and shaken, couldn't concentrate with her always on his mind. By day, he went about his tasks in a zombie-like condition where he could see and hear, but felt nothing except a longing for her. By night, he slept in short fits, tormented by the terror that he had somehow lost her. It was a hard time for him -- a time of quiet desperation.

A few days after the incident with Janet, actually at the beginning of a new week, a weekend passed, he was getting cleaned up after gym class, standing half naked in front of a changeroom locker, just showered, going through the motions of preening for a return to regular school.

"I heard they had a fight in the cafeteria," said a voice from elsewhere in the changeroom.

"Have you seen the poor bastard moping around the school?" asked a second voice.

"They were like joined at the hip," the first voice said.

"Since the ski trip," remarked the second. "Remember, he hitchhiked all the goddamned way up there."

Gawd was suddenly aware the conversation was about Janet and him -- they were talking about him, unaware that he just a row of lockers away.

"Well, you know what I heard?" asked the first voice.

"What did you hear?" asked the second voice.

"She's pregnant," responded the first voice.

But the words were loud and heavy, and hung in the air, reverberating slowly out from their point of origin and crashing in waves down over Gawd, who had frozen statuesque, underarm deodorant poised for application, not able to believe what he had heard.

"No shit," said the second voice.

"No, no shit," came the reply.

"Poor sucker," was the comment.

"Hey, you can't take the golden goose and not expect to deal with the giant," was the somewhat philosophical response.

The others must have finished their business, there was a bit of rustle and bustle and the room went quiet. Gawd collapsed onto the bench in front of him. He sat in a pose reminiscent of the Thinker -- thinking in his underwear. Pregnant. He wondered if there could be truth to what had been said. How could it be, he wondered, but knew how it could be, and in that instant he felt an odd sense of pride at his supposed accomplishment -- if it could indeed be referred to as an accomplishment.

It was the middle of the afternoon, and he had another class to go, but he bolted from that place of secondary education, and headed for Janet's. He must seek her out. He must know -- and he must know now.

Her mother answered the door.

He asked for her.

"She's sleeping," the mother answered.

"I've got to see her," Gawd insisted.

And just as the words were leaving his mouth, he caught a glimpse of her, standing back behind her mother. "It's alright, Mom," he heard her say.

The mother stepped aside, and Gawd entered the house. He could see her better now, and wanted more than anything to rush to her and hold her close. He thought she looked small and vulnerable and alone as she stood unkempt and in her housecoat.

"Are you alright?" he asked, filling his voice with obvious concern.

"Yea," she said quietly, offering him a faint smile, perhaps as proof.

"Can I talk to you?" he asked.

She didn't answer right away. There was a pause.

"I'd like to talk to you," he said.

"Sure," she answered. "We'll go out on the porch."

"I'll bring you a cold drink," the mother said, and she turned and was gone.

Janet led the way to the screened-in porch. Nothing was said. Gawd could feel an awkward tension surrounding them. He kept quiet. Delayed the inevitable. He'd wait for the porch.

"I was worried about you," he said, after they had sat opposite each other in the big, comfortable deck chairs on the porch.

"I'm sorry," she answered. "I didn't mean to upset you."

"Well, it's just that I thought we were getting to be close," he said, putting a hushed tone on his voice as if the fact should for some reason be kept secret. "I feel strongly about you."

At that moment, the mother came in with the cold drinks, so the conversation was interrupted. He waited, said nothing for a couple of minutes after she had deposited the drinks and exited the porch.

"I feel strongly about you too," Janet said after the moment of quiet.

"Then, why are you treating me like this?" he asked.

There was another silence -- it remained tense and awkward.

"Are you pregnant?" he asked bluntly.

He could see tears welling up in her eyes.

"Janet. Are you pregnant?" he repeated.

"Yes," she answered, burying her head in her hands.

It was quiet, except for her sobbing. He considered his options.

"I love you," he said.

"I didn't want it to be this way," she said, looking up, red-eyed from her weeping.

He shrugged his shoulders. "You can't always plan these things," he said.

"You're not angry?" she asked, seeming somewhat surprised.

"Why should I be angry?" he asked. "I'm going to be a father." He got up and walked around to her, knelt beside the deck chair and took her in his arms. "I love you," he said.

"You're wonderful," she answered. And they kissed.

They were married that summer, after Grade 12, and there was no consideration of going on to Grade 13 or anything beyond, because there was a family to provide for. Gawd took a job as Assistant Produce Manager at Bolander's Groceteria, and they rented a little apartment in a not-too-bad section of town, and settled in to wait for the baby.

And Gawd really was a wonderful guy. Or at least that's what everybody thought.

The Temptation

And Gawd settled in to live his life -- he used his university savings to buy a car, something he was sure he'd need after the baby came. And the baby came that summer, and it was a joyous occasion as the tiny girl burst into being, and she was named Celeste, and Gawd marvelled at her. So tiny, yet so perfect. And he showered her with attention, walked her to and fro in the buggy, sat her on his lap and spoonfed her cool tea, calling her by silly baby names. He had little recollection of his own infancy, other than to imagine it had been difficult, knowing all too well his mother's dire circumstance, and it was like he wanted his own wee child to have everything that he had not. And for the first time, he thought perhaps he knew what it might mean to be in love. He craved the infant while he sorted through radishes and lettuce at Bolander's.

But Janet was another story. Something happened to her at the moment she gave birth, so that she had not been the same since. After she came home from the hospital, after the miracle had occured, she kept to her own side of the bed, turning to face away from him with her knees tucked up under her. At first, he would cuddle close to her, pressing himself against her, touching her gently in her private places. But even when she would eventually roll over to give herself to him, she would be stiff and cold and unyielding. He could feel it. He could feel the hardness. He tried to talk to her about it -- to tell her how he felt, that he needed the closeness with her -- but she withdrew. So that he stopped making the bedtime overtures. And he lived celebate.

He threw himself into his work at the store, and Mr. Bolander seemed to like him -- gave him a small raise after his first three months. It was dreary work, but he guessed he should throw himself into it, and try to distinguish himself at something -- even if that should be building the perfect pyramid of cantelope. And, of course, he read voraciously, being a regular visitor to the Halybury Public Library. And he dreamed -- of one day getting out of Halybury and of one day going to the university -- because no one could take his dreams from him -- that much they had left him.

And five years passed. And then seven. And, finally, twelve years had passed, and Gawd lived in a kind of quiet misery. He doted on his daughter who was now on the threshhold of becoming a young woman and was growing more beautiful by the day. He and Janet slept in twin beds, and likely would have found separate rooms, if not for the child and the image that must be maintained.

One day, a new librarian came to work at the Halybury Public Library. Gawd had known that the regular librarian was going to be leaving on maternity leave -- she had gotten quite large over the past month -- and one day, she was gone and a new face had appeared in the library.

He was sitting in the lounge area, browsing the newspapers, as he sometimes did on those occasions when he wanted to escape the house -- and those had become frequent occasions indeed. Someone started straightening the papers on the table in front of him. He glanced over the top of the paper he was reading to see a person directly in front of him. A woman. And just at the moment he looked, he must also have moved, and that attracted her attention, and she also looked. So their eyes met. Gawd felt a rush of excitement wash through him. He felt himself flush, and tried to break off the contact, but couldn't. She turned away first. He looked away embarrassed.

"Hello," the woman said, and he sensed that she had also felt something in that instant their eyes had met.

"Hi," he managed to return.

"It's quiet in here tonight," she commented, returning to straightening the papers.

"Yes," he answered. "There must not be any school projects due tomorrow."

She smiled. "Yes, they do tend to come with a rush," she said.

"Hey, I remember what it was like," he said. "Even though it was a few years ago."

"It doesn't look like it was that long ago," she said.

There was a pause in the conversation, as strangers searched for appropriate dialogue. He regarded her for the first time. Liked what he saw. Attractive, but subtle. Tasteful.

"You working here?" he asked.

"Yes, I'm filling in for Shirley," she answered. "She's off to have her baby."

"Yes, I suppose so," Gawd answered. "I hope everything goes well."

"Yes, me too," she agreed. "Having babies looks like tough work."

He almost said something about his own experience with childbirth all those years ago when his daughter had been born, but something stopped him -- perhaps a fear that if he admitted family, and by implication marriage, she would terminate the interaction. And he found that he wanted to prolong it. For the first time in a very long time, he felt a sense of giddy exhileration just to be with her. Only one other woman had ever done that to him -- and it had been his wife when they had been in another life and all had been well between them.

"I haven't seen you around," he casually remarked.

"I've only been in town a month," she answered. "I'm living with my grandmother for a while -- looking after her. Getting this job was a real stroke of luck."

"You're from the city?" he asked, folding his paper across his knee and turning full attention to her, somehow flattered that she would choose to continue the exchange with him.

"Yes," she answered, also abandoning what she was doing, sitting on the edge of a chair opposite him, glancing about, perhaps to make sure she could spare this moment. "I've been here for visits since I was a little girl, but I've never lived here before," she explained.

"You must find it pretty boring," he commented. "There's not much going on around here most of the time."

"I find it charming," she answered. "My grandmother is very involved, even though she's getting up there. She has a couple of church groups, a bridge group, a reading club, the horticultural society and some other things on the go. I came here to get some rest, but she's been dragging me all over the place with her."

"She probably travels in the same circles as my Aunt Rose," Gawd answered. "She's a pretty active old lady, too. Always on the go."

"If she hangs out at the United Church, I've probably seen her," the new librarian said.

"As a matter of fact, she does," Gawd answered.

And they laughed.

"It doesn't sound like your grandmother needs that much looking after," he said.

"No, she really doesn't," she admitted. "It could really be that she's the one looking after me." And as she uttered the remark, at first so innocent, the expression on her face changed. A sudden, dark cloud appeared to spread over what had previously been such a sunny disposition.

"You need looking after?" he asked, then thought perhaps he was prying and should mind his own business.

"Lately, it seems I do," she said.

And just at that moment there was a harumph from over by the circulation desk, and they looked over and could see an elderly patron waiting for service.

"I've got to go," she said, starting to get to her feet.

He started to unfurl the paper he was holding. "Welcome to town," he said.

"Thanks," she answered, and was gone.

Gawd waited for her to get another interruption in her duties, and hoped she would again choose to straighten newspapers, so they could resume their conversation. But there was no such break, and finally it was closing time at the library, and he could see that she and the other librarian were doing the closing time tasks. He waited as long as he could possibly wait, then could wait no longer, and made for the door, hoping she'd see him, and intercept him, so he could again have the opportunity to speak with her. But she was nowhere to be seen, and he was soon out the door, starting the walk home, slowly at first, then, as he realized she would come no more on this night, a little more quickly.

He slept on the couch that night. He felt guilty, and perhaps he should have. Because although it had seemed an innocent exchange, his thoughts had not been so pure and immaculate. She was attractive -- he found her so -- and she had shown interest in him. It seemed it had been a lifetime since an attractive woman had shown interest in him. He had revelled in it. Gotten excited. And now he felt guilt for his thoughts, and wondered if he had indeed commited adultery on this evening at the library, and guessed he must have, if he felt so unclean -- and that was how he felt.

It was that same Saturday, he wasn't working for a change, and Janet and Celeste had gone on a Guiding expedition, something that was a mother/daughter thing and from which he was excluded, and he had gone over to Aunt Rose's to help her turn her mattresses; something she did regularly twice a year, even though nobody slept in five of the six beds in her great, old house.

"My heavens," the old woman was saying, "I'm so glad you haven't forgotten your Aunt Rose. I'm sorry I have to bother you from time to time, but the rest of my kinfolk have all but forgotten I'm still alive."

"Oh, Aunt Rose, they're just busy. They all love you. You know that," Gawd said, humouring her. He struggled with a big queen-size mattress in a room that had stood empty for over forty years.

"Where did you say your family were going?" Aunt Rose asked, as she waved her hands about in the air, apparently directing the motions of the mattress.

"They've gone camping for the weekend," he told her for the third time, huffing and puffing with the mattress. She was slipping, he thought.

The old woman appeared thoughtful for a moment. "You should come to the church with me," she said.

"Tomorrow?" he asked, sliding the mattress into place, neatly flipped over.

"No, tonight," she answered. "They're having a dinner."

He stood, hands on hips, gasping for air, exhausted from his effort. "A dinner at the church?" he asked. Thoughts of a woman crossed his mind.

"Home-made pie," Aunt Rose coaxed.

But his mind was already made up. He'd get a good meal............ and......you never knew who you might meet at church.

"It's a deal," he said.

He went home and got cleaned up, paying a little more attention to himself than he usually would, having an extremely rare Saturday night shave, liberally splashing after-shave on his smoother-than-silk face when he'd completed the deed. He even struggled with the iron trying to press a shirt for the occasion. Aunt Rose would have said he was getting all gussied-up.

Then, he did one more thing -- something he'd not done in more than a decade. He slipped his wedding ring off his finger. He hid it at the back of the top drawer of his dresser. He felt a twinge of guilt as he performed this simple action, but he did it just the same, and the guilt was followed by a trace of anger that he should feel he was betraying anyone or anything, when he had felt so betrayed for so long himself.

And off he went to the dinner at the church, and Aunt Rose was delighted, because she knew he didn't make attendance at church too regular an event any more, not since he'd moved out on his own. And she made such a fuss over him when they arrived, that he almost wasn't sure it was worth it. But then he caught sight of her back in the kitchen area of the Christian Education Building, and felt his heart flutter ever so slightly just to know she was here. Already he hoped there would be an opportunity for them to meet -- surely she wouldn't stay in the kitchen while he remained at the other end of the hall, having to be content with the company of old hens. He quickly formulated a plan to avoid such a catastophe.

"Here, Aunt Rose," he said to his elderly companion, "let me take that back to the kitchen for you." He gently relieved her of the lemon meringue pie she was carrying.

"That would be so nice of you," she said, smiling, not suspecting his ulterior motive for the apparent good deed.

And in a flash, he was standing in the doorway to the kitchen. "Where would you like this?" he asked a little more loudly than necessary, holding the pie aloft.

One of the church ladies snatched it from his hand faster than you could say 'how do you do', but his announcement had the desired effect on the busy kitchen, as everyone in the room stopped what they were doing and looked up to see who had arrived. They all took a quick glance toward the door, but he saw only one of them.

"How are you?" asked the new librarian, smiling, recognizing him right away, up to her elbows in the roast beef she was carving.

"Hi," he answered, offering a slight wave and a smile of his own. Then, even though he knew he really shouldn't, he took the liberty of deking and dodging his way through the kitchen to where she was carving the meat.

"Imagine meeting you in a place like this?" he deadpanned.

She smiled again. "I guess you've just got to know the right people," she said.

There was a moment of silence, and the two of them stood still, and he felt they were suddenly and magically alone, so transfixed was he just to be in her presence. He could see nothing but her soft beauty, radiating out to him, ebbing over him in a delicious wash of emotion.

"They're getting ready for grace," interrupted an anxious woman's voice. "How's the meat coming, Barbara?"

They were startled back to the reality of the kitchen. "Fine, Grandma," answered the librarian, whose name he'd now discovered was Barbara.

"I should be going," he said. "Aunt Rose is probably holding a seat for me. Maybe I can see you after dinner."

"I'd like that, but I'll have quite a few dishes to help wash after the hungry horde have chowed down," she answered.

And at that moment, a swarm of church ladies appeared and whisked the platters of meat away, and the contact was broken. He was kind of carried away toward the door, and she had grabbed up the gravy and was going in the other direction. She glanced back toward him, just as she was disappearing. They smiled at each other and he offered a small wave.

It was a long and hectic dinner, with the old hens cackling merrily away, spreading tales about the various people who were out of earshot, and he wondered that he might become a topic for one of those tales if he followed through with his apparent plan -- and he had no doubt that he would.

Finally, though, it was time for the pie and coffee, and he was glad because it was a more social time, with people taking time to visit with those they'd not been sitting close to during the meal, so he was able to take his pie and coffee and leave the table to stand off in a corner by himself. He'd had enough making pleasant chit-chat for one day. He guessed Barbara had eaten in the kitchen with the rest of the church ladies. He'd watched out for her during dinner, but had not caught so much as a glimpse.

He finished his dessert, and walked the dirty plate and cup back toward the kitchen. He passed through the doorway and saw her immediately, this time up to her elbows in dishwater -- by herself, at the moment.

"You look like you could use a hand," he remarked.

She looked up to see him, and offered her customary pleasant smile.

"I'm sure I'll have plenty in a minute or two," she said. "I think the ladies are busy gabbing."

"Do you think they'd mind if I helped out?" he asked.

She smiled warmly, brushing a soapy hand across her brow. "Oh, I don't think so," she answered.

And, soon, they were both up to their elbows in dishwater. And he reflected during a load of silverware that he'd not had such a good time in quite a long while, and he found himself hoping that the church ladies would keep right on gabbing. But, of course, they didn't. And soon there was a flurry of activity around them, dishes clattering, cupboard doors slamming, as a veritable army of well-intentioned souls descended on the kitchen and proceeded to begin to get it ship shape.

But the ladies chose to leave the two to their dishwater, and they washed away in quiet, only with the help of a couple of others, who started in at the drying. Gawd was in his glory, with the woman by his side, and even though there was no real conversation, he thought he felt a closeness to her. But he kept to himself, almost sure, but not quite, that she returned his feeling, yet afraid to utter any word for fear it might be the wrong one and could possibly offend.

"Well, that is a strange sight," broke in Aunt Rose's voice from the doorway overlooking the cleanup.

"Aunt Rose," Gawd said, looking over at her, shaking the soap off his hands into the sink. "I suppose it's time to go."

"I was wondering where you'd gotten to," the old woman said. "But I can see you're in good hands." She smiled at Barbara. "How's your grandmother, dear?" she asked.

"She's fine," Barbara answered. "She was right here a minute ago -- I don't know where she's gotten to."

"You say hello for me," Aunt Rose said.

"I'll make sure I do," Barbara replied.

"I'll be out in a minute," Gawd said to his aunt.

"I'll wait outside," Aunt Rose answered. "It's warm in here."

"I won't be long," he promised.

She turned and was gone.

Gawd turned toward Barbara. "I guess I've got to go," he said, somewhat unhappily.

"It's been fun," she said, extending a soapy hand.

He accepted it, and gave it a firm shake. He turned to go.

He walked about two steps, then stopped, and turned back toward her.

"How about a coffee?" he asked uncertainly. "After you finish here."

"Where?" she asked, again offering her warm smile.

"I think the place by the bus station will be the only one open this late," he said.

She looked at her watch. "About ten?" she asked.

"Sure," he answered. And he turned and was gone. But there was a certain spring to his step as he left.

There was quiet in the car as he drove Aunt Rose home. It was an unusual quiet, because the old woman was usually chattering about this, that or the other thing.

"Where did you say Janet and Celeste are tonight?" she finally asked, cutting through the silence.

"They're at a Guiding thing," he said. "They're camping out."

"You could stay at my place tonight," she said. "Sleep in your old room. You won't be lonely."

"No, I'll be alright," Gawd answered. "I'm going to draw myself a hot bath, do some reading, and maybe watch one of those bad movies on the late show. It's going to be a nice, quiet night. I've been looking forward to it for a month. Don't worry about me, Aunt Rose. I sure won't be lonely." He felt a little twinge as he rhymed off the succession of lies, but he chased it quickly away.

There was a silence after he finished.

"Things are alright between you and Janet?" the old woman asked intuitively.

"Sure," he answered, choosing not to elaborate on the one-word answer.

"There's just so much divorce going around," she said. "Why just tonight Shirley Beale was telling us that Marge McGuire's son Robert is getting a divorce from that Blakeney girl -- and they've got three children. It's a crying shame. What will become of those kids?"

"Yea, but it's no good staying together if you're not happy; not just for the sake of the children," Gawd answered, perhaps more defensively than was necessary, sure the old woman had found him out. "They say that's the worst thing for the children."

"I don't know," she said. "There was a time when people made a commitment when they chose to be parents -- and they stuck together through thick and thin. It's just too easy to get a divorce these days."

Gawd was quiet. Nothing was said for a moment.

"Anyway, I'm glad to hear that you and Janet are getting along fine," Aunt Rose said. "She's a good girl. And Celeste is just the perfect little angel. You've got the perfect family there, and you should treasure it."

"I do, Aunt Rose," he said. "I do," he repeated for emphasis, but he wasn't sure he convinced himself.

And they had arrived back at her big, old, very dark house. He pulled into the driveway.

"Are you sure you won't stay?" she asked, as he reached over and opened her door for her. "I could make you a bedtime snack like I used to."

"Thanks, Aunt Rose," he said, leaning over and kissing her lightly on the cheek, "but I think I'll take a rain check if you don't mind."

"Alright," she said, getting out of the car. "You look after yourself."

"I will," he answered.

She smiled and swung the car door shut.

He waited in the driveway until he was sure she was in the house, then he waited for a light to come on inside, before he backed the car out into the street, and started on his way to the coffee shop down by the bus station. It was nine-thirty. He'd be a little early. But he was anxious to be there. So, he went anyway.

He had picked the coffee shop down by the bus station, not because it was likely the only one open -- it seemed another in a web of lies -- but because he was fairly certain there'd be no one who knew him in that area of town because he seldom went there. It was vitally important that this be a clandestine operation, because rumours would be flying everywhere if the meeting was observed by the wrong people -- and that meant pretty well anyone who knew him -- and that meant pretty well anyone -- because this was a small town.

He sat in a faraway corner of the hazy place -- it had a bit of a reputation, being nearly next door to one of the seedier bars in town, and he wondered that he had invited her here; perhaps it had not been a particularly wise decision. But what could he have done? Invited her to his place?

By ten past ten, he was losing hope that she'd come, but about a minute after he thought it, and before real disappointment started to set in, the little bell over the door gave a jangle, and she appeared. She smiled when she saw him.

He got up to meet her, paid for her coffee, embarrassing himself by dumping a pocketful of change all over the floor. She helped him retrieve it. He joked about being a clutz. She laughed. He felt better.

Finally, they were sitting opposite each other in the booth in the faraway corner of the place.

"Sorry about this place," he apologized.

"It's alright," she said. "I was glad for the chance to get out. I've been feeling a little cooped up with Grandma."

"Yea, I guess it would be kind of difficult to move to a new town," he said, taking a sip of his coffee.

"You've lived here all your life?" she asked.

"No, but I moved here when I was just a kid and I've been here since," he answered, but he offered no further explanation and hoped she'd not press him on a past that few had any inkling of. "You've moved a few times?" he asked, taking the initiative and turning the conversation back in her direction.

"My Dad was a bank manager," she explained. "He was from here originally, but he moved right after high school to take a job with the bank, met my Mom, swept her off her feet, got her pregnant, and the rest is history -- as they say......... but we moved a million times."

"Did you come here when you were a kid?" he asked.

"Oh, yea," she answered. "Some of my fondest memories are of coming here in the summers to stay with Grandma and Grandpa. I had a great time coming here -- and I met a few people so I'm not a total stranger."

"And how did you come to be here this time?" he asked, continuing the line of questioning. "Your grandmother doesn't look like she needs too much help. She seems pretty spry."

She didn't answer, but looked away. He had pressed. He regretted it.

"I'm sorry," he said. "I didn't mean to pry."

"No, it's alright," she said, looking back at him. "It's stupid." But tears started to well up in the corners of her eyes.

"I'm sorry. I didn't mean to upset you," he offered.

"It's not your fault," she said. "I was in a long relationship; I thought for the rest of my life. But it ended. We decided it was for the best because we'd grown apart. He said he wasn't happy anymore." She produced a Kleenex and dabbed at her eyes.

"I'm sorry," he said for the third time. "It must be a hard time for you."

"I don't know," she said. "It's strange. I felt relief when we first separated, but it's bothered me that he's living with someone else. I phoned his apartment one night just after he moved out and a woman answered the phone. I just hung up. But I didn't sleep at all that night. I thought I would die from a broken heart. I didn't think I loved him any more. But I decided that night to take a leave from my job and get away."

"Life can be unkind," he said, but he felt a growing sense of uncomfortableness at his current circumstance.

"Yes, I suppose it can," she answered.

He thought he had been ready to pour out to her what a miserably, unhappy marriage he was trapped in, and how he had been so struck by her, and he was sure she felt it too, and it was like they were meant for each other, and all that other gushy, romantic stuff that people in this situation usually pour out.

But he didn't. He swallowed hard. He knew she had felt it too.

"So, do you work as a librarian in the city?" he asked instead, overwhelming himself with morality.

"Actually, I'm a school librarian," she answered, following his lead away from an emotional minefield. "I took a sabatical this year. Grandma said she could use the company."

"You'll have a good year here," he said. "This is a good community."

"Oh, I know," she answered. "I may complain about being cooped up, but I'm on the go now more than I was before I moved here -- just trying to keep up with Grandmother -- and this is what I need right now. It keeps my mind off things."

"I'm sure everything will work out," he told her, and he meant it.

"You're a nice guy," she told him, and he believed it.

They sat through a second cup of coffee, and then a third, but it was only a pleasant conversation, and there was nothing more. He could not bring himself to break a trust he held with Janet. He remembered how he'd loved her -- and he wanted to love her again. He wondered if he could try talking to her again.

He went home and drew himself a hot bath, and dug out an old, tattered copy of a favourite book, and burrowed down into the steamy water, until he felt relaxation flow through him. After the bath, he fixed himself a cup of tea, and settled in to watch one of the old movies on TV. It was a Western. He was glad to see that the hero saved the day, got the girl and lived happily ever after. That's the way it should be, he thought. That's the way it should be.

And Gawd Is Cast Out

But it was the girl, Celeste, who was the apple of his eye. When she was a wee child, he took her everywhere with him, showing her off to everyone in the community, brimming with pride when she accomplished each small task associated with her own lengthening journey along the road of life. As she grew, he taught her to skate, and swim, and to ride a bike, and to do all the things of childhood. He loved her with all his heart, and showered her with affection.

And there was one special thing they did together. From the time she was extremely tiny, he took her to the library, where he would gather a great stack of books, and she would help him choose, although not too much in the beginning, and they would return home burdened with a wonderful treasure. And they would curl up in a corner of the couch and he would read to her of strange faraway lands and knights in shining armour, and it was his favourite time in the whole world, with the child cuddled in the crook of his arm. And it was a time where the wife had no business -- and it was like she knew that was the case, and made herself scarce when father and daughter were so engaged. And it could have been that in those special moments, there were memories of another time for Gawd.

And once he wept at the memories. Wept to think of what had come before.

"Daddy, why are you crying?" the small child had asked.

"It's nothing, honey," he answered. "Daddy's just being foolish."

"But you must be sad, Daddy," she reflected.

"I guess maybe I am," he answered.

There was a pause. He wiped away another tear.

"What's making you sad, Daddy?" the child questioned.

"I was just thinking about somebody I used to know," he said, and a vision of his mother and her life of abuse came to him, and he thought he saw her image in the young girl who was cuddled in the crook of his arm.

"I want you to be happy, Daddy," the child said, her face shimmering with youthful innocence.

"I am, baby," he said softly, and he leaned over and kissed her on the forehead. "I'm happy when I'm with you. You make me happy."

But he wasn't happy, and even the girl couldn't truly change how he felt. She provided him with some few moments of joy in his otherwise drab life that consisted mostly of avoiding the woman he had once tried to love so very much, but who he now felt only anger toward. In the beginning, when she had first pulled back from him, he had tried to understand what she was feeling. But she would have none of his attempted understanding, and would not even discuss their relationship except in the angry exchanges he precipitated. Why had she become so cold? He could not answer that question and in the end, he stopped trying. So that there was a constant coolness about the home. And no affection. No affection between the husband and wife.

And as the daughter grew older, it was like she sensed the icy tension between the mother and father. She knew of the profound unhappiness that pervaded the home but was only a child, and could not understand the reason for it. At first, when she was still small, she seemed to try to pull the two together, but then it was like she realized they were having none of it, but were growing further apart, so she stopped. She withdrew. Became a quiet, moody child, speaking almost only when spoken to, always politely -- she wasn't a rude child -- and keeping mostly to herself. Gawd was troubled by her, but by the time she reached her teenage years he had sunk into a sea of self-pity over his own dark circumstance. Still, he loved her dearly. She seemed like all he had.

The father and daughter continued to spend time together, but it became more of a tradition that something to be looked forward to, and he seemed oblivious to her slipping away. But it was like Gawd was numbed by his life -- that he could not somehow believe that this was it -- that he had struggled to make a place for himself in a world where he felt so little satisfaction at his lot. It was like the humdrum of life had finally taken even his hopes and dreams.

And it was about this time, when the girl had reached her sixteenth birthday, that there were troubles at the store. Mr. Bolander was over eighty, and even though he'd always run a tight ship, he'd perhaps not kept up with the times like he should. Even so, he had survived the onslaught of the first of the giant food chains, when it had built a huge superstore on the edge of town. But when the second chain came to town a few short years later, seeking to buy out one of the existing grocery stores, then demolish it and build their own superstore, Mr. Bolander wouldn't sell, even though it was his location they were after, and it was Ernie Sandlos, another local grocer, who hatched a deal with the mega market. After that, the writing was on the wall for the couple of local grocery stores that were left. And old Mr. Bolander wasn't as sharp as he used to be, so there were troubles at the store.

Gawd was spraying down the lettuce one Thursday afternoon, when Vi DaCosta came rushing back into the store about twenty minutes before her lunch break was over. Gawd watched her march over to where the other check-out girl and Herb, the assistant manager, were standing. The three of them huddled, discussing something intensely, and it was obvious Vi was upset. She was waving something about in the air. Gawd put down the sprayer, and walked over, interested to see what was bothering the poor woman.

"Oh, man, I was afraid of this," Herbie, the assistant manager was saying, as Gawd approached.

"My husband, Fred, just got laid off from his job," Vi was lamenting.

"What do you think it means?" asked Betty, the other check-out girl.

"What's the matter?" Gawd asked innocently.

"We're all going to be out of a job," Vi sobbed. "That's what's the matter."

"Why?" Gawd asked, but there was a knot in his stomach. "What's going on?"

"They wouldn't honour Vi's pay cheque at the bank," Herbie answered.

"I just came from there," she said, her mascara running down her face, giving her a clownish look. "They wouldn't cash it. They've been cashing my cheque there for the last thirteen years." She brandished the cheque aloft.

"Maybe there's some kind of mistake," Gawd offered. "Maybe the old man forgot to make a deposit, or transfer some money, or something."

The other three paused in their misery for a moment, eyeing Gawd suspiciously.

"Do you think so?" asked Betty.

"Hey, you know what he's getting like," Gawd said. "I mean, he's getting up there, and he just forgets once in a while. I'll bet if we go tell him what happened, he'll straighten the whole thing out."

"Do you think so?" Betty asked for the second time.

And the four of them set off to find Mr. Bolander, who, at this time of day, could usually be found up in his office, sitting behind his huge, oaken desk, eating the bag lunch his wife of sixty years had made for him, and reading the paper he'd picked up early that morning at Heuhn's Drug Store.

They climbed the stairs and approached the office door a little hesitantly, knowing the old man enjoyed his quiet time each noon hour. Finally, they reached the door, and Gawd knocked quietly. There was no reply. He knocked again, a little more loudly. Still, no reply.

"I saw him go up here at lunch," Herbie said.

Gawd knocked a third time, still louder. "Mr. Bolander," he called through the door. But there was still no answer.

"Maybe he's sleeping," Vi offered.

"Maybe he's passed out or something," Betty suggested.

There was a moment of quiet indecision.

Gawd tried the door. It was unlocked. He turned the knob and slowly pushed it open. "Mr. Bolander?" he called out. "Are you in here, sir?"

But the question was barely out of his mouth. A shadow fell across the partially opened door. Gawd turned to see what had caught the light. Mr. Bolander looked back. Empty, lifeless eyes, protruding toward him. It was death. Mr. Bolander, an old man who had seen his eightieth birthday, had hung himself.

Gawd pulled back, quickly swinging the door closed, crashing back into the others, forcing them to retreat to the top of the stairs.

"What's the matter?" cried out Betty, seeing his obvious distress.

And he had been shaken, but it passed. He told Herbie to go call the police, and told the women to go back downstairs and watch the store in case a customer came in.

"The old man's dead," he told them. "I guess we are out of a job."

And Gawd was cast out among the ranks of the jobless. And it was a poor time, because there were few jobs around, and, in any case, Gawd had few qualifications for any reasonable type of employment. So, his already miserable life took a decided turn for the worse.

And as he searched for work, but was unsuccessful, he became frustrated and angry. He took to sleeping on the couch, no longer caring what his daughter might think about the situation between mother and father, stopped shaving every day as he'd done faithfully since he couldn't remember when, and watched hour after hour of the type of mind-numbing television he had never had time for.

One day, as Gawd was watching some particularly mind-numbing television, and Janet was out doing a good deed for some charity or another, the phone rang. Gawd answered it. It was a vice principal from Celeste's school. Did he know his daughter had missed several days of school over the past few weeks? They just thought he should know. Thanks, he said, hanging up the phone. He closed his eyes and swallowed. He was angry. Mad angry.

That night, the three of them, father, mother and daughter gathered for the evening meal. It was quiet as they ate.

"How are things going at school?" Gawd asked the girl between mouthfuls, breaking the silence that hung over the supper table.

"Okay," she answered quietly.

"You're sure?" he asked, persisting.

"Yes," she answered, and again her voice was quiet, and she didn't look up to meet his gaze.

There was more quiet. He chewed slowly.

"How would you know?" he asked deliberately.

"What do you mean?" she asked back, looking up uncertainly.

"The school called today," he said, and he could see her bristle.

"Those bastards," she said angrily.

"Why haven't you been going to school?" he asked, and there was anger in his voice as well.

She shrugged her shoulders, but said nothing.

"I think we deserve an explanation," Gawd said, and there was severity in his voice.

"Young lady, is this true?" asked the mother, obviously surprised by the revelation that her daughter had been delinquent.

But the daughter said nothing, instead getting brusquely to her feet.

"I want to know what you've been doing with your time," Gawd roared.

"Go to hell!" she snapped back, and she stormed out of the room and bounded up the stairs.

Gawd sat, arms outstretched, trembling with rage, unable to move.

The door to the girl's room slammed shut upstairs. A moment later, it opened, and she started to come back down the stairs. Gawd rose and went out to meet her, knowing she was making for the door to escape the house.

"Where do you think you're going?" he asked loudly.

"I'm going out," she barked.

"I don't think so," he answered sharply.

"Just try to stop me," she said threateningly.

He strode toward her, and grabbed her by the wrist. "You're not going anywhere unless I say so," he said, and there was true venom in his voice -- he had forgotten his little girl.

The girl shrieked and tried to pull away, but he held firm, so she collapsed, going limp, catching him by surprise so he couldn't support her, and she fell to the floor in a heap. The mother appeared from the dining room.

"What are you doing?" she cried at Gawd, going to be with the girl, crouching to her, embracing her.

"She won't listen," Gawd said, regarding the two of them huddled together, knowing he was beaten, that he had somehow been mistaken in his actions. "I'm sorry," he managed, and he felt like something had changed in his life, and he was profoundly sad because of it.

And he turned and went to the door himself, grabbing his coat off the hook, and he left the house. He walked deep into the night; out to the place where he and his grandfather had come -- to his special place -- but he found he could not stay there because of a feeling that he was somehow unclean -- that he shouldn't have treated her so -- the one who had been the centre of his life for all of her life.

Finally, he came back to the house. He entered quietly, it was early morning. He silently climbed the stairs and crept into her room, where he sat on the edge of her bed. He watched her sleep, but it was as usually happens and she who slept seemed to sense the presence of another, so that her eyes fluttered open, and she saw him there.

She started, but he placed his hand reassuringly on her shoulder, and she was calmed.

"I'm sorry," he said. "I'm so very sorry."

She said nothing. Her countenance staid, unmoved.

"I didn't mean to hurt you," he said. "I'm angry right now.......but it's not at you. I shouldn't have taken it out on you. I'm sorry."

A small smile broke across her face. He smiled back.

"I'm concerned about the school stuff, though," he said, with a serious tone to his voice. "You've got to get an education. Look what's happened to me. You've got to get out of this one-horse town, and the best way to do it is by hitting the books."

"I know, Dad," she said softly, but she kept her mind to herself, not looking up to meet his look.

"I don't know what's wrong with us," he said. "We used to be so close." He paused. "Remember the stuff we used to do together?" he asked, not really expecting an answer.

She regarded him, but this time said nothing, yet her look confirmed that she remembered.

Gawd felt tears come to him. She wouldn't talk to him. It was like a wall had been built between them, and that while he might scale his side, he could not cross over the top and so descend to where she was, and she would not climb her side of the structure, so he could not reach out to her. He tasted tears of sadness, but also of frustration.

The girl continued to regard him. She reached out and touched him, but still said nothing.

"Remember, princess, that I've nothing to give you but myself," he said. "I know you're going to go your own way in life, but you've got to know that I'm always here for you. No matter what comes up, you've got to know that all you've got to do is come to me and I'll listen."

She gave his hand a slight squeeze. "I know that, Daddy," she finally said.

He thought he felt sincerity in her voice. He leaned forward and kissed her lightly on the forehead. "I love you, princess," he said softly.

"I love you, Daddy," she responded.

Then, there was silence. He felt drained, tired for the first time since he had set out the night before.

"Sorry for getting you up so early," he said, breaking the silence. "You must be tired."

She gave a wide yawn, and smiled.

He got up from the edge of the bed, and started toward the door. He turned back just before he closed her bedroom door behind him. "I'm sorry about last night," he apologized once more. There was no answer. She's probably already sleep, he thought.

And things were better around the household. It was like the tension had been cut, and even the husband and wife seemed more amiable toward each other. Gawd got a job. It was just pumping gas at the Fina station up by where he used to live with Aunt Rose, but it was better than nothing, so he accepted it greatfully, and took a certain satisfaction from cleaning a person's car windows 'til they sparkled. If you're going to do something, you might as well do it right. He remembered his grandfather saying that back all those years ago, during the brief period in his life when he and the old man had been bosom companions. Besides that, he had been given to understand that if he worked out he had a chance to advance to doing oil and lube jobs where the money was better and the hours were a little more regular.

It was about that time that Janet secured employment at an insurance office in town, and this made Gawd feel somewhat peculiar to think that his wife was helping to support the family. He knew that was an old-fashioned approach to life, but he still felt that way, and that was a fact. But the offer of employment she received from Fred Murdoch, who was an old classmate of theirs from Hampton High, and who was now the most successful insurance man in Hampton, came at a fortuitous time for them, because unemployment insurance was running out and the job pumping gas wouldn't have paid all the bills. Also, their child was well on her way to growing up and the wife now seemed to have considerable free time on her hands. So, Gawd acquiesed in the decision and she went to work.

When he started working at the service station and Janet started working at the insurance agency, there could have been a problem because they were a one-car household and both of their jobs were across town. But Gawd volunteered to walk to work, saying it would do him good to get some much-needed exercise.

When Aunt Rose found out that Gawd was working nearby and walking to work, she rolled out the welcome mat for him, offering to make him lunch. Glad for the company, she said. He readily accepted, glad to go back to the home of his youth, a place where he had always felt considerable comfortableness just at being there.

He was glad to see Aunt Rose so robust when he called on her for lunch that first day. She was truly a charm -- that was what he now thought, despite the shaky start he'd gotten off to with her all those years ago when he and grandfather had regarded her as a bit of a meddling battleaxe. He well remembered the trepidation he'd felt coming to live with her in her big, old Victorian house.

"It's just so fortunate that you got that job at the Fina," Aunt Rose said, as she ladled him a bowl of her famous cream of asparagus soup. "Things must have been getting tight for you and Janet. That was an awful thing that happened to Mr. Bolander. He was such a nice man. Why, I was a check-out girl there myself when I was just a girl -- nearly every girl in town worked for Mr. Bolander at one time or another. Such a kind, old man. Such a terrible thing."

Gawd agreed with her between spoonfuls of his most excellent repast.

"Well, I'm not sure I agree with that wife of yours going out to work," Aunt Rose said, brandishing a piece of her homemade bread at him. "I think a woman's place is in the home. I realize your child is getting older, but she still needs her mother at home. Children need their mothers. That much I know." She took a bite of the bread.

"We needed the money, Aunt Rose," Gawd said, but he said it halfheartedly, because although it was true, he knew he felt the same way as the old woman.

"Money or no money, it's not good to have your child coming home to an empty house," she said.

He shrugged his shoulders, knowing he felt she was right, but also feeling he might somehow be betraying his wife if he came right out and said it.

And so he went to Aunt Rose's for lunch, and he enjoyed going there. He didn't mind her offering her opinion on just about anything under the sun. And that was just about what she did. She had a tiny black and white TV on the end of her kitchen counter, so they often watched it while they ate, and because he worked peculiar hours, they ate at odd times and so watched everything from the news to various sporting events, and she had a comment for everything. Not only didn't he mind her prattling on about this, that or the other thing, he looked forward to it, and found joy in it as it reminded him of when he was a youth and had first come to live with her.

And there was again a period of blissful calm in Gawd's life, and he went merrily about his business and was able to work his way up to the lube and oil job at the Fina. Janet seemed happier than she had been for some time now that she was a working woman, and so it seemed a detente developed between them. The daughter, Celeste, was again a part of the family, and seemed to conduct her business in a polite and courteous fashion, even leaving some time for the mother and father, for which Gawd was thankful. It was truly a period of blissful calm and he was greatful.

It was a truly satisfying time in his life, and he would have continued with it for a considerable length of time. But all good things must come to an end. Or so the saying goes. At least that's the way he remembered it. And it surely must be true.

One day, he was going to Aunt Rose's for lunch like he always did, and it was a rare day because it was actually about noon hour. But he found himself hurrying down the street toward her big, old Victorian house, when he saw what he thought might be a police car parked out front. He went quickly past the car, and up the walk to the front door. He was intercepted by a young police officer.

"What's the problem here, officer? Is everything alright? Is something wrong with my Aunt Rose?" He rattled out the questions in rapid succession, trying to push past the officer, feeling sure he knew the answers.

"You're her family?" the officer asked, and just then another officer appeared, older than the first and one who'd been around town for longer, and he recognized Gawd.

"It's alright, let him in," he told his younger counterpart.

"Is there a problem?" Gawd asked.

"It's your Aunt," the senior officer replied. "A couple of her lady friends dropped by for lunch, and they found her in the basement where she'd been doing the laundry. Appears she had a heart attack or a stroke. She wasn't a young woman."

Gawd felt weakness in his knees, but he held firm. Aunt Rose, he thought. Aunt Rose. Dead.

"Looks like it was real sudden and real quick," the officer said. "She didn't suffer."

"Can I see her?" Gawd asked.

"She smashed her head a bit from taking a fall when it hit her," he answered. "I don't think it's a good idea."

And so Gawd went and sat on the front verandah of the big, old Victorian house he'd once called home. And he saw her before him. And he wept for her. But he also wept for himself. Because another piece of his life had been taken from him.

He got through her funeral, and it was on with his life. They got a nice settlement from her estate, which was good, and Gawd used part of it to pay off an assortment of bills, but he used the greater part of it to pay off the mortgage on their little nest and that called for a celebration where they decided it would be appropriate to officially ignite the expired document and render it to ash.

Even Celeste was there for the mortgage burning. It was a pleasant family time. Janet seemed to smile more than he had seen her do for many years, and he again found himself attracted to her -- having feelings for her which he'd thought were gone forever, because he no longer allowed them to get the better of him. They laughed together, the three of them, and it was good. Gawd felt warmth in that circumstance, and wished that it could last for such a very long time.

But the girl announced she was going out with some friends. They were going swimming at the quarry.

Be careful, he told her. I've seen them fish kids out of that quarry back when I was a boy.

"Yea, right, old man," she said, and she was gone out the door.

Janet had gone upstairs. He wondered why, and could only hope that he knew the answer. He brushed his teeth in the downstairs bathroom, and headed for the stairs. He felt light and confident as he climbed them. He opened the door to their bedroom, filled with anticipation.

He saw only the suitcase at first.

"What are you doing?" he remembered asking.

"I'm leaving," she answered. "I'm leaving you." She was jamming stuff into the suitcase.

"Why?" he asked.

"Because I'm not happy," she answered. "Because I'm in love with Fred Murdoch."

"Fred?" he remembered sort of stupidly asking, wanting confirmation that his ears hadn't deceived him.

"Yes," she answered. "I was going to tell you weeks ago, but there was the business with your Aunt Rose. I didn't want to upset you."

He said nothing. Sat on the edge of the bed. Felt sort of numb.

She grabbed the suitcase off the bed. "I'll be back for the rest of my stuff," she said, as she started toward the door. Then, she wheeled back toward him. "Look, I'm sorry about this," she said, "but it's for the better. We're both miserable. I'll be in touch so we can sort things out. You know, like who gets what." She turned partway toward the door. "I'll be seeing you," she said.

"Yea, see you," he answered woodenly. And he listened to her descend the stairs and leave through the front door. He heard it close behind her, and just like that she shut him out of her life. Just like that.

He went and had a shower. He wept and the water washed away his tears. And as he stood towelling himself dry, the doorbell to the house rang, so that he threw on his housecoat, and made for the front door. It was ten o'clock. Who'd be at the door at this hour?

He swung it open, and was surprised to see a police officer.

"There's been an accident out at the quarry," the officr said. "There's been a drowning."

And Gawd was cast out among the heathen.

Into the Wilderness

And Gawd returned to the place from whence he had come -- the city -- and to that part of it that contained mainly vermin and refuse. He wanted no more to do with the town where he'd spent the greater part of his life. He could no longer bear the places that had been special to him, because each held a gentle memory of a moment captured in his heart. He wept as he sat on the bus that took him from Halybury, knowing that he had once been, at the very least, content to have lived there. But he knew there was now nothing for him. Some uncles and aunts and cousins were left about the town, and he had acquaintances after so many years spent there, so there were plenty of well wishers as he laid his daughter to rest in the cemetery by the river. People were scandalized by his wife's behaviour. And they knew how close he'd been to Aunt Rose. So he received more than his share of well-meaning pitying for a couple of weeks. He even got a couple of offers of fairly decent jobs.

But it was like his life had somehow ended on that fateful night, and he could no longer imagine a need to carry on with it. So he cast it away and went out to live among the vermin and refuse, to be a solitary soul, who would keep no other company than himself. He signed sole title to the house over to his wife, and gave her pretty well everything he owned, much to the chagrin of some of the relatives who might have stood to make gains at the expense of his apparently broken life. But he bore Janet no ill will, and thought of her as a kind person for having put up with him for as long as she had. It had been a great sacrifice on her part. He remembered their parting conversation.

"You're going away?" she'd asked.

"Yea, it looks that way," he answered.

"To the city?" she asked.

"Yea, I guess," he answered.

"Are you going to go to school?" she asked.

"I might," he answered. "I haven't decided."

"You should go," she said. "You've always wanted to."

There was a pause. They were standing in their old bedroom, only it was just her bedroom now, and he guessed she and Fred would be sleeping in their bed from now on. The pause continued, and it was somewhat awkward.

"I'm sorry if I hurt you," she finally said, her voice quiet, furtive. "I really didn't mean to hurt you." She hesitated. There were tears welling up in her eyes.

"It's okay," he said with little emotion in his voice.

"I'll always love you, you know," she said.

He felt empty. He was quiet.

She reached out and took his hand. He left it limp, uncommitted. "We'll always be soulmates, you know," she said, pushing out with her voice to make it sound more sincere.

"Yea, I guess," he answered flatly. He looked up to meet her eyes, and he looked through her, and into her -- to try to know what had happened between them.

"I'm sorry about Celeste," the woman said. "I know you and her had a special relationship."

He smiled, but said nothing.

"I've got to go," she said rather suddenly, looking at her watch, shifting up the atmosphere in the room by a couple of notches. Letting him know the special moment was over. She had done what she had felt compelled to do.

He watched from the bedroom window as she walked out to her car. Good-bye, he thought. But he also thought that he really didn't care. He was numb toward her after so many years of so little.

He gathered up a few things from around the house, a picture of his daughter, a toothbrush and a clean pair of underwear, stuffed them into the old duffle bag he'd brought with him to his Grandfather's back all those years ago when he'd first come to this place. It seemed fitting that he would go out with just about exactly what he had come in with.

And he boarded a bus for the city -- back from whence he had come.

But while he had divested himself of most of his earthly possessions, he'd kept what was left of his inheritance from Aunt Rose -- his ex-wife didn't even quibble about it, she was so glad to get all the rest of his stuff, such as it was. He tucked the money from Aunt Rose carefully away, in a place where he could get at it, but in a place where the getting at it was somewhat difficult. He took none of it with him on the bus, except for a few dollars to buy a few supplies at the other end, and that he pinned to the inside of his shirt. He took a heavier coat than he needed for this time of year, and he wore his work boots, because he knew he'd need to be prepared for most things in his new life. And he went out into the streets.

It was actually pleasant enough for the first few months, it being summer and then fall, so there was little need to worry about the weather. He found himself a place under a railway trestle, out and away from where most others could usually be found. He quickly found a branch library that was friendly and welcoming, even to those such as he, who had become uncomfortable with the normal way of things, and who were on vacation from responsibility. He visited a mission or two and the food bank to obtain sustenance on his journey. He settled in.

And even in the winter it seemed somehow all right. He found some casual work shovelling snow at an apartment complex, and the superintendent let him sleep in the garbage room when it was really cold out. It smelled pretty bad, and the truck that picked up the garbage came at about four in the morning. But he was thankful. Sometimes he found perfectly good magazines in among the trash. And he was thankful even for that.

He read a lot and visited the library, but he liked to go down into the centre of the city and watch people. He took to thinking of this as an activity called street watching, which he regarded as sort of a job. He would sit stone still for hours at a busy intersection, usually until the police asked him to move on, and simply watch people as they passed by, examining them to find what clues they revealed about who they might really be besides the made-up creatures currently on parade for all the world to see. He would see them walking by and he'd wonder how they had come to pass this way in life -- what set of circumstances had happened to them since they were nothing but tiny children, to have brought them to this particular intersection on this particular day. Even as he watched.

One day, as he sat watching, an interesting set of circumstances unfolded. A young woman was standing at the corner waiting for the "walk" signal so she could cross the street. While she was standing there, a youth suddenly appeared, grabbed her purse and started to run. The young woman shrieked, alerting everyone on the street to her dilemma, and the youth immediately became a major centre of attention on the crowded street. One passerby, a well-built young man in a muscle shirt, threw himself into the path of the fleeing delinquent, bringing him to ground almost right in front of where Gawd was sitting watching.

And just as quickly as the tangled twosome skidded onto the pavement, the youth who had grabbed the purse squirted free, and came quickly back to his feet. He reached up under his coat and produced a huge and very dangerous looking gun. He levelled it at the approaching crowd, led by the young woman whose purse had been stolen.

The youth was defiant. He cocked the gun.

Gawd felt himself tense up, expecting the worst.

"Don't nobody move!" commanded the youth.

The crowd froze. The youth froze. Gawd watched from almost between them. Then, a strange thing happened. Gawd pulled himself up to a standing position, attracting the attention of all concerned. He looked thoughtfully over at the youth, who had kept the gun levelled at the crowd, but was watching Gawd nervously out of the corner of one eye.

"Don't move, man," the youth snarled threateningly at Gawd, almost turning the gun from the crowd to point at the derelict who was so obviously interfering with the stand-off.

At first, Gawd said nothing, but continued to regard the youth thoughtfully, as if he might be studying an exhibit in a museum. Then, he spoke slowly and deliberately. "I'm not sure you should be doing this," he said to the young man with the gun.

"Who the hell are you? You're nothin' but a bum," he challenged. "And you're gonna be a dead bum," he threatened.

Gawd could see behind the youth, to where a couple of police officers had manouvered in behind the parked cars, and were making their way ever so secretly down the street to where the confrontation was taking place. "You should think about what you're doing," he said steadily, no trace of tension in his voice. "These people have families."

Those words had hardly departed Gawd's mouth, and the youth turned suddenly and violently toward him. "You goddammned bastard bum!" he cried out, lunging at Gawd, grabbing him by the lapel of his coat, pressing the gun to his temple. "But I'll bet you don't have a family, eh bum?" he hissed into Gawd's face. Gawd could taste the young man's breath.

And it was at that precise moment that the police felt they had the best chance to try to grab the delinquent, while his attention was turned to Gawd. So two officers hurtled themselves over the car they'd been crouching behind, and crashed heavily into Gawd and the young man with the gun, and all four of them went smashing into a large plate glass window in the storefront immediately behind where the altercation had been taking place. Gawd remembered hearing a loud crack as they fell through the window. He remembered thinking about the gun. Then, everything went dark.

He came to in a hospital emergency room about fifteen minutes later. At first, they thought he'd been shot, but it turned out he just taken a hit on the head when they'd fallen into the window. A doctor gave him the once over, and declared him basically fit, except for the bump on his head, but told him to lay still for a few moments, until they could be absolutely sure he hadn't suffered some internal injury.

While he was laying still, his eyes closed, he felt another in the examination room. He opened his eyes, expecting to see a doctor or nurse fussing about with some of the array of wires and knobs protruding from the medical equipment. Instead, he saw a young woman in street clothes.

"Hello," she said softly.

Gawd smiled, but said nothing.

"I wanted to thank you," the young woman said.

Gawd continued to lay quietly, watching her.

"It was my purse," she explained. "I thought he was going to shoot. I thought someone was going to get shot." She paused. "I could have been the one if you hadn't distracted him. That was a very brave thing you did. You're a very brave man."

Gawd remained quiet.

"Look, you look like you're a little down on your luck, and I'd like to repay you," the young woman said. "Here's my business card and I want you to get in touch with me in the next couple of days." She slipped the card into his hand.

"I've got to go now," she started. "But thanks again. That was really something special." And she turned and left the examination room.

Gawd held up the business card, examining it. She was a lawyer. Nice young woman, he thought.

And he climbed down off the bed. It was time to go. And he slipped out of the emergency department and back onto the street. He had a bit of a headache, but figured he'd live. He didn't want any attention. He wanted quiet and calm.

Of course, he didn't call the lady lawyer. He settled back into life on the street. And the years passed. He moved from the railway trestle out to a piece of bush behind one of the city's cemeteries. And he managed to hang onto his winter shovelling job during all those years, and slept snug and secure among the refuse of others on the coldest of winter nights. And while others might have said that his was a mean and miserable lot, he did not once complain that he was somehow treated unfairly, and even on those nights when he went to sleep hungry because he could not bear another sermon at the mission, he did not lament his existence.

And after some years had passed, and he was really none the worse for wear, something happened. One day, as he was walking down the street, perhaps more shuffling than walking because of the heavy boots he wore, he came across a boy, who was sitting on the front steps of an apartment building looking extremely unhappy. As Gawd approached to pass, the young man rose to meet him.

"You don't know anybody who'd like to buy a camera?" he asked Gawd, glancing about nervously.

"I don't think so," Gawd answered, looking curiously at the young man who had part of a camera protruding out from under his jacket. "Where did you get it?" Gawd asked, breaking with his usual habit of asking nothing of anyone.

"I won it," the young man answered.

"You must be lucky," Gawd replied, and he turned and continued on his way.

Some time later, Gawd was again walking and he came upon the same boy, who was again sitting on the front steps of the apartment building and again looking most unhappy.

"Did you sell the camera?" Gawd asked, as he approached to pass.

The boy looked up, appearing surprised.

"The camera you won," Gawd said. "Did you sell it?"

"Oh.......no," answered the boy. "I couldn't. It wasn't mine."

"What do you mean?" Gawd asked. "I thought you won it."

"I took it from my Dad's stuff," the boy answered. "I was getting even with him because he divorced my mom -- that's what my counsellor would say."

"That's too bad -- I mean about your mom and dad," Gawd observed.

"I hate it," the boy said. "My mom and dad split up, so I've got to move halfway across the city -- away from everything. And I'm stuck living with my mom because my dad's with his new family. Nobody seems to really give a care about me or what I think."

Gawd decided to pause in his daily travels. He sat down on the step near the boy.

"That's tough what you're going through," he offered. "The adults are all mixed up and they don't see the kids. I'm sure they still care about you just like they always have -- but they're just so caught up in their own lives that they can't see anything else."

"I don't know," answered the boy. "I just want them to know that I'm not part of the furniture."

"I'm sure they'll realize that," Gawd said.

"I hope so," answered the young man.

Gawd got to his feet. "I should go," he said. "It's good that you put your Dad's camera back. Your counsellor would probably have been right -- you were probably getting even. Don't be too hard on your parents. I'm sure they love you."

Just then a car drove up in front of the apartment building. Gawd could see someone peering curiously out of the car window, perhaps wondering what interest a derelict creature such as this might have with a young boy, and perhaps even thinking the worst.

"Take care," he said to the boy. "Be strong." And he turned and walked away, rejoining his daily travels where they had been left off.

The next day, he went to the library, as was his custom, but instead of sitting in amongst the newspapers and magazines, he went to the study tables over by the reference section, where he was resolved that he would produce a letter. He had not forgotten the boy he had met the previous day, and he felt that he should somehow make an attempt to help the lad in his struggles. He would do what he could.

He had an idea that he would try to write a letter to the boy's parents, telling them how their son felt, so that they might have some chance to recognize the error of their ways and make some effort to appease their child. He was sure the parents were just so caught up in their own lives that they had lost sight of the boy. They just needed a reminder that he was also part of the family.

Just as he was about to start to write, he sensed another standing by him. He turned to see the very boy who was in his thoughts.

"Hello," the young man said.

"Hi," Gawd answered.

There was a pause.

"You looking for something to read?" Gawd asked.

"I have a project to do," the boy answered somewhat glumly.

"That's too bad," Gawd said sympathetically.

"My dad was supposed to help me but he had to go to his office," the boy said, retaining his glum tone of voice.

"Where's your mom?" Gawd asked.

"She's working," the boy said. "She's always working."

There was another pause.

"I might be able to help," Gawd said quietly.

"Do you think you could?" the boy asked.

"I used to help my daughter with her projects," Gawd said, and he became somewhat pensive after he spoke the words.

And so Gawd helped the young man, whose name was Joshua, or Josh for short, with his school project and they were soon sitting at the study table surrounded by huge stacks of reference materials. And for the first time in many years -- a very considerable length of time -- Gawd felt some true enjoyment in his life. But even as he went about digging through the research materials, he was aware that others in the library were watching the odd twosome, the unshaven, unkempt derelict and the boy, and were no doubt wondering at the coupling. And for a moment -- just the tiniest of moments -- he was ashamed of what he'd become. But he continued to help the boy, who was oblivious to the busy bodyness currently going on in the place and directed at the two of them.

And it was a delicious afternoon for Gawd, who felt no harm was done to be with the boy in such a public place. But, as with all good things, time eventually ran out on the afternoon, and the library was due to close. So, they returned some of their reference materials, and the boy gathered up the notes he had made, and they started for the door.

"There, do you think you've got enough to get a start?" Gawd asked, as they walked.

"Oh, I'm sure I do," answered the boy.

They were soon outside on the sidewalk in front of the building. Gawd had decided they should part once they left the library, so he bade Joshua farewell, and started away from the direction of the apartment building where he knew the boy lived. "See you," he said, as he started off.

"Why are you going that way?" asked the boy.

"I've got some things to do downtown," Gawd lied.

"Come this way," the boy said. "Let's walk part way together."

"I really shouldn't," Gawd maintained.

"Comeon, please," pleaded the boy. "You can still turn off and go downtown."

"Maybe just a little ways," Gawd said, relenting, unable to say no the boy, perhaps still feeling the glow of helping him in the library.

"Great," answered the boy.

And they set off.

They'd walked only a short distance when Gawd was aware of a car coming up beside them, and slowing to a stop. He turned to see what was up.

"Oh, great, it's my dad," the boy said, and it was obvious that he was less than pleased.

They stopped on the sidewalk beside the car, and watched as its driver's side door opened and a tall, athletic-looking man got out.

"Josh," the man started. "I've been looking for you. Your mother's been frantic. I had to leave a business meeting." He rattled out the statements machine gun style and the boys recoiled each time he was hit with a new volley. He punctuated the attack with a look of disgust in Gawd's direction.

"I was at the library," the boy snapped back angrily. "I was doing my project -- the one you were supposed to help me with."

"I know you were at the library -- I went there -- and they told me you'd been with a filthy old man," the father said, his voice now also filled with anger. "I had to deal with something at work. I explained about that to you" He paused, giving Gawd another look-over. "Who is this, anyway?" he asked the boy.

"He's my friend," answered the boy defiantly. "He helped me with my project."

There was a moment of quiet uneasiness.

"Josh, wait in your Dad's car," Gawd said to the boy, suddenly deciding to act out of character, to get involved.

"But....." the boy started to protest.

"Please, Josh?" Gawd asked.

And the boy hung his head, but he went and got into the car.

"I don't mean your boy any harm," Gawd said to the father, once the car door had closed.

"I think you'd better move along," the father said. "I don't know what you were doing with Josh, but I'd appreciate it if you'd stay away from him. He's going through a tough time right now, and he's a little mixed up."

"I'm not sure he's the one who's mixed up," Gawd answered. "I think you've got a really bright, eager kid there, and I think you're mixed up about where your priorities lie."

"I don't think you know what you're talking about," the father answered, and there was anger in his voice again. "How dare you intefere with my family."

"I may not know what I'm talking about," Gawd answered, "but I know a boy who needs a little attention when I see him. I know a boy who's very close to the edge -- and who's very unhappy with things. And I'd be thankful if somebody told me about it."

"You better get the hell out of here," the father said forcefully, starting for the driver's side of the car, bearing an awful countenance. "And don't come near my son again," he threatened, as he got into the car and slammed the door.

The car roared off, spraying up loose gravel, while the boy and Gawd looked helplessly at each other.

Gawd sighed. He'd tried.

Some weeks later, he was sitting in a downtown park, reading a newspaper he'd found in the trash, and paying little attention to what was transpiring about him. He didn't see the man approach. He sensed his presence. Looked up. He saw the father.

The man looked somewhat fidgety and uncomfortable. He cleared his throat.

"I saw you sitting here," the father started. "I wanted to talk to you. I was hoping I might get to see you again."

Gawd regarded him, but said nothing.

"I was wrong when I talked to you before," the father confessed. "You were so right about what I was doing with Josh. God, what a bastard I was being. I don't know what got into me."

Still, Gawd was quiet. He watched the man.

"Anyway, I just wanted to say thanks and that I was sorry for being less than kind the other day," the father said. "I can't patch things up with Josh's mom -- things are over between us -- but I can try to make sure the boy doesn't get caught in a crossfire." He paused. "Listen, you look like you're a little down on your luck," he continued. "I don't know if there's anything I can do, but I owe you a lot -- and here's my card. You just call my secretary." He paused again. "Thanks," he concluded, reaching out and grasping Gawd's hand, giving it a firm shake.

Then, he started to walk off. Before had gone too far, he turned back. "He got an "A" on that project," he called, smiling, then continuing on his way.

Gawd returned the smile. He glanced at the business card. A vice president in charge of finance. A captain of industry. Strange how some things work out.

The years passed, and they were kind to Gawd. He suffered the occasional humiliation of poverty. There was more hunger than not, and he lost his winter accommodation in the refuse room at the apartment complex when the kindly superintendent was arrested and convicted of scamming money out of the tenants monthly rental fees, so it was cold in winter. But it was a peaceful period for him. He lived quietly, continuing to frequent the library, where he was able to spirit himself away from the drab ordinariness of his reality, and into exotic locales and faraway faerie lands.

The torturous remembrances of his earlier life had even seemed to fade somewhat. He still carried the girl's picture close to his heart, his fair daughter who had been the love of his life. And over the years, he had sometimes been reminded of her, and had been caused to come up short by the sight of another young face, so fresh and innocent. But he tried not to dwell on the past and went on about his life, such as it was, until he had reached a point near three score years.

And it happened that one day, as he was sitting in a coffee shop sipping a cup of tea, having been fortunate enough to have salvaged an old chesterfield suite that was in good enough shape to get a couple of bucks for, that something happened. A young girl, possibly a teenager, came to sit beside him -- or actually at the table directly across from him, so it was difficult for him to avoid appearing to stare at her.

She was a pretty girl, but he quickly saw that she seemed in some distress, was red-eyed, perhaps from weeping, and even now, as she toyed with her coffee, she seemed to be stifling yet another sob. He wondered what could make one so young so apparently miserable at an age when there should be few concerns and life should be bright and rosey.

She fought back tears, even as he watched, thinking he should look away and allow her some privacy in her moment of anguish, but he was as unable to do so as she was able to win the battle to prevent the tears.

She wept, holding her hand up over her face, trying to hide her grief. Finally, he could take no more.

"Are you alright?" he asked, getting up and approaching her.

She looked up, a picture of misery.

"Are you alright?" he asked again, putting a gentle hand on her shoulder, taking a chance.

She wiped away the tears, tried to compose herself. "I think so," she answered. "Thanks," she added, taking his hand and giving it a tiny squeeze.

He went back to his own table. After he had gotten situated he looked up, and saw the girl looking straight back at him. She smiled. He smiled.

"You could talk about it," he suggested, and he again broke with his usual habit of keeping only to himself.

"It won't do any good," she answered.

"It usually does some good," he said.

She smiled again. "You look like you need to talk about it," she said.

He smiled, but said nothing.

A couple who'd been sitting down at the other end of the place got up and left, so Gawd, the girl and the guy behind the counter were the only ones who remained. There was quiet for a few moments.

Gawd glanced back toward the girl, and saw she appeared deep in thought. "God, what a mess," he thought he heard her mumble.

"It can't be that bad," Gawd said.

"It's that bad," the girl said. "I'm pregnant," she added matter-of-factly. "How much worse could it be?"

Gawd was taken aback by her news. She looked so young -- too young. "That's a tough one," he said. "That's a real tough one."

There was silence. The guy behind the counter had disappeared, probably into the kitchen.

"What are you going to do?" Gawd asked, knowing it was none of his business, but remembering back to another time to another young girl in a similiar circumstance.

"I came here to get rid of it," she said, her voice flat, even and hushed.

"An abortion?" he asked, already knowing the answer.

She looked over at him, a picture of misery.

"Who knows?" Gawd asked.

"Just my boyfriend," the girl said.

"And where's he?" Gawd asked.

"He didn't think it would look right if we both missed school on the same day," she said. "He gave me the money and told me where to go."

Gawd remembered another. He felt sadness at the remembrance. "Your parents don't know?" he asked.

"I don't have parents. I live with my grandmother," she answered. "I could never tell her. It would kill her." Another look of grief came over her at the thought of her dear grandmother. "And after she took me in."

"She should know," Gawd said. "She won't stop loving you. She might be able to help you. I'm not sure you're doing the right thing."

"I can't tell her," the girl said. "She wouldn't know what to do. She'd die."

"You might be surprised," Gawd said.

There was a silence. The girl seemed deep in thought.

"I can't," she finally said. "I've got to get rid of it. I've got to go for the abortion."

"Look, maybe you should go for the abortion," Gawd answered, "but you should do it under the right circumstances. You should tell your grandmother, and let her help you through it. You shouldn't do it like this. It's a mistake. A serious mistake." Again there were memories from his past -- when he had sat in such a place waiting for another to do the deed. Only it had ended in tragedy.

Still, he wondered that he should speak so, when he had borne such an aversion to doing so to others of his kind over his years of solitude. He had seen a thousand decrepit children dwelling in misery and anguish on the streets of this city, but he had said nothing to any of them -- he had not helped their cause one iota, but had watched from a distance. But for this young girl, he was overwhelmed with empathy and a desire to assist, if only he could.

"How could I ever go to her?" the girl said. "She trusted me." She looked directly at Gawd. "You know I've had sex once, and it was almost an accident the way it happened, and my life is ruined," she said, with a tone of seriousness to her voice.

"Your life doesn't have to be ruined," Gawd said, his voice also serious, an earnestness to it. "You could go to your grandmother, or even a teacher at school, or your doctor -- get somebody to help you through this. There are some things that you should have help with. This is one of them. Don't throw your life away over one mistake."

Gawd's voice had risen in volume and become more intense as he'd spoken, swelling to a magnificent crescendo in the last line, and when he finished it was dead silent in the coffee shop, the girl chewing nervously on the ends of her hair, no sign of the counter guy.

The silence persisted for several moments, until the counter guy came out of the kitchen area and crashed a fresh tray of donuts into their position behind the counter.

"Will you help?" said a quiet, uncertain voice.

More silence. Gawd thought.

"I'll go to your grandmother's with you," he finally said.

"I don't know if I can do that," she said fearfully.

"It's your only option," Gawd said. "I'll try to help you through that."

More silence. The girl thought.

"I'll try," she finally said. "If you'll come, I'll try to tell her." She gave a hint of a smile.

"There, you feel better already," Gawd said, breaking into a broad grin himself.

She smiled more warmly.

So, they set off for the other side of the city where the grandmother lived, Gawd paying their bus fare with the last of his money, even though she offered to pay from the money her boyfriend had given her for the abortion. There was mostly silence between them as they rode. Both were with their thoughts, perhaps wondering how they had come to be in such a position.

Soon, they were standing on the sidewalk in front of the grandmother's house.

"I'm not sure I should be doing this," the girl said uncertainly.

"Let's go," Gawd said, gently taking her by the arm and starting up the sidewalk.

Gawd followed her into the house, feeling uneasy about again being in what might be called a home, but he trailed along behind her, certain that he wouldn't waver in this task.

When the grandmother heard someone in the house, she came out to see who it was, so they met in the dining room. When Gawd first saw her, he was taken aback, because he'd been expecting a gray-haired, bespectacled, wrinkled-up, elderly sort of person, and what he got was an extremely attractive woman who was obviously comfortably enjoying the autumn of her years.

"Grandma," the girl said, when the older woman entered, rushing to embrace her.

"Why aren't you in school, child?" the grandmother asked. "And who's this with you?"

The girl stepped back, suddenly serious, she took her grandmother's hand. "I've got something important to talk to you about," she said quietly. "This kind gentleman came to help me tell you."

Gawd felt himself flush as the woman's attention focussed on him, and he could feel her looking him over, and he felt naked and vulnerable and uncomfortable before her. He was ashamed of the disreputable condition of his attire. He wanted for a shower, a razor, a comb and a change of clothes.

"Hello, ma'am," he said respectfully.

"Hello," the woman said back, then turned her attention back to the girl. "Now, what's this that's so important that you've missed school."

"Oh, grandma," the girl sort of sighed, in a way that showed this was a serious topic indeed. "I'm pregnant."

There was silence for a moment after she said the words. The older woman said nothing. Then, she reached out and put an arm around her grandchild, and held her close.

"She needs your help, ma'am," Gawd said softly.

"Of course she does," the grandmother said rather fiercely. "And she shall have it."

"Oh, grandma," the girl wept, melting into the older woman's comforting embrace.

"You poor child," the grandmother said to the girl. "How you must have suffered keeping this all to yourself."

Gawd started to quietly withdraw. He took a couple of small steps back toward the doorway that led out of the room.

"Wait," the grandmother said when she saw his intent. He stopped his retreat. "What's this man's involvement in this?" she asked her granddaughter.

"He's the one who told me to tell you," the girl said. "I was going to have an abortion -- I was upset, and he asked me what was wrong."

"An abortion!" the older woman exclaimed. "Without talking to me about it?"

"He told me I should come to you," the girl said. "He told me that I shouldn't let it ruin my life."

"It seems you may have saved my granddaughter's life," the grandmother said to Gawd.

"I was just someone she could talk to, ma'am," Gawd answered. "She made the right choice herself."

"Well, would you consider staying to dinner for your trouble?" the grandmother asked. Gawd felt his heart jump.

"I really probably should be going," Gawd answered. But he knew he surely didn't mean it.

"Come now," the woman said, "you can certainly stay for dinner. I can even give you a ride home after."

"I don't know, ma'am," Gawd continued to protest.

"Please stay," the girl interjected.

Gawd looked sheepishly toward his shoes, feeling awkward and embarrassed.

"There, it's settled," the grandmother said with finality. "I'll set an extra place."

The exchange was followed by a moment of silence, as if everyone was now unsure what to do next – Gawd because he was a stranger in the house, and the two women because they had invited a derelict into their home and were now unsure what to do with him.

"Would you like to get cleaned up?" the grandmother suddenly asked, perhaps sensing the embarrassment he felt at his general condition and appearance. "Come with me," she instructed, not waiting for him to answer.

Gawd followed her up the stairs to the second storey of the well-kept house, and into a large bedroom.

"Look," she was saying, "here's what you'll be needing." She pushed open a door leading off the bedroom to reveal a bathroom. "You could probably use a shower," she said, offering him a wide smile.

He felt small and petty for being nothing and having nothing.

"Don't be embarrassed," the grandmother said. "You're obviously a very special man to have helped my granddaughter the way you did. I'm sure there's a perfectly logical explanation for the way you look. You have a shower and get cleaned up."

She seemed to eye him up for a moment. "I'm going to go up into the attic and get down some of my Henry's clothes for you. I think you're about the same size." She paused for a moment as if thinking about something. "He was my husband," she explained. "He died a few years ago. It's about time I got some use out of those clothes."

And soon Gawd was luxuriating in the hottest of showers, letting the water course over him, washing away the years of filth and grime. And when he finally got out of the shower, fearful that he had emptied the hot water heater, there were fresh towels, a razor and everything else he needed, including his choice from a huge wardrobe that had been laid out on the bed.

And once he had cleaned and groomed and dressed himself, he descended to the main floor of the house, where he found the women had prepared a veritable feast. And as he sat and ate, he felt so absolutely contented that he engaged in pleasant chit chat and conversation with his dinner companions and they laughed and joked about the state of the weather and other innane subjects. But they also broached the difficult topic of the pregnancy, and Gawd found himself invited to participate in that discussion as if he might have been one of the family. He relished the occasion

After dinner, he helped to clear the dishes, and went into the kitchen to see if there was anything he could help with there. Just as he made his offer, the phone rang and it was one of the girl's friends, so she disappeared to make gossip about schoolmates, and he found himself in possession of a dish towel, which he immediately set about using.

"You know you're charming company," the grandmother said to him, as they did the dishes. "It's hard to believe........" She started to say, but stopped in mid-sentence.

"What's the matter?" he asked.

"I was going to call you a bum," she said apologetically.

"I suppose that would be fair," he answered, "considering that I am one."

"How could......." she started to ask, then stopped.

"What's the matter?" he asked again.

She smiled. "I was going to ask how a nice guy like you ended up in a predicament like this -- or something like that. That would be kind of a cliched question, eh?"

He smiled back. But said nothing. They washed and dried in silence for a moment.

"It was really great of you to help my granddaughter out," the grandmother finally said, just as he was drying the last dish, and she was wiping down the counter. "I don't know what I could do to thank you."

"It's alright," he answered. "I was just glad to do it."

"Do you want to stay for a while longer, or can I give you a ride home?" she asked. "It would be nice if you stayed."

"Oh, I've probably outstayed my welcome now," he replied. "I should probably go. But I can walk. It's not very far."

"Well, alright, if you're sure," she said.

"Thanks anyway," he said.

"Let me give you a few of Henry's things before you go," she offered.

Soon, he was loaded down with a couple of bags of clothes and was saying his farewells at the door. The grandmother had given him their telephone number, and told him to call if he ever needed anything. When she asked for his number and he had to explain that he didn't have a telephone at his place she looked at him strangely but said nothing.

Finally, he was gone from the place. And he went back out into he streets just as night was falling. But he smiled that he had accomplished so much on this day. It had been a good day. Good indeed.

He had walked for some time and was lost in his thoughts, so didn't notice a car pull up alongside of him until it was right beside him. He watched as the driver's side door opened. It was the grandmother.

"I've had quite a time finding you," she said. "It's pitch black out here."

He looked at her, was somewhat confused that she should have appeared.

"It's no wonder you have no phone," she said. "You have no place to live do you?"

He looked about awkwardly.

"Listen," the woman started, "come and stay with us for a while. We talked about it after you left. We've got all kinds of space in that big, old house. We'd be happy for the company."

He turned and started to walk away.

"I had a great time tonight," she said. "It was so very nice to have someone of similiar interests to talk to over dinner again. Come and give it a try for a while. Just call it a vacation for yourself. You can just lounge around the house all day if you like."

"I'm not sure," he answered. But he knew he was sure. He wanted to accept -- he wanted to scream out that he accepted -- but something would not let him -- and he struggled with it.

"Come with me," the grandmother said. "We'd both love to have you as part of the household. For as long or as short as you like."

"You really don't mind?" he asked uncertainly.

"You're welcome with us," she said, smiling.

"Okay," Gawd said. And he smiled.

And he got into her car. And his time in the wilderness was at an end.

Revelations

And so began the golden period of Gawd's existence. It turned out that he became more than just a house guest as he and Ruth, as the grandmother was called, came to know one another on a more than casual basis and were even intimate in their relationship. They were about the same age, and both had known loneliness in their lives, so it was a natural sort of thing that they came together. She was a beautiful and loving woman and Gawd revelled in the affection she constantly showered upon him. He had not imagined that life could be such as it was with her. He wanted to be with her always, but they hid it from the granddaughter for some time, and he was forced to creep about the house in the dead of night to pursue the dear, sweet woman. And, finally, when they thought they were being so clever in their subterfuge, it turned out the girl had been aware of their goings-on for a considerable time, and once the relationship did finally come out in the open, she supported it whole-heartedly.

Gawd spent some time living on Ruth's good graces, but, finally, even he realized that he had again begun his life, after so much time in the netherworld, where he was neither dead or alive. So, he called a lady lawyer he'd met in another life to help start getting his affairs in order. And he called a vice president in charge of finance at one of the larger investment houses in the city. His inheritance from Aunt Rose had grown into a considerable fortune and it would have to be managed. Both of those he called were glad for the opportunity to renew his acquaintance, knowing him to be of good and noble character. He and

Ruth met with them for dinner and the four of them hit it off remarkably well and were soon conversing like the oldest of friends.

And so it was indeed Gawd's golden period. He settled in. The girl had the baby, and Gawd and Ruth resolved to give both her and the child the best of lives. And, indeed, the tiny boy was a delight to have around the house, and he made it seem even more a home, and he made them seem even more a family. They lived in comfort and style and enjoyed life to the fullest. Gawd hated even to sleep knowing that what he had today could be gone tomorrow and he didn't want to let any of the precious time slip away or be wasted.

The years passed. The granddaughter met a fine young man, who worked at a bank and seemed to have a solid future, and got married, and she and the child moved out so she could be with her new husband. Soon she was pregnant again, only this time it was a more joyous occasion. Two other children followed, and Gawd and Ruth were as grandparents to all of them, even though they had a special place in their hearts for the firstborn, who had in fact brought them together.

And Gawd buried Ruth when he was near to his ninetieth birthday, and she was of a similiar old age. They'd been talking about moving out of the big, old house for over ten years, knowing it was too large for them, and that they would have increasing difficulty managing in it on their own. One night, after they'd had one of their frequent discussions about moving into a retirement residence, Gawd thought Ruth looked unusually tired.

"I didn't sleep very well last night," she said, as they laid together in the same bed they'd shared for almost thirty years.

"Sexy dreams?" he said jokingly.

"Yea, you old coot. I was dreaming about when we could still do it more than once a month," she said.

He snuggled up to her, felt her against him.

"I love you," he said softly into her ear, kissing her gently on the neck.

"Watch it, old fool," she said affectionately, twisting her neck around, until they could kiss.

"Just don't you forget it," he said.

"How could I?" she asked. "You've been showing me how much you love me for thirty years, and you've told me that very thing every night before bed for just as long."

They kissed again. Then, he laid back down, pulled himself up close to her, so he could feel her against him. And he went to sleep. He remembered waking up once in the night, and thinking something didn't seem quite right, but it didn't bother him enough to keep him awake and he quickly fell back asleep.

In the morning, she was dead. He wept tears of sadness for the first time in many years.

After her death, he knew finally that he was near his end. The scene had been acted out, and even the final curtain call had been given. The granddaughter invited him to come and live with she and the banker, but he declined the offer, and went instead to the Spring Valley Retirement Home to live out what time remained to him. And when he was first in the Home, he was sociable enough, playing checkers, the odd game of euchre and such, even attending the parties and other events the staff held to keep the old folks occupied while they waited to die. It was a curious sort of existence.

His family – the granddaughter and her offspring and banker husband – came to visit him often when he was first in the Home. But, as time passed, Gawd got older and more infirm, until he could no longer acknowledge each visitor, but only caught glimpses of memory that helped him identify just a lucky few. And he could no longer remember to go to the washroom, but he could clearly see back to when he and his mother had snuggled on the couch and read stories together. He saw his grandfather and Sid and Aunt Rose and Janet and Celeste. They came to him as often as any others. And when they left, he wept.

And, finally, all that remained was Gawd. As it had been in the beginning. He laid in his bed, moved only by the nurses, fed only by the nurses, cleaned only by the nurses. His physical self tired, broken, almost dead from its long journey. Still, he could see, but he could no longer distinguish between actual reality and what had become his own personal reality, where visions from past and present came and went and mixed and mingled freely together.

And so it was that Gawd finally came to rest. He lay in his bed and only existed to exist. The world became his fiction, and he became the fact. And all that was left for him to do was to look within himself. To see if he had come this far with any purpose. And if he had not, why should any others? Why indeed?

And he found himself as a young child back with his mother. He sat upon her knee and was in awe of her great beauty and shining radiance. She no longer appeared to be the beaten, broken wretch of a woman he'd known in his youth. She seemed angelic in her countenance, as if by living a life of misery and suffering, she had indeed secured her place in the mythical heaven.

"Gawd, you have finally come home," the woman said to him.

Gawd said nothing.

"We have been worried about you," she said. "We were afraid that you had lost your way."

Still, he did not answer.

"Your grandfather wants to take you fishing," his mother said. "He said he knows a good spot."

"You're with grandfather?" Gawd asked, breaking his silence, speaking with a child's voice.

"Oh, yes," she answered. "Grandfather and I have been waiting for you. We were all waiting for you."

"Aunt Rose?" he asked.

"She's here," was the answer. "She's got a batch of cookies baked for you."

And then it became dark. The woman, his mother, faded into the coming blackness, and he was left alone. And there was only the pain of reality with him, and it was usually when the doctors and nurses came upon him with their poking and prodding that he came back to that reality. And it was when he was in that state that he wondered that his life would not go away and leave him alone, for he was sure that he had had enough of it, and it had likely tired of him as well. But he could not find an eternal peace, and still his heart was troubled as it had almost always been.

He was with his grandfather. They were fishing.

"So, boy, you think you've been hard done by in life?" the old man asked, casting his line into a river that wasn't there.

"I'm not sure, grandfather," he answered. "I've seen the bad and the good, and I'd rather have the good than the bad. But I'm not sure you can have one without the other."

"There's always somebody worse off than you," the old man reflected.

"I'm not sure there's truth to that," Gawd answered. "Each person lives according to himself, and you can never truly know what another might be feeling. Hell is hell. Personal or otherwise."

"You did well with your life?" the old man questioned.

"I did as well as I could," Gawd answered. "And that's as well as you can ever do."

"Those are wise words," the grandfather said.

And the vision departed, and he was again left alone and in the dark, blackness of reality. But he exerted huge energy to open his eyes and could see the grey, hazy shapes of people as they went about the room.

"I don't know why we have to be here," he heard a young woman say impatiently. "He doesn't even know we're here."

"It's his birthday," he heard another voice say.

"Oh, look, he's waking up," said still another, and suddenly he was aware of the shapes coming closer, so that he could eventually make out some of their features.

"Old Grandpa," said a young voice. "Are you awake?"

Gawd fought to try to wake up out of the slumber his body rested in, but he could not make himself stir, other than to partly lift a hand, and to open his toothless mouth gaping wide.

"Look, he is awake," squealed the youngster.

"Do you think he does know we're here?" he heard the young woman ask.

"Yes, he knows," said a voice.

"It can't be much of a life," said the young woman.

"Oh, I wish you could have known him," said an older woman's voice. "He was such a good and kind man. He was a loving husband, always looked out for his family, and he never had a bad word to say about anyone. I'd be happy to know most people if they were half the person he was."

And Gawd remembered, finally, a smile.

"Look, he's happy," the youngster said.

And Gawd found himself back on the church roof and was surprised to see his old friend, Sid, happened to also be there.

"Hey, man, did you ever get laid?" Sid asked.

"Once or twice," Gawd answered.

There was a moment of silence.

"Did you ever get closer to god?" Gawd asked.

"I don't know," Sid answered. "I think that maybe each of us has a bit of god in us and it may depend on how you live whether you're close to him or not."

"Good answer," Gawd said. "That's deep."

The two friends sat in silence on the edge of the roof.

"Did you learn anything else in life?" Gawd finally asked.

"It's either don't take it too serious, because you're here for a good time not a long time, or you better take it real serious, because it's the only shot you get," Sid answered.

"Maybe you could take it moderately seriously," Gawd answered.

"Doesn't seem to be the case," Sid answered thoughtfully.

"Strange," Gawd responded.

Gawd thought he could hear a fire siren, and as he started to look out to see if there was anything to see, he felt himself fall back into himself and lose the vision. He came crashing back to reality. Noise had come from the outside -- the sound of people laughing and clapping -- a television. He breathed as deeply as he could, exhaling from the bottoms of his feet, relaxing himself.

"Oh, Mrs. Johnson, how are you today?" boomed a loud female voice, causing him to start. "Are we watching some television? It's time for medication."

It was the duty nurse with the evening pill parade. Gawd would get his share, there was no doubt about that, for he had his share of bodily ailments, even with a tired, beaten old body like his.

The time passed slowly when he was in this state, conscious of the world, but not part of it; unable to come fully out from under the veil of inertia that seemed to weigh so heavily upon him. He had struggled with it, but it had not mattered, so that now he laid in quiet, as a silent stone statue in a graveyard. Except when he was turned to avoid bedsores -- which he got anyway.

But he soon departed again. And he found himself on a bus. He looked beside him. It was the fair Julia, who had once saved him from humiliation at the hands of the dreaded Gerald. She looked back at him and smiled a soft, warm smile.

"Hi, there," he said.

"Hi," she answered.

"You look tired," he said.

She smiled, but said nothing.

They rode for a moment in silence.

"You were sweet," she said.

"I was stupid," he answered.

"You tried to help," she said.

"I killed you," he said.

"You helped me," she answered.

There was silence after the brief exchange.

"Don't have any regrets," she said.

"I killed you," he said.

"You did what you thought was right," she said. "You were just a kid."

"I loved you," he said.

"I know," she answered.

"I wanted to protect you," he said.

"You did," she said.

"How?" he asked.

"You protected me from life," she said. "You were sweet."

"I was stupid," he repeated.

"Don't have any regrets," she said. "They'll poison you."

"I love you," he said.

There was silence. He held her hand and she laid her head on his shoulder, and it was a scene of peaceful bliss. He would stay forever with her. But already he could feel her fading, disappearing from his view, slipping from his grasp.

Farewell, fair Julia. That's what he thought he remembered thinking.

He came back into reality, but his stays in the world were becoming all the shorter with each visit, and he struggled less to stay on the surface of his consciousness, and let himself slide smoothly under its skin, to where his past was, to the memories that brought him peace and perhaps even some understanding of what had been.

The characters from his past paraded before him. Some of the memories were terrible and awful and others were radiant and shining, but all brought the peace and understanding, so he looked forward to each excursion into the realm of what had been. Even though it would have been easy to imagine that some of the scenes would have been difficult for him to experience, he had no trepidation at feeling them come. In fact, he relished them.

And each time he transcended the reality, he seemed to have more difficulty finding it again. And one day he'd gone into his past, only to discover that it was now more the reality, and he no longer wanted to go back. So, he struggled to stay away. He had finally realized the futility of existence. He tried to die.

The doctors came. He was an old man, but they savaged him nonetheless, in an attempt to salvage him for one more hour upon the scrap heap of humanity. It was their duty to save life -- all life is sacred -- that's what they would have said. They couldn't understand that he had lived, but that was now past, and there was no future. Gawd knew that he would not have chosen life, even could they promise to make him young once more, because he had tired of life. He wanted to depart from it.

They hooked him to a machine. He lingered on, hoses and tubes and wires coming from him in every direction. He could not protest, and perhaps even if he could have, he'd have chosen not to, just so the doctors could have their way with him. And while he was so connected, he found he could not depart from the here and now, but was always trapped in that space and time. And it was like hell because he had no desire to be in that place.

But he had not laid long, and he became aware that someone other than one of the hospital staff had come into the room and was standing close by to him.

"I always called you Grandpa," a woman's voice said. "But you weren't really my Grandpa. You were just a person off the street when I met you. But I loved you like a Grandpa. And now I have to decide whether you live or die." She paused. "I don't think you'd consider this really living, anyway. I've signed the papers. I just wanted a moment alone with you.

"I wish I knew more about you," she continued. "I know you were a good and kind man, but you never talked about what you did or who you were before you came into my life all those years ago in the coffee shop. I don't know if you told Grandma that kind of stuff or not."

There was silence. He could hear weeping. He wanted to reach out, but could not because he had not enough life left in him. He felt her come close and offer him a soft, light kiss on his cheek. "I love you," she whispered to him. "You changed my life."

Then, she withdrew. And he was left alone to die. There was no ceremony. They just switched him off. There was no appointed time. The doctor and nurse talked about having a beer and pizza after shift. It was all rather casual.

He came this way only once, and he found it a difficult journey he had taken. He had perhaps not counted on the degree of difficulty it would offer. But it had come to this. He could not see them suffer so, unless he had knowledge of why they suffered. And he could not have that knowledge without life. So, life had come. And life had gone. And only he remained. The moment his heart stopped, there was only him -- all other being throughout the universe stopped.

He stood, fully naked in the glare of a thousand galaxies, stretching out his arms, letting the stars sprinkle through his fingers as if they might be elfin dust. From his fingertips flashed bolts of jagged lightning, and he bore an awful countenance, and he was terrible to behold. He was the truth and the light. And he was no longer part of existence, but he also was existence.

And in that moment of his death, he stood as one with all being. He breathed in and out an atmosphere saturated with all life. He felt himself stretching out across the whole of reality, knowing that he was becoming part of every thing, and every thing was becoming part of him. His consciousness was being shared with the consciousness of the ages and he was becoming an indistinguishable part of the whole. He could feel himself slipping away. He rose up out of his body, and watched it rot and decay and turn to dust, and soon there was none of him left -- he was all used up.

He wanted to know if he had done well in his life. "Who can answer me that?" he asked.

"Only you can answer that," came the answer.

"There must be someone who can tell me if I was right," Gawd said.

"There is no one," came the answer.

"I did my best," Gawd said.

"What does it matter?" came the question.

"I tried to be good," Gawd said.

"What does it matter?" came the question.

"I am dead," Gawd said.

"What does it matter?" came the question.

And maybe it didn't matter.

And it came to pass that Gawd was buried with little fanfare. His tiny family from the last of his life stood about on the crest of a small hill in the secluded cemetery he and Ruth had chosen some years before as a final resting place. It was fall and it was raining one of those rains that's actually more of an endless, soggy drizzle, and it was a most unhappy occasion. A minister read from the good book, and he said it was really a most joyous occasion -- that Gawd had now gone to live in glorious splendor with his heavenly father.

And there is no way of knowing whether Gawd actually achieved that residence, or whether he went fishing with his grandfather again, or tasted some of Aunt Rose's cookies. But it was certain that he had lived, and by living, he had been, and perhaps that is all we can hope for as we pass this way. For we are as creaturous as the lion and the wolf and the cunning fox. And to think that we could somehow be more is to mock the meanness of our spirit. Every street in the world is paved with gold, but there is serious misery in the houses along the way. And that is the way with us.

"For I have walked a thousand miles, and seen a thousand kindnesses, and felt a thousand deaths, yet I am," said the man.

And that mattered for sure.

And that is that…